Nora Roberts is the *New York Times* bestselling author of more than one hundred and ninety novels. A born storyteller, she creates a blend of warmth, humour and poignancy that speaks directly to her readers and has earned her almost every award for excellence in her field. The youngest of five children, Nora Roberts lives in western Maryland. She has two sons.

Visit her website at www.noraroberts.com

Also available by Nora Roberts

Nora Roberts

Snow is Falling

Published in Great Britain 2015
by Mills & Boon, an imprint of Harlequin (UK) Limited,
Eton House, 18-24 Paradise Road, Richmond, Surrey, TW9 1SR

SNOW IS FALLING © 2015 Harlequin Books S.A.

Gabriel's Angel © 1989 Nora Roberts
Blithe Images © 1981 Nora Roberts

ISBN: 978-0-263-91555-6

29-1015

Harlequin (UK) Limited's policy is to use papers that are natural, renewable and recyclable products and made from wood grown in sustainable forests. The logging and manufacturing processes conform to the legal environmental regulations of the country of origin.

Printed and bound in Spain
by CPI Group, Croydon

Gabriel's Angel

Chapter 1

Damn snow. Gabe downshifted to second gear, slowed the Jeep to fifteen miles an hour, swore and strained his eyes. Through the frantic swing of the wipers on the windshield all that could be seen was a wall of white. No winter wonderland. Snow pelted down in flakes that looked as big and as mean as a man's fist.

There would be no waiting out this storm, he thought as he took the next curve at a crawl. He considered himself lucky that after six months he knew the narrow, winding road from town so well. He could drive almost by feel, but a newcomer wouldn't stand a chance. Even with that advantage, his shoulders and the back of his neck were tight with tension. Colorado snows could be as vicious in spring as they were in the dead of winter, and they could last for an hour or a day. Apparently this one had been a surprise to everyone—residents, tourists and the National Weather Service.

He had only five miles to go. Then he could unload his supplies, stoke his fire and enjoy the April blizzard from the comfort of his cabin, with a hot cup of coffee or an ice-cold beer.

The Jeep chugged up the incline like a tank, and he was grateful for its sturdy perseverance. The unexpected snowfall might force him to take three times as long to make the twenty-mile trip from town to home, but at least he'd get there.

The wipers worked furiously to clear the windshield. There were seconds of white vision followed by seconds of white blindness. At this rate there would be better than two feet by nightfall. Gabe comforted himself with the thought that he'd be home long before that, even as the air in the Jeep turned blue from his cursing. If he hadn't lost track of the time the day before, he'd have had his supplies and been able to laugh at the weather.

The road went into a lazy S and Gabe took it cautiously. It was difficult for him to move slowly under any circumstances, but over the winter he had gained a healthy respect for the mountains and the roads that had been blasted through them. The guardrail was sturdy enough, but beneath it the cliffs were unforgiving. He wasn't worried so much about making a mistake himself—the Jeep was solid as a rock—but he thought of others who might be traveling north or south on the pass, pulling over to the side or stopping dead in the middle of the road.

He wanted a cigarette. His hands gripping the wheel

hard, he all but lusted for a cigarette. But it was a luxury that would have to wait. Three miles to go.

The tension in his shoulders began to ease. He hadn't seen another car in more than twenty minutes, and he wasn't likely to now. Anyone with any sense would have taken shelter. From this point on he could almost feel his way home. A good thing. Beside him the radio was squawking about roads closed and activities canceled. It always amazed Gabe that people planned so many meetings, luncheons, recitals and rehearsals on any given day.

But that was human nature, he supposed. Always planning on drawing together, if only to sell a bunch of cakes and cookies. He preferred to be alone. At least for now. Otherwise he wouldn't have bought the cabin and buried himself in it for the past six months.

The solitude gave him freedom, to think, to work, to heal. He'd done some of all three.

He nearly sighed when he saw—or rather felt—the road slant upward again. This was the final rise before his turnoff. Only a mile now. His face, which had been hard and tight with concentration, relaxed. It wasn't a smooth or particularly handsome face. It was too thin and angular to be merely pleasant, and the nose was out of alignment due to a heated disagreement with his younger brother during their teens. Gabe hadn't held it against him.

Because he'd forgotten to wear a hat, his dark blond hair fell untidily around his face. It was long and a bit shaggy over the collar of his parka and had been styled hastily with his fingers hours before. His eyes, a dark, clear green, were starting to burn from staring at the snow.

While his tires swished over the cushioned asphalt he glanced down at his odometer, saw that there was only a quarter mile left, then looked back to the road. That was when he saw a car coming at him out of control.

He didn't even have time to swear. He jerked the Jeep to the right just as the oncoming car seemed to come out of its spin. The Jeep skimmed over the snow piled on the shoulder, swaying dangerously before the tires chewed down to the road surface for traction. He had a bad moment when he thought the Jeep was going to roll over like a turtle. Then all he could do was sit and watch and hope the other driver was as lucky.

The oncoming car was barreling down the road sideways. Though only seconds had passed, Gabe had time to think of how nasty the impact would be when the car slammed into him. Then the driver managed to straighten out. With only feet between them the car fishtailed and swerved to avoid the collision, then began to slide helplessly toward the guardrail. Gabe set his emergency brake and was out of the Jeep when the car rammed into the metal.

He nearly fell on his face, but his boots held as he raced across the road. It was a compact—a bit more compact now, with its right side shoved in and its hood sprung like an accordion, also on the passenger side. He had another moment to think, and he grimaced at the thought of what would have happened if the car had hit on the driver's side.

Fighting his way through the snow, he managed to

make it to the wrecked car. He saw a figure slumped over the wheel, and he yanked at the door. It was locked. With his heart in his throat, he began to pound against the window.

The figure moved. A woman, he saw from the thick wave of wheat-blond hair that spilled onto the shoulders of a dark coat. He watched her reach up and drag a ski cap from her head. Then she turned her face to the window and stared at him.

She was white, marble-white. Even her lips were colorless. Her eyes were huge and dark, the irises almost black with shock. And she was beautiful, stunningly, breathtakingly beautiful. The artist in him saw the possibilities in the diamond-shaped face, the prominent cheekbones, the full lower lip. The man in him rejected them and banged on the glass again.

She blinked and shook her head as if to clear it. As the shock passed out of them, he saw that her eyes were blue, a midnight-blue. They filled now with a rush of concern. In a quick movement she rolled down the window.

"Are you hurt?" she demanded before he could speak. "Did I hit you?"

"No, you hit the guardrail."

"Thank God." She let her head slump back on the seat for a moment. Her mouth was as dry as dust. And her heart, though she was already fighting to control it, was thudding in her throat. "I started to skid coming down the incline. I thought—I hoped—I might be able to ride it out. Then I saw you and I was sure I was going to hit you."

"You would have if you hadn't swerved away toward

the rail." He glanced at the front of her car again. The damage could have been worse, much worse. If she'd been going any faster... There was no use speculating. He turned to her again, studying her face for signs of shock or concussion. "Are you all right?"

"Yes. I think so." She opened her eyes again and tried to smile at him. "I'm sorry. I must have given you quite a scare."

"At least." But the scare was over now. He was less than a quarter of a mile from hearth and home, and stuck in the snow with a strange woman whose car wasn't going anywhere for several days. "What the hell are you doing out here?"

She took the furiously bitten-off words in stride as she unhooked her seat belt. The long, deep breaths she'd been taking had gone a long way toward steadying her. "I must have gotten turned around in the storm. I was trying to get down to Lonesome Ridge to wait it out, find a place for the night. That's the closest town, according to the map, and I was afraid to pull over on the shoulder." She glanced over at the guardrail and shuddered. "What there is of it. I don't suppose there's any way I'm going to get my car out of here."

"Not tonight."

Frowning, Gabe stuck his hands in his pockets. The snow was still falling, and the road was deserted. If he turned around and walked back to his Jeep, leaving her to fend for herself, she might very well freeze to death before an emergency vehicle or a snowplow came along. However much he'd have liked to shrug off the obligation, he couldn't leave a woman stranded in this storm.

"The best I can do is take you with me." There wasn't an ounce of graciousness in his tone. She hadn't expected any. If he was angry and impatient about nearly being plowed into, and inconvenienced on top of it, he was entitled.

"I'm sorry."

He moved his shoulders, aware that he'd been rude. "The turnoff for my cabin's at the top of the hill. You'll have to leave your car and ride in the Jeep."

"I'd appreciate it." With the engine off and the window open, the cold was beginning to seep through her clothes. "I'm sorry for the imposition, Mr.—?"

"Bradley. Gabe Bradley."

"I'm Laura." She slipped out of the safety harness that had undoubtedly saved her from injury. "I have a suitcase in the trunk, if you wouldn't mind giving me a hand with it."

Gabe took the keys and stomped back toward the trunk, thinking that if he'd only left an hour earlier that afternoon he'd be home—alone—at this moment.

The case wasn't large, and it was far from new. The lady with only one name traveled light, he thought. He muttered to himself as he hefted it out of the trunk. There was no use being angry with her, or being snotty. If she hadn't managed to skid quite so well, if she hadn't avoided him, they might have been needing a doctor now instead of a cup of coffee and dry feet.

Deciding to be more civil, Gabe turned to tell her to go across to the Jeep. She was standing, watching him, with the snow falling on her uncovered hair. That was when he saw she was not only beautiful, she was very, very pregnant.

"Oh, God" was all he could manage.

"I'm really sorry to be so much trouble," Laura began. "And I want to thank you in advance for the lift. If I could call from your cabin and find a tow truck, maybe we could clear this whole thing up quickly."

He hadn't heard a word she'd said. Not one. All he could do was stare at the ripe slope beneath her dark coat. "Are you sure you're all right? You didn't tell me you were— Are you going to need a doctor?"

"I'm fine." This time she smiled, fully. The cold had brought the color back into her face. "Really. The baby wasn't hurt. He's annoyed a bit, I'd say from the way he's kicking me, but we hardly felt the impact. We didn't ram the guardrail, we sort of slid into it."

"You might have…" What? he wondered. "Jarred something."

"I'm fine," she said again. "I was strapped in, and the snow, though it started it all, cushioned the hit." Noting that he still seemed unconvinced, she tossed back her snow-covered hair. Her fingers, though they were tucked into subtle, silk-lined leather, were going numb. "I promise, I'm not going to give birth in the middle of the road—unless you plan on standing here for a few more weeks."

She was all right…he hoped. And the way she was smiling at him made him feel like an idiot. Deciding to take her word for it, he offered her a hand. "Let me help you."

The words, such simple words, went straight to her

heart. She could have counted on her hands the number of times she had heard them.

He didn't know how to deal with pregnant women. Were they fragile? It had always seemed to him that the opposite must be true, given what they had to go through, but now, faced with one, he was afraid she'd shatter at a touch.

Mindful of the slippery road, Laura took a firm grip on his arm as they started across. "It's beautiful here," she said when they reached the Jeep. "But I have to admit, I'm going to appreciate the snow more from inside." She glanced at the high step below the door of the Jeep. "I think you're going to have to give me a bit of a boost. I'm not as agile as I used to be."

Gabe stowed her case, wondering exactly where to grab her. Mumbling, he put a hand under her elbow and another on her hip. Laura slid into the seat with less fuss than he'd expected.

"Thanks."

He grunted a response as he slammed the door. He skirted the hood, then took his place behind the wheel. It took a little maneuvering, but with a minimum of effort they inched back onto the road.

The dependable Jeep started up the hill. Laura uncurled her hands as they moved along at a steady pace. They'd finally stopped shaking. "I wasn't sure anyone lived along here. If I'd known, I'd have begged a roof long before this. I wasn't expecting a snowstorm in April."

"We get them later than this." He said nothing for a moment. He respected other people's privacy as zealously as his own. But these were unusual circumstances. "You're traveling alone?"

"Yes."

"Isn't that a little risky in your condition?"

"I'd planned on being in Denver in a couple of days." She laid a hand lightly on her belly. "I'm not due for six weeks." Laura took a deep breath. It was a risk to trust him, but she really had no other option. "Do you live alone, Mr. Bradley?"

"Yes."

She shifted her gaze just enough to study him as he turned down a narrow, snow-covered lane. At least she assumed a lane was buried somewhere under all the white. There was something tough and hard about his face. Not rugged, she thought. It was too lean and fine-boned for that. It was coldly sculpted, as she imagined a mythic warrior chief's might be.

But she remembered the stunned male helplessness in his eyes when he'd seen she was pregnant. She believed she'd be safe with him. She had to believe that.

He felt her gaze and read her thoughts easily enough. "I'm not a maniac," he said mildly.

"I appreciate that." She smiled a little, then turned to look out the windshield again.

The cabin could barely be seen through the snow, even when he stopped in front of it. But what Laura could see, she loved. It was a squat rectangle of wood with a covered porch and square-paned windows. Smoke puffed from the chimney.

Though it was buried under snow, there was a path of flat rocks leading from the lane to the front steps. Evergreens mantled with white trooped around the corners. Nothing had ever looked as safe and warm as this snow-decked little cabin in the mountains.

"It's lovely. You must be happy here."

"It does the job." Gabe came around to help her down. She smelled like the snow, he thought, or perhaps more like water, the pure, virginal water that poured down the mountain in the spring. "I'll take you in," he told her, knowing both his reaction and his comparison were ridiculous. "You can warm up by the fire." Gabe opened the front door and waved her in. "Go ahead. I'll bring in the rest."

He left her alone, snow dripping wet from her coat onto the woven mat inside the door.

The paintings. Laura stood just where she was and stared openmouthed at the paintings. They covered the walls, they were stacked in corners, they were piled on tables. Only a few were framed. They didn't need the ornamentation. Some were half finished, as though the artist had lost interest or motivation. There were oils, in colors vivid and harsh, and watercolors in soft, misty hues that might have sprung from dreams. Shrugging out of her coat, Laura moved in for a closer look.

There was a scene from Paris, the Bois de Boulogne. She remembered it from her honeymoon. Looking at it made her eyes swim and her muscles tense. Breathing deeply, she forced herself to look at it until her emotions settled.

An easel was set near the window, where the light would come in and fall on the canvas. She resisted the temptation to go over and steal a look. She already had the sensation that she was trespassing.

What was she going to do? Laura gripped her hands together tightly as she let the despair come. She was stranded, her car wrecked, her money dwindling. And the baby— The baby wasn't going to wait until she made things right.

If they found her now…

They weren't going to find her. Deliberately she unlaced her hands. She'd come this far. No one was going to take her baby, now or ever.

She turned as the door to the cabin opened. Gabe shifted the bags he'd carried inside, leaving them jumbled together in a pile. He, too, shrugged out of his coat and hung it on a hook by the door.

He was as lean as his face had indicated. Though he might have been a bit under six feet, the spare toughness of his build gave the illusion of more height, more power. More like a boxer than an artist, Laura thought as she watched him kick the clinging snow from his boots. More like a man of the outdoors than one who came from graceful mansions and gentle blood.

Despite what she knew of his aristocratic background, he wore flannel and corduroy and looked perfectly suited to the rustic cabin. Laura, who came from humbler stock, felt fussy and out of place in her bulky Irish knit sweater and tailored wool.

"Gabriel Bradley," she said, and gestured widely toward the walls. "My brain must have been scrambled before. I didn't put it together. I love your work."

"Thanks." Bending, he hefted two of the bags.

"Let me help—"

"No." He strode off into the kitchen, leaving Laura biting her lip.

He wasn't thrilled to have her company, she thought. Then she shrugged. It couldn't be helped. As soon as it was reasonably safe for her to leave, she would leave. Until then... Until then Gabriel Bradley, artist of the decade, would have to make do.

It was tempting just to take a seat and passively stay out of his way. Once she would have done just that, but circumstances had changed her. She followed him into the adjoining kitchen. Counting the baby she carried, there were three of them in the little room, and it was filled to capacity.

"At least let me make you something hot to drink." The ancient two-burner stove looked tricky, but she was determined.

He turned, brushed against her belly and was amazed at the wave of discomfort he felt. And the tug of fascination. "Here's the coffee," he mumbled, handing her a fresh can.

"Got a pot?"

It was in the sink, which was filled with water that had once been sudsy. He had been trying to soak out the stains from the last time he'd used it. He moved to get it, bumped her again and stepped back.

"Why don't you let me take care of it?" she suggested. "I'll put this stuff away and start the coffee, and you can call a tow truck."

"Fine. There's milk. Fresh."

She smiled. "I don't suppose you have any tea."

"No."

"Milk's fine, then. Thank you."

When he left, Laura busied herself in the kitchen. It was too small for it to be complicated. She used her own system in storing the goods since it appeared Gabe had none. She'd only emptied the first bag when he reappeared in the doorway.

"Phone's out."

"Out?"

"Dead. We lose service a lot when there's a storm."

"Oh." Laura stood holding a can of soup. "Is it usually out for long?"

"Depends. Sometimes a couple hours, sometimes a week."

She lifted a brow. Then she realized that he was perfectly serious. "I guess that puts me in your hands, Mr. Bradley."

He hooked his thumbs in his front pockets. "In that case, you'd better call me Gabe."

Laura frowned down at the can in her hand. When things got bad, you made the best of them. "Want some soup?"

"Yeah. I'll, ah…put your things in the bedroom."

Laura simply nodded, then began to search for a can opener.

She was a piece of work, all right, Gabe decided as he carried Laura's suitcase into his room. Not that he was an expert when it came to women, but he wasn't what anyone would have called a novice, either. She hadn't batted an eye when he'd told her that the phone was dead and they were effectively cut off from the outside world. Or, to put it more precisely, that she was cut off from everyone but him.

Gabe glanced into the streaked mirror over his battered dresser. As far as he knew, no one had ever considered him harmless before. A quick, cocky smile flashed over his face. He hadn't always been harmless, when it came right down to it.

This, of course, was an entirely different situation.

Under other circumstances he might have entertained some healthy fantasies about his unexpected guest. That face. There was something haunting, something indefinable, about that kind of beauty. When a man looked at it, he automatically began to wonder and imagine. Even if she hadn't been carrying a child, the fantasies would have remained only that. Fantasies. He'd never been enthusiastic about flings and one-night stands, and he certainly wasn't in any shape for a relationship. Celibacy had been the order of the day for the past few months. The desire to paint had finally seduced him again. Gabe needed no other love affair.

But as for more practical matters, he did have a guest, a lone woman who was very pregnant—and very secretive. He hadn't missed the fact that she'd told him only her first name and hadn't volunteered any information about who she was and where and why she was traveling. Since it was unlikely that she'd robbed a bank or stolen secrets for terrorists, he wouldn't press too hard right now.

But, given the strength of the storm and the seclusion of the cabin, they were likely to be together for a few days. He was going to find out more about the calm and mysterious Laura.

What was she going to do? Laura stared at the empty plate in her hand and saw a hint of her reflection. How could she get to Denver or Los Angeles or Seattle—or any huge, swallowing city that was far enough away from Boston—when she was trapped here? If only she hadn't felt that urgent need to move on this morning. If she'd stayed in that quiet little motel room another day she might still have had some control over what was happening.

Instead, she was here with a stranger. Not just any stranger, Laura reminded herself. Gabriel Bradley, artist—wealthy, respected artist from a wealthy, respected family. But he hadn't recognized her. Laura was certain of that. At least he had yet to recognize her. What would happen when he did, when he found out who she was running from? For all she knew, the Eagletons might be close family friends of the Bradleys. The gesture of her hand over the mound of her stomach was automatic and protective.

They wouldn't take her baby. No matter how much money and how much power they wielded, they wouldn't take her baby. And if she could manage it they would never find her or the child.

Setting down the plate, she turned her attention to the window. How odd it was to look out and see nothing. It gave her a nice, settled feeling to know that no one could see in, either. She was effectively curtained off from everyone. Or nearly everyone, she corrected, thinking again of Gabe.

Perhaps the storm had been a blessing. When there was no choice, she found it best to look on the bright side. No one could follow her trail in this kind of weather. And who would think of looking for her in some tiny, out-of-the-way cabin in the mountains? It felt safe. She would cling to that.

She heard him moving around in the next room, heard the sound of his boots on the hardwood, the thud of a log being added to the fire. After so many months alone she found even the sound of another human being a comfort.

"Mr. Bradley...Gabe?" She stepped through the doorway to see him adjusting the screen in front of the fire. "Could you clear off a table?"

"Clear off a table?"

"So we could eat...sitting down."

"Yeah."

She disappeared again while he tried to figure out what to do with the paints, brushes, canvas stretchers and general disorder on the picnic table that had once served as a dining area. Annoyed at having his space compromised, he spread his equipment throughout the room.

"I made some sandwiches, too." Using a bent cookie sheet as a makeshift tray, she carried in bowls and plates and cups. Embarrassed and edgy, Gabe snatched it from her.

"You shouldn't be carrying heavy things."

Her brows lifted. Surprise came first. No one had ever pampered her. And certainly her life, which had rarely been easy, had been hardest over the past seven months. Then gratitude came, and she smiled. "Thanks, but I'm careful."

"If you were careful, you'd be in your own bed with your feet up and not snowbound with me."

"Exercise is important." But she sat and let him set out the dishes. "And so's food." With her eyes closed, she breathed in the scents. Hot, simple, fortifying. "I hope I didn't put too much of a dent in your supplies, but once I got started I couldn't stop."

Gabe picked up half a sandwich that was thick with cheese, crisp bacon and sliced hothouse tomatoes. "I'm not complaining." The truth was, he'd gotten into the habit of eating right out of the pan over the kitchen sink. Hot food made with more care than hurry tasted one hell of a lot better from a plate.

"I'd like to pay you back, for the bed and the food."

"Don't worry about it." He scooped up clam chowder while he studied her. She had a way of sticking out her chin that made him think of pride and will. It made an interesting contrast with the creamy skin and the slender neck.

"That's kind of you, but I prefer paying my own way."

"This isn't the Hilton." She wore no jewelry, he noted, not even a plain gold band on her finger. "You cooked the meal, so we'll call it even."

She wanted to argue—her pride wanted to argue—but the simple truth was, she had very little cash, except for the baby fund she'd scrupulously set aside in the lining of her suitcase. "I'm very grateful." She sipped at the milk, though she detested it. The scent of his coffee was rich and forbidden. "Have you been here long, in Colorado?"

"Six months, seven, I guess."

That gave her hope. The timing was good, almost too

good. From the looks of the cabin, he didn't spend much time poring over the newspapers, and she hadn't noticed a television. "It must be a wonderful place to paint."

"So far."

"I couldn't believe it when I walked in. I recognized your work right away. I've always admired it. In fact, my—someone I knew bought a couple of your pieces. One of them was a painting of a huge, deep forest. It seemed as though you could step right into it and be completely alone."

He knew the work, and, oddly enough, he'd had the same feeling about it. He couldn't be sure, but he thought it had been sold back east. New York, Boston, perhaps Washington, D.C. If his curiosity about her persisted, it would only take a phone call to his agent to refresh his memory.

"You didn't say where you were traveling from."

"No." She continued to eat, though her appetite had fled. How could she have been foolish enough to describe the painting? Tony had bought it, or rather had snapped his fingers and arranged for his lawyers to buy it on his behalf because Laura had admired it. "I've been in Dallas for a while."

She'd been there almost two months before she'd discovered that the Eagletons' detectives were making discreet inquiries about her.

"You don't sound like a Texan."

"No, I suppose I don't. That's probably because I've lived all over the country." That was true enough, and she was able to smile again. "You're not from Colorado."

"San Francisco."

"Yes, I remember reading that in an article about you and your work." She would talk about him. From her experience men were easily distracted when the conversation centered on themselves. "I've always wanted to see San Francisco. It seems like a lovely place, the hills, the bay, the beautiful old houses." She gave a quick gasp and pressed a hand to her stomach.

"What is it?"

"The baby's just restless." She smiled, but he noted that her eyes were shadowed with fatigue and her complexion was pale again.

"Look, I don't know anything about what you're going through, but common sense tells me you should be lying down."

"Actually, I am tired. If you wouldn't mind, I'd like to rest for a few minutes."

"The bed's through here." He rose and, not certain she could get up and down on her own, offered her a hand.

"I'll take care of the dishes later if…" Her words trailed off as her knees buckled.

"Hold on." Gabe put his arms around her and had the odd, rather humbling sensation of having the baby move against him.

"I'm sorry. It's been a long day, and I guess I pushed it further than I should have." She knew she should move away, pull back on her own, but there was something exquisite about leaning against the hard, sturdy body of a man. "I'll be fine after a nap."

She didn't shatter as he'd once thought she might, but now she seemed so soft, so delicate, that he imagined her dissolving in his hands. He would have liked to comfort her, would have liked to go on holding her like that while she leaned into him, trusting, depending. Needing him. Calling himself a fool, he picked her up.

Laura started to protest, but it felt so good to be off her feet. "I must weigh a ton."

"That's what I was expecting, but you don't."

She found she could laugh, even though the fatigue was smothering her. "You're a real charmer, Gabe."

His own awkwardness began to fade as he moved through the door to the bedroom. "I haven't had many opportunities to flirt with pregnant ladies."

"That's all right. You redeemed yourself by rescuing this one from a snowstorm." With her eyes half-closed, she felt herself being lowered onto a bed. It might be nothing more than a mattress and a rumpled sheet, but it felt like heaven. "I want to thank you."

"You've been doing that on an average of every five minutes." He pulled a slightly ragged comforter over her. "If you really want to thank me, get some sleep and don't go into labor."

"Fair enough. Gabe?"

"Yeah."

"Will you keep trying the phone?"

"All right." She was nearly asleep. He had a moment's attack of guilt for wanting to press her while she was vulnerable. Right now, she didn't look as though she had the strength to brush away a fly. "Do you want me to call anyone for you? Your husband?"

She opened her eyes at that. Though they were clouded

with fatigue, they met his levelly, and he saw that she wasn't down for the count yet.

"I'm not married," she said, very clearly. "There's no one to call."

Chapter 2

In the dream she was alone. That didn't frighten her. Laura had spent a large portion of her life alone, so she was more comfortable in solitude than in a crowd. There was a soft, misty quality to the dream—like the seascape she had seen on the wall of Gabe's cabin.

Oddly, she could even hear the ocean, purring and lapping off in the distance, though a part of her knew she was in the mountains. She walked through a pearl-colored fog, listening to the waves. Under her feet sand shifted, warm and soft. She felt safe and strong and strangely unencumbered. It had been a long, long time since she had felt so free, so at ease.

She knew she was dreaming. That was the best part. If she could have managed it, she would have stayed there, in the soft-focused fantasy of it, forever. It would be so easy to keep her eyes closed and cling to the utter peace of the dream.

Then the baby was crying. Screaming. A pulse began to beat in her temple as she listened to the high, keening wails. She started to sweat, and the clean white fog changed to a dark, threatening gray. No longer warm, the air took on a chill that whipped straight to the bone.

The cries seemed to come from everywhere and nowhere, echoing and rebounding as she searched. Sobbing for breath, she fought her way through the mist as it circled and thickened. The cries became louder, more urgent. Her heart was beating in her throat, and her breath rasped and her hands shook.

Then she saw the bassinet, with its pretty white skirt and its lacy pink-and-blue ruffles. The relief was so great that her knees sagged.

"It's all right," she murmured as she gathered the child in her arms. "It's all right. I'm here now." She could feel the baby's warm breath against her cheek, could feel the weight in her arms as she rocked and soothed. The fine scent of powder surrounded her. Gently she cradled the child, murmuring and comforting as she began to lift the concealing blanket from its face.

And there was nothing, nothing in her arms but an empty blanket.

Gabe was sitting at the picnic table, sketching her face, thinking of her, when he heard her cry out. The moan was so long, so desperate, that he snapped the pencil in two before he jumped up and raced to the bedroom.

"Hey, come on." Feeling awkward, he took her by the shoulders. She jerked so hard that he had to fight back his own panic, as well as hers, to hold on to her. "Laura, take it easy. Are you in pain? Is it the baby? Laura, tell me what's going on."

"They took my baby!" There was hysteria in her voice, but it was a hysteria that was laced with fury. "Help me! They took my baby!"

"No one took your baby." She was still fighting him, with a strength that awed him. Moving on instinct, he wrapped his arms around her. "You're having a dream. No one took your baby. Here." He clamped a hand around her wrist, where her pulse was beating like a jackhammer, and dragged her hand to her belly. "You're safe, both of you. Relax before you hurt yourself."

When she felt the life beneath her palms, she slumped against him. Her baby was safe, still inside her, where no one could touch him. "I'm sorry. It was a dream."

"It's okay." Without being aware of it, he was stroking her hair, cradling her as she had cradled the baby of her imagination, rocking her gently in an age-old comforting motion. "Do us both a favor and relax."

She nodded, feeling protected and sheltered. Those were two sensations she had experienced very rarely in her twenty-five years. "I'm all right, really. It must have been the shock from the accident catching up with me."

He drew her away, angry with himself because he wanted to go on holding her, shielding her. When she had asked him for help, he had known, without understanding why, that he would do anything to protect her. It was almost as though he had been dreaming himself, or had been caught up in her dream.

The snow was still falling in sheets outside the window and the only light was what came slanting through the bedroom door from the main cabin. It was dim and slightly yellow, but he could see her clearly, and he wanted to be certain that she saw him, as well. He wanted answers, and he wanted them now.

"Don't lie to me. Under normal circumstances you'd be entitled to your privacy, but right now you're under my roof for God knows how long."

"I'm not lying to you." Her voice was so calm, so even, that he nearly believed her. "I'm sorry if I upset you."

"Who are you running from, Laura?"

She said nothing, just stared at him with those dark blue eyes. He swore at her, but she didn't flinch. He sprang up to pace the room, but she didn't shudder. Abruptly he dropped down on the bed again and caught her chin in his hand. She went absolutely still. Gabe would have sworn that for an instant she stopped breathing. Though it was ridiculous, he had the odd sensation that she was bracing for a blow.

"I know you're in trouble. What I want to know is how big. Who's after you, and why?"

Again she said nothing, but her hand moved instinctively to protect the child she carried.

Since the baby was obviously the core of the problem, they would begin there. "The baby's got a father," he said slowly. "You running from him?"

She shook her head.

"Then who?"

"It's complicated."

He lifted a brow as he jerked his head toward the

window. "We've got nothing but time here. This keeps up, it could be a week before the main roads are open."

"When they do, I'll go. The less you know, the better off we'll both be."

"That won't wash." He was silent a moment, trying to organize his thoughts. "It seems to me that the baby is very important to you."

"Nothing is or can be more important."

"Do you figure the strain you're carrying around is good for it?"

He saw the regret in her eyes instantly, saw the concern, the almost imperceptible folding into herself. "There are some things that can't be changed." She took a long breath. "You have a right to ask questions."

"But you don't intend to answer them."

"I don't know you. I have to trust you, to a point, because I have no choice. I can only ask you to do the same."

He moved his hand away from her face. "Why should I?"

She pressed her lips together. She knew he was right. But sometimes right wasn't enough. "I haven't committed a crime, I'm not wanted by the law. I have no family, no husband looking for me. Is that enough?"

"No. I'll take that much tonight because you need to sleep, but we'll talk in the morning."

It was a reprieve—a short one, but she'd learned to be grateful for small things. With a nod, she waited for him to walk to the door. When it shut and the darkness was full again, she lay down. But it was a long, long time before she slept.

* * *

It was silent, absolutely silent, when Laura woke. She opened her eyes and waited for memory to return. There had been so many rooms, so many places where she'd slept, that she was used to this confusion upon waking.

She remembered it all...Gabriel Bradley, the storm, the cabin, the nightmare. And the sensation of waking in fear to find herself safe, in his arms. Of course, the safety was only temporary, and his arms weren't for her. Sighing, she turned her head to look out the window.

The snow was still falling. It was almost impossible to believe, but she lay and watched it, thinner now, slower, but still steady. There would be no leaving today.

Tucking her hand under her cheek, she continued to watch. It was easy to wish that the snow would never stop and that time would. She could stay here, cocooned, isolated, safe. But time, as the child she carried attested, never stopped. Rising, she opened her suitcase. She would put herself in order before she faced Gabe.

The cabin was empty. She should have felt relieved at that. Instead, the cozy fire and polished wood made her feel lonely. She wanted him there, even if it was just the sound of his movements in another room. Wherever he had gone, she reminded herself, he would be back. She started to walk into the kitchen to see what could be done about breakfast.

She saw the sketches, a half dozen of them, spread out on the picnic table. His talent, though raw in pencil or charcoal drawing, was undeniable. Still, it made her both uneasy and curious to see how someone else—no, how Gabriel Bradley—perceived her.

Her eyes seemed too big, too haunted. Her mouth was too soft, too vulnerable. She rubbed a finger over it as she frowned at the drawing. She'd seen her face count-less times, in glossy photographs, posed for the best angle. She'd been draped in silks and furs, drenched in jewels. Her face and form had sold gallons of perfume, hawked fortunes in clothes and gems.

Laura Malone. She'd nearly forgotten that woman, the woman they'd said would be the face of the decade. The woman who had, briefly, held her own destiny in her hands. She was gone, erased.

The woman in the sketches was softer, rounder and infinitely more fragile. And yet she seemed stronger. Laura lifted a sketch and studied it. Or did she just want to see the strength, need to see it?

When the front door opened, she turned, still hold-ing the pencil sketch. Gabe, covered with snow, kicked the door shut again. His arms were loaded with wood.

"Good morning. Been busy?"

He grunted and stomped the worst of the snow from his boots, then walked, leaving a wet trail, to the firebox to dump his wood. "I thought you might sleep longer."

"I would have." She patted her belly. "He wouldn't. Can I fix you some breakfast?"

Drawing off his gloves, he tossed them down on the hearth. "Already had some. You go ahead."

Laura waited until he'd stripped off his coat. Appar-ently they were back on friendly terms again. Cautiously friendly. "It seems to be letting up a little."

He sat on the hearth to drag his boots off. Snow was caked in the laces. "We've got three feet now, and I wouldn't look for it to stop before afternoon." He drew out a cigarette. "Might as well make yourself at home."

"I seem to be." She held up the sketch. "I'm flattered."

"You're beautiful," he said offhandedly as he set his boots on the hearth to dry. "I can rarely resist drawing beautiful things."

"You're fortunate." She dropped the sketch back on the table. "It's so much more rewarding to be able to depict beauty than it is to be beautiful." Gabe lifted a brow. There was a trace, only a trace, of bitterness in her tone. "Things," she explained. "It's strange, but once people see you as beautiful, they almost always see you as a thing."

Turning, she slipped into the kitchen, leaving him frowning after her.

She brewed him fresh coffee, then idled away the morning tidying the kitchen. Gabe gave her room. Before night fell again, he would have some answers, but for now he was content to have her puttering around while he worked.

She seemed to need to be busy. He had thought a woman in her condition would be content to sleep or rest or simply sit and knit for most of the day. He decided it was either nervous energy or her way of avoiding the confrontation he'd promised her the night before.

She didn't ask questions or stand over his shoulder, so they rubbed along through the morning without incident. Once, he glanced over to see her tucked into a corner of the sagging sofa reading a book on childbirth. Later she threw some things together in the kitchen and produced a thick, aromatic stew.

She said little. He knew she was waiting, biding her time until he pushed open the door he'd unlocked the night before. He, too, was waiting, biding his time. By midafternoon he decided she looked rested. Taking up his sketch pad and a piece of charcoal, he began to work while she sat across from him peeling apples.

"Why Denver?"

The only sign of her surprise was a quick jerk of the paring knife. She didn't look up or stop peeling. "Because I've never been there."

"Under the circumstances, wouldn't you be better off in some place that's familiar?"

"No."

"Why did you leave Dallas?"

She set the apple down and picked up another. "Because it was time."

"Where's the baby's father, Laura?"

"Dead." There wasn't even a shadow of emotion in her voice.

"Look at me."

Her hands stilled as she lifted her gaze, and he saw that that much, at least, was true.

"You don't have any family who could help you?"

"No."

"Didn't he?"

Her hand jerked again. This time the blade nicked her finger. The blood welled up as Gabe dropped his pad to take her hand. Once again she saw her face in the sweeping charcoal lines.

"I'll get you a bandage."

"It's only a scratch," she began, but he was already

up and gone. When he returned he dabbed at the wound with antiseptic. Again Laura was baffled by the care he displayed. The sting came and went; his touch remained gentle.

He was kneeling in front of her, his brows drawn together as he studied the thin slice in her finger. "Keep this up and I'll think you're accident-prone."

"And I'll think you're the original Good Samaritan." She smiled when he looked up. "We'd both be wrong."

Gabe merely slipped a bandage over the cut and took his seat again. "Turn your head a little, to the left." When she complied, he picked up his pad and turned over a fresh sheet. "Why do they want the baby?"

Her head jerked around, but he continued to sketch.

"I'd like the profile, Laura." His voice was mild, but the demand in it was very clear. "Turn your head again, and try to keep your chin up. Yes, like that." He was silent as he formed her mouth with the charcoal. "The father's family wants the baby. I want to know why."

"I never said that."

"Yes, you did." He had to hurry if he was going to capture that flare of anger in her eyes. "Let's not beat that point into the ground. Just tell me why."

Her hands were gripped tightly together, but there was as much fear as fury in her voice. "I don't have to tell you anything."

"No." He felt a thrill of excitement—and, incredibly, one of desire—as he stroked the charcoal over the pad. The desire puzzled him. More, it worried him. Pushing it aside, he concentrated on prying answers from her. "But since I'm not going to let it drop, you may as well."

Because he knew how to look, and to see, he caught the subtle play of emotions over her face. Fear, fury, frustration. It was the fear that continued to pull him over the line.

"Do you think I'd bundle you and your baby off to them, whoever the hell they are? Use your head. I haven't got any reason to."

He'd thought he would shout at her. He'd have sworn he was on the verge of doing so. Then, in a move that surprised them both, he reached out to take her hand. He was more surprised than she to feel her fingers curl instinctively into his. When she looked at him, emotions he'd thought unavailable to him turned over in his chest.

"You asked me to help you last night."

Her eyes softened with gratitude, but her voice was firm. "You can't."

"Maybe I can't, and maybe I won't." But as much as it went against the grain of what he considered his character, he wanted to. "I'm not a Samaritan, Laura, good or otherwise, and I don't like to add someone else's problems to my own. But the fact is, you're here, and I don't like playing in the dark."

She was tired, tired of running, tired of hiding, tired of trying to cope entirely on her own. She needed someone. When his hand was covering hers and his eyes were calm and steady on hers, she could almost believe it was him she needed.

"The baby's father is dead," she began, picking her way carefully. She would tell him enough to satisfy him, she hoped, but not all. "His parents want the baby. They want...I don't know, to replace, to take back, something that they've lost. To...to ensure the lineage. I'm sorry for them, but the baby isn't their child." There was that look again, fierce, protective. A mother tiger shielding her cub. "The baby's mine."

"No one would argue with that. Why should you have to run?"

"They have a lot of money, a lot of power."

"So?"

"So?" Angry again, she pushed away. The contact that had been so soothing for both of them was broken. "It's easy to say that when you come from the same world. You've always had. You've never had to want and to wonder. No one takes from people like you, Gabe. They wouldn't dare. You don't know what it's like to have your life depend on the whims of others."

That she had was becoming painfully obvious. "Having money doesn't mean you can take whatever you want."

"Doesn't it?" She turned to him, her face set and cold. "You wanted a place to paint, somewhere you could be alone and be left alone. Did you have to think twice about how to arrange it? Did you have to plan or save or make compromises, or did you just write a check and move in?"

His eyes were narrowed as he rose to face her. "Buying a cabin is a far cry from taking a baby from its mother."

"Not to some. Property is property, after all."

"You're being ridiculous."

"And you're being naive."

His temper wavered, vying with amusement. "That's

a first. Sit down, Laura, you make me nervous when you swing around."

"I'm not going to break," she muttered, but she eased into a chair. "I'm strong, I take care of myself. I had an examination just before I left Dallas, and the baby and I are fine. Better than fine. In a few weeks I'm going to check into a hospital in Denver and have my baby. Then we're going to disappear."

He thought about it. He almost believed the woman sitting across from him could accomplish it. Then he remembered how lost and frightened she'd been the night before. There was no use pointing out the strain she'd been under and its consequences for her. But he knew now what button to push.

"Do you think it's fair to the baby to keep running?"

"No, it's horribly, horribly unfair. But it would be worse to stop and let them take him."

"Why are you so damn sure they would, or could?"

"Because they told me. They explained what they thought was best for me and the child, and they offered to pay me." The venom came into her voice at that, black and bitter. "They offered to give me money for my baby, and when I refused they threatened to simply take him." She didn't want to relive that dreadful, terrifying scene. With an effort she cleared it from her mind.

He felt a swift and dark disgust for these people he didn't even know. He buried it with a shake of his head and tried to reason with her. "Laura, whatever they want, or intend, they couldn't just take what isn't theirs. No court would just take an infant from its mother without good cause."

"I can't win on my own." She closed her eyes for a moment because she wanted badly to lay her head down and weep out all the fear and anguish. "I can't fight them on their own ground, Gabe, and I won't put my child through the misery of custody suits and court battles, the publicity, the gossip and speculation. A child needs a home, and love and security. I'm going to see to it that mine has all of those things. Whatever I have to do, wherever I have to go."

"I won't argue with you about what's right for you and the baby, but sooner or later you're going to have to face this."

"When the time comes, I will."

He rose and paced over to the fire to light another cigarette. He should drop it, just leave it—her—alone and let her follow her own path. It was none of his business. Not his problem. He swore, because somehow, the moment she'd taken his arm to cross the road, she'd become his business.

"Got any money?"

"Some. Enough to pay a doctor, and a bit more."

He was asking for trouble. He knew it. But for the first time in almost a year he felt as though something really mattered. Sitting on the edge of the hearth, he blew out smoke and studied her.

"I want to paint you," he said abruptly. "I'll pay you the standard model's fee, plus room and board."

"I can't take your money."

"Why not? You seem to think I have too much for my own good, anyway."

Shame brought color flooding into her cheeks. "I didn't mean it—not like that."

He brushed her words aside. "Whatever you meant, the fact remains that I want to paint you. I work at my own pace, so you'll have to be patient. I'm not good at compromise, but owing to your condition I'm willing to make some concessions and stop when you're tired or uncomfortable."

It was tempting, very tempting. She tried to forget that she'd traded on her looks before and concentrate on what the extra money would mean to the baby. "I'd like to agree, but the fact is, your work is well-known. If the portrait was shown, they'd recognize me."

"True enough, but that doesn't mean I'd be obliged to tell anyone where we'd met or when. You have my word that no one will ever trace you through me."

She was silent for a moment, warring with herself. "Would you come here?"

Hesitating only a moment, he tossed his cigarette into the fire. He rose, walked over, then crouched in front of her chair. She, too, had learned how to read a face. "Your word?"

"Yes."

Some risks were worth taking. She held both hands out to his, putting her trust into them.

With the continuing fall of snow, it was a day without a sunrise, a sunset, a twilight. The day stayed dim from morning on, and then night closed in without fanfare. And the snow stopped.

Laura might not have noticed if she hadn't been standing by the window. The flakes didn't appear to have tapered off, but to have stopped as if someone had thrown a switch. There was a vague sense of disappointment, the same she remembered feeling as a young girl when a storm had ended. On impulse, she bundled herself in her boots and coat and stepped out onto the porch.

Though Gabe had shoveled it off twice during the day, the snow came almost to her knees. Her boots sank in and disappeared. She had the sensation of being swallowed up by a soft, benign cloud. She wrapped her arms around her chest and breathed in the thin, cold air.

There were no stars. There was no moon. The porch light tossed its glow only a few feet. All she could see was white. All she could hear was silence. To some the high blanket of snow might have been a prison, something to chafe against. To Laura it was a fortress.

She'd decided to trust someone other than herself again. Standing there, soaking up the pure dark, the pure quiet, she knew that the decision had been the right one.

He wasn't a gentle man, or even a contented man, but he was a kind one, and, she was certain, a man of his word. If they were using each other, her for sanctuary, him for art, it was a fair exchange. She needed to rest. God knew she needed whatever time she could steal to rest and recover.

She hadn't told him how tired she was, how much effort it took for her just to keep on her feet for most of the day. Physically the pregnancy had been an easy one. She was strong, she was healthy. Otherwise she would have crumpled long before this. But the past few months had drained every ounce of her emotional and mental reserves. The cabin, the mountains, the man, were going to give her time to build those reserves back up again.

She was going to need them.

He didn't understand what the Eagletons could do, what they could accomplish with their money and their power. She'd already seen what they were capable of. Hadn't they paid and maneuvered to have their son's mistakes glossed over? Hadn't they managed, with a few phone calls and a few favors called in, to have his death, and the death of the woman with him, turned from the grisly waste it had been into a tragic accident?

There had never been any mention in the press about alcohol and adultery. As far as the public was concerned, Anthony Eagleton, heir to the Eagleton fortune, had died as a result of a slippery road and faulty steering, and not his criminally careless drunk driving. The woman who had died with him had been turned from his mistress into his secretary.

The divorce proceedings that Laura had started had been erased, shredded, negated. No shadow of scandal would fall over the memory of Anthony Eagleton or over the family name. She'd been pressured into playing the shocked and grieving widow.

She had been shocked. She had grieved. Not for what had been lost—not on a lonely stretch of road outside of Boston—but for what had been lost so soon after her wedding night.

There was no use looking back, Laura reminded herself. Now, especially now, she had to look forward. Whatever had happened between her and Tony, they had created a life. And that life was hers to protect and to cherish.

With the spring snow glistening and untouched as far as she could see, she could believe that everything would work out for the best.

"What are you thinking?"

Startled, she turned toward Gabe with a little laugh. "I didn't hear you."

"You weren't listening." He pulled the door closed behind him. "It's cold out here."

"It feels wonderful. How much is there, do you think?"

"Three and a half, maybe four feet."

"I've never seen so much snow before. I can't imagine it ever melting and letting the grass grow."

His hands were bare. He tucked them in the pockets of his jacket. "I came here in November and there was already snow. I've never seen it any other way."

She tried to imagine that, living in a place where the snow never melted. No, she thought, she would need the spring, the buds, the green, the promise. "How long will you stay?"

"I don't know. I haven't thought about it."

She turned to smile at him, though she felt a touch of envy at his being so unfettered. "All those paintings. You'll need to have a show."

"Sooner or later." He moved his shoulders, suddenly restless. San Francisco, his family, his memories, seemed very far away. "No hurry."

"Art needs to be seen and appreciated," she murmured, thinking out loud. "It shouldn't be hidden up here."

"And people should?"

"Do you mean me, or is that what you're doing, too? Hiding?"

"I'm working," he said evenly.

"A man like you could work anywhere, I think. You'd just elbow people aside and go to it."

He had to grin. "Maybe, but now and again I like to have some space. Once you make a name, people tend to look over your shoulder."

"Well, I, for one, am glad you came here, for whatever reason." She brushed the hair away from her face. "I should go back in, but I don't want to." She was smiling as she leaned back against the post.

His eyes narrowed. When he cupped her face in his hands, his fingers were cold and firm. "There's something about your eyes," he murmured, turning her face fully into the light. "They say everything a man wants a woman to say, and a great deal he doesn't. You have old eyes, Laura. Old, sad eyes."

She said nothing, not because her mind was empty, but because it was suddenly filled with so many things, so many thoughts, so many wishes. She hadn't thought she could feel anything like this again, and certainly not this longing for a man. Her skin warmed with it, even though his touch was cool, almost disinterested.

The sexual tug surprised her, even embarrassed her a little. But it was the emotional pull, the slow, hard drag of it, that kept her silent.

"I wonder what you've seen in your life."

As if of their own volition, his fingers stroked her cheek. They were long, slender, artistic, but hard and strong. Even so, he might merely have been familiarizing himself with the shape of her face, with the texture of her skin. An artist with his subject.

The longing leaped inside her, the foolish, impossible longing to be loved, held, desired, not for her face, not for the image a man could see, but for the woman inside.

"I'm getting tired," she said, managing to keep her voice steady. "I think I'll go to bed now."

He didn't move out of her way immediately. And his hand lingered. He couldn't have said what kept him there, staring at her, searching the eyes he found so fascinating. Then he stepped back quickly and shoved the door open for her.

"Good night, Gabe."

"Good night."

He stayed out in the cold, wondering what was wrong with him. For a moment, damn it, for a great deal longer than a moment, he'd found himself wanting her. Filled with self-disgust, he pulled out a cigarette. A man had to be sinking low to think about making love to a woman who was more than seven months along with another man's child.

But it was a long time before he could convince himself he'd imagined it.

Chapter 3

He wondered what she was thinking. She looked so serene, so quietly content. The pale pink sweater she wore fell into a soft cowl at her throat. Her hair shimmered to her shoulders. Again she wore no jewelry, nothing to draw attention away from her, nothing to draw attention to her.

Gabe rarely used models in his work, because even if they managed to hold the pose for as long as he demanded they began to look bored and restless. Laura, on the other hand, looked as though she could sit endlessly with that same soft smile on her face.

That was part of what he wanted to capture in the portrait. That inner patience, that…well, he supposed he could call it a gracious acceptance of time—what had come before, and what was up ahead. He'd never had much patience, not with people, not with his work, not with himself. It was a trait he could admire in her without having the urge to develop it himself.

Yet there was something more, something beyond the utterly feminine beauty and the Madonna-like calm. From time to time he saw a fierceness in her, a warrior-like determination. He could see that she was a woman who would do whatever was necessary to protect what was hers. Judging from her story, all that was hers was the child she carried.

She had more to tell, he mused as he ran the pencil over the pad. The bits and pieces she'd offered had only been given to keep him from asking more. He hadn't asked for more. It wasn't his usual style, once he'd decided an explanation was called for, to accept a partial one. He couldn't quite make himself push for the whole when even the portion she'd given him had plainly cost her so much.

There was still time. The radio continued to squawk about the roads that were closed and the snow that was yet to come. The Rockies could be treacherous in the spring. Gabe estimated it would be two weeks, perhaps three, before a trip could be managed with real safety.

It was odd, but he would have thought the enforced company would annoy him. Instead, he found himself pleased to have had his self-imposed solitude broken. It had been a long time since he'd done a portrait. Maybe too long. But he hadn't been able to face flesh and blood, not since Michael.

In the cabin, cut off from memories and reminders, he'd begun the healing process. In San Francisco he hadn't been able to pick up a brush. Grief had done more than make him weak. For a time it had made him…blank.

But here, secluded, solitary, he'd painted landscapes, still lifes, half-remembered dreams and seascapes from old sketches. It had been enough. Not until Laura had he felt the need to paint the human face again.

Once he'd believed in destiny, in a pattern of life that was meant to be even before birth. Michael's death had changed that. From that point, Gabe had had to blame something, someone. It had been easiest, and most painful, to blame himself. Now, sketching Laura, thinking over the odd set of circumstances that had brought her into his life, he began to wonder again.

And what, he asked himself yet again, was she thinking?

"Are you tired?"

"No." She answered, but she didn't move. He'd stationed a chair by the window, angling it so that she was facing him but still able to look out. The light fell over her, bringing no shadows. "I like to look at the snow. There are tracks in it now, and I wonder what animals might have passed by without us seeing. And I can see the mountains. They look so old and angry. Back east they're more tame, more good-natured."

He absently murmured his agreement as he studied his sketch. It was good, but it wasn't right, and he wanted to begin working on canvas soon. He set the pad aside and frowned at her. She stared back, patient and—if he wasn't reading her incorrectly—amused. "Do you have anything else to wear? Something off-the-shoulder, maybe?"

The amusement was even more evident now. "Sorry, my wardrobe's a bit limited at the moment."

He rose and began to pace, to the fire, to the window, back to the table. When he strode over to take her face in his hand and turn it this way and that, she sat obligingly. After three days of posing, she was used to it. She might have been an arrangement of flowers, Laura thought, or a bowl of fruit. It was as if that one moment of awareness on the snow-covered porch had never happened. She'd already convinced herself that she'd imagined that look in his eyes—and, more, her response to it.

He was the artist. She was the clay. And she'd been there before.

"You have a completely feminine face," he began, talking more to himself than to her. "Alluring and yet composed, and soft, even with the angular shape and those cheekbones. It's not threatening, and yet, it's utterly distracting. This—" his thumb brushed casually over her full lower lip "—says sex, even while your eyes promise love and devotion. And the fact that you're ripe—"

"Ripe?" She laughed, and the hands that had clenched in her lap relaxed again.

"Isn't that what pregnancy is? It only adds to the fascination. There's a promise and a fulfillment and—despite education and progress—a compelling mystery to a woman with child. Like an angel."

"How?"

As he spoke, he began to fuss with her hair, drawing it back, piling it up, letting it fall again. "We see angels as ethereal creatures, mystic, above human desires and flaws, but the fact is, they were human once."

His words appealed to her, made her smile. "Do you believe in angels?"

His hand was still in her hair, but he'd forgotten, totally forgotten, the practical reason for it. "Life wouldn't be worth much if you didn't." She had the hair of an angel, shimmery-blond, cloud-soft. Feeling suddenly awkward, he drew his hand away and tucked it in the pocket of his baggy corduroys.

"Would you like to take a break?" she asked him. Her hands were balled in her lap again.

"Yeah. Rest for an hour. I need to think this through." He stepped back automatically when she rose. When he wasn't working, he took great care not to come into physical contact with her. It was disturbing how much he wanted to touch her. "Put your feet up." When she lifted a brow at that, he shifted uncomfortably. "It recommended it in that book you leave lying around. I figured it wouldn't hurt for me to glance through it, under the circumstances."

"You're very kind."

"Self-preservation." Things happened to him when she smiled like that. Things he recognized but didn't want to acknowledge. "The more I make sure you take care of yourself, the less chance there is of you going into labor before the roads are clear."

"I've got more than a month," she reminded him. "But I appreciate you worrying about me—about us."

"Put your feet up," he repeated. "I'll get you some milk."

"But I—"

"You've only had one glass today." With an impatient

gesture, he motioned her to the sofa before he walked into the kitchen.

With a little sigh of relief, Laura settled back against the cushions. Putting her feet up wasn't as easy as it once had been, but she managed to prop them on the edge of the coffee table. The heat from the fire radiated toward her, making her wish she could curl up in front of it. If she did, she thought wryly, it would take a crane to haul her back up again.

He was being so kind, Laura thought as she turned her head toward the sound of Gabe rummaging in the kitchen. He didn't like her to remind him of it, but he was. No one had ever treated her quite like this—as an equal, yet as someone to be protected. As a friend, she thought, without tallying a list of obligations, a list of debts that had to be paid. Whether he listed them or not, someday, when she was able, she'd find a way to pay him back. Someday.

She could see the future if she closed her eyes and thought calm thoughts. She'd have a little apartment somewhere in the city. Any city. There would be a room for the baby, something in sunny yellows and glossy whites, with fairy-tale prints on the walls. She'd have a rocking chair she could sit in with the baby during the long, quiet nights, when the rest of the world was asleep.

And she wouldn't be alone anymore.

Opening her eyes, she saw Gabe standing over her. She wanted, badly, to reach up, to take his hands and draw in some of the strength and confidence she felt radiating from him. She wanted, more, for him to run his thumb along her lip again, slowly, gently, as though she were a woman, rather than a thing to be painted.

Instead, she reached up to take the glass of milk he held. "After the baby's born and I finish nursing, I'm never going to drink a drop of milk again."

"This is the last of the fresh," he told her. "Tomorrow you go on powdered and canned."

"Oh, joy." Grimacing, she downed half the contents of the glass. "I pretend it's coffee, you know. Strong, black coffee." She sipped again. "Or, if I'm feeling reckless, champagne. French, in fluted crystal."

"It's too bad I don't have any wineglasses handy. It would help the illusion. Are you hungry?"

"It's a myth about eating for two, and if I gain much more weight I'll begin to moo." Content, she settled back again. "That painting of Paris…did you do it here?"

He glanced over at the work. So she'd been there, he thought. It was a moody, almost surreal study of the Bois de Boulogne. "Yes, from old sketches and memory. When were you there?"

"I didn't say I'd been to Paris."

"You wouldn't have recognized it otherwise." He took the empty glass out of her hand and set it aside. "The more secretive you are, Laura, the more it makes me want to dig."

"A year ago," she said stiffly. "I spent two weeks there."

"How did you like it?"

"Paris?" She ordered herself to relax. It had been a lifetime ago, almost long enough that she could imagine it had all happened to someone else. "It's a beautiful city, like an old, old woman who still knows how to flirt. The flowers were blooming, and the smells were incredible. It rained and rained, for three days, and you could sit and watch the black umbrellas hurrying by and the blossoms opening up."

Instinctively he put a hand over hers to calm the agitated movement of her fingers. "You weren't happy there."

"Paris in the spring?" She concentrated on making her hands go limp. "Only a fool wouldn't be happy there."

"The baby's father...was he with you there?"

"Why does it matter?"

It shouldn't have mattered. But now, whenever he looked at the painting, he would think of her. And he had to know. "Did you love him?"

Had she? Laura looked back at the fire, but the only answers were within herself. Had she loved Tony? Her lips curved a little. Yes, she had, she had loved the Tony she'd imagined him to be. "Very much. I loved him very much."

"How long have you been alone?"

"I'm not." She laid a hand on her stomach. When she felt the answering movement, her smile widened. Taking Gabe's hand, she pressed it against her. "Feel that? Incredible, isn't it? Someone's in there."

He felt the stirring beneath his hand, gentle at first, then with a punch that surprised him. Without thinking, he moved closer. "That felt like a left jab. Makes you feel as though it's fighting to get out." He knew the feeling, the impatience, the frustration at being trapped in one world while you longed for another. "How does it feel from the other side?"

"Alive." Laughing, she left her hand over his. "In Dallas they put a monitor on, and I could hear the baby's heartbeat. It was so fast, so impatient. Nothing in the world ever sounded so wonderful. And I think…"

But he was looking at her now, deeply, intently. Their hands were still joined, their bodies just brushing. Even as the life inside her quickened, so did her pulse. The warmth, the intimacy, of the moment washed over her, leaving her breathless and full of needs.

He wanted to hold her, badly. The urge to gather her close and just hold on was so sharp, so intense that he hurt. He dreamed of her every night when he struggled for sleep on the floor of the spare room. In his dreams they were curled in bed together, with her breath warm on his cheek and her hair tangled in his hands. And when he woke from the dreams he told himself he was mad. He told himself that again now and moved aside.

Though they were no longer touching, he could feel, as well as hear, her long, quiet sigh.

"I'd like to work some more, if you're up to it."

"Of course." She wanted to weep. That was natural, she told herself. Pregnant women wept easily. Their emotions ran on the surface, to be bruised and battered without effort, and often without cause.

"I've got something in mind. Hold on a minute."

She waited, still sitting, while he went into the spare room. Moments later he came back holding a navy blue shirt.

"Put this on. I think the contrast between the man's shirt and your face might be the answer."

"All right." Laura went into the bedroom and stripped off the big pink sweater. She started to draw an arm through the sleeve and then she caught his scent. It was there, clinging to the heavy cotton. Tough, and unapologetically sexual. Man. Unable to resist, she rubbed her cheek over it. The material was soft. The scent was not, but somehow even the scent of him made her feel safe. And yet, foolish as it seemed, it made her feel a dull, deep tremor of desire.

Wasn't it wrong to want as a woman, to want Gabe as a man, when she carried such a responsibility? But it didn't seem wrong when she felt so close to him. He had sorrows, too. She could see them, sense them. Perhaps it was that common ground, and their isolation, that made her feel as though she'd known him, cared about him, for so long.

With a sigh, she slipped into the shirt. What did she know about her own feelings? The first, the only, time she'd trusted them completely had brought misery. Whatever emotions Gabe stirred in her, she would be wise to keep gratitude in the forefront.

When she stepped back into the main cabin, he was going through his sketches, rejecting, considering, accepting. He glanced up and realized that his conception of Laura fell far, far short of the mark.

She looked like the angel he'd spoken of, illusory, golden, yet tied now to the earth. He preferred to think of her as an illusion rather than as a woman, one who stirred him.

"That's more of the look I want," he said, managing to keep his voice steady. "The color's good on you, and the straight-line masculine style is a nice contrast."

"You may not get it back anytime soon. It's wonderfully comfortable."

"Consider it a loan."

He walked over to the chair as she sat and shifted into the precise pose she'd been in before the break. Not for the first time, Gabe wondered if she'd modeled before. That was another question, for another time.

"Let's try something else." He shifted her, mere inches, muttering to himself. Laura nearly smiled. She was back to being a bowl of fruit.

"Damn, I wish we had some flowers. A rose. Just one rose."

"You could imagine one."

"I may." He tilted her head a fraction to the left before he stood back. "This feels right, so I'm going to draw it on canvas. I've wasted enough time on rough sketches."

"Three whole days."

"I've completed paintings in half that time when things clicked."

She could see it, him sitting on a tall stool at an easel, working feverishly, brows lowered, eyes narrowed, those long, narrow hands creating. "There are some in here you haven't finished at all."

"Mood changed." He was already making broad strokes on canvas with his pencil. "Do you finish everything you start?"

She thought about that. "I suppose not, but people are always saying you should."

"When something's not right, why drag it out to the bitter end?"

"Sometimes you promise," she murmured, thinking of her marriage vows.

Because he was watching her closely, he saw the swift look of regret. As always, though he tried to block it, her emotions touched a chord in him. "Sometimes promises can't be kept."

"No. But they should be," she said quietly. Then she fell silent.

He worked for nearly an hour, defining, refining, perfecting. She was giving him the mood he wanted. Pensive, patient, sensuous. He already knew, even before the first brush stroke, that this would be one of his best. Perhaps his very best. And he knew he would have to paint her again, in other moods, in other poses.

But that was for tomorrow. Today, now, he needed to capture the tone of her, the feel, the simplicity. That was pencil lines and curves. Black against white, and a few shades of gray. Tomorrow he would begin filling in, adding the color, the complexities. When he had finished he would have the whole of her on canvas, and he would know her fully, as no one had ever before or would ever again.

"Will you let me see it as you go along?"

"What?"

"The painting." Laura kept her head still but shifted her eyes from the window to him. "I know artists are supposed to be temperamental about showing their work before it's finished."

"I'm not temperamental." He lifted his gaze to hers, as if inviting her to disagree.

"Anyone could see that." Though she kept her expression sober, he could hear the amusement in her voice. "So will you let me see it?"

"Doesn't matter to me. As long as you realize that if you see something you don't like I won't change it."

This time she did laugh, more freely, more richly than before. His fingers tightened on the pencil. "You mean if I see something that wounds my vanity? You don't have to worry about that. I'm not vain."

"All beautiful women are vain. They're entitled."

"People are only vain if their looks matter to them."

This time he laughed, but cynically. He set down his pencil. "And yours don't matter to you?"

"I didn't do anything to earn them, did I? An accident of fate, or a stroke of luck. If I were terribly smart or talented somehow I'd probably be annoyed with my looks, because people look at them and nothing else." She shrugged, then settled with perfect ease into the pose again. "But since I'm neither of those, I've learned to accept that looking a certain way is…I don't know, a gift that makes up for a lack of other things."

"What would you trade your beauty for?"

"Any number of things. But then, a trade isn't earning, either, so it wouldn't count. Will you tell me something?"

"Probably." He took a rag out of his back pocket and dusted off his hands.

"Which are you more vain about, your looks or your work?"

He tossed the rag aside. It was odd that she could look

so sad, so serious, and still make him laugh. "No one's ever accused me of being beautiful, so there's no contest." He started to turn the easel. When she began to rise, he motioned her back. "No, relax. Look from there and tell me what you think."

Laura settled back and studied. It was only a sketch, less detailed than many of the others he'd done. It was her face and torso, her right hand resting lightly just below her left shoulder. For some reason it seemed a protective pose, not defensive, but cautious.

He'd been right about the shirt, she realized. It made her seem more of a woman than any amount of lace or silks could have. Her hair was long and loose, falling in heavy, disordered curls that contradicted the pose. She hadn't expected to find any surprises in her face, but as she studied his conception of it, she shifted uncomfortably in her chair.

"I'm not as sad as you make me look."

"I've already warned you I wouldn't change anything."

"You're free to paint as you please. I'm simply telling you that you have a misconception."

There was a huffiness in her voice that amused him. He turned the easel around again but didn't bother to look at his work. "I don't think so."

"I'm hardly tragic."

"Tragic?" He rocked back on his heels as he studied her. "There's nothing tragic about the woman in the painting. *Valiant* is the word."

She smiled at that and pushed herself out of the chair. "I'm not valiant, either, but it's your painting."

"We agree on that."

"Gabe!"

She flung out a hand. The urgency in her voice had him crossing to her quickly and gripping her hand. "What is it?"

"Look, look out there." She turned to him, using her free hand to point.

Not urgency, Gabe realized. He was tempted to strangle her. Excitement. The excitement of seeing a solitary buck less than two yards from the window. It stood deep in snow, its head lifted, scenting the air. Arrogantly, and without a trace of fear, it stared at them through the glass.

"Oh, he's wonderful. I've never seen one so big before, or so close."

It was easy to share the pleasure. A deer, a fox, a hawk circling overhead…those were some of the things that had helped him over his own grief.

"A few weeks ago I hiked down to a stream about a mile south of here. I came across a whole family. I was downwind, and I managed three sketches before the doe spotted me."

"This whole place belongs to him. Can you imagine it? Acres and acres. He must know it, even enjoy it, or else he wouldn't look so sure of himself." She laughed again, and pressed her free hand to the frosted glass. "You know, it's as if we were exhibits and he'd come to take a quick look around the zoo."

The deer nosed down in the snow, perhaps looking for the grass that was buried far beneath, perhaps scenting another animal. He moved slowly, confident in his solitude. Around him the trees dripped with ice and snow.

Abruptly he raised his head, his crown of antlers plunging high in the air. In bounds and leaps he raced across the snow and disappeared into the woods beyond.

Laughing, Laura turned, then instantly forgot everything.

She hadn't realized they had moved so close together. Nor had he. Their hands were still linked. Beside them the sun streamed in, losing power as the afternoon moved toward evening. And the cabin, like the woods beyond, was absolutely silent.

He touched her. He hadn't known he would, but the moment his fingers grazed her cheek he knew he needed to. She didn't move away. Perhaps he would have accepted it if she had. He wanted to believe he would have accepted it. But she didn't move.

There were nerves. He felt them in the hand that trembled in his. He had them, too. Another new experience. How did he approach her, when he knew he had no business approaching her? How did he resist what common sense told him he had to resist?

Yet her skin was warm under his touch. Real. Not a portrait, but a woman. Whatever had happened in her life, whatever had made her into the woman she was, that was yesterday. This was now. Her eyes, wide and more than a little frightened, were on his. She didn't move. She waited.

He swore at himself even as he slowly, ever so slowly, lowered his lips to hers.

It was madness to allow it. It was more than madness

to want it. But even before his lips touched hers she felt herself give in to him. As she gave, she braced herself, not knowing what to expect for herself, or for him.

It might have been the first. That was her one and only thought as his mouth closed over hers. Not just the first with him but the first with anyone. No one had ever kissed her like this. She had known passion, the quick, almost painful desire that came from heat and frenzy. She had known demands, some that she could answer, some that she could not. She had known the anger and the hunger a man could have for a woman, but she had never known, had never imagined, this kind of reverence.

And yet, even with that, there were hints of darker needs, needs held down by chains, that made the embrace more exciting, more involving, than any other. His hands were in her hair, searching, exploring, while his lips moved endlessly over hers. She felt the world tip and knew instinctively that he would be there to right it again.

He had to stop. He couldn't stop. One taste, just one taste, and he craved more. It seemed he'd been empty, without knowing it, and now—incredibly, swiftly, terrifyingly—he was filled.

Her hands, hesitant, somehow innocent, slipped over his arms to his shoulders. When she parted her lips, there was that same curious shyness in the invitation. He could smell the spring, though it was still buried beneath the snow, could smell it in her hair, on her skin. Even the wood smoke that always tinted the air in the cabin couldn't overwhelm it. Logs shifted in the grate,

and the wind that came up with evening began to moan
against the window. And Laura, her mouth warm and
giving under his, sighed.

He wanted to play out the fantasy, to draw her up into
his arms and take her to bed. To lie with her, to slip his
shirt from her and feel her skin against his own. To have
her touch him, hold on to him. Trust him.

The war inside him raged on. She wasn't merely a
woman, she was a woman who was carrying a child.
And growing inside her was not merely a child, but the
child of another man, one she had loved.

She wasn't his to love. He wasn't hers to trust. Still,
she pulled at him, her secrets, her eyes, eyes that said
much, much more than her words, and her beauty, which
she didn't seem to understand went far beyond the shape
and texture of her face.

So he had to stop, until he resolved within himself exactly what he wanted—and until she trusted him enough
to tell him the whole truth.

He would have drawn her away from him, but she
pressed her face into his shoulder. "Please don't say anything, just for a minute."

There were tears in her voice, and they left him more
shaken than the kiss had. The tug-of-war increased, and
finally he lifted a hand to stroke her hair. The baby
turned, moving inside her, against him, and he wondered
what in God's name he was going to do.

"I'm sorry." Her voice was under control again, but
she didn't let go. How could she have known how badly
she needed to be held, when there had been so few

times in her life when anyone had bothered? "I don't mean to cling."

"You're not."

"Well." Drawing herself up straight, she stepped back. There were no tears, but her eyes glimmered with the effort it took to hold them in. "You were going to say that you didn't mean for that to happen, but it's all right."

"I didn't mean for that to happen," he said evenly. "But that's not an apology."

"Oh." A little nonplussed, she braced a hand on the back of the chair. "I suppose what I meant is that I don't want you to feel— I don't want you to think that I— Hell." With that, she gave in and sat. "I'm trying to say that I'm not upset that you kissed me and that I understand."

"Good." He felt better, much better than he'd thought he would. Casually he dragged over another chair and straddled it. "What do you understand, Laura?"

She'd thought he would let it go at that, take the easy way out. She struggled to say what she felt without saying too much. "That you felt a little sorry for me, and involved a bit, because of the situation, and the painting, too." Why couldn't she relax again? And why was he looking at her that way? "I don't want you to think that I misunderstood. I would hardly expect you to be..." The ground was getting shakier by the minute. She was ready to shut up entirely, but he quirked a brow and gestured with his hands, inviting her, almost challenging her, to finish.

"I realize you wouldn't be attracted to me—physically, that is—under the circumstances. And I don't want to think that I interpreted what just happened as anything other than a—a sort of kindness."

"That's funny." As if he were considering the idea, Gabe reached up and scratched his chin. "You don't look stupid. I'm attracted to you, Laura, and there's a part of that attraction that's very, very physical. Making love with you may not be possible under the circumstances, but that doesn't mean that the desire to do so isn't there."

She opened her mouth as if to speak, but ended up just lifting her hands and then letting them fall again.

"The fact that you're carrying a child is only part of the reason I can't make love with you. The other, though not as obvious, is just as important. I need the story, Laura, your story. All of it."

"I can't."

"Afraid?"

She shook her head. Her eyes glimmered, but her chin lifted. "Ashamed."

He would have expected almost any other reason than that. "Why? Because you weren't married to the baby's father?"

"No. Please don't ask me."

He wanted to argue, but he bit the words back. She was looking pale and tired and just too fragile. "All right, for now. But think about this. I have feelings for you, and they're growing much faster than either of us might like. Right now I'm damned if I know what to do about it."

When he rose, she reached up and touched his arm. "Gabe, there's nothing to do. I can't tell you how much I wish it were otherwise."

"Life's what you make it, angel." He touched her hair then stepped away. "We need more wood."

Laura sat in the empty cabin and wished more than she had ever wished for anything that she had made a better job of hers.

Chapter 4

More snow had fallen during the night. It was, compared to what had come before, hardly more than a dusting. The fresh inches lay in mounds and drifts over the rest, where the wind had blown them. In places the snow was as high as a man. Miniature mountains of it lay cozily against the windowpanes, shifting constantly in the wind.

Already the sun was melting the fresh fall, and if Laura listened she could hear the water sliding down the gutters from the roof like rain. It was a friendly sound, and it made her think of hot tea by a sizzling fire, a good book read on a lazy afternoon, a nap on the sofa in early evening.

But this was morning, only an hour or two past dawn. As usual, she had the cabin to herself.

Gabe was chopping wood. From the kitchen, where

she was optimistically heating milk and a chocolate bar in a pan, she could hear the steady thud of the ax. She knew the woodbox was full, and the stack of logs outside the rear door was still high. Even if the snow lasted into June, they would still have an ample supply. Artist or not, he was a physical man, and she understood his need to do something manual and tiring.

It seemed so...normal, she thought. Her cooking in the kitchen, Gabe splitting logs, icicles growing long and shiny on the eaves outside the window. Their little world was so well tuned, so self-contained. It was like this every morning. She would rise to find him already outdoors, shoveling, chopping, hauling. She would make fresh coffee or warm what he'd left in the pot. The portable radio would bring her news from the outside, but it never seemed terribly important. After a little while he would come in, shake and stomp the snow off, then accept the cup of coffee she offered him. The routine would continue with him taking his place in behind the easel and Laura taking hers by the window.

Sometimes they would talk. Sometimes they would not.

Beneath the routine, she sensed some kind of hurry in him that she couldn't understand. Though he might paint for hours, his movements controlled and measured, he still seemed impatient to finish. The fact was, the portrait was coming along faster than she could ever have imagined. She was taking shape on canvas—or rather the woman he saw when he looked at her was taking shape. Laura couldn't understand why he had chosen to make her look so otherworldly, so dreamy. She was very much a part of the world. The child she carried grounded her to it.

But she'd learned not to complain, because he didn't listen.

He'd done other sketches, as well, some full-length, some just of her face. She told herself he was entitled, particularly if that was all the payment she could give him for the roof over her head. A few of the sketches made her uneasy, like the one he'd drawn when she'd fallen asleep on the sofa late one afternoon. She'd looked so…defenseless. And she'd felt defenseless when she'd realized that he'd watched her and drawn her while she was unaware of it.

Not that she was afraid of him. Laura poked halfheartedly at the mixture of powdered milk, water and chocolate. He'd been kinder to her than she'd had any right to expect. And, though he could be terse and brusque, he was the gentlest man she'd ever known.

Perhaps he was attracted to her. Men had often been attracted to her face. But whether he was or not he treated her with respect and care. She'd learned not to expect those things when there was attraction.

With a shrug, she poured the liquid into a mug. Now wasn't the time to focus on the feeling Gabe might or might not have. She was on her own. Fixing a mental image of creamy hot chocolate in her mind, Laura downed half the contents of the mug. She made a face, sighed, then lifted the mug again. In a matter of days she would be on her way to Denver again.

A sudden pain had her gripping the side of the counter for support. She held on, fighting back the instinctive need to call for Gabe. It was nothing, she told herself as it began to ease. Moving carefully, she started into the living room. Gabe's chopping stopped. It was in that silence that she heard the other sound. An engine? The panic came instantly, and almost as quickly was pushed down. They hadn't found her. It was ridiculous to even think it. But she walked quickly, quietly, to the front window to look out.

A snowmobile. The sight of it, shiny and toylike, might have amused and pleased her if she hadn't seen the uniformed state trooper on it. Preparing to stand her ground if it came to that, Laura moved to the door and opened it a crack.

Gabe had worked up a warm, healthy sweat. He appreciated being outdoors, appreciated the crisp air, the rhythm of his work. He couldn't say that it kept his mind off Laura. Nothing did. But it helped him put the situation into perspective.

She needed help. He was going to help her.

There were some who knew him who would have been more than a little surprised by his decision. It wasn't that anyone would have accused him of being unfeeling. The sensitivity in his paintings was proof of his capacity for emotion, passion, compassion. But few would have thought him capable of unconditional generosity.

It was Michael who had been generous.

Gabe had always been self-absorbed—or, more accurately, absorbed in his art, driven to depict life, with all its joys and pains. Michael had simply embraced life.

Now he was gone. Gabe brought the ax down, his

breath whistling through his teeth and puffing white in the thin air. And Michael's leaving had left a hole so big, so great, that Gabe wasn't certain it could ever be filled.

He heard the engine when his ax was at the apex of his swing. Distracted, he let it fall so that the blade was buried in wood. Splinters popped out to join others on the trampled snow. With a quick glance toward the kitchen window, Gabe started around the cabin to meet the visitor.

He didn't make a conscious decision to protect the woman inside. He didn't have to. It was the most natural thing in the world.

"How ya doing?" The cop, his full cheeks reddened by wind and cold, shut off the engine and he nodded to Gabe.

"Well enough." He judged the trooper to be about twenty-five and half frozen. "How's the road?"

Giving a short laugh, the trooper stepped off the snowmobile. "Let's just say I hope you've got no appointments to keep."

"Nothing pressing."

"Good thing." He offered a gloved hand. "Scott Beecham."

"Gabe Bradley."

"I heard somebody bought the old McCampbell place." With his hands on his hips, Beecham studied the cabin. "A hell of a winter to pick for moving in. We're swinging by to check on everybody on the ridge, seeing if they need supplies or if anyone's sick."

"I stocked up the day of the storm."

"Good for you." He gestured toward the Jeep. "At least you've got a fighting chance in a four-wheel drive. Could've filled a used car lot with some of the vehicles towed in. We're checking around on a compact, an '84 Chevy that took a spin into the guardrail about a quarter mile from here. Abandoned. Driver might have wandered out and got lost in the blizzard."

"My wife," Gabe said. In the doorway, Laura opened her eyes wide. "She was worried that something had happened to me and got the idea of driving into town." Gabe grinned and drew out a cigarette. "Damn near ran into me. At the rate things were going, I figured it was best to leave the car where it was and get us back here. Haven't been able to get back out to check on the damage."

"Not as bad as some I've seen the last few days. Was she hurt?"

"No. Scared ten years off both of us, though."

"I'll bet. Afraid we're going to have to tow the vehicle in, Mr. Bradley." He glanced toward the house. His voice was casual, but Gabe sensed that he was alert. "Your wife, you say?"

"That's right."

"Name on the registration was Malone, Laura Malone."

"My wife's maiden name," Gabe said easily.

On impulse, Laura pushed open the door. "Gabe?"

Both men turned to look at her. The trooper pulled off his hat. Gabe merely scowled.

"I'm sorry to interrupt—" she smiled "—but I thought the officer might like some hot coffee."

The trooper replaced his hat. "That's mighty tempting, ma'am, and I appreciate it, but I have to get along. Sorry about your car."

"My own fault. Can you tell us when the road will be open?"

"Your husband ought to be able to manage a trip into town in a day or two," Beecham said. "I wouldn't recommend the drive for you, ma'am, for the time being."

"No." She smiled at him and hugged her elbows. "I don't think I'll be going anywhere for a little while yet."

"I'll just be on my way." Beecham straddled the snowmobile again. "You got a shortwave, Mr. Bradley?"

"No."

"Might not be a bad idea to pick one up next time you're in town. More dependable than the phones. When's your baby due?"

Gabe just stared for a moment. The pronoun had stunned him. "Four or five weeks."

"You got yourself plenty of time, then." With a grin, Beecham started the engine. "This your first?"

"Yes," Gabe murmured. "It is."

"Nothing quite like it. Got myself two girls. Last one decided to be born on Thanksgiving. Hardly had two bites of pumpkin pie when I had to drive to the hospital. My wife still says it was my mother's sausage stuffing that started her off." He raised a hand and his voice. "Take care, Mrs. Bradley."

They watched, Gabe from the yard, Laura from the doorway, as the snowmobile scooted up the lane. And then they were alone.

Clearing his throat, Gabe started up the stairs. Laura said nothing, but she stepped out of the way and closed the door behind him. She waited until he was sitting on the low stone hearth, unlacing his boots.

"Thank you."

"For what?"

"You told the trooper that I was your wife."

Still frowning, he pried off a boot. "It seemed less complicated that way."

"For me," Laura agreed. "Not for you."

He shrugged his shoulders and then rose to go into the kitchen. "Any coffee?"

"Yes." She heard the glass pot chink against the mug, heard the liquid pour into the stoneware. He'd lied for her, protected her, and all she had done was take from him. "Gabe." Praying that her instincts and her conscience were right, she walked to the doorway.

"What the hell is this?" He had the pan she'd used to heat the milk in his hand.

For a moment the tension fled. "If you're desperate enough, it's hot chocolate."

"It looks like… Well, never mind what it looks like." He set it back on the stove. "That powdered stuff tastes filthy, doesn't it?"

"It's hard to argue with the truth."

"I'll try to make it into town tomorrow."

"If you do, could you…" Embarrassed, she let her words trail off.

"What do you want?"

"Nothing. It's stupid. Listen, could we sit down a minute?"

He took her hand before she could back away. "What do you want from town, Laura?"

"Marshmallows, to toast in the fireplace. I told you it was stupid," she murmured, and tried to tug her hand away.

He wanted, God, he wanted just to fold her into his arms. "Is that a craving or just a whim?"

"I don't know. It's just that I look at the fireplace and think about marshmallows." Because he wasn't laughing at her, it was easy to smile. "Sometimes I can almost smell them."

"Marshmallows. You don't want anything to go with them? Like horseradish?"

She made a face at him. "Another myth."

"You're spoiling all my preconceptions." He wasn't sure when he'd lifted her hand to his lips, but after the faintest taste of her skin he dropped it again. "And you're not wearing the shirt."

Though he was no longer touching it, her hand felt warm, warm and impossibly soft. "Oh." She took a long breath. He was thinking of the painting, not of her. He was the artist with his subject again. "I'll change."

"Fine." More than a little shaken by the extent of his desire for her, he turned back to the counter and his coffee.

The decision came quickly, or perhaps it had been made the moment she'd heard him lie for her, protect her. "Gabe, I know you want to work right away, but I'd like… I feel like I should… I want to tell you everything, if you still want to hear it."

He turned back, his eyes were utterly clear and intent. "Why?"

"Because it's wrong not to trust you." Again the breath

seemed to sigh out of her. "And because I need some-one. We need someone."

"Sit down," he said simply, leading her to the couch.

"I don't know where to start."

It would probably be easier for her to start further back, he thought as he tossed another log in the fire. "Where do you come from?" he asked when he joined her on the couch.

"I've lived a lot of places. New York, Pennsylvania, Maryland. My aunt had a little farm on the Eastern Shore. I lived with her the longest."

"Your parents?"

"My mother was very young when I was born. Un-married. She… I went to live with my aunt until…until things became difficult for her, financially. There were foster homes after that. That isn't really the point."

"Isn't it?"

She took a steadying breath. "I don't want you to feel sorry for me. I'm not telling you this so that you'll feel sorry for me."

The pride was evident in the tilt of her head, in the tone of her voice—the same quiet pride he was trying to capture on canvas. His fingers itched for his sketch pad, even as they itched to touch her face. "All right, I won't."

With a nod, she continued. "From what I can gather, things were very hard on my mother. Even without the little I was told, it's easy enough to imagine. She was only a child. It's possible that she wanted to keep me, but it didn't work out. My aunt was older, but she had children of her own. I was essentially another mouth to feed, and when it became difficult to do so, I went into foster care."

"How old were you?"

"Six the first time. For some reason it just never seemed to work out. I would stay in one place for a year, in another for two. I hated not belonging, never being a real part of what everyone else had. When I was about twelve I went back with my aunt for a short time, but her husband had problems of his own, and it didn't last."

He caught something in her voice, something that made him tense. "What sort of problems?"

"They don't matter." She shook her head and started to rise, but Gabe put his hand firmly on hers.

"You started this, Laura, now finish it."

"He drank," she said quickly. "When he drank he got mean."

"Mean? Do you mean violent?"

"Yes. When he was sober, he was discontented and critical. Drunk, he was—could be—vicious." She rubbed a hand over her shoulder, as if she were soothing an old wound. "My aunt was his usual target, but he often went after the children."

"Did he hit you?"

"Unless I was quick enough to get out of his way." She managed a ghost of a smile. "And I learned to be quick. It sounds worse than it was."

He doubted it. "Go on."

"The social services took me away again and placed me in another home. It was like being put on hold. I re-member when I was sixteen, counting the days until I'd be of age and able to at least fend for myself. Make…

I don't know, make some of my own decisions. Then I was. I moved to Pennsylvania and got a job. I was working as a clerk in a department store in Philadelphia. I had a customer, a woman, who used to come in regularly. We got friendly, and one day she came in with a man. He was short and balding—looked like a bulldog. He nodded to the woman and told her she'd been absolutely right. Then he handed me a business card and told me to come to his studio the next day. Of course, I had no intention of going. I thought… That is, I'd gotten used to men…"

"I imagine you did," Gabe said dryly.

It still embarrassed her, but since he seemed to take it in stride she didn't dwell on it. "In any case, I set the card aside and would have forgotten about it, but one of the girls who worked with me picked it up later and went wild. She told me who he was. You might know the name. Geoffrey Wright."

Gabe lifted a brow. Wright was one of the most respected fashion photographers in the business—no, *the* most. Gabe might not know much about the fashion business, but a name like Geoffrey Wright's crossed boundaries. "It rings a bell."

"When I found out he was a professional, a well-known photographer, I decided to take a chance and go to see him. Everything happened at once. He was very gruff and had me in makeup and under the lights before I could babble an excuse. I was terribly embarrassed, but he didn't seem to notice. He barked out orders, telling me to stand, sit, lean, turn. He had a fur in his vault—a full-length sable. He took it out and tossed it around my shoulders. I thought I was dreaming. I must have said so aloud, because while he was shooting he laughed and told me that in a year I could wear sable to breakfast."

Saying nothing, Gabe settled back. With his eyes narrowed, he could see her, enveloped in furs. There was a twist in his stomach as he thought about her becoming one of Wright's young and casually disposable mistresses.

"Within a month I had done a layout for *Mode* magazine. Then I did another for *Her,* and one for *Charm.* It was incredible. One day I was selling linens and the next I was having dinner with designers."

"And Wright?"

"No one in my life had ever been as good to me as Geoffrey. Oh, I knew he saw me as a commodity half the time, but he set himself up as, I don't know, a watchdog. He had plans, he'd tell me. Not too much exposure too quickly. Then, in another two years, there wouldn't be a person in the Western world who wouldn't recognize my face. It sounded exciting. Most of my life I'd been essentially anonymous. He liked that, the fact that I'd come from nothing, from nowhere. I know some of his other models saw him as cold. He often was. But he was the closest thing I'd ever had to a father."

"Is that how you saw him?"

"I suppose. And then, after all he'd done for me, after all the time he'd invested, I let him down." She started to rise again, and again Gabe stopped her.

"Where are you going?"

"I need some water."

"Sit. I'll get it."

She used the time to compose herself. Her story was only half done, and the worst part, the most painful part, was yet to come. He brought her a clear glass with ice swimming in it. Laura took two long sips, then continued.

"We went to Paris. It was like being Cinderella and being told midnight never had to come. We were scheduled to be there for a month, and because Geoffrey wanted a very French flavor to the pictures we went all over Paris for the shoot. We went to a party one night. It was one of those gorgeous spring nights when all the women are beautiful and the men handsome. And I met Tony."

He caught the slight break in her voice, the shadow of pain in her eyes, and knew without being told that she was speaking now of her baby's father.

"He was so gallant, so charming. The prince to my Cinderella. For the next two weeks, whenever I wasn't working, I was with Tony. We went dancing, we ate in little cafés and walked in the parks. He was everything I'd thought I'd wanted and knew I could never have. He treated me as though I were something rare and valuable, like a diamond necklace. There was a time when I thought that was love."

She fell silent for a moment, brooding. That had been her mistake, her sin, her vanity. Even now, a year later, it cut at her.

"Geoffrey grumbled and talked about rich young pups sowing wild oats, but I wouldn't listen. I wanted to be loved, I wanted so terribly for someone to care, to want me. When Tony asked me to marry him, I didn't think twice."

"You married him?"

"Yes." She looked at him again. "I know I led you to believe that I hadn't married the baby's father. It seemed easiest."

"You don't wear a ring."

Color washed into her face. The shame of it. "I sold them."

"I see." There was no condemnation in the two words, but she felt it nonetheless.

"We stayed in Paris for our honeymoon. I wanted to go back to the States and meet his family, but he said we should stay where we were happy. It seemed right. Geoffrey was furious with me, lectured and shouted about me wasting myself. At the time I thought he meant my career, and I ignored him. It was only later that I realized he meant my life."

She jumped when a log fell apart in the fire. It was easier to continue if she looked at the flames, she discovered. "I thought I'd found everything I'd ever wanted. When I look back I realize that those weeks we spent in Paris were like a kind of magic, something that's not quite real but that you believe because you aren't clever enough to see the illusion. Then it was time to come home."

She linked her hands together and began to fidget. He had come to recognize it as a sign of inner turmoil. Though the urge was there, he didn't take them in his to calm her. "The night before we were to leave, Tony went out. He said he had some business to tie up. I waited for

him, feeling a little sorry for myself that my new husband would leave me alone on our last night in Paris.
Then, as it got later and later, I stopped feeling sorry for
myself and started feeling frightened. By the time he
got back, it was after three and I was angry and upset."

She fell silent again. Gabe pulled the afghan from
the back of the couch and spread it over her lap. "You
had a fight."

"Yes. He was very drunk and belligerent. I'd never
seen him like that before, but I was to see him like that
again. I asked him where he'd been and he said—essentially he told me it was none of my business. We started
shouting at each other, and he told me he'd been with
another woman. At first I thought he said that just to
hurt me, but then I saw that it was true. I started to cry."

That was the worst of it, Laura thought, looking back
on the way she'd crumbled and wept. "That only made
him angrier. He tossed things around the suite, like a
little boy having a tantrum. He said things, but the gist
of it was that I'd have to get used to the way he lived,
and that I hardly had a right to be upset when I'd been
Geoffrey's whore."

Her voice broke on the last word, so she lifted the
glass and cooled her throat with the water. "That hurt the
most," she managed. "Geoffrey was almost like a father
to me, never, never anything else. And Tony knew, he
knew that I'd never been with anyone before our wedding night. I was so angry then, I stood up and began to
shout at him. I don't even know what I said, but he went
into a rage. And he—"

Gabe saw her fingers tighten like wires on the soft

folds of the afghan. Then he saw how she deliberately, and with great care, relaxed them again. With an effort, he kept his voice calm. "Did he hit you, Laura?"

She didn't answer, couldn't seem to push the next words out. Then he touched a hand to her cheek and turned her face to his. Her eyes were brimming over.

"It was so much worse than with my uncle, because I couldn't get away. He was so much stronger and faster. With my uncle, he'd simply struck out at anyone who didn't get out of the way in time. With Tony, there was something viciously deliberate in the way he tried to hurt me. Then he—" But she couldn't bring herself to speak of what had happened next.

It was a moment before she went on, and Gabe sat in silence as the rage built and built inside him until he thought he'd explode. He understood temper, he had a hair-trigger one of his own, but he could never understand, never forgive, anyone who inflicted pain on someone smaller, weaker.

"When it was over," she continued, calmer now, "he just went to sleep. I lay there, not knowing what to do. It's funny, but later, when I talked with other women who had had some of the same experiences, I found out that it's fairly common to believe you had it coming somehow.

"The next morning, he wept and he apologized, promised that it would never happen again. That became the pattern for the time we were together."

"You stayed with him?"

The color came and went in her face, and part of that, too, was shame. "We were married, and I thought

I could make it work. Then we went back to his parents' home. They hated me right from the start. Their son, the heir to the throne, had gone behind their back and married a commoner. We lived with them, and though there was talk about getting our own house, nothing was ever done about it. You could sit at the same table, hold a conversation with them, and be totally ignored. They were amazing. Tony got worse. He began to see other women, almost flaunting them. They knew what he was doing, and they knew what was happening to me. The cycle got uglier and uglier, until I knew I had to get out. I told him I wanted a divorce.

"That seemed to snap him out of it for a while. He made promises, swore he'd go into therapy, see a marriage counselor, anything I wanted. We even began to look at houses. I have to admit that I'd stopped loving him by this time, and that it was wrong, very wrong, for me to stay with him, to make promises myself. What I didn't realize was that his parents were pulling on the other end. They held the financial strings and were making it difficult for him to move out. Then I discovered I was pregnant."

She laid a hand over her belly, her fingers spread. "Tony was, well, at best ambivalent about the idea of having a child. His parents were thrilled. His mother immediately started redecorating a nursery. She bought antique cribs and cradles, silver spoons, Irish linen. Though it made me nervous, the way she was taking over, I thought that the baby might be the way to help us come together. But they weren't looking at me as the baby's mother, any more than they'd looked at me as

Tony's wife. It was *their* grandchild, *their* legacy, *their* immortality. We stopped looking for houses, and Tony began to drink again. I left the night he came home drunk and hit me."

She drew a careful breath and continued to stare at the fire. "It wasn't just me he was hitting now, but the child. That made all the difference. In fact, it made it incredibly easy to walk out. I called Geoffrey, buried my pride and asked for a loan. He wired me two thousand dollars. I got an apartment of my own, found a job and started divorce proceedings. Ten days later, Tony was dead."

The pain came, dull and low. Laura shut her eyes and rode it out. "His mother came to see me, begged me to bury the divorce papers, to come to the funeral as Tony's widow. His reputation, his memory, were all that was important now. I did what she asked, because—because I could still remember those first days in Paris. After the funeral I went back to their house. They'd told me there were things we needed to talk about. That was when they told me what they wanted, what they intended to have. They said they would pay all my medical expenses, that I would have the best possible care. And that after the baby was born they would give me a hundred thousand dollars to step aside. When I refused, when I had the nerve to be angry at what they were suggesting, they explained that if I didn't cooperate they would simply take the baby. Tony's baby. They made it very clear that they had enough money and influence to win a custody suit. They would bring out the 'fact' that I had been Geoffrey's mistress, that I had taken money from him. They'd checked my background and would show that due to my upbringing I would be an unstable influence on a child. That they, as the child's grandparents, could provide a better environment. They gave me twenty-four hours to think it over. And I ran."

He didn't speak for several minutes. What she had told him had left a bitter taste in his mouth. He had asked for her story, had all but demanded it. Now that he had it, he wasn't at all sure he could handle it.

"Laura, no matter what you were told, how you were threatened, I don't believe they could take the child."

"That isn't enough? Don't you see? As long as there's a chance, I can't risk it. I'd never be able to fight them on their terms. I don't have the money, the connections."

"Who are they?" When she hesitated, he took her hand again. "You've trusted me with this much."

"Their name is Eagleton," she said. "Thomas and Lorraine Eagleton of Boston."

His brows drew together. He knew the name. Who didn't? But because of his family's position, it was more than a name, more than an image. "You were married to Anthony Eagleton?"

"Yes." She turned to him then. "You knew him, didn't you?"

"Not well. Barely. He was more—" More Michael's age, he'd started to say. "He was younger. I met him once or twice when he came to the Coast." And what he had seen hadn't impressed him enough to have him form any opinion. "I read that he had been killed in a car accident, and I suppose a wife was mentioned, but this past year has been a little difficult, and I didn't pay attention. My family has socialized with the Eagletons occasionally, but they aren't well acquainted."

"Then you know they're an old, well-established family with old, well-established money. They consider this child a part of their…holdings. They've had me followed all across the country. Every time I would settle in a place and begin to relax I'd discover that detectives were making inquiries about me. I can't—I won't—let them find me."

He rose, to pace, to light a cigarette, to try to organize his thoughts and, more, his feelings. "I'd like to ask you something."

She sighed tiredly. "All right."

"Once before, when I asked you if you were afraid, you said no, that you were ashamed. I want to know why."

"I didn't fight back, and I didn't try hard enough to fix what was wrong. I just let it happen to me. You have no idea how difficult it is to sit here and admit that I let myself be used, that I let myself be beaten, that I let myself be driven down so low that I accepted it all."

"Do you still feel that way?"

"No." Her chin lifted. "No one's ever going to take control of my life again."

"Good." He sat on the hearth. The smoke from his cigarette disappeared up the draft. "I think you've had a hell of a time, angel, worse than anyone deserves. Whether you brought some of it on yourself, as you choose to think, or if it was just a matter of circumstances, doesn't really matter at this point. It's over."

"It's not as easy as that, Gabe. I don't just have my-self to worry about now."

"How far are you willing to go to fight them?"

"I've told you I can't—"

He interrupted her with a wave of his hand. "If you had the means. How far?"

"All the way. As far and as long as it takes. But that isn't the point, because I don't have the means."

He drew on his cigarette, studied it with apparent interest, then tossed it into the fire. "You would, if you were married to me."

Chapter 5

She said nothing, could say nothing. He sat on the hearth, his legs folded up, his eyes very cool, very calm, on her face. Part of the enormity of his talent was his ability to focus on an expression and draw the underlying emotions out of it. Perhaps because he did it so well, he also knew how to mask emotions when they were his own.

She could hear the logs sizzling behind him. The midmorning sunlight sparkled through the frost on the windowpanes and landed at his feet. He seemed totally at ease, as though he'd just suggested that they have soup for lunch. If her life had depended upon it, Laura couldn't have said whether it meant any more to him than that.

Using the table for leverage, she rose.

"I'm tired. I'm going in to lie down."

"All right. We can talk about this later."

She whirled around, and it wasn't anguish or fear he saw on her face now, it was fury, livid and clear. "How could you sit there and say something like that to me after everything I've told you?"

"You might consider that I said it because of everything you've told me."

"Oh, the Good Samaritan again." She detested the bitterness in her voice, but she could do nothing to stop it. "The white knight, riding in full of chivalry and good intentions to save the bumbling, inept female. Do you think I should fall on my knees and be grateful? That I would blindly let myself be taken over again, fall back into the same pitiful, destructive pattern a second time, because a man offers me a way out?"

He thought about controlling his temper, then rose, deciding to let her see it. "I have no desire to control you, and I'll be damned if you're going to stand there and compare me with some weak-minded alcoholic wife-beater."

"What then—the knight on a white charger, selflessly rescuing damsels in distress?"

He laughed at that, but his anger was still on the edge. "No one's ever accused me of that. I'm very selfish, which is another reason for my suggestion. I'm moody—you've been around me long enough to know that. I have a temper and I can get angry. But I don't hit women, and I don't use them."

With an effort, she pulled her emotions back in and forced them to settle. "I didn't mean to imply that you did, or to compare you with someone else. It's the situation that's comparable."

"One has nothing to do with the other. The fact that I have money only works to your advantage."

"I didn't marry Tony for his money."

"No." His tone softened. "No, I'm sure you didn't. But in this case I'm willing to accept that you marry me for mine."

"Why?"

Something flickered in his eyes and was gone before she could read it. "That might have been the wisest question to ask first."

"Maybe you're right." She already regretted the outburst of temper and harsh words, as she invariably did. "I'm asking it now."

With a nod, he roamed the room, stopping before the nearly completed portrait. He stared at it, as he had stared at it countless times before, trying to understand, to define, not only Laura, but himself.

"I feel something for you. I'm not sure what it is, but it's very strong. Stronger than anything I've felt before." He lifted a finger to the face on canvas. He wished he could explain himself completely, to himself, to her, but he'd always expressed himself best through painting. "I'm attracted to you, Laura, and I've discovered recently that I've been alone long enough."

"That might be enough, almost enough, for marriage, but not for me, not to me. Not with what you'd be taking on."

"I have some debts to pay," he murmured, then turned

to her again. "Helping you, and the child, might just clear the slate."

Whatever anger she'd felt evaporated. It only took the kindness and the grief in his eyes. "You've already helped us, more than I can ever repay."

"I don't want payment." The impatience, the edge, was back in his voice. "What I want is you. How many ways do you want me to say it?"

"I don't think I want you to say it." The nerves began to eat at her again, and she twisted her fingers together. He meant it. She had no doubt that he meant what he said. The prospect of being wanted by him both thrilled and terrified her. "Don't you see, I've already made one terrible mistake."

He crossed to her, gently drawing her hands apart and into his. "You're not indifferent to me?"

"No, but—"

"You're not afraid of me?"

Some of the tension seeped out of her. "No."

"Then let me help you."

"I'm going to have another man's child."

"No." He took her face in his hands because he wanted her eyes on his. "Marry me, and the child is ours. Privately, publicly, totally."

The tears came back. "They'll come."

"Let them. They won't touch you again, and they won't take the baby."

Safety. Could what had always eluded her really be only a promise away? She opened her mouth, knowing that agreement was on her tongue. Then her heart turned over in her chest and she lifted a hand to his cheek. "How could I do this to you?"

For an answer, he put his lips to hers. The need was there, she couldn't deny it, couldn't pretend it away. She tasted it as his mouth drew from hers. She felt it when his hand skimmed through her hair to brace, both possessive and supportive, at the back of her neck. Instinctively, wanting to give, she lifted her other hand to his face. They rested there, comforting.

She wasn't the only one who had demons, Laura thought. She wasn't the only one who needed love and understanding. Because he was strong, it was easy to forget that he, too, might have pain. Seeking to soothe, she drew him closer into her arms.

He could have sunk into her, into the softness, the generosity. This was what he wanted to capture on canvas, her warmth, her spirit. And this was what he was forced to admit he would never have the skill to translate. This part of her beauty, this most essential part, could never be painted. But it could be cherished.

"You need me," he murmured as he drew her away. "And I need you."

She nodded, then rested her head on his shoulder, because that seemed to say it all.

Due to fresh flurries, it was three days before Gabe risked a trip into town. Laura watched him as he downed a final cup of coffee before pulling on his coat.

"I'll be as quick as I can."

"I'd rather you took your time and paid attention to the roads."

"The Jeep drives like a tank." He accepted the gloves she held out to him but didn't put them on. "I don't like leaving you alone."

"Gabe, I've been taking care of myself for a long time."

"Things have changed. My lawyers have probably sent the marriage license."

Immediately she began to fuss with the breakfast dishes. "That would be quick work."

"They get paid to work fast, and it's been three days since I contacted them. If I can arrange it, I'd like to bring a justice of the peace back here with me."

A cup slipped out of her hand and plopped into the soapy water. "Today?"

"You haven't changed your mind?"

"No, but—"

"I want my name on the birth certificate." He had a moment of panic, vague and disturbing, at her hesitation. "It would be less complicated if we were married before the baby's born."

"Yes, that makes sense." It seemed so rushed. She plunged her hands into the water and began to wash. Her first wedding had been rushed, too, a whirlwind of flowers and champagne and white silk.

"I realize you might prefer something a little more festive, but under the circumstances—"

"No." She turned and managed a smile. "No, I don't care about that. If you can arrange it for today, here, that's fine."

"All right, then. Laura, I'd feel better if you rested until I got back. You didn't sleep well."

She turned back again. No, she hadn't slept well. The

nightmare had come back, and she hadn't rested until Gabe had come in and finally slipped into bed with her. "I won't overdo."

"I don't think it would tax your strength for you to kiss me goodbye."

That made her smile. She turned, her hands still dripping, to lift her lips to his.

"Not even married yet and you're already kissing me as though we've been together twenty years." He changed the mood simply by nipping her lip. In seconds she was clinging to him, and there was nothing casual about the embrace.

"Better," he murmured. "Now go lie down. I'll be back in less than two hours."

"Be careful."

He closed the door. In moments she heard the sound of the Jeep's engine chugging to life. Moving into the living room, she watched Gabe drive away.

Strangely enough, even as the quiet settled over the cabin, she didn't feel alone. She felt nervous, she admitted with a little laugh. Brides were entitled to nerves. If Gabe had his way—and she'd come to believe that he nearly always did—they would be married that afternoon.

And her life, Laura realized, would change yet again. This time it would be better. She would make it better.

As the ache in her lower back grew worse, she pressed her hand against it. Blaming the discomfort she'd been feeling all morning on the mattress and a restless night, she walked over to the portrait.

He'd finished it the day before. She knew, because

he'd explained it to her, that the paint would take a few days to set and dry completely, so she didn't touch it. She sat on the stool Gabe sometimes used and studied her own face.

So this was how he saw her, she thought. Her skin was pale, with only a faint shadow of color along her cheekbones. It was partly that whiteness, that translucence, that made her appear like the angel he sometimes called her. She looked as though she were caught in a daydream, one of the many she'd indulged in during the hours Gabe had painted. As she had told him—as she had complained—there was too much vulnerability. It was in her eyes, around her mouth. There was something strong and independent about the pose, about the way her head was tilted, but that lost, sad look in her eyes seemed to negate the strength.

She was reading too much into it, Laura decided as the pain dug, deep and dull, into her back. Rubbing at it, she rose to look around the cabin.

She would be married here, in a matter of hours. There would be no crowd of well-wishers, no pianist playing romantic songs, no trail of rose petals. Yet, with or without the trimmings, she would be a bride. She might not be able to make it look festive, but at least she could tidy up.

The pain in her back drove her to lie down. Two hours later she heard the Jeep coming down the lane. For a moment longer she lay there, working to block out the discomfort. Later, she told herself, she would soak the ache away in a hot tub. She walked into the living room just as Gabe ushered an elderly couple into the cabin.

"Laura, this is Mr. and Mrs. Witherby. Mr. Witherby is a justice of the peace."

"Hello. It's so nice of you to come all this way."

"Part of the job," Mr. Witherby said, adjusting his fogging glasses. "'Sides that, your young man here wasn't going to take no for an answer."

"Don't you worry about this old man here." Mrs. Witherby patted her husband's arm and studied Laura. "He loves to complain."

"Can I get you something, some coffee?"

"Don't you fuss. Mr. Bradley's got a carload of supplies. You just sit down and let him take care of it." She had already walked over to lead Laura to the couch with her frail hands. "Man's nervous as a goose at Christmas," she confided. "Let him keep busy for a spell."

Though she couldn't imagine Gabe being nervous about anything, she thought the Witherbys would expect such emotion from a man about to marry. Laura listened to Gabe rattling bags and cans in the kitchen. "Maybe I should help him."

"Now, you sit right here." Mrs. Witherby motioned to her husband to sit, as well. "A woman's entitled to be waited on when she's carrying. The good Lord knows you won't have much time to sit once that baby's born."

Grateful, Laura shifted to ease the throbbing in her back. "You have children?"

"Had six of them. Now we've got twenty-two grandchildren and five great-grandchildren."

"And another on the way," Mr. Witherby stated, pulling out a pipe.

"You can just put that smelly thing away," his wife

told him. "You aren't smoking up this room with this lady expecting."

"I wasn't going to light it," he said, and began to chew on the stem.

Satisfied that her husband had been put in his place, Mrs. Witherby turned back to Laura. "That's a pretty picture there." She indicated a sprawling landscape that might very well sell for an amount in six figures. "Your man's an artist fellow?"

Her man. Laura experienced a twinge of panic and a glow of pleasure at the phrase. "Yes, Gabe's an artist."

"I like pictures," she said comfortably. "Got me one of the seashore over my sofa."

Gabe walked back in carrying an armful of flowers. Feeling awkward, he cleared his throat. "They sold them at the market."

"And he bought them out, too," Mrs. Witherby cackled. Then, with a few wheezes, she heaved herself off the couch. "You got a vase? She can't be carrying all of them."

"No, at least…I don't know."

"Men." She sighed and then winked at Laura. "Give them to me and let me take care of it. You can do something useful, like putting more wood on that fire. Wouldn't want your lady to catch a chill."

"Yes, ma'am."

If he'd ever felt more of a fool, he couldn't remember when. Wanting to keep his hands busy, he moved to the fire.

"Don't let her browbeat you, boy," Mr. Witherby advised him from the comfort of his chair. "She's already spent fifty-two years nagging me."

"Somebody had to," Mrs. Witherby called out from the kitchen, and he chuckled.

"Sure you two know what you're getting into?"

Gabe dusted his hands on the thighs of his jeans and grinned. "No."

"That's the spirit." Witherby laughed and rested his head against the back of the chair. "Essie, get that bag of bones you call a body moving, will you? These two people want to get married while they're still young."

"Keep your tongue in your mouth," she muttered. "Already lost his teeth." She came in carrying a watering can filled with flowers. She set it in the middle of the coffee table, nodded her approval, then handed Laura a single white carnation.

"Thank you. They're lovely." She started to rise and nearly winced at the stab of pain in her back. Then Gabe was there to take her hand and draw her to his side.

They stood in front of the fire with wood crackling and the scent of the flowers merging with that of the smoke. The words were simple and very old. Despite the countless weddings she'd been to, Mrs. Witherby dabbed at her eyes.

To love. To honor. To cherish.

For richer. For poorer.

Forsaking all others.

The ring he slipped onto her finger was very plain, just a gold band that was a size too large. Looking at it, Laura felt something grow inside her. It was warm and sweet and tremulous. Curling her hand into his, she repeated the words, and meant them, from her heart.

Let no man put asunder.

"You may kiss the bride," Witherby told him, but Gabe didn't hear.

It was done. It was irrevocable. And until that moment he hadn't been completely aware of how much it would mean to him.

With her hand still caught in his, he kissed her and sealed the promise.

"Congratulations." Mrs. Witherby brushed her dry lips over Gabe's cheek, then Laura's. "Now you sit down, Mrs. Bradley, and I'm going to fix you a nice cup of tea before we drag your husband off again."

"Thank you, but we don't have any tea."

"I bought some," Gabe put in.

"That and everything else he could lay his hands on. Come on, Ethan, give me a hand."

"You ought to be able to fix a cup of tea by yourself."

Mrs. Witherby rolled her eyes. "You'd think the old goat would have a little more romance, seeing as he's married more'n five hundred couples in his time. In the kitchen, Ethan, and give these young people five minutes alone."

He grumbled about wanting his supper, but he followed her.

"They're wonderful," Laura murmured.

"I don't think I'd have gotten him away from his TV if she hadn't shoved him out the door."

Silence followed, awkward. "It was nice of you to think of flowers…and the ring."

He lifted her hand and studied it. "They don't have a jewelry store in Lonesome Ridge. They sell these at the hardware in a little case next to sixpenny nails. It may just turn your finger green."

She laughed and knew she'd treasure it even more now. "You may not believe it, but you may have saved my life by buying that tea."

"I got some marshmallows, too."

She hated it, despised herself for not being able to control it, but she started to cry. "I'm sorry. I can't seem to do anything about this."

Discomfort surged through him. He was feeling edgy himself, and tears did nothing to help matters. "Look, I know it wasn't exactly the wedding of the century. We can have some sort of party or reception back in San Francisco."

"No, no, that's not it." Though she urged her hands over her face, the tears kept coming. "It was lovely and sweet and I don't know how to thank you."

"Not crying would be a good start." He had a bandanna in his pocket, one that he used more often than not as a paint rag. He drew it out and offered it to her. "Laura, we're legally married. That means you don't have to be grateful for every bunch of daisies I hand you."

She sniffled into the cloth and tried to smile. "I think it was the marshmallows that did it."

"Keep this up and you won't get any more."

"I want you to know..." She dried her face and managed to compose herself. "I want you to know that I'm going to do everything I can to make you happy, to make you comfortable, so that you never regret what you did today."

"I'm going to regret it," he said suddenly impatient, "if you keep making it sound as though I gave someone else the last life jacket as the ship was sinking. I married you because I wanted to, not to be noble."

"Yes, but I—"

"Shut up, Laura." To make certain she did, he closed his mouth over hers. And for the first time she felt the true strength of his passion and need and desire. With a little murmur of surprise, she drew him closer.

This was what he had needed, all he had needed, to settle him. Yet even as the first layer of tension dissolved, a new layer, one built on desire, formed.

"Before too much longer," he said against her mouth, "we're going to finish this. I want to make love with you, Laura. And after I do you won't have the strength to thank me."

Before she could think of a response, Mrs. Witherby came in with her tea. "Now let the poor thing rest and drink this while it's hot." She set the cup on the table in front of Laura. "I hate to drag you out on your wedding day, Mr. Bradley, but the sooner you drive us back to town, the sooner you can get back and fix your wife that nice steak you bought for supper."

She moved over to gather up her coat. On impulse, Laura drew one of the flowers from the watering can and took it to her. "I'm never going to forget you, Mrs. Witherby."

"There now." Touched, she sniffed at the flower. "You

just take care of yourself and that baby of yours. Shake a leg, Ethan."

"I should only be an hour," Gabe told her. "The roads aren't too bad. I really think you should rest, Laura. You look exhausted."

"I'm supposed to look glowing, but I promise I won't lift anything heavier than a teacup until you get back."

This time she watched the Jeep drive away, running her finger over and over her wedding ring. It took so little, she thought, to change so much. She bent, trying to ease the ache in her back, then she crossed the room to finish her tea.

Her back had never ached like this, not even after she'd worked a full day on her aunt's farm. The pain was constant and deep. She tried stretching out, then curling up, then stretching out again. Impatient with herself, she tried to ignore it, concentrating instead on roasting marshmallows and warming tea.

She'd been alone less than ten minutes when the first contraction hit.

It wasn't the vague warning pain she'd read about. It was sharp and long. Caught off guard, she had no time to breathe her way over it. Instead, she tensed, fought against it, then collapsed against the cushions when it faded.

It couldn't be labor. Her forehead broke out in sweat as she tried to dismiss the idea. It was too early, a month too early, and it had come on so suddenly. False labor, she assured herself. Brought on by nerves and by the excitement of the day.

But the back pain. Struggling to keep calm, she

pushed herself into a sitting position. Was it possible she'd been having back labor all morning?

No, it had to be false labor. It had to be.

But when the second contraction hit she began to time them.

She was in bed when Gabe returned, but she couldn't call out to him, because she was riding out the latest contraction. The fear that had gripped her in a stranglehold for the past hour faded a bit. He was here, and somehow that meant that everything would be all right. She heard him toss a log on the fire, took a last cleansing breath as the pain passed and called out.

The urgency in her voice had him across the room in three strides. At the bedroom door he paused, and his heart jumped into his throat.

She was propped against the pillows, half lying, half sitting. Her face was bathed in sweat. Her eyes, always dark, were sheened with moisture and nearly black.

"I have to go back on our deal," she managed, struggling with a smile because she saw the same blank fear she felt reflected on his face. "The baby's decided to come a little early."

He didn't ask if she was sure or fumble with reasons why it wasn't a good idea. He wanted to, but he found himself beside the bed, with her hand gripped in his. "Take it easy. Just hold on and I'll phone for a doctor."

"Gabe, the phone's out." Nerves skipped in and out of her voice. "I tried it when I realized this was happening so fast."

"Okay." Fighting for calm, he brushed the damp hair

away from her face. "There was an accident on the way into town. Lines must have gone down. I'll get some extra blankets and I'll take you in."

She pressed her lips together. "Gabe, it's too late. I couldn't make the trip." She tried to swallow, but fear had dried up the moisture in her mouth and throat. "I've been in labor for hours, all morning, and I didn't know it. It was back labor, and I didn't pay attention. With everything that was going on, I thought it was nerves and the restless night I'd had."

"Hours," he murmured, and eased himself down on the edge of the bed. His mind went blank, but then her fingers tightened on his. "How far apart are the pains?"

"Five minutes. I've been—" She let her head fall back and began to breathe in short, deep gasps. Gabe slipped his hand over her and felt the hardening of her abdomen.

He'd glanced through the birth and baby books she'd brought with her. To pass the time, he'd told himself, but there had been something deep inside him that had been compelled to understand what she was going through. Perhaps it was instinct that had had him absorbing the advice, the details, the instructions. Now, seeing her in pain, everything he'd read seemed to slip away from him.

When the contraction passed, her face was shiny with fresh sweat. "Getting closer," she whispered. "There's not much time." Though she bit down on her lips, a sob escaped her. "I can't lose the baby."

"The baby's going to be fine, and so are you." He squeezed her hand once reassuringly. They would need towels, lots of them. String and scissors had to be sterilized. It was really very simple when you thought about it. He only hoped it was as simple when you put it into practice.

"Just hang on. I have to get some things." He saw the doubt flash in her eyes, and he leaned over her. "I'm not going to leave you. I'm going to take care of you, Laura. Trust me."

She nodded, and with her head slumped back on the pillow, she closed her eyes.

When he came back, her eyes were focused on the ceiling and she was panting. After setting fresh towels on the foot of the bed, he spread another blanket over her. "Are you cold?"

She shook her head. "The baby will need to be kept warm. He's not full-term."

"I've built up the fire, and there are plenty of blankets." Gently he wiped her face with a cool, damp cloth. "You've talked to doctors, you've read the books. You know what to expect."

She looked up at him, trying to swallow past a dry throat. Yes, she knew what to expect, but reading about it, imagining it, was a far cry from the experience.

"They lied." Her mouth moved into a weak smile when his brows drew together. "They try to tell you it doesn't hurt so much if you ride out the pain."

He brought her hand to his lips and held it there. "Yell all you want. Scream the roof down. Nobody's going to hear."

"I'm not screaming this baby into the world." Then she gasped, and her fingers dug into his. "I can't—"

"Yes, you can. Pant. Pant, Laura. Squeeze my hand.

Harder. Concentrate on that." He kept his eyes locked on hers while she pushed air out. "You're doing fine, better than fine." When her body went lax, he moved to the foot of the bed. "The pains are closer?" As he spoke, he knelt on the mattress and shifted the blanket.

"Almost on top of each other."

"That means it's almost over. Hold on to that."

She tried to moisten her dry lips, but her tongue was thick. "If anything happens to me, promise you'll—"

"Nothing's going to happen." He bit off the words. Their eyes met again, hers glazed with pain, his dark with purpose. "Damn it, I'm not going to lose either of you now, understand? The three of us are going to pull this off. Now, you've got work to do, angel."

Each time the pains hit her, he shuddered with it. Time seemed to drag as she struggled through them, then race again as she rested. Gabe moved back and forth, to arrange her pillows, to wipe her face, then knelt again to check the progress of birth.

He could hear the fire roaring in the next room, but he still worried that the cabin would be too cold. Then he worried about the heat, because Laura's laboring body was like a furnace.

He hadn't known birth could be so hard on a woman. He knew she was close to total exhaustion, but she managed to pull herself through time after time, recharging somehow during the all-too-brief moments between contractions. Pain seemed to tear through her, impossibly hard, impossibly ruthless. His own shirt was soaked with sweat, and he swore constantly, silently, as he urged her to breathe, to pant, to concentrate. All his ambitions, his joys, his griefs, whittled down to focus on that one room, that one moment, that one woman.

It seemed to him that she should weaken, with her body being battered by the new life fighting to be born. But as the moments passed she seemed to draw on new reserves of strength. There was something fierce and valiant about her face as she pushed herself forward and braced for whatever happened next.

"Do you have a name picked out?" he asked, hoping to distract her.

"I made lists. Sometimes at night I'd try to imagine what the baby would look like and try to— Oh, God."

"Hold on. Breathe, angel. Breathe through it."

"I can't. I have to push."

"Not yet, not yet. Soon." From his position at the foot of the bed, he ran his hands over her. "Pant, Laura."

Her concentration kept slipping in and out. If she stared into his eyes, if she pulled the strength from them, she would make it. "I can't hold off much longer."

"You don't have to. I can see the head." There was wonder in his voice when he looked back at her. "I can see it. Push with the next one."

Giddy, straining with the effort, she bore down. She heard the long, deep-throated moan, but she didn't know it was her own voice. Gabe shouted at her, and in response she automatically began to pant again.

"That's good, that's wonderful." He barely recognized his own voice, or his own hands. Both were shaking. "I have the head. Your baby's beautiful. The shoulders come next."

She braced herself, desperate to see. "Oh, God." Tears

mixed with sweat as she steepled her hands over her mouth. "It's so little."

"And strong as an ox. You have to push the shoulders out." Sweat dripped off his forehead as he cupped the baby's head in his hand and leaned over it. "Come on, Laura, let's have a look at the rest of it."

Her fingers dug into the blankets, and her head fell back. And she gave birth. Over her own gasping breaths she heard the first cry.

"A boy." Gabe's eyes were wet as he held the squirming new life in his hands. "You have a son."

As the tears rolled, she began to laugh. The pain and the terror were forgotten. "A boy. A little boy."

"With a loud mouth, ten fingers and ten toes." He reached for her hand and gripped it hard. "He's perfect, angel."

Their fingers linked over the baby, and the cabin echoed with the high, indignant wails of the newborn.

She couldn't rest. Laura knew Gabe wanted her to sleep, but she couldn't shut her eyes. The baby, nearly an hour old now, was wrapped in blankets and tucked in the curve of her arm. He was sleeping, she thought, but she couldn't stop herself from tracing a fingertip over his face.

So tiny. Five pounds, seven ounces, on the vegetable scale that Gabe had unearthed and scrubbed down. Seventeen and a half inches tall, and with only a bit of pale blond peach fuzz covering his head. She couldn't stop looking at him.

"He's not going to disappear, you know."

Laura glanced up at the doorway and smiled. Fatigue had left her skin almost pale enough to see through. Triumph had given her eyes a rich glow. "I know." She held out a hand in invitation. "I'm glad you came in," she said as he sat on the bed. "I know you must be exhausted, but I'd like you to stay a minute."

"You did all the work," he murmured, running a finger down the baby's cheek.

"That's not true, and that's the first thing I want to say. We wouldn't have made it without you."

"Of course you would have. I was basically a cheerleader."

"No." Her hand tightened on his, demanding that he look at her. "You were as responsible for his life as I was. I know what you said about having your name on the birth certificate, about helping us, but I want you to know it's more than that. You brought him into the world. There's nothing I can ever do or say that could be enough. Don't look like that." She gave a quiet laugh and settled back among the pillows. "I know you hate to be thanked, and that's not what I'm doing."

"Isn't it?"

"No." She shifted the baby from her arm to his. It was a gesture that said more, much more, than the words that followed it. "I'm telling you that you got more than a wife today."

The baby went on sleeping peacefully, cupped between them.

He didn't know what to say. He touched the tiny hand and watched it curl reflexively. As an artist he'd thought he understood the full range of beauty. Until today.

"I've been reading about preemies," he began. "His weight is good, and from what the book says a baby born after the thirty-fourth week is in pretty good shape, but I want to get you both into a hospital. Will you be strong enough to travel into Colorado Springs tomorrow?"

"Yes. We'll both be strong enough."

"We'll leave in the morning, then. Do you think you could eat now?"

"Only a horse."

He grinned, but he couldn't quite bring himself to give her back the baby. "You may have to settle for beefsteak. Isn't he hungry?"

"I imagine he'll let us know."

Just as Laura had been, he was compelled to trace the shape of the child's face. "What about that name? We can't keep calling him *he*."

"No, we can't." Laura stroked the soft down on his head. "I was wondering if you'd like to pick his name."

"Me?"

"Yes, you must have a favorite, or a name of someone who's important to you. I'd like you to choose."

"Michael," he murmured, looking down at the sleeping infant.

Chapter 6

San Francisco. It was true that Laura had always wanted to see it, but she had never expected to arrive there with a two-week-old son and a husband. And she had never expected to be shown into a tall, gracious house near the Bay.

Gabe's house. Hers, too, she thought as she rubbed her thumb nervously over her wedding ring. It was foolish to be jumpy because the house was beautiful and big. It was ridiculous to feel small and insecure because you could taste the wealth and the prominence just by breathing the air.

But she did.

She stepped into the tiled foyer and wished desperately for the comfort of the tiny cabin. It had begun to snow again the day they'd left Colorado, and though the mild spring breeze and the tiny buds here were wonderful, she found herself wishing for the cold and ferocity of the mountains.

"It's lovely," she managed, glancing up at the gentle curve of the stairs.

"It was my grandmother's." Gabe set down the luggage and took in the familiar surroundings. It was a house he'd always appreciated for its beauty and its balance. "She held on to it after her marriage. Shall I show you around, or would you rather rest?"

She nearly winced. It was as though he were talking to a guest. "If I rested as much as you'd like, I'd sleep my way through the rest of the year."

"Then why don't I show you the upstairs." He knew he sounded polite, overly polite, but he'd been edgy ever since they'd stepped off the plane. The farther away from Colorado they'd gotten, the further Laura had withdrawn from him. It was nothing he could put his finger on, but it was there.

Hefting two cases, he started up the stairs. He was bringing his wife, and his son, home. And he didn't know quite what to say to either of them. "I've used this bedroom." He strode in and set the cases at the foot of a big oak bed. "If there's another you'd prefer, we can arrange it."

She nodded, thinking that though they'd shared a motel room while the baby had been in the hospital they had only shared a bed in the cabin, the night before Michael had been born. It would be different here. Everything would be different here.

"It's a beautiful room."

Her voice was a little stiff, but she smiled, trying to

soften it. The room was lovely, with its high ceilings and the glossy antiques. There was a terrace, and through the glass doors she could see a garden below, with green leaves already formed. The floors were dark with age and gleaming, just as the Oriental rug was faded with age and rich with heritage.

"The bath's through there," Gabe told her as she ran a finger down the carving in an old chifforobe. "My studio's at the end of the hall. The light's best there, but there's a room next to this that might do as a nursery."

When they spoke of the baby, things always relaxed between them. "I'd love to see it. After all those days in the incubator, Michael deserves a room of his own."

She followed Gabe out and into the next room. It was decorated in blues and grays with a stately four-poster and a many-cushioned window seat. As with the other rooms she'd seen, paintings hung on the wall, some of them Gabe's, others by artists he respected.

"It's beautiful, but what would you do with all these things?"

"They can be stored." He dismissed the furnishings with a shrug. "Michael can stay in our room until his is finished."

"You don't mind? He's bound to wake during the night for weeks yet."

"I could stick the pair of you in a hotel until it's convenient."

She started to speak, but then she recognized the look in his eyes. "Sorry. I can't get used to it."

"Get used to it." He moved over to cup her face in his hand. Whenever he did that, she was almost ready to believe that dreams came true. "I may not have the equipment to feed him, but I figure I can learn to change a diaper." He stroked a thumb under her jawline. "I've been told I'm clever with my hands."

The heat rushed into her face. She was torn between stepping into his arms and backing away. The baby woke and decided for her. "Speaking of feeding..."

"Why don't you use the bedroom, where you can be comfortable? I have some calls to make."

She knew what was coming. "Your family?"

"They're going to want to meet you. Are you up to it this evening?"

She wanted to snap that she wasn't an invalid, but she knew he wasn't speaking of her physical health. "Yes, of course."

"Fine. I'll make arrangements about the nursery. Did you have any colors in mind?"

"Well, I..." She expected to paint the room herself. She'd wanted to. Things were different now, she reminded herself. The cabin had easily become theirs, but the house was his. "I'd like yellow," she told him. "With white trim."

She sat in a chair by the window while Michael suckled hungrily. It was so good to have him with her all the time instead of having to go to the hospital to feed him, touch him, watch him. It had been so hard to leave him there and go back to a hotel room and wait until she could go back and see him again.

Smiling, she looked down at him. His eyes were closed, and his hand was pressed against her breast.

He was already gaining weight. Healthy, the doctor

in Colorado Springs had said. Sound as a dollar. And the tag on his little wristband had read Michael Monroe Bradley.

Who was Michael? she wondered. Gabe's Michael. She hadn't asked, but knew that the name, the person, was important.

"You're Michael now," she murmured as the baby began to doze at her breast.

Later she laid him on the bed, surrounding him with pillows though she knew he couldn't roll yet. Going to her suitcase, she took out her hairbrush. It was silly, of course, to feel compelled to leave some mark of herself on the room. But she set the brush on Gabe's bureau before she left.

She found him downstairs, in a dark-paneled library with soft gray carpet. Because he was on the phone, she started to back out, but he waved her in and continued to talk.

"The paintings should be here by the end of the week. Yes, I'm back in harness again. I haven't decided. You take a look first. No, I'm going to be tied up here for a few days, thanks anyway. I'll let you know." He hung up, then glanced at Laura. "Michael?"

"He's asleep. I know there hasn't been time, but he's going to need his own bed. I thought I could run out and buy something if you could watch him for a little while."

"Don't worry about it. My parents are coming over soon."

"Oh."

He sat on the edge of the desk and frowned at her. "They're not monsters, Laura."

"Of course not, it's just that… It seems we're so out in the open," she blurted out. "The more people who know about Michael, the more dangerous it is."

"You can't keep him in a glass bubble. I thought you trusted me."

"I did. I do," she amended quickly, but not quickly enough.

"Did," Gabe repeated. It wasn't anger he felt so much as pressing regret. "You made a decision, Laura. On the day he was born, you gave him to me. Are you taking him back?"

"No. But things are different here. The cabin was—"

"An excellent place to hide. For both of us. Now it's time to deal with what happens next."

"What does happen?"

He picked up a paperweight, an amber ball with darker gold streaks in the center. He set it down again, then crossed to her. She'd shed weight quickly. Her stomach was close to flat, her breasts were high and full, her hips were impossibly narrow. He wondered how it would feel to hold her now, now that the waiting was over.

"We might start with this."

He kissed her, gently at first, until he felt her first nerves fade into warmth. That was what he'd been desperate for, that promise, that comfort. When he gathered her close, she fitted against him as he'd once imagined she would. Her hair, bound up, was easily set free with a sweep of his hand. She made a small sound—a murmur of surprise or acceptance—and then her arms went around him.

And the kiss was no longer gentle.

Passion, barely restrained, and hunger, far from sated, rippled from him into her. An ache, long buried, grew in her until she was straining against him, whispering his name.

Then his lips were roaming over her face, raking over her throat, searing her skin, then cooling it, then searing it again, while his hands stroked and explored with a new freedom.

Too soon. Some sane part of him knew it was too soon for anything more than a touch, a taste. But the more he indulged in her, the more his impatience grew. Taking her by the shoulders, he drew her away and fought to catch his breath.

"You may not trust me as you once did, angel, but trust this. I want you."

Giving in to the need, she held on to him, pressing her face into his shoulder. "Gabe, is it so wrong of me to wish it was just the three of us?"

"Not wrong." He stared over the top of her head as he stroked her hair. "Just not possible, and less than fair to Michael."

"You're right." Drawing a breath, she stepped back. "I want to go check on him."

Shaken by the emotions he pulled out of her, she started back up the stairs. Halfway up, she stopped, stunned.

She was in love with him. It wasn't the love she'd come to accept, the kind that came from gratitude and dependence. It wasn't even the strong, beautiful bond that had been forged when they'd brought Michael into the world. It was more basic than that, the most elemental love of woman for man. And it was terrifying.

She had loved once before, briefly, painfully. That love had kept her chained down. All her life she'd been a victim, and her marriage had both accented that and ultimately freed her. She'd learned through necessity how to be strong, how to take the right steps.

She couldn't be that woman again, she thought as her fingers gripped the banister. She wouldn't. That was what had bothered her most about the house, about the things in it. She had stepped into a house like this before, a house in which she had been out of place and continually helpless.

Not again, she told herself, and shut her eyes. Never again.

Whatever she felt for Gabe, she wouldn't allow it to change her back into that kind of woman. She had a child to protect.

The doorbell rang. Laura sent one swift look over her shoulder, then fled up the stairs.

When Gabe opened the door, he was immediately enveloped in soft fur and strong perfume. It was his mother, a woman of unwavering beauty and unwavering opinions. She didn't believe in brushing cheeks, she believed in squeezing, hard and long.

"I've missed you. I didn't know what it would take to drag you off that mountain, but I didn't think it would be a wife and a baby."

"Hello, Mother." He smiled at her, giving her a quick sweeping look that took in her stubbornly blond hair and her smooth cheeks. She had Michael's eyes. They were a darker green than his own, with touches of gray. Seeing them brought a pang and a pleasure. "You look wonderful."

"So do you, except for the fact that you've lost about ten pounds and can't afford to. Well, where are they?" With that, Amanda Bradley marched inside.

"Give the boy a chance, Mandy." Gabe exchanged bear hugs with his father, a tall, spare man with a hang-dog expression and a razor-sharp mind. "Glad you're back. Now she'll take to rattling your cage instead of mine."

"I can handle you both." She was already slipping off her gloves with short, quick little motions. "We brought a bottle of champagne over. I thought since we missed the wedding, the birth and everything else, we should at least toast the homecoming. For heaven's sake, Gabe, don't just stand there, I'm dying to see them."

"Laura went up to check the baby. Why don't we go in and sit down?"

"This way, Mandy," Cliff Bradley said, taking his wife's arm when she started to object.

"Very well, then. You can hold me off for five minutes by telling me how your work's been going."

"Well." He watched his parents sit but couldn't relax enough to follow suit. "I've already called Marion. The paintings I finished in Colorado should be delivered to her gallery by the end of the week."

"That's wonderful. I can't wait to see them."

His hands were in his pockets as he moved around the room with a restlessness both of his parents recognized.

"There's one piece in particular I'm fond of. I plan to hang it in here, over the fire."

Amanda lifted a brow and glanced at the empty space above the mantel. Gabe had always claimed that nothing suited that spot. "It must be very special."

"You'll have to judge for yourself." He drew out a cigarette, then set it down when Laura moved into the doorway.

She said nothing for a moment, just studied the couple on the couch. His parents. His mother was lovely, her smooth skin almost unlined, her hair swept back to accent her aristocratic features and fine bones. There were emeralds at her ears and at her throat. She wore a rose silk suit with a fox stole carelessly thrown over her shoulders.

His father was tall and lean, like Gabe. Laura saw a diamond wink at his pinky. He looked sad and quiet, but she saw his eyes sharpen as he studied her.

"This is my wife, Laura, and our son."

Braced for whatever was to come, holding the baby protectively against her breasts, she stepped into the room. Amanda rose first, only because she always seemed to move quicker than anyone else.

"It's so nice to meet you at last." Amanda had reservations, a chestful of them, but she offered a polite smile. "Gabe didn't mention how lovely you were."

"Thank you." She felt a little trip-hammer of fear in her throat. Laura knew formidable when she saw it. Instinctively she lifted her chin. "I'm glad you could come. Both of you."

Amanda noted the little gesture of pride and defiance

and approved. "We wanted to meet you at the airport, but Gabe put us off."

"Rightly so," Cliff added in his soothing, take-your-time voice. "If I'd been able to, I'd have held Mandy off another day."

"Nonsense. I want to see my grandchild. May I?"

Laura's arms had tightened automatically. Then she looked at Gabe and relaxed her hold. "Of course." With care and caution, she shifted the slight weight into Amanda's arms.

"Oh, how beautiful." The cool, sophisticated voice wavered. "How precious." The scents, the baby scents of talc and mild soap and fragile skin, made her sigh. "Gabe said he was premature. No problems?"

"No, he's fine."

As if to prove it, Michael opened his eyes and stared out owlishly.

"There, he looked right at me." With emeralds glowing on her skin, Amanda grinned foolishly and cooed. "Looked right at your gran, didn't you?"

"He looked at me." Cliff leaned closer to chuck the baby under the chin.

"Nonsense. Why should he want to look at you? Do something useful, Cliff, like opening the champagne." She clucked and cooed at the baby while Laura stood twisting her hands. "I hope you don't object to the wine. I didn't ask if you were nursing."

"Yes, I am, but I don't think a sip would hurt either of us."

Approving a second time, Amanda started for the couch. Laura took an instinctive step forward, then made herself stop. This wasn't Lorraine Eagleton, and she wasn't the same woman who had once cowered. But as hard as she tried to dispel the image, she saw herself standing just outside the family circle.

"I'd get glasses," she said lamely, "but I don't know where they are."

Saying nothing, Gabe went to a cabinet and drew out four champagne flutes.

Cliff took Laura's arm. "Why don't you sit down, dear? You must be tired after traveling."

"You sound like Gabe." Laura found herself smiling as she eased into a chair.

Glasses were passed. Amanda lifted hers. "We'll drink to— For goodness' sake, I don't know the child's name."

"It's Michael," Laura offered. She saw the grief flash into Amanda's eyes before she closed them. When she opened them again, they were wet and brilliant.

"To Michael," she murmured, and after a sip she leaned down to kiss the baby's cheek. Looking up, she smiled at Gabe. "Your father and I have something in the car for the baby. Would you get it?"

Though they didn't touch, and the glance lasted only a moment, Laura saw something pass between them. "I'll just be a minute."

"We won't eat her, for heaven's sake," Amanda muttered as her son left the room.

With a laugh, Cliff rubbed her shoulder. There was something familiar about the gesture. It was Gabe's, Laura realized. The same casual intimacy.

"Have you been to San Francisco before?" he asked Laura, snapping her back to the present.

"No, I— No. I'd like to offer you something, but I don't know what we have." Or even where the kitchen is, she thought miserably.

"Don't worry about it." Cliff draped his arm comfortably over the back of the chair. "We don't deserve anything after barging in on your first day home."

"Families don't barge," Amanda put in.

"Ours does." Grinning, he leaned over and chucked the baby under the chin again. "Smiled at me."

"Grimaced, you mean." With a laugh of her own, Amanda kissed her husband's cheek. "Granddad."

"I take it the cradle's for Michael and the roses are for me." Gabe strode in, carrying a dark pine cradle heaped with frilly sheets and topped with a spray of pink roses.

"Oh, the flowers. I completely forgot. And no, they're certainly not for you, but for Laura." Amanda handed the baby to her husband and rose. Though she moved to rise, Laura saw Cliff tuck the baby easily in the crook of his arm. "We'll need some water for these," Amanda decided. "No, no, I'll get it myself."

No one argued with her as she marched out of the room, carrying the flowers.

"It's very lovely," Laura began, bending from the chair to run a finger along the smooth wood of the cradle. "We were just talking about the baby needing a bed of his own."

"The Bradley bed," Cliff stated. "Fix those sheets, Gabe, and let's see how he takes to it."

"This cradle's a family tradition." Obediently Gabe

lifted out the extra sheets and smoothed on white linen. "My great-grandfather built it, and all the Bradley children have had their turn rocking in it." He took the baby from his father. "Let's see how you fit, old man."

Laura watched Gabe set the baby down and give the cradle a gentle push. Something seemed to break inside her. "Gabe, I can't."

Crouched at her feet beside the cradle, he looked up. There was a dare in his eyes, a challenge, and, she was certain, a buried anger. "Can't what?"

"It isn't right, it isn't fair." She drew the baby from the cradle into her arms. "They have to know." She might have fled right then and there, but Amanda came back into the room holding a crystal vase filled with roses. Sensing tension, and intrigued by it, she continued in.

"Where would you like these, Laura?"

"I don't know, I can't— Gabe, please."

"I think they'll look nice by the window," she said mildly, then moved over to arrange them to her satisfaction. "Now, then, don't you three gentlemen think you could find something to occupy yourselves while Laura and I have a little talk?"

Panic leaping within, Laura looked from one to the other, then back at her husband. "Gabe, you have to tell them."

He took the baby and settled him on his shoulder. His eyes, very clear and still sparking with anger, met hers. "I already have." Then he left her alone with his mother.

Amanda settled herself on the sofa again. She crossed her legs and smoothed her skirts. "A pity there isn't a fire. It's still cool for this time of year."

"We haven't had a chance——"

"Oh, dear, don't mind me." She waved a hand vaguely at a chair. "Wouldn't you rather sit?" When Laura did so without a word, she lifted a brow. "Are you always so amenable? I should certainly hope not, as I liked you better when you stuck your chin out at me."

Laura folded her hands in her lap. "I don't know what to say. I hadn't realized Gabe had explained things to you. The way you were acting..." She let her words trail off. Then, when Amanda continued to wait patiently, she tried again. "I thought you believed that Michael was, well, biologically Gabe's."

"Should that make such a big difference?"

She was calm again, at least outwardly, and able to meet Amanda's eyes levelly. "I would have expected it to, especially with a family like yours."

Amanda drew her brows together as she thought that through. "Shall I tell you that I'm acquainted with Lorraine Eagleton?" She saw the instant, overwhelming fear and backed up. She wasn't often a tactful woman, but she wasn't cruel. "We'll save talk of her for another time. Right now, I think I should explain myself instead. I'm a pushy woman, Laura, but I don't mind being pushed back."

"I'm not very good at that."

"Then you'll have to learn, won't you? We may be friends, or we may not, I can't tell so soon, but I love my son. When he left all those months ago, I wasn't sure I'd ever have him back. You, for whatever reason, brought him back, and for that I'm grateful."

"He would have come when he was ready."

"But he might not have come back whole. Let's leave that." Again, the vague gesture. "And get to the point. Your son. Gabe considers the child his. Do you?"

"Yes."

"No hesitation there, I see." Amanda smiled at her, and Laura was reminded of Gabe. "If Gabe considers Michael his son, and you consider Michael his son, why should Cliff and I feel differently?"

"Bloodlines."

"Let's leave the Eagletons out of this for the time being," Amanda said. Laura merely stared, surprised that the mark had been hit so directly. "If Gabe had been unable to have children and had adopted one, I would love it and think of it as my grandchild. So, don't you think you should get past this nonsense and accept it?"

"You make it sound very simple."

"It sounds to me as though your life's been complicated enough." Amanda picked up the glass of champagne she'd discarded before. "Do you have any objections to our being Michael's grandparents?"

"I don't know."

"An honest woman." Amanda sipped.

"Do you have any objections to me being Gabe's wife?"

With the slightest of smiles, Amanda raised her glass to Laura. "I don't know. So I suppose we'll both have to wait and see. In the meantime, I'd hate to think that I'd be discouraged from seeing Gabe or Michael because we haven't made up our minds about each other."

"No, of course not. I wouldn't do that. Mrs. Bradley,

no one's ever been as kind or as generous with me as Gabe. I swear to you I won't do anything to hurt him."

"Do you love him?"

Uneasy, Laura cast a look toward the doorway. "We haven't...Gabe and I haven't talked about that. I needed help, and I think he needed to give it."

Pursing her lips, Amanda studied her glass. "I don't believe that's what I asked you."

The chin came up again. "That's something I should discuss with Gabe before anyone else."

"You're tougher than you look. Thank God for that." Finishing off the sparkling beverage, she set down the empty glass. "I might just like you at that, Laura. Or, of course, we might end up detesting each other. But whatever is between the two of us doesn't change the fact that Gabe has committed himself to you and the child. You're family." She sat back, lifting both brows, but inside she felt a faint twist of sympathy. "From the look on your face, that doesn't thrill the life out of you."

"I'm sorry. I'm not used to being in a family."

"You've had a very rough time, haven't you?" There was compassion there, but not so much that it made Laura uncomfortable. Mentally Amanda made a note to do a little digging on the Eagletons.

"I'm trying to put that behind me."

"I hope you succeed. Some things in the past need to be remembered. Others are best forgotten."

"Mrs. Bradley, may I ask you something?"

"Yes. On the condition that after this question call me Amanda or Mandy or anything—except, please God, Mother Bradley."

"All right. Who was Michael named for?"

Amanda's gaze drifted to the empty cradle and lingered there. There was a softening, a saddening, in her face that compelled Laura to touch her hand. "My son, Gabe's younger brother. He died just over a year ago." With a long sigh, she rose. "It's time we left you to settle in."

"Thank you for coming." She hesitated because she was never quite sure what people expected. Then listening to her heart, she kissed Amanda's cheek. "Thank you for the cradle. It means a great deal to me."

"And to me." She brushed her hand over it before she left the room. "Clifton, aren't you the one who said we shouldn't stay more than a half hour?"

His voice carried, muffled, from upstairs. Clucking her tongue, Amanda pulled on her gloves. "Always poking around in Gabe's studio. The poor dear doesn't know a Monet from a Picasso, but he loves to look over Gabe's work."

"He did some beautiful things in Colorado. You must be so proud of him."

"More every day." She heard her husband coming and glanced upstairs. "Do let me know if you want any help setting up the nursery or finding a good pediatrician. I also expect you'll understand if I buy out the baby boutiques."

"I don't—"

"Not understand, then, but you'll have to tolerate. Kiss your new daughter-in-law goodbye, Cliff."

"You don't have to tell me that." Rather than the formal, meaningless kiss she was expecting, Laura received a hearty hug that left her dazed and smiling. "Welcome to the Bradleys, Laura."

"Thank you." She had an urge to hug him back, to just throw her arms around his neck and breath in that nice, spicy aftershave she'd caught on his throat. Feeling foolish, she folded her hands instead. "I hope you'll come back, maybe next week for dinner, when I've had a chance to find things."

"Cooks, too?" He pinched Laura's cheek. "Nice work, Gabe."

When they were gone, she stood in the foyer, rubbing a finger over her cheek. "They're very nice."

"Yes, I've always thought so."

The sting was still in his voice, so she steadied herself and looked at him. "I owe you an apology."

"Forget it." He started to stride back into the library, then stopped and turned around. He'd be damned if he'd forget it. "Did you think I would lie to them about Michael? That I would have to?"

She accepted his anger without flinching. "Yes."

He opened his mouth, rage boiling on his tongue. Her answer had him shutting it again. "Well, you shoot straight from the hip."

"I did think so, and I'm glad I was wrong. Your mother was very kind to me, and your father..."

"What about my father?"

He hugged me, she wanted to say, but she didn't believe he could possibly understand how much that had affected her. "He's so much like you. I'll try not to disappoint them, or you."

"You'd do better not to disappoint yourself." Gabe

dragged a hand through his hair. It fell in a tumble of dark blond disorder, the way she liked it best. "Damn it, Laura, you're not on trial here. You're my wife, this is your home, and for better or worse the Bradleys are your family."

She set her teeth. "You'll have to give me time to get used to it," she said evenly. "The only families I've ever known barely tolerated me. I'm through with that." She swung away to start up the stairs, then called over her shoulder, "And I'm painting Michael's nursery myself."

Not certain whether to laugh or swear, Gabe stood at the foot of the stairs and stared after her.

Chapter 7

Laura brushed the glossy white enamel paint over the baseboard. In her other hand she held a stiff piece of cardboard as a guard against smearing any of the white over the yellow walls she'd already finished.

On the floor in the far corner was a portable radio that was tuned to a station that played bouncy rock. She'd kept the volume low so that she could hear Michael when he woke. It was the same radio Gabe had kept on the kitchen counter in the cabin.

She wasn't sure which pleased her more, the way the nursery was progressing or the ease with which she could bend and crouch. She'd even been able to use part of her hospital fund to buy a couple of pairs of slacks in her old size. They might still be a tad snug in the waist, but she was optimistic.

She wished the rest of her life would fall into order as easily.

He was still angry with her. With a shrug, Laura dipped her brush into the paint can again. Gabe had a temper, he had moods. He had certainly never attempted to deny or hide that. And the truth was, she'd been wrong not to trust him to do the right thing. So she'd apologized. She couldn't let his continuing coolness bother her. But, of course, it did.

They were strangers here, in a way that they had never been strangers in the little cabin in Colorado. It wasn't the house, though a part of her still blamed the size and the glamour of it. Before, the simple mechanics of space had required them to share, to grow close, to depend on each other. Being depended on had become important to Laura, even if it had only been to provide a cup of coffee at the right time. Now, beyond her responsibilities to Michael, there was little for her to do. She and Gabe could spend hours under the same roof and hardly know each other existed.

But it wasn't walls and floors and windows that made the difference. It was quite simply the difference—the difference between them. She was still Laura Malone, from the wrong side of the tracks, the same person who had been moved and shuffled from house to house, without ever being given the chance to really live there. The same person who had been handed from family to family without ever being given the chance to really belong.

And he was… Her laugh was a bit wistful. He was Gabriel Bradley, a man who had known his place from the moment he'd been born. A man who would never wonder if he'd have the same place tomorrow.

That was what she wanted for Michael, only that.

The money, the name, the big, sprawling house with the stained-glass windows and the graceful terraces, didn't matter. Belonging did. Because she wanted it, was determined to have it for her son, she was willing to wait to belong herself. To Gabe.

The only time they were able to pull together was when Michael was involved. Her lips curved then. He loved the baby. There could be no doubt about that. It wasn't pity or obligation that had him crouching beside the cradle or walking the floor at three in the morning. He was a man capable of great love, and he had given it unhesitatingly to Michael. Gabe was attentive, interested, gentle and involved. When it came to Michael.

It was only with her, when they had to deal with each other one on one, that things became strained.

They didn't touch. Though they lived in the same house, slept in the same bed, they didn't touch, except in the most casual and impersonal of ways. As a family they had gone out to choose all the things Michael would need—the crib and other nursery furniture, blankets, a windup swing that played a lullaby, soft stuffed animals that Michael would undoubtedly ignore for months. It had been easy, even delightful, to discuss high chairs and playpens and decide together what would suit. Laura had never expected to be able to give her son so much or to be able to share in that giving.

But when they'd come home the strain had returned.

She was being a fool, Laura told herself. She'd been given a home, protection and care, and, most of all, a kind and loving father for her son. Wishing for more was what had always led her to disappointment before.

But she wished he would smile at her again—at her, not at Michael's mother, not at the subject of his painting.

Perhaps it was best that they remained as they were, polite friends with a common interest. She wasn't entirely sure how she would manage when the time came for him to turn to her as a woman. The time would come, his desire was there, and he was too physical a man to share the bed with her without fully sharing it much longer.

Her experience with lovemaking had taught her that man demanded and woman submitted. He wouldn't have to love her, or even hold her in affection, to need her. God, no one knew better how little affection, how little caring, there could be in a marriage bed. A man like Gabe would have many demands, and loving him as she did she would give. And the cycle she'd finally managed to break would begin again.

Gabe watched her from the doorway. Something was wrong, very wrong. He could see the turmoil on her face, could see it in the set of her shoulders. It seemed that the longer they were here the less she relaxed. She pretended well, but it was only pretense.

It infuriated him, and the harder he held on to his temper the more infuriated he became. He hadn't so much as raised his voice to her since their first day in the house, and yet she seemed continually braced for an outburst.

He'd given her as much room as was humanly possible, and it was killing him. Sleeping with her, having her turn to him during the night, her skin separated from his only by the fragile cotton of a nightgown, had given new meaning to insomnia.

He'd taken to working during the middle of the night and spending his free time in the studio or at the gallery, anywhere he wouldn't be tempted to take what was his only legally.

How could he take when she was still so delicate, physically, emotionally? However selfish he'd always been, or considered himself, he couldn't justify gratifying himself at her expense—or frightening her by letting her see just how desperately, how violently, he wanted her.

Yet there was passion in her, the dark, explosive kind. He'd seen that, and other things, in her eyes. She needed him, as much as he needed her. He wasn't sure either of them understood where their need might take them.

He could be patient. He was aware that her body needed time to heal, and he could give her that. But he wasn't sure he could give her the time it might take for her mind to heal.

He wanted to cross to her, to sit down beside her and stroke his hand over her hair. He wanted to reassure her. But he had no idea what words to use. Instead, he tucked his hands into his pockets.

"Still at it?"

Laura started, splattering paint on her hand. She sat back on her heels. "I didn't hear you come in."

"Don't get up," he told her. "You make quite a picture." He stepped into the room, glancing at the sunny walls before looking down at her. She wore an old pair of jeans, obviously his. He could see the clothesline she'd used to secure the waist. One of his shirts was tented over her, its hem torn at her hip.

"Mine?"

"I thought it would be all right." She picked up a rag to wipe the paint from her hand. "I could tell from the splatters on them they'd already been worked in."

"Perhaps you don't know the difference between painting and—" he gestured toward the wall "—painting."

She'd nearly fumbled out an apology before she realized he was joking. So the mood had passed. Perhaps they were friends again. "Not at all. I thought your pants would give me artistic inspiration."

"You could have come to the source."

She set the brush on top of the open paint can. Relief poured through her. Though he didn't know, Gabe had found exactly the right words to reassure her. "I would never have suggested that the celebrated Gabriel Bradley turn his genius to a lowly baseboard."

It seemed so easy when she was like this, relaxed, with a hint of amusement in her eyes. "Obviously afraid I'd show you up."

She smiled, a bit hesitantly. He hadn't looked at her in quite that way for days. Then she was scrambling back up on her knees as he joined her on the floor. "Oh, Gabe, don't. You'll get paint all over you, and you look so nice."

He had the brush in his hand. "Do I?"

"Yes." She tried to take it away from him, but he didn't give way. "You always look so dashing when you go to the gallery."

"Oh, God." The instant disgust on his face made her laugh.

"Well, you do." She checked the urge to brush at

the hair on his forehead. "It's quite different from the rugged-outdoorsman look you had in Colorado, though that was nice, too."

He wasn't certain whether to smile or sneer. "Rugged outdoorsman?"

"That's right. The cords and the flannel, the untidy hair and the carelessly unshaven face. I think Geoffrey would have loved to photograph you with an ax…." She was staring at him, seeing him as he'd been and as he was. Abruptly she became aware that her hand was still covering his on the handle of the brush. Drawing it away, she struggled to remember her point. "You're not dressed for work now, and I was in the fashion business long enough to recognize quality. Those pants are linen, and you'll ruin them."

He was well aware of the sudden tension in her fingers and the look that had come into her eyes, but he only lifted a brow. "Are you saying I'm sloppy?"

"Only when you paint."

"Pot calling the kettle," he murmured, ignoring the way she jumped when he ran a finger down her cheek. He held it up to prove his point.

Laura wrinkled her nose at the smear of white paint on his fingertip—and tried to ignore the heat on her skin where his finger had brushed. "I'm not an artist." With a rag in one hand, she took his wrist in the other to clean the paint from his fingertip.

Such beautiful hands, she thought. She could imagine how it would feel to have them move over her, slowly, gently. To have them stroke and caress the way a man's might if he cared deeply about the woman beneath the skin he was touching. Her imagination had her moistening her lips as she lifted her gaze to his.

They knelt knee to knee on the drop cloth, with his hand caught in hers. It amazed her when she felt his pulse begin to thud. In his eyes she saw what he hadn't allowed her to see for days. Desire, pure and simple. Unnerved by it, drawn to it, she leaned toward him. The rag slipped out of her hand.

And the baby cried out.

They both jerked, like children caught raiding the cookie jar.

"He'll be hungry, and wet, too, I imagine," she said as she started to rise. Gabe shifted his hand until it captured hers.

"I'd like you to come back here after you've tended to him."

Longing and anxiety tangled, confusing her. "All right. Don't worry about the mess. I'll finish up later."

She was more than an hour with Michael, and she was a bit disappointed that Gabe didn't come in, as he often did, to hold the baby or play with him before he slept again. Those were the best times, those simple family times. Tucking the blankets around her son, she reminded herself that she couldn't expect Gabe to devote every free minute to her and the child.

Satisfied that the baby was dry and content, she left him to go into the adjoining bath and freshen up. After she'd washed the paint from her face, she studied herself in the mirrored wall across from the step-down tub. She didn't look seductive in baggy, masculine clothes, with her hair tugged back in a ponytail. Regardless of that, for an instant in the nursery, Gabe had been seduced.

Was that what she wanted?

How could she know what she wanted? She pressed her fingers to her eyes and tried to sort out her feelings. Confusion, and little else. One moment she imagined what it would be like, being with Gabe, making love with him. The next moment she was remembering the way it had been before, when love had had little to do with it.

It was wrong to continually let memories intrude. She told herself she was too sensible for that. Or wanted to be. She'd been in therapy, she'd talked to counselors and other women who had been in situations all too similar to her own. Because she'd had to stay on the move, she hadn't been able to remain with any one group for long, but they had helped her. Just learning that she wasn't alone in what had happened to her, seeing and talking with others who had turned their lives around again, had given her the strength to go on.

She knew—intellectually she knew—that what had happened to her was the result of a man's illness and her own insecurity. But it was one thing to know it and another to accept it and go on, to risk another relationship.

She wanted to be normal, was determined to be. That had been the communal cry from all the sessions in all the towns. Along with the fear and the anger and the self-disgust, there had been a desperate mutual need to be normal women again.

But that step, that enormous, frightening step from past to future, was so difficult to take. Only she could do it, Laura told herself as she continued to stare into her own eyes. With Gabe, and her feelings for him, she had a chance. If she was willing to take it.

How could she know how close they could be, how much they could mean to each other, if she didn't allow herself to want the intimacy?

Catching her lower lip between her teeth, she turned to study the lush bath. It was nearly as large as many of the rooms she'd lived in during her life. White on white on white, it gleamed and glistened and invited indulgence. She could sink into hot, deep water in the tub and soak until her skin was soft and pink. She still had most of a bottle of perfume, French and suggestive, that Geoffrey had bought her in Paris. She could dab it on her damp skin so that the scent seeped into her pores. Then she could…what?

She had nothing lovely or feminine to wear. The only clothes she hadn't taken to thrift shops or secondhand stores during her cross-country flight were maternity clothes. The two pairs of slacks and the cotton blouses didn't count.

In any case, what would it matter if she had a closetful of lace negligees? She wouldn't know what to do or say. It had been so long since she'd thought of herself strictly as a woman. Perhaps she never had. And surely it was better to try to reestablish that early friendship with Gabe before they attempted intimacy.

If that was what he wanted. What she wanted.

Turning away from the mirror, she went to find him.

She couldn't have been more surprised when she walked into the nursery and found the painting finished, the cans sealed and the brushes cleaned. As she stared, Gabe folded the drop cloth.

"You finished it," she managed.

"I seem to have struggled through without doing any damage."

"It's beautiful. The way I'd always imagined." She stepped into the empty room and began arranging furniture in her head. "There should be curtains, white ones, though I suppose dotted swiss is too feminine for a boy."

"I couldn't say, but it sounds like it. It's warm enough, so I've left the windows open." He tossed the drop cloth over a stepladder. "I don't want to put Michael in here until the smell of the paint's gone."

"No," she agreed absently, wondering if the crib should go between the two windows.

"Now that this is out of the way, I have something for you. A belated Mother's Day present."

"Oh, but you gave me the flowers already."

He took a small box out of his pocket. "There wasn't the time or the opportunity for much else then. We were living out of a suitcase and spending all of our time at the hospital. Besides, the flowers were from Michael. This is from me."

That made it different. Intimate. Again she found herself drawn to him, and again she found herself pulled away. "You don't have to give me anything."

The familiar impatience shimmered. He barely suppressed it. "You're going to have to learn how to take a gift more graciously."

He was right. And it was wrong of her to continue to compare, but Tony had been so casual, so lavish, in his gifts. And they had meant so little. "Thank you." She took the box, opened it and stared.

The ring looked like a circle of fire, with its channel-linked diamonds flashing against its gold band and nestled in velvet. Instinctively she ran a fingertip over it and was foolishly amazed that it was cool to the touch.

"It's beautiful. Absolutely beautiful. But—"

"There had to be one."

"It's just that it's a wedding ring, and I already have one."

He took her left hand to examine it. "I'm surprised your finger hasn't fallen off from wearing this thing."

"There's nothing wrong with it," she said, and nearly snatched her hand away.

"So sentimental, angel?" Though his voice had gentled, his hand was firm on hers. Now, perhaps, he would be able to dig a bit deeper into what she was feeling for him, about him. "Are you so attached to a little circle of metal?"

"It was good enough for us before. I don't need anything else."

"It was a temporary measure. I'm not asking you to toss it out the window, but be a little practical. If you weren't always curling your finger up, it would fall right off."

"I could have it sized."

"Suit yourself." He slipped it from her finger, then replaced it with the diamond circle. "Just consider that you have two wedding rings." When he offered her the plain band, Laura curled it into her fist. "The new one holds the same intentions."

"It is beautiful." Still, she pushed the old ring onto the index finger of her right hand, where it fit more snugly. "Thank you, Gabe."

"We did better than that before."

She didn't have to be reminded. Yet the memories flooded back when he slipped his arms around her. Emotions poured through with those memories the moment his mouth was on hers. His lips were firm and warm and hinted, just hinted, at his impatience as they slanted across hers. Though his arms remained gentle around her, his touch light and testing, she sensed a volcano in him, simmering and smoking.

As if to soothe, she leaned into him and lifted a hand to his cheek. Understanding. Acceptance.

Her touch triggered the need crawling inside him, and his arms tightened and his mouth crushed down on hers. She responded with a moan that he barely heard, with a shudder that he barely felt. Tense, hungry, he fell victim to her as much as to his own demands.

He had wanted before, casually and desperately and all the degrees in between. Why, then, did this seem like a completely new experience? He had held women before, known their softness, tasted their sweetness. But he had never known a softness, never experienced a sweetness, like Laura's.

He took his mouth on a slow, seeking journey over her face, along her jawline, down her throat, drinking in, then devouring. His hands, long and limber, slipped under her full shirt, then roamed upward. At first the slender line of her back was enough, the smooth skin and the quick tremors all he required. Then the need to touch, to possess, grew sharper. As his mouth came back to hers, he slid his hand around to cup, then claim, her breast.

The first touch made her catch her breath, pulling air in quickly, then letting it out again in a long, unsteady sigh. How could she have known, even blinded by love and longings, how desperately she'd need to have his hands on her? This was what she wanted, to be his in every way, in all ways. The confusion, the doubts, the fears, drained away. No memories intruded when he held her like this. No whispers of the past taunted her. There was only him, and the promise of a new life and an enduring love.

Her knees were trembling so she braced her body against his, arching in an invitation so instinctive that only he recognized it.

The room smelled of paint and was bright with the sun that streamed through the uncurtained windows. It was empty and quiet. He could fantasize about pulling her to the floor, tugging at her clothes until they were skin-to-skin on the polished hardwood. He could imagine taking her in the sun-washed room until they were both exhausted and replete.

With another woman he might have done so without giving a thought to where or when, and little more to how. But not with Laura.

Churning, he drew her away from him. Her eyes were clouded. Her mouth was soft and full. With a restraint he hadn't known he possessed, Gabe swore only in his mind.

"I have work to do."

She was floating, drifting on a mist so fine it could only be felt, not seen. At his words, she began the quick, confused journey back to earth. "What?"

"I have work to do," he repeated, stepping carefully away from her. He detested himself for taking things so far when he knew she was physically unable to cope with his demands. "I'll be in the studio if you need me."

If she needed him? Laura thought dimly as his footsteps echoed down the hall. Hadn't she just shown him how much she needed him? It wasn't possible that he hadn't felt it, that he hadn't understood it. With an oath, she turned and walked to the window. There she huddled on the small, hard seat and stared down at the garden, which was just beginning to bloom.

What was there about her, she wondered, that made men look at her as a thing to be taken or rejected at will? Did she appear so weak, so malleable? She curled her hands into fists as frustration spread through her. She wasn't weak, not any longer, and a long time, in some ways a lifetime, had passed since she had been malleable. She wasn't a young girl caught up in fairy-tale lies now. She was a woman, a mother, with responsibilities and ambitions.

Perhaps she loved, and perhaps this time would be as unwise a love as before. But she wouldn't be used, she wouldn't be ignored, and she wouldn't be molded.

Talk was cheap, Laura thought as she propped her chin on her knees. Doing something about it was a little costlier. She should go in to Gabe now and make herself clear. She cast a look at the door, then turned back to the window. She didn't have the courage.

That had always been her problem. She could say what she would or would not do, but when it came down to acting on it she found passivity easier than action. There had been a time in her life when she'd believed that the passive way was best for her. That had been until her marriage to Tony had fallen viciously apart. She'd done something then, Laura reminded herself, or had begun to do something, then had allowed herself to be pressured and persuaded to erase it.

It had been like that all her life. As a child she hadn't had a choice. She'd been told to live here or live there, and she had. Each house had had its own sets of rules and values, and she'd had to conform. Like one of those rubber dolls, she thought now, that you could bend and twist into any position you liked.

Too much of the child had remained with the woman, until the woman had been with child.

The only positive action she felt she'd ever taken in her life had been to protect the baby. And she had done it, Laura reminded herself. It had been terrifying and hard, but she hadn't backed down. Didn't that mean that buried beneath years of quiet compliance was the strength she'd always wanted to have? She had to believe that and, if she did, to act on it.

Loving Gabe didn't mean, couldn't mean, that she would sit quietly by while he made decisions for her. It was time to take a stand.

Rising, she walked out of the empty nursery and started down the hall. With each step her resolve wavered and had to be shored up again. At the door to his studio, she hesitated again, rubbing the heel of her hand on her chest, where the ache of uncertainty lodged. Taking one last breath, she opened the door and walked in.

He was by the long bank of windows, a brush in his hand, working on one of the paintings that had been stacked half-finished against the wall of the cabin. She remembered it. It was a snow scene, very stark and lonely and somehow appealing. The whites and cold blues and silvers gave a sense of challenge.

Laura was glad of it. A sense of challenge was precisely what she needed.

He hadn't heard her come in, so intent was he on his work. There were no sweeping strokes or bold slashes now, only a delicacy. He was adding details so minute, so exact, that she could almost hear the winter wind.

"Gabe?" It was amazing how much courage it could take to say a name.

He stopped immediately, and when he turned the annoyance on his face was very apparent. Interruptions were never tolerated here. Living alone, he hadn't had to tolerate them.

"What is it?" He clipped the words off, and he didn't set down his brush or move from the painting. It was obvious that he intended to continue exactly where he'd left off the moment he'd nudged her out of his way.

"I need to talk to you."

"Can't it wait?"

She nearly said yes, but then she brought herself up short. "No." She left the door open in case the baby should cry out, and walked to the center of the room. Her stomach twisted, knotted. Her chin came up. "Or, if it can, I don't want it to."

He lifted a brow. He'd heard that tone in her voice only a handful of times in the weeks they'd been together. "All right, but make it fast, will you? I want to finish this."

Her temper flared too quickly to surprise her. "Fine, then, I'll sum it up in one sentence. If I'm going to be your wife, I want you to treat me like one."

"I beg your pardon?"

She was too angry to see that he was stunned, and too angry to recognize her own shock at her words. "No, you don't. You've never begged anyone's pardon in your life. You don't have to. You do exactly what suits you. If that means being kind, you can be the kindest man I've ever known. If it means being arrogant, you take that just as far."

With deliberate care, he set his brush down. "If there's a point to this, Laura, I'm missing it."

"Do you want me or don't you?"

He only stared at her. If she continued to stand in the pool of light, her eyes dark and defiant, her cheeks flushed with color, he might beg. "That's the point?" he said steadily.

"You tell me you want me, then you ignore me. You kiss me, then you walk away." She dragged a hand through her hair. When her fingers tangled with the ribbon that held it back, she tugged it out in annoyance. Pale and fragile, her hair fell around her shoulders. "I realize the main reason we're married is because of Michael, but I want to know where I stand. Am I to be a guest here who's alternately indulged and ignored, or am I to be your wife?"

"You are my wife." With his own temper rising, he

pushed himself off his stool. "And it's not a matter of me ignoring you. I've simply got a lot of work to catch up on."

"You don't work twenty-four hours a day. At night—" Her courage began to fail. She thrust out the rest of the words. "Why won't you make love with me?"

It was fortunate that he'd set his brush down, or else he might have snapped it in half. "Do you expect performance on demand, Laura?"

Embarrassed color flooded her cheeks. That had once been expected of her, and it shamed her more than she could say to think she'd demanded it. "No. I didn't mean it to sound that way. I only thought it was best that you know how I felt." She took a step back, then turned to go. "I'll let you get back to work."

"Laura." He preferred, much preferred, her anger to the humiliation he'd seen. And caused. "Wait." He started after her when she whirled around.

"Don't apologize."

"All right." There was still fire in her, he saw, and he wasn't entirely sure he should be relieved. "I'll just give you a more honest explanation."

"It isn't necessary." She started toward the door again, but he grabbed her arm and yanked her around. He saw it and cursed at it—the instant fear that leaped into her eyes.

"Damn it, don't look at me like that. Don't ever look at me like that." Without his realizing it, his fingers had tightened on her arm. When she winced, he released her, dropping his hands to his side. "I can't make myself over for you, Laura. I'll yell when I need to yell and fight when I need to fight, but I told you once before, and I'll say it again. I don't hit women."

The fear had risen, a bitter bile in her throat. It was detestable. She waited for it to pass before she spoke. "I don't expect you to, but I can't make myself over for you, either. Even if I could, I don't know what you want. I know I should be grateful to you."

"The hell with that."

"I should be grateful," she continued, calm again. "And I am, but I've found out something about myself this past year. I'll never be anyone's doormat ever again. Not even yours."

"Do you think that's what I want?"

"I can't know what you want, Gabe, until you know yourself." She'd gone this far, Laura told herself, and she would finish. "Right from the beginning you expected me to trust you. But after everything we've been through you still haven't been able to make yourself trust me. If we're ever going to be able to make this marriage work you're going to have to stop looking at me as a good deed and start seeing me as a person."

"You have no idea how I see you."

"No, I probably don't." She managed a smile. "Maybe when I do it'll be easier for both of us." She heard the baby crying and glanced down the hall. "He doesn't seem to be able to settle today."

"I'll get him in a minute. He can't be hungry again. Wait." If she could be honest, he told himself, then so could he. He put a hand on her arm to hold her there. "It's easy enough to clear up one misunderstanding. I haven't made love with you, not because I haven't wanted to, but because it's too soon."

"Too soon?"

"For you."

She started to shake her head. Then his meaning became clear. "Gabe, Michael's over four weeks old."

"I know how old he is. I was there." He held up a hand before she could speak. "Damn it, Laura, I saw what you went through. How hard it was on you. However I feel, it simply isn't possible for me to act on it until I know you're fully recovered."

"I had a baby, not a terminal illness." She let out a huff of breath, but she found it wasn't annoyance or even amusement she felt. It was pleasure, the rare and wonderful pleasure of being cared for. "I feel fine. I am fine. In fact, I've probably never been better in my life."

"Regardless of how you feel, you've just had a baby. From what I've read—"

"You've read about this, too?"

That infuriated him—that wide-eyed wonder and the trace of humor in her eyes. "I don't intend to touch you," he said stiffly, "until I'm sure you're fully recovered."

"What do you want, a doctor's certificate?"

"More or less." He started to touch her cheek, then thought better of it. "I'll see to Michael."

He left her standing in the hall, unsure whether she was angry or amused or delighted. All that she was sure of was that she was feeling, and her feelings were all for Gabe.

Chapter 8

"I can't believe how fast he's growing." Feeling very grandmotherly but sporting a sleek new hairstyle, Amanda sat in the bentwood rocker in Michael's new nursery and cuddled the baby.

"He's making up for being premature." Still not quite certain how she felt about her mother-in-law, Laura continued to fold tiny clothes that were fresh from the laundry. "We had our checkup today, and the doctor said Michael was healthy as a horse." She pressed a sleeper to her cheek. It was soft, almost as soft as her son's skin. "I wanted to thank you for recommending Dr. Sloane. She's wonderful."

"Good. But I don't need a pediatrician to tell me this child's healthy. Look at this grip." Amanda chuckled as Michael curled his fingers around hers, but she stopped short of allowing him to suck on her sapphire ring. "He has your eyes, you know."

"Does he?" Delighted, Laura moved to stand over them. The baby smelled of talc—Amanda of Paris. "It's too early to tell, I know, but I'd hoped he did."

"No doubt about it." Amanda continued to rock as she studied her daughter-in-law. "And what about *your* checkup? How are you?"

"I'm fine." Laura thought about the slip of paper she'd tucked into the top drawer of her dresser.

"Looking a bit tired to me." There wasn't any sympathy in the voice; it was brusque and matter-of-fact. "Haven't you done anything about getting some help?"

Laura's spine straightened automatically. "I don't need any help."

"That's absurd, of course. With a house this size, a demanding husband and a new baby, you can use all the help you can get, but suit yourself." Michael began to coo, pleasing Amanda. "Talk to Gran, sweetheart. Tell Gran just how it is." The baby responded with more gurgles. "Listen to that. Before long you'll have plenty to say for yourself. Just make sure 'My gran's beautiful' is one of the first. There's a sweet boy." She dropped a kiss on his brow before looking up at Laura. "I'd say a change is in order here, and I'm more than happy to leave that to you." With what she considered a grandmother's privilege, Amanda handed the wet baby to Laura. She continued to sit as Laura took Michael to the changing table.

There was a great deal she'd have liked to say. Amanda was accustomed to voicing her opinions loud and clear—and, if necessary, beating anyone within reach over the head with it. It chafed a bit to hold back, but she'd learned enough in the past few weeks about the Eagletons and about Laura's life with them. Treading carefully, she tried a new tactic.

"Gabe's spending a lot of time at the gallery."

"Yes. I think he's nearly decided to go ahead with a new showing." Almost drowning in love, Laura leaned over to nuzzle Michael's neck.

"Have you been there?"

"The gallery? No, I haven't."

Amanda tapped a rounded, coral-tipped nail on the arm of the rocker. "I'd think you'd be interested in Gabe's work."

"Of course I am." She held Michael over her head, and he began to bubble and smile. "I just haven't thought it wise to take Michael in and interrupt."

It was on the tip of Amanda's tongue to remind Laura that Michael had grandparents who would delight in having him to themselves for a few hours. Again she bit the words back. "I'm sure Gabe wouldn't mind. He's devoted to the boy."

"Yes, he is." Laura retied the ribbons on Michael's pale blue booties. "But I also know he needs some time to organize his work, his career." She handed her son a small cloth bunny, and he stuck it happily in his mouth. "Do you know why Gabe is hesitating about a showing?"

"Have you asked him?"

"No, I—I didn't want to pressure him about it."

"A little pressure might be just what he needs."

Frowning, Laura turned. "Why?"

"It has to do with Michael, my son Michael. I'd prefer it if you asked Gabe the rest."

"They were close?"

"Yes." She smiled. She'd learned it hurt less to remember than to try to forget. "They were very close, though they were very different. He was devastated when Michael was killed. I believe the time in the mountains helped Gabe get back his art. And I believe you and the baby helped him get back his heart."

"If that's true, I'm glad. He's helped me more than I can ever repay."

Amanda gave Laura an even look. "Payments aren't necessary between a husband and wife."

"Perhaps not."

"Are you happy?"

Stalling, Laura laid the baby in the crib and wound the musical mobile so that he could shake his fists and kick at it. "Of course I am. Why wouldn't I be?"

"That was my next question."

"I'm very happy." She went back to folding and storing baby clothes. "It was nice of you to visit, Amanda. I know how busy your schedule is."

"Don't think you can politely show me out the door before I'm ready to go."

Laura turned and saw the faint, amused smile on Amanda's lips. Bad manners were enough out of character for her to make her flush. "I'm sorry."

"Don't be. I don't expect for you to be comfortable with me yet. I'm not entirely sure I'm comfortable with you, either."

A bit more relaxed, Laura smiled back. "I'm sure you're always comfortable. I envy that about you. And I am sorry."

Amanda brushed aside the apology and rose to roam

the room. She liked what her daughter-in-law had done here. It was a bright, cheerful place, not overly fussy, and just traditional enough to make her remember the nursery she had set up herself so many years before. There were the scents of powder and fresh linen.

A loving place, she thought. She knew she wouldn't have wanted any more for her son. It was very obvious to her that Laura had untapped stores of love.

"This is a charming room. I think so every time I step into it." Amanda patted the head of the four-foot lavender teddy bear. "But you can't hide here forever."

"I don't know what you mean." But she did.

"You said you'd never been to San Francisco, and now you're here. Have you gone to a museum, to the theater? Have you strolled down to Fisherman's Wharf, ridden a streetcar, explored Chinatown, any of the things a newcomer would surely do?"

Defensive now, Laura spoke coolly. "No, I haven't. But it's only been a few weeks."

It was time, Amanda decided, to stop circling and get to the point. "Let's deal woman-to-woman a moment, Laura. Forget the fact that I'm Gabe's mother. We're alone. Whatever is said here doesn't have to go any further."

Laura's palms were starting to sweat. She brushed them dry on the thighs of her slacks. "I don't know what you want me to say."

"Whatever needs to be said." When Laura remained silent, Amanda nodded. "All right, I'll begin. You've had some miserable spots in your life, some of them tragic. Gabe gave us the bare essentials, but I learned a good deal more by knowing who and what to ask." Amanda sat down again and crossed her legs. She didn't miss the flash in Laura's eyes. "Wait until I've finished. Then you can be as offended as you like."

"I'm not offended," Laura said stiffly. "But I don't see the purpose in discussing what used to be."

"Until you look what used to be square in the face, you won't be able to go on with what might be." She tried to keep her voice brisk, but even her solid composure wavered. "I know that Tony Eagleton abused you, and that his parents overlooked what was monstrous, even criminal, behavior. My heart breaks for you."

"Please." Her voice was strangled as she shook her head. "Don't."

"No sympathy allowed, Laura, even woman-to-woman?"

Again she shook her head, afraid to accept it and, more, to need it. "I can't bear to think back on it. And I can't stand pity."

"Sympathy and pity are entirely different things."

"All that's behind me. I'm a different person than I was then."

"I have no way of agreeing, as I didn't know you before. But I can say that anyone who stood on her own all these months must have great reserves of strength and determination. Isn't it time you used them, and fought back?"

"I have fought back."

"You've taken sanctuary, a much-needed one. I won't argue that running as you did took courage and stamina. But there comes a time to take a stand."

Hadn't she said that to herself time and time again? Hadn't she hated herself for only saying it? She looked at her son, who gurgled and reached for the colorful birds circling over his head.

"And what? Go to court, to the press, drag the whole ugly mess out for everyone to gawk at?"

"If necessary." Her voice took on a tone of pride that carried to all corners of the room. "The Bradleys aren't afraid of scandal."

"I'm not a—"

"But you are," Amanda told her. "You're a Bradley, and so is that child. It's Michael I'm thinking of in the long run, but I'm also thinking of you. What difference does it make what anyone thinks, what anyone knows? You have nothing to be ashamed of."

"I let it happen," Laura said, with a kind of dull fury. "I'll always be ashamed of that."

"My dear child." Unable to prevent herself, Amanda rose to put her arms around Laura. After the first shock, Laura felt herself being drawn in. Perhaps it was because the comfort came from a woman, but it broke down her defences as nothing else ever had.

Amanda let her weep, even wept with her. The fact that she did, that she could, was more soothing than any words could have been. Cheek-to-cheek, woman-to-woman, they held each other until the storm passed. The bond that Laura had never expected to know was forged in tears. With her arm still around Laura, Amanda led her to the gaily striped daybed.

"That's been coming on for a while, I'd say," Amanda

murmured. She drew a lace-edged handkerchief out of her breast pocket and unashamedly wiped her eyes.

"I don't know." Laura used the back of her wrist to smear away already-drying tears. "I suppose. Crying isn't something I should need, not anymore. It's only when I look back and remember."

"Now listen to me," Amanda said. All the softness had been erased from her voice. "You were young and alone, and you have nothing, nothing, to be ashamed of. One day you'll realize that for yourself, but for now it might be enough to know you're not alone anymore."

"Sometimes I'm so angry, just so angry that I was used as a convenience, or a punching bag, or a status symbol." It was amazing to her that fury could bring calm and wipe out pain. "When I am I know that no matter what it costs I'll never go back to that."

"Then stay angry."

"But…the anger for me, that's personal." She looked across the room at the crib. "It's when I think of Michael and I know they're going to try to take him…then I'm afraid."

"They don't just have to go through you now, do they?"

Laura looked back. Amanda's face was set. Her eyes glittered. So this was where Gabe got his warrior look, Laura thought, and felt a new kind of love stir. It was the most natural thing in the world for Laura to reach out and take her hand. "No, they don't."

They both heard the door open and close on the first floor. Immediately Laura began to brush her hands over her face. "That must be Gabe, home from the gallery. I don't want him to see me like this."

"I'll go down and keep him occupied." On impulse, she glanced at her watch. "Do you have plans for this afternoon?"

"No. Just to—"

"Good. Come down when you're tidied up."

Ten minutes later, Laura came down to find Gabe cornered in the living room, scowling into a glass of club soda.

"Then it's all settled." Amanda fluffed a hand through her hair, well satisfied. "Laura. Good. Are you ready?"

"Ready?"

"Yes. I've explained to Gabe that we're going shopping. He's absolutely delighted with the reception I've planned for the two of you next week." The reception she'd only begun to plan on her way downstairs.

"Resigned," he corrected, but he had to smile at his mother. The smile faded when he glanced over at Laura. "What's wrong?"

"Nothing." It had been foolish to think that a quick wash and fresh makeup could hide anything from him. "Your mother and I were getting sentimental over Michael."

"What your wife needs is an afternoon out." Amanda rose, then leaned over to kiss Gabe. "I'd scold you for keeping her locked up this way, but I love you too much."

"I never—"

"Never once nudged her out of the house," his mother finished for him. "So it's up to me. Get your purse, dear.

We have to find you something wonderful for the reception. Gabe, I imagine Laura needs your credit cards."

"My— Oh." Feeling like a tree blowing in a strong
wind, he reached for his wallet.

"These should do." Amanda plucked two of them and
handed them to Laura. "Ready?"

"Well, I... Yes," she said on impulse. "Michael's just
been fed and changed. You shouldn't have any trouble."

"I can handle things," he told her, feeling more than a
little put out. In the first place, he'd have taken her shopping himself if she'd asked. And in the second, though
he didn't want to admit it, he wasn't totally sure of himself alone with the baby.

Reading her son perfectly, Amanda kissed him again.
"Behave and we may bring you back a present."

He couldn't suppress the grin. "Out," he ordered. Then
he caught Laura in turn and kissed her with the same
light affection. It surprised him when she returned the
embrace so ardently.

"Don't let her talk you into anything with bows," he
murmured. "They wouldn't suit you. You should try to
find something to match your eyes."

"If you don't let the girl go, we won't buy anything at
all," Amanda said dryly, but she was pleased and a bit
misty-eyed to see that her son was indeed in love with
his wife.

It wasn't anyone's fault that Michael chose that particular afternoon to demand all the time and attention
an infant could possibly demand. Gabe walked, rocked,
changed, coddled and all but stood on his head. For his

part, Michael gurgled, stared owlishly—and wept piteously whenever he was set down. He did everything but sleep.

In the end, Gabe gave up any idea of working for the rest of the day and carted Michael around with him. With the baby nestled in the crook of his arm, he ate a chicken leg and scanned the newspaper. Since no one was around to chuckle at him behind their hands, he discussed world politics and the major-league box scores with Michael while the baby shook a rattle and blew bubbles.

They took a walk in the garden once Gabe located one of the small knit hats Laura had bought to protect Michael from spring breezes. It gave him enormous pleasure to watch the baby's cheeks turn pink and his eyes look around, alert and interested.

He had Laura's eyes, Gabe thought as he studied them. The same shape, the same color, but without the shadows that made hers both sad and fascinating. Michael's eyes were clear and innocent of sorrow.

Michael whimpered at first, then decided to accept his fate, when Gabe slipped him into the little baby swing. After tucking his blankets in around him, Gabe sat crosslegged in front of him and began to stretch.

The daffodils were up in a glory of white and yellow trumpets. Baby irises poked through, purple and exotic. Lilacs, though still shy of their full bloom, offered their scent. For the first time since his own tragedy, Gabe felt at peace. In the mountains, all through the winter, he'd begun to heal. But here, at home, with spring all around, he could finally see and accept that life did go on.

The baby continued to rock, pink-cheeked and bright-eyed, his hands lifting and falling to the rhythm. His little face was already filling out, taking on his own personal look and shape. Gone was the terrifying fragility of the newborn. He was, Gabe supposed, already growing up.

"I love you, Michael."

And when he spoke he spoke both to the one who was gone and to the one who rocked contentedly in front of him.

She hadn't meant to be gone so long, but the chaotic few hours breezing through the shops had brought back the way she had felt during that brief period when she'd been on her own and eager to test life.

There had been a moment or two of guilt over using Gabe's credit cards so freely. Then it had been almost too easy, with Amanda lending support, to justify the purchases. She was Laura Bradley now.

She had an eye for color and line that came naturally and had been sharpened by her time as a model, so what she had chosen was neither extravagant nor fussy. It had given Laura a great deal of satisfaction to see Amanda nod with approval over her selections.

It was a step, Laura told herself as she carried her bags and boxes through the front door. It might be a step only a woman would understand, but it was definitely a step. She was taking her life in hand again, if only by acknowledging that she needed clothes—clothes that suited her own taste and style—to live it. She was humming when she walked upstairs.

It was there that she found them together, Gabe

sprawled over the bed, with Michael snuggled in the curve of his arm. Her husband was sound asleep. Her son had kicked free of his light blanket and was shaking a rattle at the ceiling.

Quietly she set down her bags and crossed to them. It was a purely male scene, the man stretched across the bed, shoes still on, a spy thriller lying facedown on the coverlet, a glass of something that had once been cold leaving a ring on the antique nightstand.

The child, as if he understood that he was a part of this man's world, lay quietly and thought his own thoughts.

She wished she had even a portion of Gabe's skill. If she had, she would have drawn them together like this. Then the scene, the sweetness of it, would never be lost. For a while she sat on the edge of the bed and watched them.

It was so intimate, she thought, watching a man while he slept. She wanted to brush at the dark blond hair on his forehead, to trace the roughly hewn lines of his face, but she was afraid it would disturb him. Then the vulnerability would be gone, and this look at the private side of him would be over.

He was a beautiful man, though he didn't like to hear it. The compassion in him, which he often coated over with sarcasm or temper, ran deep. When she looked at him now, freely, without his being aware, she could see every reason why she'd fallen in love with him.

When Michael began to fret, she murmured and leaned over him, trying to pick him up without waking Gabe. At the first movement, Gabe's eyes opened. They were drowsy and very close to hers.

"I'm sorry. I didn't want to wake you."

He said nothing. Going with a dream she couldn't see but was very much a part of, he cupped a hand at the back of her head and drew her lips to his. There was a tenderness there that she hadn't felt for a very long time, an offering, a promise.

It was a promise she wanted, if only he would give it. It was a promise she would believe in.

Michael, scenting his mother, decided it was time to eat.

Unsettled and wishing they'd had just a moment more, Laura eased back. When Michael began to root at her breast, she undid two buttons and let him have his way.

"Did he wear you out?"

"We were taking a short break." It never failed to fascinate him how perfectly beautiful she looked when she was nursing the baby. He'd already sketched her like this, but that was for himself. "I didn't realize how much energy you need to handle someone so small."

"It gets worse. When we were shopping I saw a woman with a toddler. She never stopped running. Your mother tells me she used to collapse every afternoon when you'd finally worn down enough to take a nap."

"Lies." He shoved a couple of pillows behind his back and settled comfortably. "I was a perfectly behaved child."

"Then it was some other child who drew with crayon all over the silk wallpaper."

"Artistic expression. I was a prodigy."

"No doubt."

He just lifted a brow. Then he spotted her bags across

the room. "I was going to ask if you had a good time with my mother, but the answer's obvious."

She caught herself on the verge of an apology. That had to stop, she reminded herself. "It was wonderful to buy shoes and actually see them when I stood up, and a dress that had a waist in it."

"I suppose that's difficult for a woman, losing her figure during pregnancy."

"I loved every minute of it. The first time I couldn't hook a pair of slacks I was ecstatic." She started to go on, then stopped. That was something he would never be a part of, she realized. The first joys and fears, the first movements. Looking down at Michael, she wished with all her heart that he was Gabe's child in every way. "Still, I'm happy now not to look like an aircraft carrier."

"It was more like a dirigible."

"You give the most charming compliments."

He waited until she shifted Michael to her other breast. There was an urge inside of him to trace his finger there, just above where the baby suckled. It wasn't sexual, or even romantic, it was more a wondering. Instead, he tucked his hands behind his head.

"I tossed some leftovers together. I've no idea if they're edible."

Again there was the urge to apologize. Determined, Laura merely smiled. "I'm hungry enough for marginally edible."

"Good." Now he did lean forward, but only to trace a fingertip over Michael's head. "Come on down when he's settled. After this afternoon, I have a feeling he'll go out like a light when his belly's full."

"I won't be long." She waited until she was alone, then closed her eyes, hoping she had the courage to carry out her plans for the rest of the evening.

She hadn't been just a woman in so long. Laura stood in front of the mirrored wall, fogged now from the steam of her bath. She looked like a woman. Her nightgown was the palest blue, nearly white. She'd chosen it because it had reminded her of the way the snow had looked on the mountains in Colorado. It fell down her body from thin straps and a lacy bodice. She ran her hand down it experimentally. The material was very thin and very soft.

Should she wear her hair up, or wear it down? Did it matter?

What would it be like to be Gabe's wife...really his wife? She pressed a hand to her stomach, waiting for the nerves to ebb. Memories threatened to surface, and she fought them back. Tonight she would take Amanda's advice. She would think not of what had been, but of what could be.

She loved him so much, but she didn't know how to tell him. Words were so difficult, so irrevocable. Worse, she was afraid that he would take her love with the same discomfort and disregard as he did her gratitude. But tonight...she hoped tonight she could begin to show him.

He was stripping off his shirt when she opened the door to the adjoining bedroom. For a moment the light coming from behind her fell over her hair and ran through the thin fabric of her gown. All movement stopped as though it were a play, just as the curtain rose. He felt the heat and the tightening in his stomach.

Then she switched off the bathroom light. He pulled off his shirt.

"I checked on Michael." Gabe was surprised he could speak at all, but the words sounded normal enough. "He's sleeping. I thought I might work for an hour or two."

"Oh." She caught herself before she could twist her hands together. She was a grown woman. A grown woman should know how to seduce her husband. "I know you lost time this afternoon when I went out."

"I liked taking care of him." She was so slim, so beautifully frail, with her milky white skin and that blue-white gown. The angel again, with a fall of blond curls instead of a halo.

"You're a wonderful father, Gabe." She took a step toward him. She was already beginning to tremble.

"Michael makes it easy."

Should she have known it would be so difficult to simply cross a room? "Do I make it hard, to be a husband?"

"No." He lifted the back of his hand to her cheek. Her eyes were shades upon shades darker than the flow of silk she wore. He drew back, surprised by his own nerves. "You must be tired."

She bit off a sigh as she turned away. "It's obvious I'm not very good at this. Since seducing you isn't working, we'll try the more practical approach."

"Is that what you were doing?" He wanted to be amused, but his muscles were tight with tension. "Seducing me?"

"Badly." Opening her drawer, she drew out a small

slip of paper. "This is my doctor's report. It says that I'm a normal, healthy woman. Would you care to read it?"

This time his lips twitched. "Covered all the bases, did you?"

"You said you wanted me." The paper crumpled in her hand. "I thought you meant it."

He had her arms before she could retreat. Her eyes were dry, but he could see, just by looking, her fractured pride. The burden he already felt grew heavier. What they had was still so tenuous. If he made a mistake it might vanish completely.

"I meant it, Laura, started meaning it from the first day you were with me. It hasn't been easy, being with you, needing you, and not being able to touch."

Gingerly she laid a hand on his chest and felt his muscles tighten. "There's no reason you can't now."

He slid his hands up to her shoulders so that his fingers brushed over the thin straps of her gown. If it was a mistake, he had no choice but to make it. "No physical one any longer. When I take you to bed, there can only be the two of us. No ghosts. No memories." When she dropped her gaze, he drew her closer, challenging her to lift it again. "You won't think of anyone but me."

Whether it was a threat or a promise, he lowered his mouth to hers. Her hands fluttered, then were trapped between their bodies.

It was only the press of lips upon lips, but her blood began to pound. The stirring he could cause so easily started in her stomach and spread, long before his hands moved over her, long before her lips parted.

Her hands were imprisoned, but she didn't feel vulnerable. His mouth wasn't gentle, but she didn't feel afraid. As the kiss deepened, as the intimacy grew, she didn't think of anyone but him.

She tasted as she had the very first time, ripe and fresh. With his tongue he plundered her mouth, greedy for the flavor of her. There would be no turning back now, not when she was caught close in his arms and the lights were dim. He could hear her shuddering breath, and the steady ticking of the pendulum clock in the hallway. It was dark, it was quiet, they were alone. And tonight he would take a wife.

Her heart thudded against his bare chest, adding excitement. He ran his hands over her, feeling the smoothness of her skin, the slickness of her gown, feeling every tremble and every sigh his touch incited.

Greedy, he nipped his teeth into her lip as his hands moved lower. Passion sprung out, from him, from her, mixing together in a sudden, breath-stopping fury. Then he felt her body give against his in the ultimate gift of trust. The emotions that rose up in him tempered his desire. Tenderness, achingly sweet, more precious than diamonds, took its place.

Her hands were free. The paper still crumpled in her palm fluttered to the floor as she slipped her arms around him. Tentatively still. Her bones seemed to liquefy, degree by degree, until she wondered why she didn't simply slide out of his hands. Her mind, which had been swirling with needs, clouded with a pleasure that was softer, truer, than any she had ever imagined.

She stroked her hands over his back, feeling the muscle, the power. Wonder filled her at the discovery that anyone with such strength could be so gentle. His lips brushed over hers, testing, almost teasing, inviting her to set the pace. Or perhaps he was challenging her.

Hunger leaped inside her until she was locked against him, her mouth seeking, avid, impatient. Then she was swept up into his arms. In the dim light she saw his eyes, only his eyes, their clear green darkened by need. Hers remained open and on his as he lowered her onto the bed.

She expected speed, a frenzy of greed and a drive for gratification. She wouldn't have thought less of him for it. Her love wouldn't have diminished. Against hers, his body was taut and straining. Circling her arms around him, she prepared to give him whatever he required.

But it wasn't speed he sought. And the greed was not only to take, but also to give.

When he ranged kisses over her throat, lingering, nibbling, she, too, went taut. She could only whisper his name as he continued the slow journey over her shoulders and down to the curve of her breasts, then up again, in teasing circles. Instinctively she turned her head, seeking his mouth, his jaw, his temple, as her body turned hot and cold with pleasure.

He needed to take care, for her. At the first touch, he'd been terrified. She had been with another man, she had had a child, but he knew the extent of her innocence. He'd seen it, hour after hour, when he'd painted her. He'd felt it each and every time he'd drawn her against him. If he was going to take that innocence, he was going to give her beauty in return.

She was so…responsive. Her body seemed to ebb and flow at the touch of his hands. Wherever he tasted, her skin grew warm. Yet even as she gave, and offered, there was a shyness about her, the slightest of hesitations. He wanted to take her beyond that.

Slowly, with movements that were little more than a whisper along her skin, he drew the gown downward, following the trail of lace with his lips. At her first moan, his blood swam. He hadn't known that a sound, only a sound, could be so alluring. With light, openmouthed kisses he sensitized her skin until she began to shiver beneath him. In the lamplight she was exquisite, her skin like marble, her hair like silver. Her eyes were full of needs and uncertainties.

As he had once used his skill, his insight, to draw her emotions on canvas, he used it now to set them free.

She had never known there could be such sensitivity between a man and a woman. Even through the clouds of pleasure and the steadily rising tide of desire, she sensed his patience. She had never been so driven to touch a man before. With her fingertips and her palms, with her lips and her tongue, she discovered him. The urge came, strong, just to hold him, to wrap tight around him and hold on.

Then, without warning, he was taking her up, making her arch and gasp in shock and indescribable delight. Her mind and body were drained of everything but sensation. For an instant there was a terror of being totally out of control. His name burst out of her as she was carried away by a climax so strong, so intense, that she was left limp and dazed in the aftermath.

"Please, I can't… I've never…"

"I know." Strangely humbled, he lowered his lips to hers. He had wanted to give, had been driven to, but he hadn't known that in giving, so much would be returned to him. "Just relax. There's no hurry."

"But you haven't—"

He laughed against her throat. "I intend to. There's time. I want to touch you," he murmured, and began the slow, seductive journey again.

It wasn't possible. She would have said it couldn't be possible for her body to leap back in response to so gentle, so light, a touch. Yet within moments she was trembling again, aching again, wanting again. His tongue skimmed over her stomach, dipped to the curve of her thigh, until she was writhing, a victim now of her own desire and of the taste of heaven he'd already given her.

Then, impossibly, incredibly, she was tossed up and over again. This time, when she gasped and faltered, he slid into her.

Her moan merged with his.

Damp flesh pressed against damp flesh as they moved together. She'd never felt so strong, so utterly free, as she did now, joined as closely as was conceivable with Gabe.

She was everything he'd ever wanted, everything he'd ever dreamed of. Indeed, it was like a dream now, with the bursts and shudders of pleasure ripping through him. With his face pressed against her throat, he could smell her lightly provocative fragrance, mixed with the pungent, earthy scent of passion. He would go to the grave remembering that dizzying combination.

Her breath was fast and frenzied in his ear. Her body

was just as fast and frenzied beneath his. He could feel her nails as she dug heedlessly into his back.

He would remember all of it.

Then he remembered nothing, and he let himself go.

Chapter 9

There had been a time, a brief time, when Laura had dressed in elegant clothes and gone to elegant parties. She had met people whose names were printed in slick magazines and flashed in bold headlines in tabloids. She'd danced with celebrities and dined with princes of fashion. However much it had seemed like a dream, it had been real.

It was true enough that she had enjoyed her time modeling for Geoffrey. The work might have been hard, but she'd been young enough, untried enough, to have been dazzled by the glamour—even after ten hours on her feet.

He had taught her how to stand, how to walk, even how to look interested when fatigue was all but pouring out of her ears. He'd shown her how to use makeup to enhance subtly or strikingly, how to use her hair to express a mood.

All the things he'd taught her had helped her maintain an image during public events with the Eagletons. She'd been able to appear sophisticated and untroubled. At times, appearances were a great comfort.

She wasn't afraid she would embarrass herself or Gabe at the reception his parents were giving at their Nob Hill estate. But she wasn't certain she wanted to step back into that life again, either.

How might things have been if Gabe had been an ordinary man, a man of ordinary means? They might have found a little house with a little backyard and been swallowed up by anonymity. A part of her yearned for that, for the simplicity of it.

But that was wrong. Laura fastened the earrings she'd bought the week before, starbursts of blue stones. If Gabe had come from a different family and a different life, he wouldn't be the man she loved. The man she was almost ready to believe was beginning to love her.

There was nothing about him she wanted to change, not his looks, not his manner. She might wish occasionally that he would share with her a bit more of his thoughts and feelings, but she continued to hope that someday he would.

She wanted to be a full part of his life—lover, wife and partner. So far, she had come to be the first two.

When the door opened, she turned.

"If you're about ready, we'll—"

And he stopped and stared. This was the woman she'd only told him about, the one who had graced the covers of magazines and modeled silks and sables. Long-limbed and slender, she stood in front of the beveled mirror in a dress of midnight-blue. It was very simple, leaving her shoulders and throat bare, then caught like a wish at her breasts to fall ruler-straight to her feet.

She'd wound her hair up, swept it back, so that only a few wheat-colored curls escaped to tease her temples.

She was beautiful, gloriously so, yet even as he was drawn to her, he felt as though he were looking at a stranger.

"You look wonderful." But he kept his hand on the knob and the room between them. "I'll have to paint you like this." *Beauty on Ice,* he thought, cool, aloof and unapproachable.

"I took your advice on the color." She picked up her purse, then clasped and unclasped it as she wondered why he was looking at her as though he'd never seen her before. "And I avoided bows."

"So I see." She should have sapphires, a collar of them, around her throat. "It's still a bit cool. Do you have a wrap?"

"Yes." Irked by his tone, she walked to the bed and snatched up a wide silk scarf in a riot of jewel-like colors. It was then that he noticed that the back of the skirt was slit to the thigh.

"I imagine you'll create quite a stir in that little number."

She cringed inwardly, but, falling back on appearances, she managed to keep her face calm. "If you don't like the dress, why don't you just say so?" She swirled the scarf over her shoulders. "It's too late to change, but believe me, I won't wear it again."

"Just a minute." He grabbed her hand as she started through the doorway. He could feel the smooth gold of her plain wedding ring on the index finger of her right hand. She was still his Laura, he thought as he linked his fingers with hers. He'd only had to look in her eyes to see it.

"I have to get Michael ready," she mumbled, and tried again to move past him.

"Do you expect an apology because I'm human enough to be jealous?"

Her face went still, her eyes blank. "I'm not wearing it to attract other men. I bought it because I liked it and I thought it suited me."

He brought a hand to her face and swore roundly when she jerked. "Look at me. No, damn it, not at him, at me." Her eyes lashed back up to him. "Remember who I am, Laura. And remember this—I won't tolerate having my every mood, my every word, compared with someone else's."

"I'm not trying to do that."

"Maybe you're not trying to, but you do."

"You expect me to turn my life around overnight. I can't."

"No." He ran his thumb over the ring again. "I don't suppose you can. But you can remember that I'm part of your new life, not your old one."

"You're nothing like him." It was becoming easier to let her hand relax in his. "I know that. I guess sometimes it's easier to expect the worst than to hope for the best."

"I can't promise you the best."

No, he wouldn't make promises he couldn't keep. That was the beauty of him. "You could hold me. That's as close as I need to get."

When his arms came around her, he pressed her cheek against the shoulder of his black evening jacket. It smelled of him, and that made the last twists of tension dissolve.

"I suppose I was jealous, too."

"Oh?"

She smiled as she drew back enough to look into his face. "You look so good tonight."

"Really?" There was both discomfort and amusement in his tone.

"I've never seen you in evening clothes." She ran her finger down the dark lapel, which rested against a crisp white shirt. "Sort of like Heathcliff in a tux."

He laughed and cupped her face in his hands. "What a mind you have, angel. There's no hero in here."

"You're wrong." Her eyes were very solemn, very serious. "You're mine." He shrugged, but she kept him close. "Please, just this once, let me say it without you brushing it aside."

He just flicked a finger down her nose. "Don't expect me to walk around in armor too long. Let's get the baby. My mother knows how to make you miserable if you're late."

He wasn't a hero. He certainly wasn't comfortable being seen as one. Gabe was much more at ease discussing his work or speculating on the Giants' chances during the rest of the baseball season. He preferred arguments to good deeds.

When someone saw you as heroic, you invariably let them down. They expected you to have the right answers, the key to the lock, the light in the dark.

Michael had seen him as a hero. And, of course, he had let his brother down.

Michael had loved parties like this, Gabe thought as he sipped at the champagne that seemed to flow endlessly. He had loved the laughter, the people and the gossip. Michael had been unashamedly fond of rumors and whispers.

People had loved him moments after meeting him. He had been outgoing, funny, and as warm with strangers as with friends. It was Michael who had been the hero, doing favors without tallying the score, always willing to help or simply to be enthusiastic about a project.

Yet he'd had that streak of temper and toughness that had balanced him, prevented him from being overly... overly good, Gabe supposed.

God, he missed him still, at times unbearably.

There were people here who had known Michael, who had raised a glass with him or swapped stories with him. Perhaps that was what made it seem worse tonight, being in their parents' home, where they had grown up and shared so much and knowing that Michael would never walk into that room again.

Somehow you went on. One part of your life closed up, and another opened. Gabe looked across the room to where Laura stood talking to his father.

Sometime between the moment she'd rolled down the

window of a wrecked car and the moment she'd placed a newborn child in his arms he'd fallen in love with her. It had come not with trumpets and flares but with quiet, soothing murmurs.

If there were such things as angels, one had sent Laura to him when he'd needed her most.

She was grateful to him, and open enough to give him love and affection in return for what he had given her. There were days when he believed that would be enough, for today, and for the tomorrows they would have together.

Then there were the other times.

He wanted to grab her, to demand again and again that she look at him, see who he was, what he felt. That she forget what had happened before and trust in what was happening now. He wanted to erase, the way he might have blanked out a canvas, what had gone on before, all the things that had put shadows in her eyes, all the things that made her hesitate just that split second before she smiled.

But he knew better than most that when you painted over part of someone's life you stole something. Bad experience or good, what had happened to Laura had made her what she was, the woman he loved.

But loving as he did, and being a selfish man, he wanted to be loved back, completely, without the strings of gratitude or the shadows of vulnerability. Wanting wouldn't make it so, but time might. He could give her a little more of that.

Someone laughed across the room. Glasses chinked. There was a scent of wine, flowers and women's fragrances. The night had cooperated with a full moon, and its glow shimmered just outside the open terrace doors. The room was ablaze with lamplight. Wanting a few moments away from the crowd and the noise, he slipped upstairs to check on his son.

"The boy looks more like you every time I see him," Cliff was saying.

"Do you think so?" The thought had Laura lighting up. Perhaps she was vain after all.

"Absolutely. Though no one would believe you were a new mother, the way you're looking tonight." He patted her cheek in the way that always made her feel shy and delighted. "My Gabe has excellent taste."

"Shame on you, Cliff, flirting with a beautiful woman when your wife's not looking."

"Marion." Cliff bent down from his rangy height to give the newcomer a kiss. "Late as always."

"Amanda's already scolded me." She turned, sipping at her champagne, to give Laura a thorough study. "So this is the mysterious Laura."

"My new daughter." Cliff gave Laura a quick squeeze around the shoulders. "An old friend, Marion Trussalt. The Trussalt Gallery handles Gabe's paintings."

"Yes, I know. It's nice to meet you." She wasn't a beautiful woman, Laura thought, but she was oddly striking, with her sleek cap of black hair and her dark eyes. She wore a flowing rainbow-colored sheath that managed to be both arty and sophisticated.

"Yes, it is, since we have Gabe in common." Marion tapped a finger on the rim of her glass and smiled, but her eyes didn't warm. Laura recognized carefully polished disdain when she saw it. "You have his heart, and I his soul, you might say."

"Then it would seem we both want the best for him."

"Oh." Marion raised her glass. "Absolutely. Cliff, Amanda told me to remind you that hosts are supposed to mingle."

He grimaced. "Slave driver. Laura, be sure to work your way over to the buffet. You're getting too thin already." With that he went to do his duty.

"Yes, you're amazingly slender for someone who had a child—what was it? A month ago?"

"Almost two." Laura shifted her glass of sparkling water to her other hand. She didn't deal well with subtle attacks.

"Time flies." Marion touched her tongue to her upper lip. "It's odd that in all that time you haven't stirred yourself to come down to the gallery."

"You're right. I'll have to come down and see Gabe's work in a proper setting." She steadied herself. Under no circumstances was she going to allow herself to be intimidated or to fall into the trap of reading between the lines. If Gabe had ever had any kind of romantic involvement with Marion, it had ended. "He relies on you, I know. And I hope you'll be able to persuade him to go through with a new showing."

"I haven't decided that's really a good idea for the time being." Marion turned to smile at someone across the room who had called her name.

"Why? The paintings are wonderful."

"That isn't the only issue." She turned back to give

Laura a quick, glittering look. She hadn't been Gabe's lover, nor had there every been any urge on either side to make it so. Her feelings for Gabriel Bradley went far beyond the physical. Gabe was an artist, a great one, and she had been—and intended to go on being—the catalyst for his success.

If he had married within his circle, or chosen someone who could have enhanced or furthered his career, she would have been pleased. But for him to have wasted himself, and her ambitions, on a beautiful face and a smeared reputation was more than Marion could bear.

"Did I mention that I knew your first husband?"

If she had thrown her drink into Laura's face she would have been no less shocked. The cocoon that she had been able to draw around herself and Michael suffered its first crack.

"No. If you'll excuse me—"

"A fascinating man, I always thought. Certainly young, and a bit wild, but fascinating. A tragedy that he died so young, before he ever saw his child." She tilted her glass back until only a sheen of bubbles remained.

"Michael," Laura said evenly, "is Gabe's child."

"So I'm told." She smiled again. "There were the oddest rumors just before and just after Tony died. Some said that he was on the verge of divorcing you, that he'd already removed you from the family home because you were, well, indiscreet." With a shrug, Marion set her glass aside. "But that's all in the past now. Tell me, how are the Eagletons? I haven't spoke with Lorraine for ages."

She was going to be ill, violently and humiliatingly ill,

unless she succeeded in fighting back her rolling nausea. "Why are you doing this?" she whispered. "Why should you care?"

"Oh, my dear, I care about anything that has to do with Gabe. I intend to see him reach the very top, and I don't intend to watch him be dragged down. That's a lovely dress," she added. Then she saw Amanda approaching and slipped away.

"Laura, are you all right? You're white as a sheet. Come, let me find you a chair."

"No, I need some air." Turning, she fled through the open glass doors and onto the smooth stone terrace beyond.

"Here, now." Coming up behind her, Amanda took her arm and steered her to a chair. "Sit a minute before Gabe comes along. He'll take one look at you and pounce on me for insisting you come out and socialize too soon."

"It's nothing to do with that."

"And something to do with Marion." Amanda took the water glass out of Laura's tightening grip. "If she led you to believe that there was something—personal—between herself and Gabe, I can only say its totally untrue."

"That wouldn't matter."

With a little laugh, Amanda cast a look back inside. "If you mean that, then you're a better woman than I. I've known one of my husband's former...interests for over thirty-five years. I'd still like to spit in her eye."

With a laugh of her own, Laura drew in the softly scented evening. "I know Gabe's faithful to me."

"And so you should. You should also know that Marion and Gabe were never lovers." She moved her shoulders a bit. "I can't say that I know about all of my son's affairs, but I do know that he and Marion only have art in common. Now, what did she say to upset you?"

"It was nothing." Laura brushed her fingers over her temples, as if to soothe away an ache. "Really, it was my own fault, overreacting. She only mentioned that she'd met my first husband."

"I see." Annoyed, Amanda turned her sharp-eyed glance into the drawing room again. "Well, I have to say I find it very insensitive to bring up the subject at your wedding reception. One would have thought a woman like Marion would have more taste."

"It's over and it's best forgotten." Straightening her shoulders, Laura prepared to go back in. "I'd appreciate it if you wouldn't mention any of this to Gabe. There's no reason to annoy him."

"No, I agree. I'll speak with Marion myself."

"No." Laura picked up her glass again and sipped slowly. "If there's anything that needs to be said, I'll say it myself."

Amanda's smile spread and she said easily, "If that's what you'd like."

"Yes. Amanda…" A decision made quickly, she thought, was sometimes the best. "Could I leave Michael with you one day next week? I'd like to go into the gallery and see Gabe's paintings."

Laura woke up out of breath and shivering. She struggled her way out of the nightmare to find herself in Gabe's arms.

"Just relax. You're all right."

She drew in a big gulp of air, then let it out slowly. "Sorry," she muttered, dragging a hand through her hair.

"Want anything? Some water?"

"No." As the fear passed, annoyance took its place. The glowing dial of the alarm clock read 4:15. They'd been in bed for only three hours, and now she was wide-awake and restless.

With his arm still around her, Gabe lay back on his pillow. "You haven't had a nightmare since Michael was born. Did something happen at the party tonight?"

She thought of Marion and gritted her teeth. "Why do you ask?"

"I noticed that you seemed upset, and my mother annoyed."

"Did you think that I had an argument with your mother?" That made her smile and settle more comfortably against him. "No, in fact we get along very well."

"You sound surprised."

"I didn't expect to make friends with her. I kept waiting for her to bring out her broom and pointed hat."

He laughed and kissed her shoulder. "Just try criticizing my work."

"I wouldn't dare." Unconsciously she began to stroke her fingers through his hair. When she was here, like this, she believed she could handle anything that threatened her new family. "She showed me the mural in the parlor. The one with all the mythical creatures."

"I was twenty, and romantic." And he'd asked his mother a dozen times to have it painted over.

"I like it."

"No wonder you get along with her."

"I did like it." She shifted so that she could rest her arms on his chest. There was only a little moonlight, but she could see him. She didn't realize that it was her first completely unstudied move toward him, but he did. "What's wrong with unicorns and centaurs and fairies?"

"They have their place, I suppose." But all he was currently interested in was making love with her.

"Good. Then don't you think the side wall in Michael's room is the perfect place for a mural?"

He tugged at a curl that fell over her cheek. "Are you offering me a commission?"

"Well, I've seen a few samples of your work, and it's not bad."

He tugged harder. "Not bad?"

"Shows promise." With a quick laugh, she ducked before he could pull her hair again. "Why don't you submit some sample sketches for consideration?"

"And my fee?"

He was smiling; her skin was warming. Laura began to think the nightmare had been a blessing in disguise. "Negotiable."

"Tell you what. I'll do the mural on one condition."

"Which is?"

"That you let me paint you again, nude."

Her eyes widened. Then she laughed, sure he was joking. "You should at least let me wear a beret."

"You've been watching too many old movies, but you can wear a beret if you like—just nothing else."

"I couldn't."

"All right, then, scratch the beret."

"Gabe, you're not serious."

"Of course I am." To prove it, and to please himself, he ran a hand over her. "You have a beautiful body... long dancer's limbs, smooth white skin, a narrow waist."

"Gabe." She spoke to stop not his roaming hands but his conversation. She stopped neither.

"I've wanted to paint you nude since the first time we made love. I can still see the way you looked when I drew the nightgown away. Capturing that femininity, that subtle sexuality, would be a triumph."

She laid her cheek on his heart. "I'd be embarrassed."

"Why? I know what you look like. Every inch of you." He cupped her breasts, scraping his thumbs lightly over her nipples. Her instant response rippled through him.

"No one else does." Her voice was husky now. Hardly realizing it, she began to run her hands over him. The journey was long, lazy, thorough.

There was something incredibly exciting about the idea. No one else knew the secrets of her body, the dips and curves. No one else knew how a touch here, a stroke there, could make her shyness melt into passion. He did want to capture that on canvas, the beauty of her, the sweetness of her inhibitions. The fire of passion just discovered. But he could wait.

"I suppose I could just hire a model."

Her head came up at that. "You—" The jealousy rose, so swift and powerful that it left her momentarily speechless.

"It's art, angel," he said, amused and not at all displeased. "Not a centerfold."

"You're trying to blackmail me."

"You're very sharp."

Her eyes narrowed. In deliberate seduction that surprised them both, she shifted so that her body rubbed tantalizingly over his. "Only if I get to choose the model."

His pulse was thudding. As she lowered her head to brush kisses over his chest, he closed his eyes. "Laura."

"No, Mrs. Drumberry. I met her tonight."

He opened his eyes. But when she used her teeth to tug on his nipple he arched beneath her. "Mabel Drumberry is a hundred and five."

"Exactly." She chuckled but continued her explorations, with a growing sense of power and discovery. "I wouldn't trust you closed up in your studio with some sexy young redhead with lush curves."

He started to laugh, but the sound became a moan as her hand ranged lower. "Don't you think I can resist a sexy young redhead?"

"Of course, but she wouldn't be able to resist you." She rubbed her cheek along his jawline, which was already roughened with morning stubble. "You're so beautiful, Gabe. If I could paint, I'd show you."

"What you're doing is driving me crazy."

"I hope so," she murmured, and lowered her mouth to his.

She'd never had the confidence to take charge, had never been sure enough of her skill or her appeal. Now it seemed right and wonderfully fulfilling to tease and taunt her man in passion.

His hands were in her hair, his fingers tangled and tense, as she dipped her tongue into his mouth and explored. Her moves were instinctive rather than experienced, and all the more seductive for it.

The power came to her not in a wild burst but with quiet certainty. She could be his partner here, his full partner. It was easy to show love, almost as easy as it was to feel it.

As she discovered him, she discovered herself. She wasn't as patient as he, not here. Strangely, in the daylight, the opposite was true. She saw him as a man who needed to move quickly, decisively, and if mistakes were made because of hurry they could be corrected or just as easily ignored. She was more cautious, more prone to think through alternatives before acting.

But in bed, in the role of the seductress, she found little patience in herself.

She was wild and wanton. Gabe found himself reaching for her, then being rocked helplessly by the sensations she brought to him. It was like having a different woman in bed, one who felt like Laura, smelled like Laura, one he wanted as desperately as he wanted Laura.

When her mouth came down on his, it was Laura's taste, yet somehow darker, riper. And her body was like a furnace as she moved over him.

He tried to remember that this was his wife, his shy and still-innocent wife, who required infinite care and gentleness. He had yet to release his full range of passion with her. With Laura he had taken his time, used every drop of his sensitivity.

Now she was stripping him down to the nerve ends.

She could feel the power, and it was glorious. Despite her excitement, her mind was clear as a bell. She could make him weak, she could make him desperate. She could make him tremble. Breathlessly she pressed her lips to pulse points that she found by instinct. His heart was racing. For her. She could feel his body shudder at her touch. When he groaned, it was her own name she heard.

She heard herself laugh, and there was something sultry in the sound. A feminine triumph. The clock in the hallway struck five, and the echo went on and on in her head.

Then his arms were locked around her and the sound that was coming from his throat was long and primitive. His control snapped like a rubber band stretched too far. Needs only half satisfied, so long held in check, flooded free. His mouth covered hers, bruisingly. But it wasn't a skip of fear she felt. It was a leap of victory.

Trapped in madness, they rolled across the bed, seeking, taking, demanding, with a kind of greed that made the mouth go dry and the soul shudder. The modest gown she wore was torn aside, seams ripping, lace shredding. His hands were everywhere, and they were far from gentle.

There was no shame. There was no shyness. This was freedom, a different kind from what he had already shown her. As desperate as he, she opened for him. When he plunged into her, the shock vibrated, wave after wave.

Fast and furious, they locked into their own rhythm, each driving the other.

Endless pleasure, sharp and edgy. Insatiable need spreading like wildfire. As she gave herself to him, as she asked and received more, Laura realized that, for the lucky, time could indeed stop.

Chapter 10

When the sky darkened, Laura was in the garden. It had become her habit to spend her mornings there while the baby slept or sat rocking in his swing in the sunlight. Since her arrival in Gabe's home, she'd found little to do indoors. The house almost took care of itself and, as she had once told him, Gabe was only sloppy when he painted.

More than that, there were too many rooms, too much space that she didn't yet feel a part of. In the nursery, which she'd decorated herself and where, through necessity, she spent many hours during the day and night, she felt at home. The rest of the house, with its heirlooms and its beautiful old rugs, its polished wood and its faded wallpaper, remained aloof to her.

But as spring had taken hold she had discovered an affinity and a talent for gardening, as well as a need for space and air. She liked the sunlight and the smells and the feel of the earth under her hands. She devoured books on plants, much as she had on childbirth, so that she could become familiar with flowers and shrubs and the care they required.

The tulips were beginning to bloom, and the azaleas were already ripe with blossoms. Someone else had planted them, but Laura had no trouble taking them to heart as her own. They flowered afresh every year. Nor did she feel awkward adding her own touches with moss roses and snapdragons.

Already she was planning to plant new bulbs in the fall, daylilies, windflowers, poppies. Then, over the winter, she would root her own spring flowers from seed, starting them in little peat pots that she would set in the sunroom on the east side of the house.

"I'll teach you how to plant them next year," she told Michael. She could already imagine him toddling around the garden on short, sturdy legs, patting at the dirt, trying to snatch butterflies off blossoms.

He would laugh. There would be so much for him to laugh about. She would be able to catch him up in her arms and swing him around so that his eyes, which were still as stubbornly blue as hers, glowed and his laughter bounced on the air. Then Gabe would stick his head out of his studio window and demand to know what all the ruckus was about.

But he wouldn't really be annoyed. He'd come down, saying that if there was going to be so much noise he might as well forget about working for the morning. He'd sit on the ground with Michael in his lap and they'd laugh together about nothing anyone else would understand.

Sitting back on her heels, Laura wiped her brow with the back of a gloved hand. Dreaming had always been her escape, her defense, her survival. Now it didn't seem like any of those things, because she was beginning to believe dreams could come true.

"I love your daddy," she told Michael, as she told him at least once every day. "I love him so much that it makes me believe in happy endings."

When the shadow fell over her, Laura glanced up and saw the first dark clouds roll over the sun. She was tempted to ignore them, and she might have if she hadn't known it took more than a quick minute to gather up all her gardening tools, Michael's supplies and the baby himself.

"Well, the rain's good for the flowers, isn't it, sweetie?" She stored the tools and bags of peat moss and fertilizers in the small shed near the back door, then drew Michael out of the swing. With the acquired coordination of motherhood, she carried the baby, his little cache of toys and the folded swing indoors.

She'd barely started upstairs when the first crack of thunder had both her and Michael jumping. As he began to wail, she fought back her own longstanding fear of storms and soothed him.

He calmed down much more quickly than she as she walked and rocked and murmured reassurances. Though the rain held off, she could watch the fury raging in the sky through Michael's windows. Lightning slashed, turning the light from gray to mauve, then back to gray, in the blink of an eye.

Eventually he began to doze, but she continued to hold him, as much for her own comfort as his.

"Silly, isn't it?" she murmured. "A grown woman more afraid of thunder than a tiny baby." As the rain began to lash at the house, she made herself set the sleeping child in his crib so that she could close the windows.

At least that would keep her busy, Laura told herself as she moved from room to room to shut the windows against the pelting rain. Still, each time thunder boomed she jerked back. It wasn't until she started back into the nursery, telling herself she'd curl up on the daybed and read until the storm passed, that she remembered Gabe's studio. Thinking only of his work, she rushed down the hall.

She was grateful that the storm hadn't knocked out the power. The lights flared on at a touch. It seemed that her luck had held. The floor was wet by the ribbon of windows, but none of his paintings were stored there. Laura hurried down the line, shutting each one until the rain was muffled by the glass.

She started to do the practical thing and go for a mop, but then it struck her that this was the first time she had been in Gabe's studio alone. He'd never asked her not to go in, but the lack of privacy she'd lived with most of her life had made her fastidious about respecting that of others. Now, though, with the lights bright overhead and the thunder rolling in the distance, she felt comfortable there, as she did in the nursery. As she had in the cabin in the mountains.

The room smelled of him, she realized. It held that mixture of paint and turpentine, with the powdery addition of chalk, that often clung to his clothes and his hands. It was a scent that invariably put her at ease, even though it was also a scent that invariably aroused her. Like the man, she thought, the scent drew her emotions. She could love him and be comforted by him, just as she could be excited and confused by him.

What did he want from her? she wondered. And why? She thought she understood part of it. He wanted the solidity of family, an end to his own loneliness and passion in bed. He'd chosen her for those things because she'd been as anxious to give them as he was to take them.

It could be enough, or nearly enough. Her problem was, and continued to be, a quiet longing for more.

Shaking off the mood, she tried to picture him there in that room, alone, working, envisioning.

So much had been done here, she thought, so many hours creating, perfecting, experimenting. What made one man different from another in the way he saw and expressed what he saw? Crossing to his easel, she studied his work in progress.

A painting of Michael. The deep and simple pleasure of it had her hugging herself. There was a rough sketch tacked to the easel, and the portrait on canvas was just beginning to take shape. She could see that even since the sketch, which he'd drawn perhaps a week before, Michael had changed and grown. But because of this she would always be able to look back and see him exactly as he'd been in that one precious moment of time.

With her arms still crossed over her breasts, she

turned to study the room. It was different without Gabe in it. Less…dramatic, she thought. Then she laughed a little, knowing he would hate that description.

Without him it was a wide, airy room, largely empty. On the floor were dried drops and smears of paint that could have been there for a week or a year. A small pedestal sink was built into one corner. She saw a towel tossed carelessly over its lip. There were shelves and a worktable with equipment scattered on them. Paints and bottles, jars crammed with brushes, pallet knives, hunks of charcoal and balled-up rags. Unframed canvases were stacked against the walls, much as they had been in Colorado. He hadn't hung anything here.

She wondered why she hadn't thought before to ask Gabe if he had anything she might hang in Michael's room. The posters she'd chosen were colorful, but one of Gabe's paintings would mean more. With that in mind, she knelt down and began to go through canvases.

How easily he drew out emotion. One of his pastel landscapes would make you dreamy. Next an edgy, too-realistic view of a slum would make you shudder. There were portraits, too—an impossibly old man leaning on a cane at a bus stop, three young girls giggling outside a boutique. There was a spectacular nude study of a brunette sprawled on white satin. Instead of jealousy, it raised a feeling of awe in Laura.

She went through more than a dozen, wondering why he'd stacked them so carelessly. Many were unframed, and all were facing the wall. Each one she held left her more astonished that she could be married to a man who could do so much with color and brush. More, each painting gave her a closer look at who he was. She could sense the mood that had held him as he'd worked. Rage for this, humor for that. Sorrow, impatience, desire, delight. Whatever he could feel, he could paint.

These didn't belong here, she thought, frustrated that he would close them up in a room where no one could see them or appreciate them or be touched by them. His signature was dashed in each corner, with the year just below. Everything she found had been painted no more than two years before, and no less than one year.

She turned the last canvas over and was caught immediately. It was another portrait, and this one had been painted with love.

The subject, a young man of no more than thirty, was grinning, a bit recklessly, as though he had all the time in the world to accomplish what he wanted to do. His hair was blond, a few shades lighter than Gabe's, and brushed back from a lean, good-looking face. It was a casual study, full-length, with the subject sprawled in a chair, legs spread out and crossed at the ankle. But, despite the relaxing pose, there was a sense of movement and energy.

She recognized the chair. It sat in the parlor of the Bradley mansion on Nob Hill. And she recognized the subject by the shape of the face, which was so much like her husband's. This was Gabe's brother. This was Michael.

For a long time she sat there, holding the painting in her lap, no longer hearing the storm. The lights flickered once, but she didn't notice.

It was possible, she discovered, to grieve for someone

you hadn't even known, to feel the loss and the regret. That Gabe had loved his brother deeply was obvious in each brush stroke. Not only loved, she thought, but respected. Now more than ever she wished he trusted her enough to speak of this Michael, his life and his death. In the sketch of the baby Gabe had tacked on the easel she had seen this same kind of unconditional love.

If he was using the baby to help him get over the loss of his brother, should she begrudge him that? It didn't mean he loved their Michael any less. Still, it made her sad to think of it. Until he talked to her, opened up his emotions to her as he did in his work, she would never really be his wife and Michael would never really be his son.

Gently she turned the canvas back to the wall and replaced the others.

When the rain stopped, Laura decided to call Amanda and follow through with her decision to visit the gallery. If she wanted Gabe to take another step toward her, she would have to take another toward him. She'd avoided going to the gallery, not for all the reasons she had given, but because she hadn't felt comfortable in her role as wife to the public person, the well-known artist. Insecurity, she knew, could only be overcome by taking a confident step forward, even if that step took all the courage you could muster.

She'd grown, Laura told herself. In the past year she'd learned not just to be strong but to be as strong as she needed to be. She might not have reached the peak, but she was no longer scrambling for a foothold at the bottom of the hill.

It was as easy as asking. After her thanks were brushed aside Laura hung up the phone and glanced at her watch. If Michael stuck to his usual schedule, he would wake within the hour and demand to be fed. She could take him to Amanda—the first big step—then drive to the gallery. She glanced down at the dirt-stained knees of her jeans. First she had to change.

The doorbell caught her halfway up the stairs. Feeling too optimistic to be annoyed by the interruption, she went to answer it.

And the world crashed silently at her feet.

"Laura." Lorraine Eagleton gave a brisk nod, then strode into the hall. She stood and glanced idly around as she drew off her gloves. "My, my, you've certainly landed on your feet, haven't you?" She tucked her gloves tidily in a buff-colored alligator bag. "Where is the child?"

She couldn't speak. Both words and air were trapped in her lungs, crowding there so that her chest ached. Her hand, still gripping the doorknob, was ice-cold, though the panicked rhythm of her heart vibrated in each fingertip. She had a sudden, horrible flash of the last time she had seen this woman face-to-face. As if they had just been spoken, she remembered the threats, the demand and the humiliation. She found her voice.

"Michael's asleep."

"Just as well. We have business to discuss."

The rain had cooled the air and left its taste in it. Watery sunlight crept through the door, which Laura still hadn't closed. Birds were beginning to chirp optimistically again. Normal things. Such normal things. Life, she reminded herself, didn't bother to stop for personal crises.

Though she couldn't make her fingers relax on the doorknob, she did keep her eyes and her voice level. "You're in my home now, Mrs. Eagleton."

"Women like you always manage to find rich, gullible husbands." She arched a brow, pleased that Laura was still standing by the door, tense and pale. "That doesn't change who you are, what you are. Nor will your being clever enough to get Gabriel Bradley to marry you stop me from taking what's mine."

"I have nothing that belongs to you. I'd like you to leave."

"I'm sure you would," Lorraine said, smiling. She was a tall, striking woman with dark, sculpted hair and an unlined face. "Believe me, I have neither the desire nor the intention to stay long. I intend to have the child."

Laura had a vision of herself standing in the mist, holding an empty blanket. "No."

Lorraine brushed the refusal aside as she might have brushed a speck of lint from her lapel. "I'll simply get a court order."

The cold fear was replaced by heat, and she managed to move then, though it was only to stiffen. "Then do it. Until you do, leave us alone."

Still the same, Lorraine thought as she watched Laura's face. She spit a bit now when she was backed into a corner, but she was still easily maneuvered. It infuriated her now, as it always had, that her son had settled for so little when he could have had so much. Even in fury she never raised her voice. Lorraine had always considered derision a better weapon than volume.

"You should have taken the offer my husband and I made to you. It was generous, and it won't be made again."

"You can't buy my baby, any more than you can buy back Tony."

Pain flashed across Lorraine's face, pain that was real enough, sharp enough, to make Laura form words of sympathy. They could talk, had to be able to talk now, as one mother to another. "Mrs. Eagleton—"

"I won't speak of my son with you," Lorraine said, and the pain vanished into bitterness. "If you had been what he needed, he'd still be alive. I'll never forgive you for that."

There had been a time when she would have crumbled at those words, ready to take the blame. But Lorraine had been wrong. Laura was no longer the same. "Do you want to take my baby to punish me or to bind your wounds? Either reason is wrong. You have to know that."

"I know I can and will prove that you're unfit to care for the child. I'll produce documentation that you made yourself available to other men before and after your marriage to my son."

"You know that's not true."

Lorraine continued as if Laura hadn't spoken. "Added to that will be the record of your unstable family background. If the child proves to be Tony's, there'll be a custody hearing, and the outcome is without question."

"You won't take Michael, not with money, not with

lies." Her voice rose, and she fought to bring it back down. Losing her temper would get her nowhere. Laura knew all too well how easily Lorraine could bat aside emotion with one cold, withering look. She believed, she had to believe, there was still a way of reasoning with her. "If you ever loved Tony, then you'll know just how far I'll go to keep my son."

"And you should know just how far I'll go to see to it that you have no part in raising an Eagleton."

"That's all he is to you, a name, just a symbol of immortality." Despite her efforts, her voice was growing desperate and her knees were beginning to shake. "He's just a baby. You don't love him."

"Feelings have nothing to do with it. I'm staying at the Fairmont. You have two days to decide whether or not you want a public scandal." Lorraine drew out her gloves again. The terror on Laura's face assured her that there was no risk of that. "I'm sure the Bradleys would be displeased, at the least, to learn of your past indiscretions. Therefore, I have no doubt you'll be sensible, Laura, and not risk what you've so conveniently acquired." She walked out the door and down the steps to where a gray limo waited.

Without waiting for it to drive away, Laura slammed the door and bolted it. She was panting as though she'd been running. And it was running that occurred to her first. Dashing up the stairs, she raced into the nursery and began to toss Michael's things into his carryall.

They'd travel light. She'd only pack what was absolutely necessary. Before sundown they could be miles away. Headed north, she thought quickly. Maybe into

Canada. There was still enough money left to help them get away, to buy them enough time to disappear. A rattle slipped out of her hand and landed with a clatter. Giving in to despair, she sunk onto the daybed and buried her face in her hands.

They couldn't run. Even if they had enough funds to keep them for a lifetime, they couldn't run. It was wrong, wrong for Michael, for Gabe, even for herself. They had a life here, the kind she'd always wanted, the kind she needed to give her son.

But what could she do to protect it?

Take a stand. Ride out the attack. Not cave in. But caving in was what she'd always done best. Lifting her head, she waited until her breathing had calmed. That was the old Laura's thinking, and that was exactly what Lorraine was counting on. The Eagletons knew how easily manipulated she had been. They expected her to run, and they would use that impulsive, erratic behavior to take her baby. They thought that if she was too tired to run she would sacrifice her child to protect her position with the Bradleys.

But they didn't know her. They had never taken the time or effort to really know her. She wouldn't cave in. She wouldn't run with her son. She was damn well going to fight for him.

The anger came then, and it felt wonderful. Anger was a hot, animate emotion, so unlike the icy numbness of fear. She'd stay angry, as Amanda had advised, because angry she would not only fight but fight rough and dirty. The Eagletons were in for a surprise.

* * *

By the time she reached the gallery she was in control again. Michael was safe with Amanda, and Laura was taking the first step of the route she'd already mapped out to see that he stayed safe.

The Trussalt Gallery was in a gracefully refurbished old building. Flowers, neatly trimmed and still wet from the recent rain, were grouped near the main entrance. Laura could smell roses and damp leaves as she pulled the door open.

Inside, skylights offered an open view of the still-cloudy sky, but the gallery itself was brilliant with recessed and track lighting. It was as quiet as a church. Indeed, as Laura paused to look, she could see that this was a place designed for the worship of art. Sculptures in marble and wood, in iron and bronze, were placed lovingly. Rather than competing with each other, they harmonized. As did the paintings aligned stylishly on the walls.

She recognized one of Gabe's, a particularly solemn view of a garden going to seed. It wasn't pretty; it certainly wasn't joyful. Looking at it, she thought of the mural he'd painted for his mother. The same man who believed enough in fantasies to bring them to life also saw reality, perhaps a bit too clearly. They had that in common, as well.

There were only a few patrons here on this rainy weekday afternoon. They had time to browse, Laura reminded herself. She didn't. Spotting a guard, she moved toward him.

"Excuse me, I'm looking for Gabriel Bradley."

"I'm sorry, miss. He wouldn't be available. If you have a question about one of his paintings, you may want to see Ms. Trussalt."

"No. You see, I'm—"

"Laura." Marion breezed out of an alcove. She was wearing pastels today, a long, slim skirt in baby blue that reached to her ankles, with a hip-skimming sweater in soft pink. The quiet colors only accentuated her exotic looks. "So you decided to pay us a visit after all."

"I'd like to see Gabe."

"What a pity." Without so much as a glance, Marion motioned the guard aside. "He's not here at the moment."

Laura curled her fingers tighter around the clasp of her purse. Intimidation from this quarter meant less than nothing now. "Do you expect him back?"

"As a matter of fact, he should be back before too long. We're booked for drinks in, oh—" she glanced at her watch "—half an hour."

Both the glance and the tone were designed to dismiss her, but Laura was far beyond worrying about games. "Then I'll wait."

"You're welcome to, of course, but I'm afraid Gabe and I have business to discuss. So boring for you."

Weariness was a dull throb at the base of her skull. She had no desire to cross swords now. Her energy had to remain focused for a much more vital fight. "I appreciate your concern, but nothing about Gabe's art is boring for me."

"Spoken like a little Trojan." Marion tilted her head. There was a smile that had nothing to do with friendship in her eyes. "You're looking a bit pale. Trouble in paradise?"

And she knew. As clearly as if Marion had said it out loud, she knew how Lorraine had found her. "Nothing that can't be dealt with. Why did you call her, Marion?"

The smile remained in place, cool and confident. "I beg your pardon?"

"She was already paying good money for detectives. I only had a week or two longer at most."

Marion considered a moment, then turned to fuss with the alignment of a painting. "I've always thought time was better saved than wasted. The sooner Lorraine deals with you, the sooner I can get Gabe back on track. Let me show you something."

Marion moved across the gallery in a separate room, where the walls and floors were white. A sweeping spiral staircase, again in white, rose up in one corner. Above, balconies ran in a circle. A trio of ornamental trees grew under the staircase, fronted by a towering ebony sculpture of a man and a woman in a passionate, yet somehow despairing, embrace.

But it was the portrait that caught her attention, that drew it and demanded it. It was her own face that looked serenely back at Laura, from the portrait Gabe had painted during those long, quiet days in Colorado.

"Yes, it's stunning." Marion rubbed a finger over her lip as she studied it. She'd been tempted to take a knife to the canvas when Gabe had first unpacked it, but the temptation had faded quickly. She was too much a patron of the arts to let personal feelings interfere. "It's one of his best and most romantic pieces. It's been hanging only three weeks and I've already had six serious offers for it."

"I've already seen the painting, Marion."

"Yes, but I doubt you understand it. He calls it *Gabriel's Angel*. That should tell you something."

"Gabriel's Angel," Laura repeated in a murmur. The warmth spread through her as she took a step closer. "What should that tell me?"

"That he, like Pygmalion, fell a bit in love with his subject. That's expected now and again, even encouraged, as it often inspires great work such as this." She tapped a finger against the frame. "But Gabe's much too practical a man to string out the fantasy for long. The portrait's finished, Laura. He doesn't need you any longer."

Laura turned her head so that she could look directly at Marion. What was being said had run through her mind countless times. She told Marion what she had already told herself. "Then he'll have to tell me that."

"He's an honorable man. That's part of his charm. But once things come to a head, once he realizes his mistake, he'll cut his losses. A man only believes in an image," she said, with a gesture toward the portrait, "as long as the image is unsmeared. From what Lorraine tells me, you don't have much time."

Laura fought back the urge to turn and run. Oddly, she discovered it didn't take as much effort this time. "If you believe that, why are you taking so much trouble to move me along?"

"No trouble." She smiled again and let her hand fall away from the painting. "I consider it part of my job to encourage Gabe to concentrate on his career and avoid the kind of controversies that can only detract from it. As I've already explained, his involvement with you isn't acceptable. He'll realize that soon enough himself."

No wonder she had called Lorraine, Laura thought. They were two of a kind. "You're forgetting something, Marion. Michael. No matter what Gabe feels or doesn't feel for me, he loves Michael."

"It takes a particularly pitiful woman to use a child."

"You're right." Laura met her eyes levelly. "You couldn't be more right." When Laura saw that retort had hit home, she continued calmly, "I'll wait here for Gabe. I'd appreciate it if you'd tell him when he gets back."

"So you can run and hide behind him?"

"I can't see that Laura's reasons for coming to see me are your concern."

Gabe spoke from the entranceway. Both women turned toward him. He could read fury on Marion's face and distress on Laura's. Even as he watched, both women composed themselves in their own way. Marion lifted her brow and smiled. Laura folded her hands and raised her chin.

"Darling. You know it's part of my job to protect my artists from panicky spouses and lovers." Crossing to him, Marion laid a hand on his arm. "We're going to be meeting with the Bridgetons in a few minutes about the three paintings. I don't want you distracted and out of sorts."

He spared her only the briefest of glances, but in it Marion saw that he had heard too much. "I'll worry about my moods. If you'll excuse us now?"

"The Bridgetons—"

"Can buy the paintings or go to hell. Leave us alone, Marion."

She aimed a vicious glare at Laura, then stormed out of the room. Her heels echoed on the tile. "I'm sorry," Laura said after a long breath. "I didn't come here to make waves."

"Why, then? From the look of you, you didn't come to spend an afternoon in art appreciation." Before she could answer, he was striding to her. "Damn it, Laura, I don't like having the two of you standing here discussing me as though I were some prize to be awarded to the highest bidder. Marion's a business associate, you're my wife. The two of you are going to have to resolve that."

"I understand that completely." Her voice had changed, hardened to match his. "And you should understand that if I believed you were involved with her in any way I would already have left you."

Whatever he'd been about to say slipped completely away from him. Because he recognized the unshakable resolve in the statement, he could only stare at her. "Just like that?"

"Just like that. I've already lived through one marriage where fidelity meant nothing. I won't live through another."

"I see." Comparisons again, he thought. He wanted to shout at her. Instead, he spoke softly, too softly. "Then I've been warned."

She turned away so that she could close her eyes for a moment. Her head was pounding ruthlessly. If she didn't take the time to draw herself in, she would throw herself into his arms and beg for help. "I didn't come here to discuss the terms of our marriage."

"Maybe you should have. It might be time for us to go back to square one and spell it out."

She shook her head and made herself turn to face him again. "I wanted to tell you that I'm going to see a lawyer in the morning."

He felt the life drain out of him in one swift flood. She wanted a divorce. Then, as quickly as he'd been left limp, the fury came. Unlike Laura, he had never had to prime himself for a fight. "What the hell are you talking about?"

"It can't be put off any longer. I can't keep pretending it's not necessary." Again she wanted to step into his arms, to feel them close around her, make her safe. She kept an arm's length away and stood on her own. "I didn't want to start what will be a difficult and ugly period without letting you know."

"That's big of you." Spinning away, he dragged a hand through his hair. Above him, her portrait smiled gently down. As he stood between them, he felt as though he were caught between two women, between two needs. "What in the hell brought this on? Do you think you can kiss me goodbye at the door, then talk about lawyers a few hours later? If you haven't been happy, why haven't you said so?"

"I don't know what you're talking about, Gabe. We knew this would probably happen eventually. You were the one who told me there'd come a time when I'd have to face it. Now I'm ready to. I just want to give you the option of backing off before it's too late to turn back."

He started to snap at her, then stopped himself. It occurred to him that what he had thought they were talking about, and what was actually being discussed were two different things. "Why do you need to see a lawyer in the morning?"

"Lorraine Eagleton came to the house this afternoon. She wants Michael."

No relief came at the realization that they weren't speaking of divorce. There was no room for it. He recognized a flash of panic before fury replaced it. "She may as well want the moon, because she won't have that, either." He reached out to touch a hand to her cheek. "Are you all right?"

She nodded. "I wasn't, but I am now. She's threatening a custody suit."

"On what grounds?"

She pressed her lips together, but her gaze didn't waver. "On the grounds that I'm not fit to care for him. She told me she'll prove that I was...that there were other men before and during my marriage to Tony."

"How can she prove what isn't true?"

So he believed in her. It was just that easy. Laura reached for his hand. "You can get people to do or say a great many things if you pay them enough. I've seen the Eagletons do that kind of thing before."

"Did she tell you where she was staying?"

"Yes."

"Then it's time I talked with her."

"No." She had his hand before he could stride from the room. "Please, I don't want you to see her yet. I need to talk with a lawyer first, make certain what can and can't be done. We can't afford the luxury of making a mistake in anger."

"I don't need a lawyer to tell me she can't walk into my house and threaten to take Michael."

"Gabe, please." Again she had to stop him. When her fingers curled around his arms, she felt the fury vibrating in him. "Listen to me. You're angry. So was I, and frightened, too. My first impulse was to run again. I'd even started to pack."

He thought of what it would have done to him to have come home to find the house empty. The score he had to settle with the Eagletons was getting bigger. "Why didn't you?"

"Because it wouldn't have been right, not for Michael, not for you or for me. Because I love both of you too much."

He stopped and cupped her face in his hands, trying to read what was behind her eyes. "You wouldn't have gotten very far."

The smile came slowly as she wrapped her fingers around his wrists. "I hope not. Gabe, I know what I have to do, and I also know that I can do it."

He paused, taking it in. She spoke of love one moment, then of what she would do, not of what they would do. "Alone?"

"If necessary. I know you've taken Michael as your own, but I want you to understand that if she pursues the suit it's going to get ugly, and what's said about me will affect you and your family." There was a moment's hesitation as she worked up the courage to give him a choice. "If you'd rather not be involved in what's going to happen now, I understand."

His choices had narrowed from the moment he'd seen her. They'd disappeared completely when she'd first put Michael in his arms. Because he didn't know how to explain, he cut through to the bottom line.

"Where's Michael?"

Relief made her giddy. "He's with your mother."

"Then let's pick him up and take him home."

Chapter 11

She couldn't sleep. Both memory and imagination worked against Laura as her mind insisted on racing over what had happened, and what might happen the next day. It was almost a year since she had fled Boston. Now, thousands of miles away, she had chosen to take her stand. But she was no longer alone.

Gabe hadn't waited to make an appointment with his lawyer during regular business hours. He had made a phone call and requested—demanded—a meeting that evening.

Her life, her child, her marriage and her future had been discussed over coffee and crumb cake in the parlor while a low, wispy fog had rolled in from the bay. Her initial embarrassment about speaking with a stranger about her life, her first marriage and her mistakes had sharpened painfully, then vanished. It had seemed as though they were talking about someone else's experiences. The more openly it was discussed, with details meticulously examined and noted, the less shame she'd felt.

Matthew Quartermain had been the Bradleys' attorney for forty years. He was crusty and shrewd and, despite his stuffy exterior, not easily shocked. He'd nodded and made notes and asked questions until Laura's mouth had dried up from answering.

Because he hadn't sympathized or condemned, it had become easier to talk plainly. The truth, spoken in simple, unemotional terms, had been easier to face than it had to keep hidden. In the end she hadn't spared herself or Tony. And in the end she'd felt a powerful sense of having been cleansed.

At last she'd said it all, put all the misery and pain into words. She'd purged her heart and her mind in a way that her lingering sense of shame had never permitted before. Now that it was done, she understood what it was to wipe the slate clean and begin again.

Quartermain hadn't been happy with her final decision, but she'd been firm. Before papers of any kind were served or answered, she would see Lorraine again, face-to-face.

Beside Laura, Gabe lay sleepless. Like her, he was thinking back over the scene in the parlor. With every word that played back in his head his fury inched higher. She had spoken of things there that she had never told him, going into detail she had glossed over before. He'd thought he understood what she'd been through, and he'd thought his feelings about it had already peaked. He'd been wrong.

She hadn't told him about the black eye that had prevented her from leaving the house for nearly a week, or about Lorraine explaining away Laura's split lip by speaking of her daughter-in-law's clumsiness. She hadn't told him about the drunken attacks in the middle of the night, the jealous rages if she'd spoken with another man at a social function, the threats of revenge and violence when she'd finally found the courage to leave.

They'd come out tonight, in excruciating detail.

He hadn't touched her when they'd prepared for bed. He wondered how she could bear to be touched at all.

What she had been through was all too clear now. How could he expect her to put it aside, when he was no longer certain he could? No matter how gentle he was, how much care he took with her, the shadow of another man and another time was between them.

She'd said she loved him. As much as he wanted to believe it, he couldn't understand how anyone who had lived through that kind of hell could ever trust a man again, much less love him.

Gratitude, devotion, with Michael as the common ground. That he could understand. And that, Gabe thought as he lay in the dark, was more than many people were ever given.

He'd wanted more for them, had been on the verge of believing they could have more. That had been before all those words had been spoken downstairs while the quiet spring breeze had ruffled the curtains.

Then she turned toward him, her body brushing his. He stiffened.

"I'm sorry. Did I wake you?"

"No." He started to shift so that they were no longer touching, but she moved again until her head rested on his shoulder.

The gesture, the easy, uncomplicated movement toward him, tore him in two. The one who needed, and the one who was afraid to ask.

"I can't sleep, either. I feel as though I've run an obstacle course, and my body's exhausted from it. But my mind keeps circling."

"You should stop thinking about tomorrow."

"I know." Laura brushed her hair aside, then settled more comfortably. She felt the slight drawing away, the pulling back. With her eyes shut tight, she wondered if he thought less of her now that he knew everything.

"There's no need for you to worry. It's going to be all right."

Was it? Taking a chance, she reached through the dark for his hand. "The trouble is, different scenes keep popping into my head. What I'll say, what she'll say. If I don't..." Her words trailed off when the baby started crying. "Sounds like someone else is restless."

"I'll get him."

Though she'd already tossed the covers aside, Laura nodded. "All right. I'll nurse him in here if he's hungry."

She sat up and hugged her knees to her chest as Gabe tossed on a robe and strode to the nursery. A moment later the crying stopped, then started again. Under it, she could hear Gabe's voice, murmuring and soothing.

It was so easy for him, so natural. Sensitivity, tenderness, were as much a part of him as temper and arrogance. Wasn't that why she'd finally been able to admit that she loved him? There would be no cycle of despair, submission and terror with Gabe, as there had been with Tony. She could love him without giving up the pieces of herself that she'd so recently discovered.

No, he didn't think less of her. She couldn't be sure of all of his feelings, but she could be sure of that. It was just that he was as worried as she and felt obligated to pretend otherwise.

The light from the nursery slanted into the hallway. In it she could see Gabe's shadow as he moved. The crying became muffled, then rose in a wail. Recognizing the tone of the crying, Laura leaned back and shut her eyes. It was going to be a long night.

"Teething," she murmured when Gabe brought a sobbing Michael into the bedroom. Switching on the bedside lamp she smiled at him. All of them needed support tonight. "I'll nurse him and see if that helps any."

"There you go, old man. Best seat in the house." Gabe settled him in Laura's arms. The crying faded to a whimper, then disappeared completely as he suckled. "I'm going down for a brandy. Do you want anything?"

"No. Yes, some juice. Whatever's in there."

Alone, she held Michael with one arm and arranged her pillows behind her back with the other. It seemed so normal, so usual, just like any other night. Though there were nights when Michael was restless when her body craved sleep, there were others when she prized these hours in the middle of the night. These were the times she and Gabe would remember years down the road, when Michael took his first steps, when he started school, when he rode a two-wheeler for the first time. They'd look back and remember how they'd walked the floor, half dozing themselves. Nothing could change that.

They needed this, needed the normalcy of it. And, if only for a few hours, they would have it.

When Gabe came back in, he set her glass on the table beside her. Smiling, she lifted a hand to his arm. "Can I smell your brandy?"

Amused, he tilted the snifter for her and let her draw in the scent. "Enough?"

"Thanks. I always loved the taste of brandy late at night." Lifting her juice glass, she clinked it against his snifter. "Cheers." He didn't join her in bed, as she'd hoped he would, but turned to stand by the window. "Gabe?"

"Yes?"

"I'd like to make a deal with you. You tell me what's on your mind, ask any question you need to ask, and I'll tell you the absolute truth. Then, in return, I'll ask you and you'll do the same."

"Haven't you answered enough questions for one night?"

So that was it. Laura set her glass aside before she gently shifted Michael to her other breast. "You're upset because of the things I told Mr. Quartermain."

"Did you expect I would take them with a shrug?" When he whirled, the brandy sloshed dangerously close to the lip of the snifter. Laura said nothing as he tossed back half the contents and began to pace.

"I'm sorry it had to be brought up. I'd have preferred another way myself."

"It's not a matter of its being brought up." The words lashed out. He drank more brandy, but it did nothing to soothe him. "My God, it's killing me to think of it, to imagine it. I'm afraid to touch you, because it might bring it back."

"Gabe, you've been telling me all along that it's over, that things are different now. I know they are. You were right when you said I compared you with Tony, but maybe you don't understand that by doing that I helped myself realize that things could change."

He looked at her then, only for a moment, but long enough for her to see that her words weren't enough, not yet. "Things are different now, but I wonder why you don't hate any man who puts his hands on you."

"There was a time when I wouldn't have let any man within ten feet of me, but I was able to start putting things in perspective, through therapy, listening to other women who'd pulled themselves out of the spin." She watched him as he stood in the shadow, his hands thrust in the pockets of his robe and clenched into fists. "When you touch me, when you hold me, it doesn't bring any of that back. It makes me feel the way I've always wanted to feel about myself, about my husband."

"If he were alive," Gabe said evenly, "I'd want to kill him. I find myself resenting the fact that he's already dead."

"Don't do that to yourself." She reached out a hand to him, but he shook his head and walked back to the window. "He was ill. I didn't know that then, not really. And I prolonged it all by not walking away."

"You were afraid. You had nowhere to go."

"That's not enough. I could have gone to Geoffrey. I knew he would have helped me, but I didn't go, because I was pinned there by my own shame and insecurities. When I finally did leave, it was because of the baby. That's when I began to get well myself. Finding you was the best medicine of all, because you made me feel like a woman again."

He remained silent while she searched for the right words. "Gabe, there's nothing either of us can do to change things that have already happened. Don't let it change what we have now."

Calmer now, he swirled his brandy and continued to look out of the window. "When you talked of lawyers in the gallery today, I thought you wanted a divorce. It scared me to death."

"But I wouldn't have— Did it?"

"There you were, standing under the portrait, and I couldn't imagine what I would do if you walked away. I may have changed your life, angel, but no more than you've changed mine."

Pygmalion, she thought. If he loved the image, he might eventually love the woman. "I won't walk away. I love you, Gabe. You and Michael are my whole life."

He came to her then, to sit on the edge of the bed and take her hand. "I won't let anyone hurt either one of you."

Her fingers tightened on his. "I need to know that whatever we have to do we'll do it together."

"We've been in this together right from the start."

Leaning forward, he kissed her, while the baby dozed between them. "I need you, Laura, maybe too much."

"It can't be too much."

"Let me go put him down," Gabe murmured. "Then maybe we can continue that."

He took the baby, but the moment he eased off the bed Michael began to cry.

They took turns walking, rocking, rubbing tender gums. Each time Michael was laid back in his crib he woke with a wail. Dizzy with fatigue, Laura leaned over the rail, patting and rubbing his back. Each time she moved her hand away he cried again.

"I guess we're spoiling him," she murmured.

Gabe sat heavy-eyed in the rocking chair and watched her. "We're entitled. Besides, he sleeps like a rock most of the time."

"I know. This teething's got him down. Why don't you go to bed? There's no sense in both of us being up."

"It's my shift." He rose and discovered that at 5:00 a.m. the body could feel decades older than it was. "You go on to bed."

"No—" Her own yawn cut her off. "We're in this together, remember?"

"Or until one of us passes out."

She would have laughed if she had had the energy. "Maybe I'll just sit down."

"You know, I've been known to watch the sun come up after a night of drinking, card playing or...other forms of entertainment." He began to pat Michael's back as Laura collapsed in the rocker. "And I can't remember ever feeling as though someone had run over me with a truck."

"This is one of the joys of parenting," she told him as she curled her legs under her and shut her eyes. "We're actually having the time of our lives."

"I'm glad you let me know. I think he's giving in."

"That's because you have such a wonderful touch," she murmured as she drifted off. "Such a wonderful touch."

Inch by cautious inch, Gabe drew his hand away. A man backing away from a tiger couldn't have taken more care. When he was a full two feet from the crib, he nearly let out a breath of relief. Afraid to push his luck, he held it and turned to Laura.

She was sound asleep, in an impossibly uncomfortable position. Hoping his energy held out for five minutes longer, Gabe walked over to pick her up. She shifted and cuddled against him instinctively. As he carried her from the room, she roused enough to murmur. "Michael?"

"Down for the count." He walked into their room, but rather than taking her to bed he moved to the window. "Look, the sun's coming up."

Laura stirred and opened her eyes. Through the window she could see the curve of the eastern sky. If she looked hard enough she could see the water of the bay, like a mist in the distance. The sun seemed to vibrate as it rose. And the echoes brought colors: pinks, mauves, golds. Softly at first, with the darker night sky still dominating above, the colors spread, then deepened. Pinks became reds, vibrant and glowing.

"Sometimes your paintings are like that," she thought

aloud. "Changing, shifting angles, with the colors intensifying from the core to the edges." She nestled her head against his shoulder as they watched the new day dawn. "I don't think I've ever seen a more beautiful sunrise."

His skin was warm beneath her cheek, his arms strong, firm with muscle, as they held her to him. She could feel the light, steady beating of his heart. She turned her face toward his as the first birds woke and began to sing. When love was so easily reached, only a fool questioned it.

"I want you, Gabe." She laid her hand on his cheek, her lips on his lips. "I've never wanted anyone the way I want you."

There was a moment's hesitation. She felt it, understood it, then coaxed him past it. This wasn't the time to think of yesterdays or tomorrows. Her lips softened and parted against his and her hand slipped back to brush through his hair.

"You were right," she murmured.

"About what?"

"I don't think of anyone but you when we make love."

He hadn't meant to ask her for anything. He found there was nothing he couldn't ask.

She was so beautifully open. It made it possible, even easy, to put that part of her life that left him angry and bitter aside. That had nothing to do with where they could take each other. With his mouth still on hers, he moved to the bed. She wrapped her arms around him as he lay beside her. For a moment that was enough.

Morning embraces, sunrise kisses, after a long, sleepless night. Her face was pale with fatigue, but still she trembled for him. The sigh that passed from her lips to his was soft and drowsy. Her body arched, lazy, limber, at the stroke of his hands.

The dawn air was balmy as it fluttered through the window and over their skin. She parted his robe, pushed it back from his shoulders, so that she could warm his skin herself. Just as slowly, he drew off her nightgown. Naked, they lay on the rumpled sheets and made long, luxurious love.

Neither of them set the pace. It wasn't necessary. Here they were in tune, without words or requests. Demands were for other moments, night moments, when passion was hot and urgent. As the light turned gray with morning, desire was deliciously cool.

Perhaps the love she felt for him was best displayed this way, with ease and affection that lasted so much longer than the flare of a flame. She moved with him and he with her, and they brought pleasure to each other that came in sighs and murmurs instead of gasps and shudders.

She felt the roughness of his cheek when she stroked her hand there. This was real. Marriage was more than the band she wore on her finger or the coming together full of need and excitement in the dark. Marriage was holding on at daybreak.

He would have scaled mountains for her. Until now, somehow, the full extent of his feelings for her had escaped him. He'd recognized the need first, the love later, but now he understood the devotion. She was his in a way no other woman could ever be. For the first time in his life, he wanted to be a hero.

When they came together, full light was pouring over the bed. Later, still entwined, they slept.

"I know I'm doing the right thing." Still, Laura hesitated when they stepped off the elevator in Lorraine's hotel. "And, no matter what happens, I'm not going to back down." She caught Gabe's hand in hers and held it tight. Lack of sleep had left her feeling light-headed and primed for action. "I'm awfully glad you're here."

"I told you before, I don't like the idea of you having to see her again, to deal with her on any level. I can easily handle this on my own."

"I know you could. But I told you, I need to. Gabe…"

"What?"

"Please don't lose your temper." She laughed a little at the way his brows rose. The tension rising inside her eased. "There's no need to look like that. I'm only trying to say that shouting at Lorraine won't accomplish anything."

"I never shout. I do occasionally raise my voice to get a point across."

"Since we've gotten that straightened out, I guess the only thing left to do is knock." She felt the familiar flutter of panic and fought it back as she knocked on the door. Lorraine answered, looking regal and poised in a navy suit.

"Laura." After the briefest of nods, she turned to Gabe. "Mr. Bradley. It's nice to meet you. Laura didn't mention that you were coming with her this afternoon."

"Everything that concerns Laura and Michael con-

cerns me, Mrs. Eagleton." He entered, as Laura could
never have done, without an invitation.

"I'm sure that's very conscientious of you." Lorraine
closed the door with a quick click. "However, some of
the things Laura and I may discuss are private family
matters. I'm sure you understand."

"I understand perfectly." He met her level gaze with
one of his own. "My wife and son are my family."

The war of wills was silent and unpleasant. Lorraine
ended it with another nod. "If you insist. Please, sit. I'll
order coffee. The service here is tolerable."

"Don't bother on our account." Laura spoke with only
the slightest trace of nerves as she chose a seat. "I don't
think this should take very long."

"As you like." Lorraine sat across from them. "My
husband would have been here, but business prevented
him from making the trip. I do, however, speak for both
of us." That said, she laid her hands on the arms of
her chair. "I'll simply repeat what has already been discussed. I intend to take Tony's son back to Boston and
raise him properly."

"And I'll repeat, you can't have him." She would try
reason one last time, Laura thought, leaning forward.
"He's a baby, not an heirloom, Mrs. Eagleton. He has
a good home and two parents who love him. He's a
healthy, beautiful child. You should be grateful for that.
If you want to discuss reasonable visitation rights—"

"We'll discuss visitation rights," Lorraine said, inter-
rupting her. "Yours. And if I have anything to say about
it, they will be short and spare. Mr. Bradley," she continued, turning away from Laura. "Surely you don't want

to raise another man's child as your own. He hasn't your blood, and he only has your name because, for whatever reason, you married his mother."

Gabe drew out a cigarette and lit it slowly. Laura had asked him not to lose his temper. Though he wouldn't be able to accommodate her, it wouldn't do to let it snap so quickly. "You're very wrong" was all he said.

She sighed, almost indulgently. "I understand you have feelings for Laura. My son had them, too."

The first chain on his temper broke clean in half. The rage could be seen in his eyes and heard in each precise, bitten-off word. "Don't you ever compare my feelings for Laura with your son's."

Lorraine paled a little, but went on evenly. "I have no idea what she may have been telling you—"

"I told him the truth." Before Gabe could speak, or move, Laura put a hand on his arm. "I told him what you know is the truth, that Tony was ill, emotionally unstable."

Now it was Lorraine who moved, rising deliberately from her chair. Her face was flushed and pinched, but her voice was held at the same even pitch. "I will not sit here and listen to you defame my son."

"You will listen." Laura's fingers dug hard into Gabe's arm, but she didn't give way. "You'll listen now the way you never listened when I was desperate for help. The way you never listened when Tony was screaming for it in the only way he knew. He was an alcoholic, an emotional wreck who abused someone weaker than he. You knew he hurt me, you saw the marks and ignored them or made excuses. You knew there were other women. By your silence, you gave him approval."

"What was between you and Tony was none of my concern."

"That's for you to live with. But I warn you, Lorraine, if you open the lid, you won't be able to handle what comes out."

Lorraine sat again, if for no other reason than the tone of Laura's voice and the fact that for the first time Laura had called her by her first name. That one change made them equals. This wasn't the same frightened, easily pressured woman she had known only a year before.

"Threats from someone like you don't worry me. The courts will decide if some loose-moraled young tramp will have custody of an Eagleton or if he'll be placed with those who can give him the proper upbringing."

"If you refer to my wife in that way again you'll have more than threats to deal with." Gabe blew out a long, narrow stream of smoke. "Mrs. Eagleton."

"It doesn't matter." Laura squeezed his hand. She knew he was on the verge of losing control. "You can't make me cringe anymore, Lorraine, and you won't make me beg. You know very well that I was faithful to Tony."

"I know that Tony didn't believe that."

"Then how do you know the child is his?"

Absolute silence fell the moment Gabe spoke. Laura started to speak but was held off by the look in Gabe's eyes. Color flooded into Lorraine's face again when she found her voice.

"She wouldn't have dared—"

"Wouldn't she? That's odd. You intend to prove that

Laura was unfaithful to your son, and now you claim she wasn't. Either way, you have a problem. If she had had an affair with anyone. Me, for example." He smiled again as he crushed out his cigarette. "Or haven't you wondered why we were married so quickly, why, as you've already asked, I accept the child as my own?" He let that thought take hold before he continued. "If she had been unfaithful, the child could be anyone's. If she wasn't unfaithful, you haven't got a case."

Lorraine clenched and unclenched her fingers on the arm of the chair. "My husband and I have every intention of determining the child's paternity. I would hardly take someone's bastard into my home."

"Be careful," Laura said, so quietly that the words seemed to vibrate in the air. "Be very careful, Lorraine. I know you have no concern for Michael as a person."

Fighting for control she so rarely lost, Lorraine settled again. "I have nothing but the gravest concern for Tony's son."

"You've never asked about him, what he looks like, if he's well. You've never demanded to see him, even a picture or a doctor's report. You've never once called him by name. If you had, if I'd seen in you one ounce of love or affection for the baby, I'd feel differently about what I'm about to say." The courage came without the need to muster it. "You're free to draw up the papers and initiate a custody suit. Gabe and I have already notified our attorney. We'll fight you, and we'll win. And in the meantime, I'll go to the press with the story of what my life was like with the Eagletons of Boston."

Lorraine's nails dug into the material on the arm of the chair. "You wouldn't have the nerve."

"I have that and more when it comes to protecting my son."

She could see it, the calm, unshakable determination in Laura's eyes. "Even if you did, no one would believe you."

"But they would," Laura told her. "People have a way of recognizing the truth."

Lorraine's face was set when she turned to Gabe. "Do you have any conception of what this kind of gossip could do to your family name? Do you want to risk your reputation, your parents' reputation, over this woman and a child who isn't even of your blood?"

"My reputation can handle it, and, to be frank, my parents are looking forward to a fight." There was a challenge in his voice now that didn't have to be feigned. "Michael may not be of my blood, but he's mine."

"Lorraine." Laura waited until they were face-to-face again. "You lost your son, and I'm sorry for you, but you won't replace him with mine. Whatever the cost to protect Michael's welfare, I'll pay. And so will you."

Putting a hand under her arm, Gabe rose, keeping Laura beside him. "Your attorney can contact us once you've made your decision. Remember, Mrs. Eagleton, you're not pitting yourself against a lone pregnant woman. You're up against the Bradleys now."

The moment they were in the hall, Gabe pulled Laura against him. He could feel the tremors coursing through her, so he held her a moment longer. "You were wonderful." He kissed her hair before he drew her away from him. "In fact, angel, you were amazing. Lorraine still doesn't know what hit her."

The flush of pride was as warm and satisfying as anything she'd ever felt. "It wasn't as bad as I thought," she said with a sigh, but she kept her hand in his as they walked to the elevator. "I used to be so terrified of her, afraid to speak two words. Now I can see her for what she really is, a lonely woman trapped by her own strict sense of family honor."

Gabe gave a quick, humorless laugh as the elevators doors opened. "Honor has nothing to do with it."

"No, but that's how she sees it."

"Tell you what." He pressed the button for the lobby. "We're going to forget about Lorraine Eagleton for the rest of the day. In fact, we're going to forget about her completely before long, but for now there's a little restaurant a few blocks away. Not too quiet, and very expensive."

"It's too early for dinner."

"Who said anything about dinner?" He slipped an arm around her waist as they walked out into the lobby. "We're going to sit at a table over the water, and I'm going to watch everyone stare at my gorgeous wife while we drink a bottle of champagne."

She loved him for that. Then her heart skipped a beat when he brought her fingers to his lips. "Don't you think we should wait to celebrate until Lorraine gives us her decision?"

"We'll celebrate then, too. Right now I want to celebrate being witness to an angel breathing fire."

She laughed and walked outside with him. "I could do it again. In fact…"

"What?"

She swept her gaze up to his. "I'd like to."

"Sounds as though I'm going to have to watch my step."

"Probably." She was giddy with success, but she was still practical. "I really shouldn't have champagne. Michael—"

Gabe kissed her, and signaled for his car.

Chapter 12

"You look exhausted." Amanda gave a quick shake of her head as she stepped into the house.

"Michael's teething." The excuse was valid enough, but more than a fretful baby was keeping Laura from sleeping at night. "He's been down all of ten minutes. With luck, he might make an entire hour straight."

"Then why aren't you napping?"

Since Amanda was already stepping into the parlor, Laura followed her in. "Because you called and said you were coming over."

"Oh." With a faint smile, Amanda took a seat, then tossed her purse on the table. "So I did. Well, I won't keep you long. Gabe's not home?"

"No. He said he had something to see to." Laura sat in the chair facing her and let her head fall back. Sometimes small luxuries felt like heaven. "Can I get you some coffee, or something cold?"

"You don't look as though you can get yourself out of that chair. And, no, I don't need a thing. How is Gabe?"

"He hasn't been getting a great deal of rest, either."

"I'm not surprised. No word from Lorraine Eagleton or her attorney?"

"Nothing."

"I don't suppose that you're able to take the attitude that no news is good news?"

Laura managed a smile. "Afraid not. The longer this goes on, the easier it gets to imagine the worst."

"And if she takes this to court?"

"Then we'll fight." Despite her fatigue, her newly discovered power came through. "I meant everything I said to her."

"That's really all I wanted to hear." Sitting back, Amanda adjusted the pin on her lapel. A little too thin, a little too pale, she thought as she studied Laura. But, all in all, she thought her daughter-in-law was holding up well. "When this is over, you and Gabe should be able to tie up a few loose ends."

Laura caught herself before she dozed off. "Loose ends?"

"Yes, little things. Such as what you intend to do with the rest of your lives."

"I don't know what you mean."

"Gabe has his art, and you both have Michael, and however many other children you choose to bring into the world."

That was something that made Laura sit up straighter. More children. They'd never discussed the possibility of more. As she began to, she wondered if Gabe even wanted any. Did she? She passed a hand over her now flat stomach and imagined it filled with another child— Gabe's child this time, from the very first moment. Yes, she wanted that. Glancing over, she saw Amanda studying her quietly and with complete understanding.

"It's difficult to make decisions with so much hanging over us."

"Exactly. But it will pass. When it does, what are you going to look for? Since I spent more than two decades under the same roof as Gabe, I know that he can, when the muse is on him, lock himself in his studio for hours and days on end."

"I don't mind. How could I, when I see what he can accomplish?"

"A woman needs a solid sense of accomplishment, as well. Children can be the best of that, but…" She reached for her purse, opened it and took out a business card. "There's an abuse clinic downtown. It's rather small, and unfortunately not well funded. Yet." She intended to correct that. "They need volunteers, women who understand, who know there can be normal life after hell."

"I'm not a therapist."

"You don't need a degree to give support."

"No." She looked at the card on the table as the idea took root. "I don't know. I…"

"Just think about it."

"Amanda, did you go to the clinic?"

"Yes, Cliff and I went there yesterday. We were very impressed."

"Why did you go?"

Amanda lifted a brow in a gesture Laura knew Gabe

had inherited. "Because there's someone we both care about who we wanted to understand better. Don't get up," she said as she rose. "I'll let myself out. Give Gabe my love and tell him his father wants to know if they're ever going to play poker again. The man thrives on losing money."

"Amanda." Laura pushed off her shoes before she curled her legs up in the chair. "I never had a mother, and the one I always imagined for myself was nothing like you." She smiled as her eyes began to close. "I'm not at all disappointed."

"You're coming along," Amanda said, and left Laura sleeping in the chair.

She was still there when Gabe came in. He tilted the bulky package against the wall. When she didn't stir at the rattle of the paper, he walked over to the couch. He didn't even have the energy to wish for his sketch pad as he stretched out his legs and almost instantly fell asleep.

The baby woke both of them. Gabe merely groaned and pulled a throw pillow over his face. Disoriented, Laura pulled herself up, blinked groggily at Gabe, then put one foot in front of the other to get upstairs.

A short time later, he went up after her.

"My timing's good," he decided when he saw that Laura was fastening a fresh diaper.

"I'm beginning to wonder about your timing." But she was smiling as she lifted Michael over her head to make him laugh. "How long have you been home?"

"Long enough to see that my wife has nothing better to do than lounge around all day." He plucked Michael from her while she pretended to glare at him. "Do you think if we kept him awake and exhausted him with attention he'd sleep tonight?"

"I'm willing to try anything."

At that, Gabe sat on the floor and began to play nonsense games. Bouncing the Baby, Flying the Baby, Tickling the Baby.

"You're so good with him." Finding her second wind, Laura sat on the floor with them. "It's hard to believe you're new at this."

"I never thought about parenthood. It certainly has its compensations." He set Michael on his knee and jiggled him.

"Like walking the ten-minute mile at 2:00 a.m."

"That, too."

"Gabe, your mother came by."

"Should I be surprised?"

She smiled a little as she leaned over to let Michael tug at her hair. "She left a card—from an abuse clinic."

"I see." He reached over himself to untangle her hair from Michael's grip. "Do you want to go back into therapy?"

"No...at least I don't think so." She looked over at him. Michael was chewing madly at his chin. All the therapy she needed was sitting across from her. "She suggested I might like to volunteer there."

He frowned as he let Michael gnaw on his knuckle. "And be reminded day after day?"

"Yes—of what I was able to change."

"I thought you'd want to go back to modeling eventually."

"No, I haven't any desire to go back to modeling. I think I could do this, and I know I'd like to try."

"If you're asking for my approval, you don't need to."

"I'd still like to have it."

"Then you do, unless I see this wearing you down."

She had to smile. He still saw her as more fragile than she was or could ever have afforded to be. "You know, I've been thinking...with everything that's happened, and everything we've had to think and worry about, we haven't had much time to really get to know a lot about each other."

"I know you take entirely too long in the bathtub and like to sleep with the window open."

She took the stuffed rabbit Michael liked to chew on and passed it from hand to hand. "There are other things."

"Such as?"

"The other night, I said that you could ask me anything and I'd tell you the truth, and then I'd ask you something. Do you remember?"

"I remember."

"I never had my turn."

He shifted so that he could rest his back against the daybed. They were avoiding speaking of the phone call they were both waiting for. And they both knew it. Perhaps that was best, Gabe mused as the baby continued to rub his sore gums against his knuckles.

"Do you want to hear about my misspent youth?"

Though she was plucking nervously at the rabbit's ears, she smiled. "Is there time?"

"You flatter me."

"Actually, I'd like to ask you about something else. A few days ago, when it rained, I went into your studio to close the windows. I looked through some of your paintings. Perhaps I shouldn't have."

"It doesn't matter."

"There was one in particular. The one of Michael. Your brother. I'd like you to tell me about him."

He was silent for so long that she had to fight back the urge to tell him that it didn't matter. But it mattered too much. She was certain it was his brother's death that had sent him to Colorado, that was preventing him, even after all these months, from having a showing of his work.

"Gabe." She laid a tentative hand on his arm. "You asked me to marry you so that you could take on my problems. You wanted me to trust you, and I have. Until you can do the same, we're still strangers."

"We haven't been strangers since the first time we laid eyes on each other, Laura. I would have asked you to marry me with or without your problems."

Now she fell silent, as surprise ran through her, chased frantically by hope. "Do you mean that?"

He shifted the baby onto his shoulder. "I don't always say everything I mean, but I do mean what I say." When Michael began to whimper, Gabe stood to walk him. "You needed someone, I wanted to be that someone. And I, though I didn't know it until you were already part of my life, needed someone, too."

She wanted to ask him how he needed her, and why, and if love—the kind she'd always hoped for—was somehow mixed up with that need. But they needed to go back further than that if they were ever to move forward.

"Please tell me about him."

He wasn't certain he could, that he wouldn't trip over the pain, and then the words. It had been so long since he'd spoken of Michael. "He was three years younger than I," he began. "We got along fairly well growing up because Michael tended to be even-tempered unless backed into a corner. We didn't have many of the same interests. Baseball was about it. It used to infuriate me that I couldn't outhit him. As we grew older, I turned to art, and Michael to law. The law fascinated him."

"I remember," she murmured, as some vague recollection stirred. "There was something about him in an article I read about you. He was working in Washington."

"As a public defender. He set a lot of tongues clucking over that decision. He wasn't interested in corporate law or big fees. Of course, a lot of people said he didn't need the money, anyway. What they didn't understand was that he would have done the same thing with or without his stock portfolio behind him. He wasn't a saint." Gabe set Michael in the crib and wound up the mobile. "But he was the best of us. The best and the brightest, my father used to say."

She had risen, but she wasn't certain he wanted her to go to him. "I could see that in the portrait. You must have loved him very much."

"It's not something you think about, one brother loving another. Either it's there or it isn't. It isn't something you say, because you don't think it needs to be said. Then all you have is time to regret."

"He had to know you loved him. He only had to see the portrait."

With his hands in his pockets, Gabe walked to the window. It was easier than he could have imagined to talk to her about it. "I'd badgered him to sit for me off and on for years. It became a family joke. I won five sittings from him in a poker game. A heart flush to his three of a kind." The pain clawed at him, no longer fresh, but still sharp. "That was the last time we played."

"What happened to him?"

"An accident. I've never believed in accidents. Luck, fate, destiny, but they called it an accident. He was researching a case in Virginia and took a small commuter plane to New York. Minutes after takeoff it went down. He was coming to New York because I was having a showing."

Her heart broke for him. This time there was no hesitation as she went to him and put her arms around him. "You've blamed yourself all this time. You can't."

"He was coming to New York for me, to be there for me. I watched my mother fall apart for the first and only time in her life. I saw my father walk through his own home as if he'd never seen it before, and I didn't know what to say or do."

She stroked his back, aching for him. There was no use telling him that being there was sometimes all that could be done. "I've never lost anyone I've loved, but having you and Michael now, I can imagine how devastating it would be. Sometimes things happen and there's no one to blame. Whether that's an accident or fate, I don't know."

He rested his cheek on her hair and looked out at the flowers she'd planted. "I went to Colorado to get away for a while, to be alone and see if I could paint again. I hadn't been able to here. When I found you, I'd begun to pull myself back. I could work again, I could think about coming home and picking up my life. But there was still something missing." He drew back and cupped her face in his hand. "You filled in those last pieces for me."

She curled her fingers around his wrist. "I'm glad."

When he held her, she closed her eyes. They would make it, Laura told herself. Whatever happened, they would make it. Sometimes need was enough.

"Gabe." She slid her hands down until they gripped his. "The paintings in your studio. They don't belong there." She squeezed his fingers with hers before he could speak or turn away. "It's wrong to keep them there, facing the wall and pretending they don't exist. If your brother was proud enough of you to want to be there for one of your showings, it's time you had one. Dedicate it to him. Maybe you didn't say the words, but there can't be any better way to show that you loved him."

He had started to brush it aside, to make excuses, but her last words hit home. "He would have liked you."

Her lips curved. "Will you do it?"

"Yes." He kissed her while she was still smiling. "Yes, it's time. I've known that, but I haven't been able to take the last step. I'll have Marion start the arrangements." She stiffened, and though the change was only slight he drew her away to study her face. "Problem?"

"No, of course not."

"You do a lot of things well, angel. Lying isn't one of them."

"Gabe, nothing could please me more than you going ahead with this. That's the truth."

"But?"

"Nothing. All of this has really put me behind schedule. I need to give Michael his bath."

"He'll hold a minute." He kept her with him by doing no more than running his hands down her arms. "I know there's some tension between you and Marion. I've already told you there's nothing between us but business."

"I understand that. I've told you what I would have done if I thought otherwise."

"Yes, you did." Amusement moved over his face. She would have packed her bags and headed for the door, but she would have gotten no more than five feet. "So what's the problem?"

"There is no problem."

"I'd prefer not going to Marion with this."

"So would I." Her chin came up. "Don't push this, Gabe. And don't push me."

"Well, well." He brought his hands to her shoulders as he nodded. "It's a rare thing for you to get that look on your face. Whenever you do, I have this deep-seated urge to drag you down on the floor and let loose." When color flooded her face, he laughed and drew her closer.

"Don't laugh at me." She would have twisted away, but his hands were firm.

"Sorry. I wasn't, really, more at the situation." He thought that perhaps delicacy was called for, but then he rejected the idea. "Want to fight?"

"Not at the moment."

"If you can't lie better than that, we'll have to keep you out of poker games," he murmured, and watched her eyes cool. "I overheard your discussion with Marion at the gallery."

"Then you obviously don't need me to spell things out for you. She believes I'm going to hold you back, prevent you from reaching your full potential, and she took steps to stop it. I realize that the Eagletons would have found us, probably in a matter of days, but I won't forgive her for calling them. The fact that you're associated with her gallery means I have to be polite to her in public, but that's the extent of it."

His hands had tightened on her shoulders, and all amusement had been wiped from his face. "You're telling me that Marion called the Eagletons?"

"You just said you'd heard us, so—"

"I hadn't heard that much." Deliberately he relaxed his hands, then took a step back. "Why didn't you explain this to me before so that we could have told her to go to hell?"

"I didn't think that you—" She stopped and stared at him. "Would you have?"

"Damn it, Laura, what more do I have to do to convince you that I'm committed totally to you and Michael?"

"But she said—"

"What difference does it make what she said? It's what I say, isn't it?"

"Yes." She folded her hands but didn't lower her gaze. It was what he said. And not once had he ever said he loved her. "I didn't want to interfere when it came to your work."

"And I won't tolerate Marion interfering in my life. I'll handle it."

"How?"

Exasperated, he tugged his hand through his hair. "One minute you talk of my work as though I had an obligation to mankind to share it, and the next you act as though I'd have to go begging to find another gallery."

"I didn't mean… You'll take your paintings out of Marion's gallery?"

"Good God," he muttered, and took another turn around the room. "Obviously we need to talk—or maybe talking's not what's called for." He took a step toward her, then swore when the phone rang. "Stay here." With that he turned on his heel and strode out.

Laura let out a long breath. He'd said something about dragging her to the floor and letting loose. That was what had been in his eyes a moment before. And what would that have proved?

She moved to the crib to hand a fretful Michael his favorite rabbit. It would only have proved that he wanted and needed her. She had no doubts about that. Why shouldn't she be surprised that he would cut himself off from Marion for her? But not for her, really, Laura thought as she leaned over to nuzzle the baby. For himself. Marion had made the mistake of interfering.

Reasons didn't matter, she told herself. Results did. A great deal had been accomplished here this afternoon. He'd finally trusted her with his feelings about his brother. She'd been able to say the right things to convince him to show his work, and Marion was out of their lives.

"That should be enough for one day," she murmured to Michael. But there was still an ache in her heart.

She wouldn't think about the Eagletons.

"He needs us, Michael." That, too, should have been enough. Perhaps they were a replacement for someone he had loved and lost, but he had already given the baby unconditional love. He had given her a promise of his fidelity. That was more than she'd ever had, more than she had come to believe she would ever have. And yet it wasn't enough.

"Laura."

She turned, annoyed because she was feeling weepy and dejected. "What is it?"

"That was Quartermain on the phone." He saw the fear come first, then saw it vanish to be replaced by determination. "It's over," he told her before she could ask. "The Eagletons' attorney contacted him a few minutes ago."

"Over?" She could only whisper. The strength she'd built up, layer by layer, began to slip.

"They've pulled back. There'll be no custody suit. Not now, not ever. They don't want anything to do with the baby."

"Oh, God." She covered her face with her hands. The tears came, but she wasn't ashamed of them, not even when Gabe gathered her close. "Is he sure? If they change their minds—"

"He's sure. Listen to me." He drew her back, just a little. He wasn't entirely certain how she would feel about the rest. "They're going to file papers claiming that Tony wasn't Michael's biological father. They want him cut off legally from any future claim to the Eagleton estate."

"But she doesn't believe that."

"She wants to believe that."

She closed her eyes while relief and regret poured through her. "I would have tried to be fair, to let them see Michael. At least I want to believe I would have tried."

"He'll lose his heritage."

"The money?" When she opened her eyes, they were dark and damp. "I don't think that will matter to him. It doesn't to me. As far as family goes, he already has one. Gabe, I don't know how to thank you."

"Then don't. You were the one who stood up to her."

"I did." She brushed the tears away, and then there was laughter as she threw her arms around him. "Yes, I did. No one's ever going to take him away from us. I want to celebrate. To go dancing, have a party." She laughed again and squeezed him hard. "After I sleep for a week."

"It's a date." He found her lips with his, then held them there as she melted into him. Another beginning, he thought, and this time they'd take the first step properly. "I want to call my parents and let them know."

"Yes, right away." She pressed against him for a moment longer. "I'll give Michael his bath, and then we'll be down."

It was nearly an hour before she came downstairs, bringing a more contented Michael with her. The baby, fresh from his bath, was awake and ready to be entertained. Because her jeans had gotten wet, she'd changed into a pale lavender shirt and slacks. Her hair was loose around her shoulders, and both she and Michael smelled of soap and soft talc. Gabe met her at the foot of the stairs.

"Here, let me have him." He curled his arm around the baby and tickled his belly. "Looks like you're ready to go field a few grounders."

"So do you." Envious, Laura muffled a yawn. "You haven't had any more sleep than I have. How do you manage it?"

"Three decades of clean living—and a body accustomed to all-night poker games."

"Your father wants to play. Maybe Michael could sit in."

"Maybe." He tipped her chin up with his finger. "You really are ready to drop, aren't you?"

"I've never felt better in my life."

"And you can barely keep your eyes open."

"That's nothing five straight hours of sleep wouldn't fix."

"I've got something to show you. Afterward, why don't you go up and take a nap? Michael and I can entertain ourselves." His thumb traced along her jawline. Until Laura, he hadn't known that the scent of soap and powder could be arousing. "Once you've rested, we can have our private celebration."

"I'll go now."

He laughed and caught her arm before she could start back up. "Come see first."

"Okay, I'm too weak to argue."

"I'll keep that in mind for later." With the baby in

one arm and the other around Laura, he walked into the parlor.

She'd seen the painting before, from the first brush strokes to the last. Yet it seemed different now, here, hung over the mantel. In the gallery, she had seen it as a beautiful piece of work, something to be studied by art students and patrons, a thing to be commented on and discussed, dissected and critiqued. Here, in the parlor, in the late afternoon, it was a personal statement, a part of all three of them.

She hadn't realized just how much she'd resented seeing it in Marion's gallery. Nor had she known that seeing it here would make her feel, as nothing else had, that she had finally come home.

"It's beautiful," she murmured.

He understood. It wasn't vanity or self-importance. "I've never done anything in my life that compares to this. I doubt I will again. Sit down, will you?"

Something in his tone had her glancing over at him before she settled on the couch. "I didn't know you intended to bring it home. I know you've had offers."

"I never had any intention of selling it. I always meant it for here." Resting the baby on his hip, he walked over to the portrait. "As long as I've lived here, I haven't done anything, or found anything, that I wanted to hang in that spot. It goes back to fate again. If I hadn't been in Colorado, if it hadn't been snowing, if you hadn't been running. It took what had happened to you, and what had happened to me, to bring us together and make this."

"When you were painting it, I wondered why you seemed so driven. I understand now."

"Do you?" With a half smile, he turned back to her. "I wonder just what you understand, angel. It wasn't until a little while ago that I realized you have no idea what I feel for you."

"I know you need me, me and Michael. Because of what happened to all of us, we're able to make things better."

"And that's it?" He wondered if he was pushing too far, but he thought that if he didn't push now it might be too late. "You said you loved me. I know gratitude's a big part of that, but I want to know if there's anything more."

"I don't know what you want me to say."

"I want you to look." He held out a hand. When she didn't move, he walked over to her and drew her to her feet. "Look at the portrait and tell me what you see."

"Myself."

It seemed to be the day for showdowns, Gabe thought. He quickly carried the sleeping Michael upstairs to the nursery and put him in the crib. Going back down to Laura, he took her by the shoulders and, holding her in front of him, made her face the portrait. "Tell me what you see."

"I see myself as you saw me then." Why was her heart hammering? "I seem a little too vulnerable, a little too sad."

Impatience had him giving her a quick shake. "You don't see enough."

"I want to see strength," she blurted out. "I think I do. And I see a woman alone who's ready to protect what's hers."

"When you look at her eyes. Look at them, Laura, and tell me what you see."

"A woman falling in love." She shut her own. "You must have known."

"No." He didn't turn her toward him. Instead, he wrapped his arms around her so that they both continued to face the portrait. "No, I didn't know, because I kept telling myself I was painting what I wanted to see. And what I was feeling myself."

Her heart leaped into her throat and throbbed there. Whatever he could feel, he could paint. That had been her own conclusion. "What are you feeling?"

"Can't you see it?"

"I don't want to see it there." She turned to grip the front of his shirt. "I want to hear it."

He wasn't sure he had the words. Words came so much less easily than emotion. He could paint his moods, and he could shout them, but it was difficult to speak them quietly when they mattered so much.

He touched her face, her hair, then her hand. "Almost from the first you pulled at me in a way no one ever had before and no one ever will again. I thought I was crazy. You were pregnant, totally dependent on me, grateful for my help."

"I was grateful. I'll always be grateful."

"Damn it" was all he could manage as he turned away.

"I'm sorry you feel that way." She was calm now, absolutely, beautifully calm, as he glared at her. She'd remember him like this always, she thought, with his hair tousled from his hands, a gray shirt with the sleeves shoved up to the elbows and his face full of impatience.

"Because I intend to be grateful for the rest of my life. And that has nothing to do with my intending to love you for the rest of my life."

"I want to be sure of that."

"Be sure. You didn't paint what you wanted to see, you never do. You paint the truth." She took one step toward him, the most important step she'd ever taken. "I've given you the truth, Gabe. Now I have to ask for it. Are your feelings for me tied up in that portrait, in that image, are they an effect of your love for Michael, or are they for me?"

"Yes." He caught her hands in his. "I'm in love with the woman I painted, with the mother of my child, and with you. Separately and together. We could have met anywhere, under any circumstances, and I would still have fallen in love with you. Maybe it wouldn't have happened as quickly, maybe it wouldn't have been as complicated, but it would have happened." She started to move into his arms, but he held her back. "When I married you, it was for purely selfish reasons. I wasn't doing you any favors."

She smiled. "Then I won't be grateful."

"Thank you." He lifted her hands to his lips, the one that wore the old wedding band, then the one that wore the new. "I want to paint you again."

She was laughing as his lips came down to her. "Now?"

"Soon."

Then his hands were in her hair, and the kiss became urgent and seeking. It was met equally as her arms went around him. Love, fully opened, added its own desperation.

There was a murmur of pleasure, then a murmur of protest as he drew her to the floor. Her laugh turned to a moan when he unbuttoned her blouse.

"Michael—"

"Is asleep." He dragged her hair back, leaving her face unframed. Everything he'd wanted to see was there. "Until he wakes up, you're mine. I love you, Laura. Every time you look at the painting, you'll see it. You were mine from the first moment I touched you."

Yours, she thought as she drew him back to her. Gabriel's angel was more than a portrait. And she finally belonged.

* * * * *

Blithe Images

To Ron's Patience

Chapter 1

The girl twisted and turned under the lights, her shining black hair swirling around her as various expressions flitted across her striking face.

"That's it, Hillary, a little pout now. We're selling the lips here." Larry Newman followed her movements, the shutter of his camera clicking rapidly. "Fantastic," he exclaimed as he straightened from his crouched position. "That's enough for today."

Hillary Baxter stretched her arms to the ceiling and relaxed. "Good, I'm beat. It's home and a hot tub for me."

"Just think of the millions of dollars in lipstick your face is going to sell, sweetheart." Switching off lights, Larry's attention was already wavering.

"Mind-boggling."

"Mmm, so it is," he returned absently. "We've got that shampoo thing tomorrow, so make sure your hair is in its usual gorgeous state. I almost forgot." He turned and faced her directly. "I have a business appointment in the morning. I'll get someone to stand in for me."

Hillary smiled with fond indulgence. She had been modeling for three years now, and Larry was her favorite photographer. They worked well together, and as a photographer he was exceptional, having a superior eye for angles and detail, for capturing the right mood. He was hopelessly disorganized, however, and pathetically absentminded about anything other than his precious equipment.

"What appointment?" Hillary inquired with serene patience, knowing well how easily Larry confused such mundane matters as times and places when they did not directly concern his camera.

"Oh, that's right, I didn't tell you, did I?" Shaking her head, Hillary waited for him to continue. "I've got to see Bret Bardoff at ten o'clock."

"*The* Bret Bardoff?" Hillary demanded, more than a little astonished. "I didn't know the owner of *Mode* magazine made appointments with mere mortals—only royalty and goddesses."

"Well, this peasant's been granted an audience," Larry returned dryly. "As a matter of fact, Mr. Bardoff's secretary contacted me and set the whole thing up. She said he wanted to discuss plans for a layout or something."

"Good luck. From what I hear of Bret Bardoff, he's a man to be reckoned with—tough as nails and used to getting his own way."

"He wouldn't be where he is today if he were a pushover," Larry defended the absent Mr. Bardoff with a shrug. "His father may have made a fortune by starting *Mode,* but Bret Bardoff made his own twice over by expanding and developing other magazines. A very successful businessman, and a good photographer—one that's not afraid to get his hands dirty."

"You'd love anyone who could tell a Nikon from a Brownie," Hillary accused with a grin, and pulled at a lock of Larry's disordered hair. "But his type doesn't appeal to me." A delicate and counterfeit shudder moved her shoulders. "I'm sure he'd scare me to death."

"Nothing scares you, Hil," Larry said fondly as he watched the tall, willowy woman gather her things and move for the door. "I'll have someone here to take the shots at nine-thirty tomorrow."

Outside, Hillary hailed a cab. She had become quite adept at this after three years in New York. And she had nearly ceased to ponder about Hillary Baxter of a small Kansas farm being at home in the thriving metropolis of New York City.

She had been twenty-one when she had made the break and come to New York to pursue a modeling career. The transition from small-town farm girl to big-city model had been difficult and often frightening, but Hillary had refused to be daunted by the fast-moving, overwhelming city and resolutely made the rounds with her portfolio.

Jobs had been few and far between during the first year, but she had hung on, refusing to surrender and escape to the familiar surroundings of home. Slowly, she had constructed a reputation for portraying the right image for the right product, and she had become more and more in demand. When she had begun to work with Larry, everything had fallen into place, and her face was now splashed throughout magazines and, as often as not, on the cover. Her life was proceeding according to plan, and the fact that she now commanded a top model's salary had enabled her to move from the third-floor walk-up in which she had started her New York life to a comfortable high-rise near Central Park.

Modeling was not a passion with Hillary, but a job. She had not come to New York with starry-eyed dreams of fame and glamour, but with a resolution to succeed, to stand on her own. The choice of career had seemed inevitable, since she possessed a natural grace and poise and striking good looks. Her coal black hair and high cheekbones lent her a rather exotic fragility, and large, heavily fringed eyes in deep midnight blue contrasted appealingly with her golden complexion. Her mouth was full and shapely, and smiled beautifully at the slightest provocation. Along with her stunning looks, the fact that she was inherently photogenic added to her current success in her field. The uncanny ability to convey an array of images for the camera came naturally, with little conscious effort on her part. After being told the type of woman she was to portray, Hillary became just that—sophisticated, practical, sensuous—whatever was required.

Letting herself into her apartment, Hillary kicked off her shoes and sank her feet into soft ivory carpet. There was no date to prepare for that evening, and she was looking forward to a light supper and a few quiet hours at home.

Thirty minutes later, wrapped in a warm, flowing azure robe, she stood in the kitchen of her apartment preparing a model's feast of soup and unsalted crackers. A ring of the doorbell interrupted her far-from-gourmet activities.

"Lisa, hi." She greeted her neighbor from across the hall with an automatic smile. "Want some dinner?"

Lisa MacDonald wrinkled her nose in disdain. "I'd rather put up with a few extra pounds than starve myself like you."

"If I indulge myself too often," Hillary stated, patting a flat stomach, "I'd be after you to find me a job in that law firm you work for. By the way, how's the rising young attorney?"

"Mark still doesn't know I'm alive," Lisa complained as she flopped onto the couch. "I'm getting desperate, Hillary. I may lose my head and mug him in the parking lot."

"Tacky, too tacky," Hillary said, giving the matter deep consideration. "Why not attempt something less dramatic, like tripping him when he walks past your desk?"

"That could be next."

With a grin, Hillary sat and lifted bare feet to the surface of the coffee table. "Ever hear of Bret Bardoff?"

Lisa's eyes grew round. "Who hasn't? Millionaire, incredibly handsome, mysterious, brilliant businessman and still fair game." These attributes were counted off carefully on Lisa's fingers. "What about him?"

Slim shoulders moved expressively. "I'm not sure. Larry has an appointment with him in the morning."

"Face to face?"

"That's right." Amusement dawned first, then dark blue eyes regarded Lisa with curiosity. "Of course, we've both done work for his magazines before, but I can't imagine why the elusive owner of *Mode* would want to see a mere photographer, even if he is the best. In the trade, he's spoken of in reverent whispers, and if gossip columns are to be believed, he's the answer to every maiden's prayer. I wonder what he's really like." She frowned, finding herself nearly obsessed with the thought. "It's strange, I don't believe I know anyone who's had a personal dealing with him. I picture him as a giant phantom figure handing out monumental corporate decisions from *Mode*'s Mount Olympus."

"Maybe Larry will fill you in tomorrow," Lisa suggested, and Hillary shook her head, the frown becoming a grin.

"Larry won't notice anything unless Mr. Bardoff's on a roll of film."

Shortly before nine-thirty the following morning, Hillary used her spare key to enter Larry's studio. Prepared for the shampoo ad, her hair fell in soft, thick waves, shining and full. In the small cubicle in the rear she applied her makeup with an expert hand, and at nine forty-five she was impatiently switching on the lights required for indoor shots. As minutes slipped by, she began to entertain the annoying suspicion that Larry had neglected to arrange for a substitute. It was nearly ten when the door to the studio opened, and Hillary immediately pounced on the man who entered.

"It's about time," she began, tempering irritation with a small smile. "You're late."

"Am I?" he countered, meeting her annoyed expression with raised brows.

Pausing a moment, she realized how incredibly handsome the man facing her was. His hair, the color of corn silk, was full and grew just over the collar of his casual polo-necked gray sweater, a gray that exactly matched large, direct eyes. His mouth was quirked in a half smile, and there was something vaguely familiar about his deeply tanned face.

"I haven't worked with you before, have I?" Hillary asked, forced to look up to meet his eyes since he was an inch or more over six feet.

"Why do you ask?" His evasion was smooth, and she felt suddenly uncomfortable under his unblinking gray glance.

"No reason," she murmured, turning away, feeling compelled to adjust the cuff of her sleeve. "Well, let's get to it. Where's your camera?" Belatedly, she observed he carried no equipment. "Are you using Larry's?"

"I suppose I am." He continued to stand staring down at her, making no move to proceed with the task at hand, his nonchalance becoming thoroughly irritating.

"Well, come on then, let's not be all day. I've been ready for half an hour."

"Sorry." He smiled, and she was struck with the change it brought to his already compelling face. It was a carelessly slow smile, full of charm, and the thought passed through her mind that he could use it as a deadly weapon. Pivoting away from him, she struggled to ignore its power. She had a job to do. "What are the pictures for?" he asked her as he examined Larry's cameras.

"Oh, Lord, didn't he tell you?" Turning back to him, she shook her head and smiled fully for the first time. "Larry's a tremendous photographer, but he is the most exasperatingly absentminded man. I don't know how he remembers to get up in the morning." She tugged a lock of raven hair before giving her head a dramatic toss. "Clean, shiny, sexy hair," she explained in the tone of a commercial. "Shampoo's what we're selling today."

"Okay," he returned simply, and began setting equipment to rights in a thoroughly professional manner that did much to put Hillary's mind at ease. At least he knows his job, she assured herself, for his attitude had made her vaguely uneasy. "Where is Larry, by the way?" The question startled Hillary out of her silent thoughts.

"Didn't he tell you anything? That's just like him." Standing under the lights, she began turning, shaking her head, creating a rich black cloud as he clicked the camera, crouching and moving around her to catch different angles. "He had an appointment with Bret Bardoff," she continued, tossing her hair and smiling. "Lord help him if he forgot that. He'll be eaten alive."

"Does Bret Bardoff consume photographers as a habit?" the voice behind the camera questioned with dry amusement.

"Wouldn't be surprised." Hillary lifted her hair above her head, pausing for a moment before she allowed it to fall back to her shoulders like a rich cloak. "I would think a ruthless businessman like Mr. Bardoff would have little patience with an absentminded photographer or any other imperfection."

"You know him?"

"Lord, no." She laughed with unrestrained pleasure. "And I'm not likely to, far above my station. Have you met him?"

"Not precisely."

"Ah, but we all work for him at one time or another, don't we? I wonder how many times my face has been in one of his magazines. Scillions," she calculated, receiving a raised-brow look from behind the camera. "Scillions," she repeated with a nod. "And I've never met the emperor."

"Emperor?"

"How else does one describe such a lofty individual?" Hillary demanded with a gesture of her hands. "From what I've heard, he runs his mags like an empire."

"You sound as though you disapprove."

"No," Hillary disagreed with a smile and a shrug. "Emperors just make me nervous. I'm plain peasant stock myself."

"Your image seems hardly plain or peasant," he remarked, and this time it was her brow that lifted. "That should sell gallons of shampoo." Lowering his camera, he met her eyes directly. "I think we've got it, Hillary."

She relaxed, pushed back her hair, and regarded him curiously. "You know me? I'm sorry, I can't quite seem to place you. Have we worked together before?"

"Hillary Baxter's face is everywhere. It's my business to recognize beautiful faces." He spoke with careless simplicity, gray eyes smoky with amusement.

"Well, it appears you have the advantage, Mr.—?"

"Bardoff, Bret Bardoff," he answered, and the camera clicked to capture the astonished expression on her face. "You can close your mouth now, Hillary. I think we've got enough." His smile widened as she obeyed without thinking. "Cat got your tongue?" he mocked, pleasure at her embarrassment obvious.

She recognized him now, from pictures she had seen of him in newspapers and his own magazines, and she was busily engaged in cursing herself for the stupidity she had just displayed. Anger with herself spread to encompass the man in front of her, and she located her voice.

"You let me babble on like that," she sputtered, eyes and cheeks bright with color. "You stood there taking pictures you had no business taking and just let me carry on like an idiot."

"I was merely following orders." His grave tone and sober expression added to her mounting embarrassment and fury.

"Well, you had no right following them. You should have told me who you were." Her voice quavered with indignation, but he merely moved his shoulders and smiled again.

"You never asked."

Before she could retort, the door of the studio opened and Larry entered, looking harassed and confused. "Mr. Bardoff," he began, advancing on the pair standing under the lights. "I'm sorry. I thought I was to meet you at your office." Larry ran a hand through his hair in agitation. "When I got there, I was told you were coming here. I don't know how I got it so confused. Sorry you had to wait."

"Don't worry about it," Bret assured him with an easy smile. "The last hour's been highly entertaining."

"Hillary." Her existence suddenly seeped into Larry's consciousness. "Good Lord, I knew I forgot something. We'll have to get those pictures later."

"No need." Bret handed Larry the camera. "Hillary and I have seen to them."

"You took the shots?" Larry looked at Bret and the camera in turn.

"Hillary saw no reason to waste time." He smiled and added, "I'm sure you'll find the pictures suitable."

"No question of that, Mr. Bardoff." His voice was tinged with reverence. "I know what you can do with a camera."

Hillary had an overwhelming desire for the floor to open up and swallow her. She had to get out of there quickly. Never before in her life had she felt such a fool. Of course, she reasoned silently, it was his fault. The nerve of the man, letting her believe he was a photographer! She recalled the fashion in which she had ordered him to begin, and the things she had said. She closed her eyes with an inward moan. All she wanted to do now was disappear, and with luck she would never have to come face to face with Bret Bardoff again.

She began gathering her things quickly. "I'll leave you to get on with your business. I have another session across town." Slinging her purse over her shoulder, she took a deep breath. "Bye, Larry. Nice to have met you, Mr. Bardoff." She attempted to brush by them, but Bret put out his hand and captured hers, preventing her exit.

"Goodbye, Hillary." She forced her eyes to meet his, feeling a sudden drain of power by the contact of her hand in his. "It's been a most interesting morning. We'll have to do it again soon."

When hell freezes over, her eyes told him silently, and muttering something incoherent, she dashed for the door, the sound of his laughter echoing in her ears.

Dressing for a date that evening, Hillary endeavored, without success, to block the events of the morning from her mind. She was confident that her path would never cross Bret Bardoff's again. After all, she comforted herself, it had only been through a stupid accident that they had met in the first place. Hillary prayed that the adage about lightning never striking twice would hold true. She had indeed been hit by a lightning bolt when he had casually disclosed his name to her, and her cheeks burned again, matching the color of her soft jersey dress as her careless words played back in her mind.

The ringing of the phone interrupted her reflections, and she answered, finding Larry on the other end. "Hillary, boy, I'm glad I caught you at home." His excitement was tangible over the wire, and she answered him quickly.

"You just did catch me. I'm practically out the door. What's up?"

"I can't go into details now. Bret's going to do that in the morning."

She noted the fact that *Mr. Bardoff* had been discarded since that morning and spoke wearily. "Larry, what are you talking about?"

"Bret will explain everything in the morning. You have an appointment at nine o'clock."

"What?" Her voice rose and she found it imperative to swallow twice. "Larry, what are you talking about?"

"It's a tremendous opportunity for both of us, Hil. Bret will tell you tomorrow. You know where his office is." This was a statement rather than a question, since everyone in the business knew *Mode*'s headquarters.

"I don't want to see him," Hillary argued, feeling a surge of panic at the thought of those steel gray eyes. "I don't know what he told you about this morning, but I made a total fool of myself. I thought he was a photographer. Really," she continued, with fresh annoyance, "you're partially to blame, if—"

"Don't worry about all that now," Larry interrupted confidently. "It doesn't matter. Just be there at nine tomorrow. See you later."

"But, Larry." She stopped, there was no purpose in arguing with a dead phone. Larry had hung up.

This was too much, she thought in despair, and sat down heavily on the bed. How could Larry expect her to go through with this? How could she possibly face that man after the things she had said? Humiliation, she decided, was simply something for which she was not suited. Rising from the bed, she squared her shoulders. Bret Bardoff probably wanted another opportunity to laugh at her for her stupidity. Well, he wasn't going to get the best of Hillary Baxter, she told herself with firm pride. She'd face him without cringing. This peasant would stand up to the emperor and show him what she was made of!

* * *

Hillary dressed for her appointment the next morning with studious care. The white, light wool cowl-necked dress was beautiful in its simplicity, relying on the form it covered to make it eye-catching. She arranged her hair in a loose bun on top of her head in order to add a businesslike air to her appearance. Bret Bardoff would not find her stammering and blushing this morning, she determined, but cool and confident. Slipping on soft leather shoes, she was satisfied with the total effect, the heels adding to her height. She would not be forced to look up quite so high in order to meet those gray eyes, and she would meet them straight on.

Confidence remained with her through the taxi ride and all the way to the top of the building where Bret Bardoff had his offices. Glancing at her watch on the elevator, she was pleased to see she was punctual. An attractive brunette was seated at an enormous reception desk, and Hillary stated her name and business. After a brief conversation on a phone that held a prominent position on the large desk, the woman ushered Hillary down a long corridor and through a heavy oak door.

She entered a large, well-decorated room where she was greeted by yet another attractive woman, who introduced herself as June Miles, Mr. Bardoff's secretary. "Please go right in, Miss Baxter. Mr. Bardoff is expecting you," she informed Hillary with a smile.

Walking to a set of double doors, Hillary's eyes barely had time to take in the room with its rather fabulous decor before her gaze was arrested by the man seated at a huge oak desk, a panoramic view of the city at his back.

"Good morning, Hillary." He rose and approached her. "Are you going to come in or stand there all day with your back to the door?"

Hillary's spine straightened and she answered coolly, "Good morning, Mr. Bardoff, it's nice to see you again."

"Don't be a hypocrite," he stated mildly as he led her to a seat near the desk. "You'd be a great deal happier if you never laid eyes on me again." Hillary could find no comment to this all-too-true observation, and contented herself with smiling vaguely into space.

"However," he continued, as if she had agreed with him in words, "it suits my purposes to have you here today in spite of your reluctance."

"And what are your purposes, Mr. Bardoff?" she demanded, her annoyance with his arrogance sharpening her tone.

He leaned back in his chair and allowed his cool gray eyes to travel deliberately over Hillary from head to toe. The survey was slow and obviously intended to disconcert, but she remained outwardly unruffled. Because of her profession, her face and form had been studied before. She was determined not to let this man know his stare was causing her pulses to dance a nervous rhythm.

"My purposes, Hillary—" his eyes met hers and held "—are for the moment strictly business, though that is subject to change at any time."

This remark cracked Hillary's cool veneer enough to bring a slight blush to her cheeks. She cursed the color as she struggled to keep her eyes level with his.

"Good Lord." His brows lifted with humor. "You're blushing. I didn't think women did that anymore." His grin widened as if he were enjoying the fact that more color leaped to her cheeks at his words. "You're probably the last of a dying breed."

"Could we discuss the business for which I'm here, Mr. Bardoff?" she inquired. "I'm sure you're a very busy man, and believe it or not, I'm busy myself."

"Of course," Bret agreed. He grinned reflectively. "I remember—*'Let's not waste time.'* I'm planning a layout for *Mode,* a rather special layout." He lit a cigarette and offered Hillary one, which she declined with a shake of her head. "I've had the idea milling around in my mind for some time, but I needed the right photographer and the right woman." His eyes narrowed as he peered at her speculatively, giving Hillary the sensation of being viewed under a microscope. "I've found them both now."

She squirmed under his unblinking stare. "Suppose you give me some details, Mr. Bardoff. I'm sure it's not usual procedure for you to interview models personally. This must be something special."

"Yes, I think so," he agreed suavely. "The idea is a layout—a picture story, if you like—on the Many Faces of Woman." He stood then and perched on the corner of the desk, and Hillary was affected by his sheer masculinity, the power and strength that exuded from his lean form clad in a fawn-colored business suit. "I want to portray all the facets of womanhood: career woman, mother, athlete, sophisticate, innocent, temptress, et cetera—a complete portrait of Eve, the Eternal Woman."

"Sounds fascinating," Hillary admitted, caught up in the backlash of his enthusiasm. "You think I might be suitable for some of the pictures?"

"I know you're suitable," he stated flatly, "for *all* of the pictures."

Finely etched brows raised in curiosity. "You're going to use one model for the entire layout?"

"I'm going to use *you* for the entire layout."

Struggling with annoyance and the feeling of being submerged by very deep water, Hillary spoke honestly. "I'd be an idiot not to be interested in a project like this. I don't think I'm an idiot. But why me?"

"Come now, Hillary." His voice mirrored impatience, and he bent over to capture her surprised chin in his hand. "You do own a mirror. Surely you're intelligent enough to know that you're quite beautiful and extremely photogenic."

He was speaking of her as if she were an inanimate object rather than a human being, and the fingers, strong and lean on her chin, were very distressing. Nevertheless, Hillary persisted.

"There are scores of beautiful and photogenic models in New York alone, Mr. Bardoff. You know that better than anyone. I'd like to know why you're considering me for your pet project."

"Not considering." He rose and thrust his hands in his pockets, and she observed he was becoming irritated. She found the knowledge rewarding. "There's no one else I would consider. You have a rather uncanny knack for getting to the heart of a picture and coming across with exactly the right image. I need versatility as well as beauty. I need honesty in a dozen different images."

"In your opinion, I can do that."

"You wouldn't be here if I weren't sure. I never make rash decisions."

No, Hillary mused, looking into his cool gray eyes, you calculate every minute detail. Aloud, she asked, "Larry would be the photographer?"

He nodded. "There's an affinity between the two of you that is obvious in the pictures you produce. You're both superior alone, but together you've done some rather stunning work."

His praise caused her smile to warm slightly. "Thank you."

"That wasn't a compliment, Hillary—just a fact. I've given Larry all the details. The contracts are waiting for your signature."

"Contracts?" she repeated, becoming wary.

"That's right," he returned, overlooking her hesitation. "This project is going to take some time. I've no intention of rushing through it. I want exclusive rights to that beautiful face of yours until the project's completed and on the stands."

"I see." She digested this carefully, unconsciously chewing on her bottom lip.

"You needn't react as if I've made an indecent proposal, Hillary." His voice was dry as he regarded her frowning concentration. "This is a business arrangement."

Her chin tilted in defiance. "I understand that completely, Mr. Bardoff. It's simply that I've never signed a long-term contract before."

"I have no intention of allowing you to get away. Contracts are obligatory, for you and for Larry. For the next few months I don't want you distracted by any other jobs. Financially, you'll be well compensated. If you have any complaints along those lines, we'll negotiate. However, my rights to that face of yours for the next six months are exclusive."

He lapsed into silence, watching the varied range of expressions on her face. She was working out the entire platform carefully, doing her best not to be intimidated by his overwhelming power. The project appealed to her, although the man did not. It would be fascinating work, but she found it difficult to tie herself to one establishment for any period of time. She could not help feeling that signing her name was signing away liberation. A long-term contract equaled a long-term commitment.

Finally, throwing caution to the winds, she gave Bret one of the smiles that made her face known throughout America.

"You've got yourself a face."

Chapter 2

Bret Bardoff moved quickly. Within two weeks contracts had been signed, and the shooting schedule had been set to begin on a morning in early October. The first image to be portrayed was one of youthful innocence and unspoiled simplicity.

Hillary met Larry in a small park selected by Bret. Though the morning was bright and brisk, the sun filtering warm through the trees, the park was all but deserted. She wondered a moment if the autocratic Mr. Bardoff had arranged the isolation. Blue jeans rolled to mid-calf and a long-sleeved turtleneck in scarlet were Hillary's designated costume. She had bound her shining hair in braids, tied them with red ribbons, and had kept her makeup light, relying on natural, healthy skin. She was the essence of honest, vibrant youth, dark blue eyes bright with the anticipation.

"Perfect," Larry commented as she ran across the grass to meet him. "Young and innocent. How do you manage it?"

She wrinkled her nose. "I am young and innocent, old man."

"Okay. See that?" He pointed to a swing set complete with bars and a slide. "Go play, little girl, and let this old man take some pictures."

She ran for the swing, giving herself over to the freedom of movement. Stretching out full length, she leaned her head to the ground and smiled at the brilliant sky. Climbing on the slide, she lifted her arms wide, let out a whoop of uninhibited joy, and slid down, landing on her bottom in the soft dirt. Larry clicked his camera from varying angles, allowing her to direct the mood.

"You look twelve years old." His laugh was muffled, his face still concealed behind the camera.

"I am twelve years old," Hillary proclaimed, scurrying onto the crossbars. "Betcha can't do this." She hung up by her knees on the bar, her pigtails brushing the ground.

"Amazing." The answer did not come from Larry, and she turned her head and looked directly into a pair of well-tailored gray slacks. Her eyes roamed slowly upward to the matching jacket and farther to a full, smiling mouth and mocking gray eyes. "Hello, child, does your mother know where you are?"

"What are you doing here?" Hillary demanded, feeling at a decided disadvantage in her upside-down position.

"Supervising my pet project." He continued to regard

her, his grin growing wider. "How long do you intend to hang there? The blood must be rushing to your head."

Grabbing the bar with her hands, she swung her legs over in a neat somersault and stood facing him. He patted her head, told her she was a good girl, and turned his attention to Larry.

"How'd it go? Looked to me as if you got some good shots."

The two men discussed the technicalities of the morning's shooting while Hillary sat back down on the swing, moving gently back and forth. She had met with Bret a handful of times during the past two weeks, and each time she had been unaccountably uneasy in his presence. He was a vital and disturbing individual, full of raw, masculine power, and she was not at all sure she wanted to be closely associated with him. Her life was well ordered now, running smoothly along the lines she designated, and she wanted no complications. There was something about this man, however, that spelled complications in capital letters.

"All right." Bret's voice broke into her musings. "Setup at the club at one o'clock. Everything's been arranged." Hillary rose from the swing and moved to join Larry. "No need for you to go now, little girl—you've an hour or so to spare."

"I don't want to play on the swings anymore, Daddy," she retorted, bristling at his tone. Picking up her shoulder bag, she managed to take two steps before he reached out and took command of her wrist. She rounded on him, blue eyes blazing.

"Spoiled little brat, aren't you?" he murmured in a

mild tone, but his eyes narrowed and met the dark blue blaze with cold gray steel. "Perhaps I should turn you over my knee."

"That would be more difficult than you think, Mr. Bardoff," she returned with unsurpassable dignity. "I'm twenty-four, not twelve, and really quite strong."

"Are you now?" He inspected her slim form dubiously. "I suppose it's possible." He spoke soberly, but she recognized the mockery in his eyes. "Come on, I want some coffee." His hand slipped from her wrist, and his fingers interlocked with hers. She jerked away, surprised and disconcerted by the warmth. "Hillary," he began in a tone of strained patience. "I would like to buy you coffee." It was more a command than a request.

He moved across the grass with long, easy strides, dragging an unwilling Hillary after him. Larry watched their progress and automatically took their picture. They made an interesting study, he decided, the tall blond man in the expensive business suit pulling the slim, dark woman-child behind him.

As she sat across from Bret in a small coffee shop, Hillary's face was flushed with a mixture of indignation and the exertion of keeping up with the brisk pace he had set. He took in her pink cheeks and bright eyes, and his mouth lifted at one corner.

"Maybe I should buy a dish of ice cream to cool you off." The waitress appeared then, saving Hillary from formulating a retort, and Bret ordered two coffees.

"Tea," Hillary stated flatly, pleased to contradict him on some level.

"I beg your pardon?" he returned coolly.

"I'll have tea, if you don't mind. I don't drink coffee; it makes me nervous."

"One coffee and one tea," he amended before he turned back to her. "How do you wake up in the morning without the inevitable cup of coffee?"

"Clean living." She flicked a pigtail over her shoulder and folded her hands.

"You certainly look like an ad for clean living now." Sitting back, he took out his cigarette case, offering her one and lighting one before going on. "I'm afraid you'd never pass for twenty-four in pigtails. It's not often one sees hair that true black—certainly not with eyes that color." He stared into them for a long moment. "They're fabulous, so dark at times they're nearly purple, quite dramatic, and the bone structure, it's rather elegant and exotic. Tell me," he asked suddenly, "where did you get that marvelous face of yours?"

Hillary had thought herself long immune to comments and compliments on her looks, but somehow his words nonplussed her, and she was grateful that the waitress returned with their drinks, giving her time to gather scattered wits.

"I'm told I'm a throwback to my great-grandmother." She spoke with detached interest as she sipped tea. "She was an Arapaho. It appears I resemble her quite strongly."

"I should have guessed." He nodded his head continuing his intense study. "The cheekbones, the classic bone structure. Yes, I can see your Indian heritage, but the eyes are deceiving. You didn't acquire eyes like cobalt from your great-grandmother."

"No." She struggled to meet his penetrating gaze coolly. "They belong to me."

"To you," he acknowledged with a nod, "and for the next six months to me. I believe I'll enjoy the joint ownership." The focus of his study shifted to the mouth that moved in a frown at his words. "Where are you from, Hillary Baxter? You're no native."

"That obvious? I thought I had acquired a marvelous New York varnish." She gave a wry shrug, grateful that the intensity of his examination appeared to be over. "Kansas—a farm some miles north of Abilene."

He inclined his head, and his brows lifted as he raised his cup. "You appear to have made the transition from wheat to concrete very smoothly. No battle scars?"

"A few, but they're healed over." She added quickly, "I hardly have to point out New York's advantages to you, especially in the area of my career."

His agreement was a slow nod. "It's very easy to picture you as a Kansas farm girl or a sophisticated New York model. You have a remarkable ability to suit your surroundings."

Hillary's full mouth moved in a doubtful pout. "That makes me sound like I'm no person on my own, sort of...inconspicuous."

"Inconspicuous?" Bret's laughter caused several heads to turn, and Hillary stared at him in dumb amazement. "Inconspicuous," he said again, shaking his head as if she had just uttered something sublimely ridiculous. "What a beautiful statement. No, I think you're a very complex woman with a remarkable affinity with her surroundings. I don't believe it's an acquired talent, but an intrinsic ability."

His words pleased Hillary out of all proportion, and she made an issue of stirring her tea, giving it her undivided attention. Why should a simple, impersonal compliment wrap around my tongue like a twenty-pound chain? she wondered, careful to keep a frown from forming. I don't think I care for the way he always manages to shift my balance.

"You do play tennis, don't you?"

Again, his rapid altering of the conversation threw her into confusion, and she stared at him without comprehension until she recalled the afternoon session was on the tennis court of an exclusive country club.

"I manage to hit the ball over the net once in a while." Annoyed by his somewhat condescending tone, she answered with uncharacteristic meekness.

"Good. The shots will be more impressive if you have the stance and moves down properly." He glanced at the gold watch on his wrist and drew out his wallet. "I've got some things to clear up at the office." Standing, he drew her from the booth, again holding her hand in his oddly familiar manner, ignoring her efforts to withdraw from his grip. "I'll put you in a cab. It'll take you some time to change from little girl to female athlete." He looked down at her, making her feel unaccustomedly small at five foot seven in her sneakers. "Your tennis outfit's already at the club, and I assume you have all the tricks of your trade in that undersized suitcase?" He indicated the large shoulder bag she heaved over her arm.

"Don't worry, Mr. Bardoff."

"Bret," he interrupted, suddenly engrossed with running his hand down her left pigtail. "I don't intend to stop using your first name."

"Don't worry," she began again, evading his invitation. "Changing images is my profession."

"It should prove interesting," he murmured, tugging the braid he held. Then, shifting to a more professional tone he said, "The court is reserved for one. I'll see you then."

"You're going to be there?" Her question was accompanied by a frown as she found herself undeniably distressed at the prospect of dealing with him yet again.

"My pet project, remember?" He nudged her into a cab, either unaware of or unconcerned by her scowl. "I intend to supervise it very carefully."

As the cab merged with traffic, Hillary's emotions were in turmoil. Bret Bardoff was an incredibly attractive and distracting man, and there was something about him that disturbed her. The idea of being in almost daily contact with him made her decidedly uneasy.

I don't like him, she decided with a firm nod. He's too self-assured, too arrogant, too... Her mind searched for a word. *Physical.* Yes, she admitted, albeit unwillingly, he was a very sexual man, and he unnerved her. She had no desire to be disturbed. There was something about the way he looked at her, something about the way her body reacted whenever she came into contact with him. Shrugging, she stared out the window at passing cars. She wouldn't think of him. Rather, she corrected, she would think of him only as her employer, and a temporary one at that—not as an individual. Her hand still felt warm from his, and glancing down at it, she sighed. It was imperative to her peace of mind that she do her job and avoid any more personal dealings with him. Strictly business, she reminded herself. Yes, their relationship would be strictly business.

The tomboy had been transformed into the fashionable tennis buff. A short white tennis dress accented Hillary's long, slender legs and left arms bare. She covered them, as she waited on the court, with a light jacket, since the October afternoon was pleasant but cool. Her hair was tied away from her face with a dark blue scarf, leaving her delicate features unframed. Color had been added to her eyes, accenting them with sooty fringes, and her lips were tinted deep rose. Spotless white tennis shoes completed her outfit, and she held a lightweight racket in her hands. The pure white of the ensemble contrasted well with her golden skin and raven hair, and she appeared wholly feminine as well as capable.

Behind the net, she experimented with stances, swinging the racket and serving the balls to a nonexistent partner while Larry roamed around her, checking angles and meters.

"I think you might have better luck if someone hit back."

She spun around to see Bret watching her with an amused gleam in his eyes. He too was in white, the jacket of his warm-up suit pushed to the elbows. Hillary, used to seeing him in a business suit, was surprised at the athletic appearance of his body, whipcord lean, his shoulders broad, his arms hard and muscular, his masculinity entirely too prevalent.

"Do I pass?" he asked with a half smile, and she flushed, suddenly aware that she had been staring.

"I'm just surprised to see you dressed that way," she muttered, shrugging her shoulders and turning away.

"More suitable for tennis, don't you think?"

"We're going to play?" She spun back to face him, scowling at the racket in his hand.

"I rather like the idea of action...shots," he finished with a grin. "I won't be too hard on you. I'll hit some nice and easy."

With a good deal of willpower, she managed not to stick out her tongue. She played tennis often and well. Hillary decided, with inner complacency, that Mr. Bret Bardoff was in for a surprise.

"I'll try to hit a few back," she promised, her face as ingenuous as a child. "To give the shots realism."

"Good." He strode over to the other side of the court, and Hillary picked up a ball. "Can you serve?"

"I'll do my best," she answered, coating honey on her tongue. After glancing at Larry to see if he was ready, she tossed the ball idly in the air. The camera had already replaced Larry's face, and Hillary moved behind the fault line, tossed the ball once more, connected with the racket, and smashed a serve. Bret returned her serve gently, and she hit back, aiming deep in the opposite corner.

"I think I remember how to score," she called out with a thoughtful frown. "Fifteen-love, Mr. Bardoff."

"Nice return, Hillary. Do you play often?"

"Oh, now and again," she evaded, brushing invisible lint from her skirt. "Ready?"

He nodded, and the ball bounced back and forth in an easy, powerless volley. She realized with some smugness that he was holding back, making it a simple matter for her to make the return for the benefit of Larry's rapidly snapping camera. But she too was holding back, hitting the ball lightly and without any style. She allowed a few more laconic lobs, then slammed the ball away from him, deep in the back court.

"Oh." She lifted a finger to her lips, feigning innocence. "That's thirty-love, isn't it?"

Bret's eyes narrowed as he approached the net. "Why do I have this strange feeling that I'm being conned?"

"Conned?" she repeated, wide-eyed, allowing her lashes to flutter briefly. He searched her face until her lips trembled with laughter. "Sorry, Mr. Bardoff, I couldn't resist." She tossed her head and grinned. "You were so patronizing."

"Okay." He returned her grin somewhat to Hillary's relief. "No more patronizing. Now I'm out for blood."

"We'll start from scratch," she offered, returning to the serving line. "I wouldn't want you to claim I had an unfair advantage."

He returned her serve with force, and they kept each other moving rapidly over the court in the ensuing volley. They battled for points, reaching deuce and exchanging advantage several times. The camera was forgotten in the focus of concentration, the soft click of the shutter masked by the swish of rackets and thump of balls.

Cursing under her breath at the failure to return a

ball cleanly, Hillary stooped to pick up another and prepared to serve.

"That was great." Larry's voice broke her concentration, and she turned to gape at him. "I got some fantastic shots. You look like a real pro, Hil. We can wrap it up now."

"Wrap it up?" She stared at him with incredulous exasperation. "Have you lost your mind? We're at deuce." She continued to regard him a moment as if his brain had gone on holiday, and shaking her head and muttering, she resumed play.

For the next few minutes, they fought for the lead until Bret once more held the advantage and once more placed the ball down the line to her backhand.

Hillary put her hands on her hips and let out a deep breath after the ball had sailed swiftly past her. "Ah, well, the agony of defeat." She smiled, attempted to catch her wind, and approached the net. "Congratulations." She offered both hand and smile. "You play a very demanding game."

He accepted her hand, holding it rather than shaking it. "You certainly made me earn it, Hillary. I believe I'd like to try my luck at doubles, with you on my side of the net."

"I suppose you could do worse."

He held her gaze a moment before his eyes dropped to the hand still captive in his. "Such a small hand." He lifted it higher and examined it thoroughly. "I'm astonished it can swing a racket like that." He turned it palm up and carried it to his lips.

Odd and unfamiliar tingles ran up her spine at his kiss,

and she stared mesmerized at her hand, unable to speak or draw away. "Come on." He smiled into bemused eyes, annoyingly aware of her reaction. "I'll buy you lunch." His gaze slid past her. "You too, Larry."

"Thanks, Bret." He was already gathering his equipment. "But I want to get back and develop this film. I'll just grab a sandwich."

"Well, Hillary." He turned and commanded her attention. "It's just you and me."

"Really, Mr. Bardoff," she began, feeling near to panic at the prospect of having lunch with him and wishing with all her heart that he would respond to the effort she was currently making to regain sole possession of her hand. "It's not necessary for you to buy me lunch."

"Hillary, Hillary." He sighed, shaking his head. "Do you always find it difficult to accept an invitation, or is it only with me?"

"Don't be ridiculous." She attempted to maintain a casual tone while she became more and more troubled by the warmth of his hand over hers. She stared down at the joined hands, feeling increasingly helpless as the contact continued. "Mr. Bardoff, may I please have my hand back?" Her voice was breathless, and she bit her lip in vexation.

"Try Bret, Hillary," he commanded, ignoring her request. "It's easy enough, only one syllable. Go ahead."

The eyes that held hers were calm, demanding, and arrogant enough to remain steady for the next hour. The longer her hand remained in his, the more peculiar she felt, and knowing that the sooner she agreed, the sooner she would be free, she surrendered.

"Bret, may I please have my hand back?"

"There, now, we've cleared the first hurdle. That didn't hurt much, did it?" The corner of his mouth lifted as he released her, and immediately the vague weakness began to dissipate, leaving her more secure.

"Nearly painless."

"Now about lunch." He held up his hand to halt her protest. "You do eat, don't you?"

"Of course, but—"

"No buts. I rarely listen to buts or nos."

In short order Hillary found herself seated across from Bret at a small table inside the club. Things were not going as she had planned. It was very difficult to maintain a businesslike and impersonal relationship when she was so often in his company. It was useless to deny that she found him interesting, his vitality stimulating, and he was a tremendously attractive man. But, she admonished herself, he certainly wasn't her type. Besides, she didn't have time for entanglements at this point of her life. Still, the warning signals in her brain told her to tread carefully, that this man was capable of upsetting her neatly ordered plans.

"Has anyone ever told you what a fascinating conversationalist you are?" Hillary's eyes shot up to find Bret's mocking gaze on her.

"Sorry." Color crept into her face. "My mind was wandering."

"So I noticed. What will you have to drink?"

"Tea."

"Straight?" he inquired, his smile hovering.

"Straight," she agreed, and ordered herself to relax.

"I don't drink much. I'm afraid I don't handle it well. More than two and I turn into Mr. Hyde. Metabolism."

Bret threw back his head and laughed with the appearance of boundless pleasure. "That's a transformation I would give much to witness. We'll have to arrange it."

Lunch, to Hillary's surprise, was an enjoyable meal, though Bret met her choice of salad with open disgust and pure masculine disdain. She assured him it was adequate, and made a passing comment on the brevity of overweight models' careers.

Fully relaxed, Hillary enjoyed herself, the resolution to keep a professional distance between herself and Bret forgotten. As they ate, he spoke of the next day's shooting plans. Central Park had been designated for more outdoor scenes in keeping with the outdoor, athletic image.

"I've meetings all day tomorrow and won't be able to supervise. How do you exist on that stuff?" He changed the trend of conversation abruptly, waving a superior finger at Hillary's salad. "Don't you want some food? You're going to fade away."

She shook her head, smiling as she sipped her tea, and he muttered under his breath about half-starved models before resuming his previous conversation. "If all goes according to schedule, we'll start the next segment Monday. Larry wants to get an early start tomorrow."

"Always," she agreed with a sigh. "If the weather holds."

"Oh, the sun will shine." She heard the absolute confidence in his voice. "I've arranged it."

Sitting back, she surveyed the man across from her

with uninhibited curiosity. "Yes." She nodded at length, noting the firm jaw and direct eyes. "I believe you could. It wouldn't dare rain."

They smiled at each other, and as the look held, she experienced a strange, unfamiliar sensation running through her—something swift, vital, and anonymous.

"Some dessert?"

"You're determined to fatten me up, aren't you?" Grateful that his casual words had eliminated the strange emotion, she summoned up an easy smile. "You're a bad influence, but I have a will of iron."

"Cheesecake, apple pie, chocolate mousse?" His smile was wicked, but she tossed her head and lifted her chin.

"Do your worst. I don't break."

"You're bound to have a weakness. A little time, and I'll find it."

"Bret, darling, what a surprise to see you here." Hillary turned and looked up at the woman greeting Bret with such enthusiasm.

"Hello, Charlene." He granted the shapely, elegantly dressed redhead a charming smile. "Charlene Mason, Hillary Baxter."

"Miss Baxter." Charlene nodded in curt greeting, and green eyes narrowed. "Have we met before?"

"I don't believe so," Hillary returned, wondering why she felt a surge of gratitude at the fact.

"Hillary's face is splashed over magazines covers everywhere," Bret explained. "She's one of New York's finest models."

"Of course." Hillary watched the green eyes narrow further, survey her, and dismiss her as inferior merchandise. "Bret, you should have told me you'd be here today. We could have had some time."

"Sorry," he answered with a casual move of his shoulders. "I won't be here long, and it was business."

Ridiculously deflated by his statement, Hillary immediately forced her spine to straighten. Didn't I tell you not to get involved? she reminded herself. He's quite right, this was a business lunch. She gathered her things and stood.

"Please, Miss Mason, have my seat. I was just going." She turned to Bret, pleased to observe his annoyance at her hasty departure. "Thanks for lunch, Mr. Bardoff," she added politely, flashing a smile at the frown that appeared at her use of his surname. "Nice to have met you, Miss Mason." Giving the woman occupying the seat she had just vacated a professional smile, Hillary walked away.

"I didn't realize taking employees to lunch was part of your routine, Bret." Charlene's voice carried to Hillary as she made her exit. Her first instinct was to whirl around and inform the woman to mind her own business, but grasping for control, she continued to move away without hearing Bret's reply.

The following day's session was more arduous. Using the brilliant fall color in Central Park for a backdrop, Larry's ideas for pictures were varied and energetic. It was a bright, cloudless day, as Bret had predicted, one of the final, golden days of Indian summer. Gold, russet, and scarlet dripped from the branches and covered the ground. Against the varied fall hues, Hillary posed, jogged, threw Frisbees, smiled, climbed trees, fed pigeons, and made three costume changes as the day wore on. Several times during the long session she caught herself looking for Bret, although she knew he was not expected. Her disappointment at his absence both surprised and displeased her, and she reminded herself that life would run much more smoothly if she had never laid eyes on a certain tall, lean man.

"Lighten up, Hil. Quit scowling." Larry's command broke into her musings. Resolutely, she shoved Bret Bardoff from her mind and concentrated on her job.

That evening she sank her tired body into a warm tub, sighing as the scented water worked its gentle magic on aching muscles. Oh, Larry, she thought wearily, with a camera in your hands you become Simon Legree. What you put me through today. I know I've been snapped from every conceivable angle, with every conceivable expression, in every conceivable pose. Thank heavens I'm through until Monday.

This layout was a big assignment, she realized, and there would be many more days like this one. The project could be a big boost to her career. A large layout in a magazine of *Mode*'s reputation and quality would bring her face to international recognition, and with Bret's backing she would more than likely be on her way to becoming one of the country's top models.

A frown appeared from nowhere. Why doesn't that please me? The prospect of being successful in my profession has always been something I wanted. Bret's face entered her mind, and she shook her head in fierce rejection.

"Oh, no you don't," she told his image. "You're not going to get inside my head and confuse my plans. You're the emperor, and I'm your lowly subject. Let's keep it that way."

Hillary was seated with Chuck Carlyle in one of New York's most popular discos. Music filled every corner, infusing the air with its vibrancy, while lighting effects played everchanging colors over the dancers. As the music washed over them, Hillary reflected on her reasoning for keeping her relationship with Chuck platonic.

It wasn't as though she didn't enjoy male companionship, she told herself. It wasn't as though she didn't enjoy a man's embrace or his kisses. A pair of mocking gray eyes crept into her mind unbidden, and she scowled fiercely into her drink.

If she shied away from more intimate relationships, it was only because no one had touched her deeply enough or stirred her emotions to a point where she felt any desire to engage in a long-term or even a short-term affair. Love, she mused, had so far eluded her, and she silently asserted that she was grateful. With love came commitments, and commitments did not fit into her plans for the immediate future. No, an involvement with a man would bring complications, interfere with her well-ordered life.

"It's always a pleasure to take you out, Hillary." Thoughts broken, she glanced over to see Chuck grin and look pointedly down at the drink she had been nursing ever since their arrival. "You're so easy on my paycheck."

She returned his grin and pushed soul-searching aside.

"You could look far and wide and never find another woman so concerned about your financial welfare."

"Too true." He sighed and adopted a look of great sadness. "They're either after my body or my money, and you, sweet Hillary, are after neither." He grabbed both of her hands and covered them with kisses. "If only you'd marry me, love of my life, and let me take you away from all this decadence." His hand swept over the dance floor. "We'll find a vine-covered cottage, two-point-seven kids, and settle down."

"Do you know," Hillary said slowly, "if I said yes, you'd faint dead away?"

"When you're right, you're right." He sighed again. "So instead of sweeping you off your feet to a vine-covered cottage, I'll drag you back to the decadence."

Admiring eyes focused on the tall, slim woman with the dress as blue as her eyes. Hillary's skirt was slit high to reveal long, shapely legs as she turned and spun with the dark man in his cream-colored suit. Both dancers possessed a natural grace and affinity with the music, and they looked spectacular on the dance floor. They ended the dance with Chuck lowering Hillary into a deep, dramatic dip, and when she stood again, she was laughing and flushed with the excitement of the dance. They wove their way back to their table, Chuck's arm around her shoulders, and Hillary's laughter died as she found herself confronted with the gray eyes that had disturbed her a short time before.

"Hello, Hillary." Bret's greeting was casual, and she was grateful for the lighting system, which disguised her change of color.

"Hello, Mr. Bardoff," she returned, wondering why her stomach had begun to flutter at the sight of him.

"You met Charlene, I believe."

Her eyes shifted to the redhead at his side. "Of course, nice to see you again." Hillary turned to her partner and made quick introductions. Chuck pumped Bret's hand with great enthusiasm.

"Bret Bardoff? *The* Bret Bardoff?" Hillary cringed at the undisguised awe and admiration.

"The only one I know," he answered with an easy smile.

"Please—" Chuck indicated their table "—join us for a drink."

Bret's smile widened as he inclined his head to Hillary, laughter lighting his eyes as she struggled to cover her discomfort.

"Yes, please do." She met his eyes directly, and her voice was scrupulously polite. She was determined to win the silent battle with the strange, uncommon emotions his mere presence caused. Flicking a quick glance at his companion, her discomfort changed to amusement as she observed Charlene Mason was no more pleased to share their company than she was. Or perhaps, Hillary thought idly as they slid behind the table, she was not pleased with sharing Bret with anyone, however briefly.

"A very impressive show the two of you put on out there," Bret commented to Chuck, indicating the dance floor with a nod of his head. His gaze roamed over to include Hillary. "You two must dance often to move so well together."

"There's no better partner than Hillary," Chuck declared magnanimously, and patted her hand with friendly affection. "She can dance with anyone."

"Is that so?" Bret's brows lifted. "Perhaps you'll let me borrow her for a moment and see for myself."

An unreasonable panic filled Hillary at the thought of dancing with him and it was reflected in her expressive eyes.

She rose with a feeling of helpless indignation as Bret came behind her and pulled out her chair without waiting for her assent.

"Stop looking like such a martyr," he whispered in her ear as they approached the other dancers.

"Don't be absurd," she stated with admirable dignity, furious that he could read her so effortlessly.

The music had slowed, and he turned her to face him, gathering her into his arms. At the contact, an overpowering childish urge to pull away assailed her, and she struggled to prevent the tension from becoming noticeable. His chest was hard, his basic masculinity overwhelming, and she refused to allow herself the relief of swallowing in nervous agitation. The arm around her waist held her achingly close, so close their bodies seemed to melt together as he moved her around the floor. She had unconsciously shifted to her toes, and her cheek rested against his, the scent of him assaulting her senses, making her wonder if she had perhaps sipped her drink too quickly. Her heart was pounding erratically against his, and she fought to control the leaping of her pulses as she matched her steps to his.

"I should have known you were a dancer," he murmured against her ear, causing a fresh flutter of her heartbeat.

"Really," she countered, battling to keep her tone careless and light, attempting to ignore the surge of excitement of his mouth on the lobe of her ear. "Why?"

"The way you walk, the way you move. With a sensuous grace, and effortless rhythm."

She intended to laugh off the compliment and tilted her head to meet his eyes. She found herself instead staring wordlessly into their gray depths. His hold on her did not lessen as they faced, their lips a breath apart, and she found the flip remark she had been about to make slip into oblivion.

"I always thought gray eyes were like steel," she murmured, hardly aware she was voicing her thoughts. "Yours are more like clouds."

"Dark and threatening?" he suggested, holding her gaze.

"Sometimes," she whispered, caught in the power he exuded. "And others, warm and soft like an early mist. I never know whether I'm in for a storm or a shower. Never know what to expect."

"Don't you?" His voice was quiet as his gaze dropped to her lips, tantalizingly close to his. "You should by now."

She struggled with the weakness invading her at his softly spoken retort and clutched for sophistication. "Really, Mr. Bardoff, are you attempting to seduce me in the middle of a crowded dance floor?"

"One must make use of what's available," he answered, then lifted his brow. "Have you somewhere else in mind?"

"Sorry," she apologized, and turned her head so their faces no longer met. "We're both otherwise engaged, and," she added, attempting to slip away, "the dance is over."

He did not release her, pulling her closer and speaking ominously in her ear. "You'll not get away until you drop that infuriatingly formal Mr. Bardoff and use my name." When she did not reply, he went on, an edge sharpening his voice. "I'm perfectly content to stay like this. You're a woman who was meant for a man's arms. I find you suit mine."

"All right," Hillary said between her teeth. "Bret, would you please let me go before I'm crushed beyond recognition?"

"Certainly." His grip slacked, but his arm remained around her. "Don't tell me I'm really hurting you." His smile was wide and triumphant as he gazed into her resentful face.

"I'll let you know after I've had my X-rays."

"I doubt if you're as fragile as all that." He led her back to the table, his arm still encircling her waist.

They joined their respective partners, and the group spoke generally for the next few minutes. Hillary felt unmistakable hostility directed toward her from the other woman, which Bret was either blissfully unaware of or ignored. Between frosty green eyes and her own disquieting awareness of the tall, fair man whose arms had held her so intimately, Hillary was acutely uncomfortable. It was a relief when the couple rose to leave, and

Bret refused Chuck's request that they stay for another round. Charlene looked on with undisguised boredom.

"Charlene's not fond of discos, I'm afraid," Bret explained, grinning as he slipped an arm casually around the redhead's shoulders, causing her to look up at him with a smile of pure invitation. The gesture caused a sudden blaze of emotions to flare in Hillary that she refused to identify as jealousy. "She merely came tonight to please me. I'm thinking of using a disco background for the layout." Bret gazed down at Hillary with an enigmatic smile. "Wasn't it a stroke of luck that I was able to see you here tonight. It gives me a much clearer picture of how to set things up."

Hillary's gaze narrowed at his tone, and she caught the gleam of laughter in his eyes. Luck nothing, she thought suddenly, realizing with certainty that Bret rarely depended on luck. Somehow he had known she would be here tonight, and he had staged the accidental meeting. This layout must be very important to him, she mused, feeling unaccountably miserable. What other reason would he have for seeking her out and dancing with her while he had the obviously willing Charlene Mason hanging all over him?

"See you Monday, Hillary," Bret said easily as he and his lady made to leave.

"Monday?" Chuck repeated when they were once more alone. "Aren't you the fox." His teeth flashed in a grin. "Keeping the famous Mr. Bardoff tucked in your pocket."

"Hardly," she snapped, irritated by his conclusion.

"Our relationship is strictly business. I'm working for his magazine. He's my employer, nothing more."

"Okay, okay." Chuck's grin only widened at her angry denial. "Don't take my head off. It's a natural mistake, and I'm not the only one who made it."

Hillary looked up sharply. "What are you talking about?"

"Sweet Hillary," he explained in a patient tone, "didn't you feel the knives stabbing you in the back when you were dancing with your famous employer?" At her blank stare, he sighed deeply. "You know, even after three years in New York, you're still incredibly naive." The corners of his mouth lifted, and he laid a brotherly hand on her shoulder. "A certain redhead was shooting daggers into you from her green eyes the entire time you were dancing. Why, I expected you to keel over in a pool of blood at any second."

"That's absurd." Hillary swirled the contents of her glass and frowned at them. "I'm sure Miss Mason knew very well Bret's purpose in seeing me was merely for research, just background for his precious layout."

Chuck regarded her thoroughly and shook his head. "As I said before, Hillary, you are incredibly naive."

Chapter 3

Monday morning dawned cool, crisp, and gray. In the office of *Mode,* however, threatening skies were not a factor. Obviously, Hillary decided, Bret had permitted nature to have a tantrum now that shooting had moved indoors.

At his direction, she was placed in the hands of a hairdresser who would assist in the transformation to smooth, competent businesswoman. Jet shoulder-length hair was arranged in a sleek chignon that accented classic bone structure, and the severely tailored lines of the three-piece gray suit, instead of appearing masculine, only heightened Hillary's femininity.

Larry was immersed in camera equipment, lighting, and angles when she entered Bret's office. Giving the room a quick survey, she was forced to admit it was both an elegant and suitable background for the morning's session. She watched with fond amusement as Larry, oblivious to her presence, adjusted lenses and tested meters, muttering to himself.

"The genius at work," a voice whispered close to her ear, and Hillary whirled, finding herself staring into the eyes that had begun to haunt her.

"That's precisely what he is," she retorted, furious with the way her heart began to drum at his nearness.

"Testy this morning, aren't we?" Bret observed with a lifted brow. "Still hungover from the weekend?"

"Certainly not." Dignity wrapped her like a cloak. "I never drink enough to have a hangover."

"Oh, yes, I forgot, the Mr. Hyde syndrome."

"Hillary, there you are." Larry interrupted Hillary's search for a suitable retort. "What took you so long?"

"Sorry, Larry, the hairdresser took quite some time."

The amused gleam in Bret's eyes demanded and received her answer. As their gazes met over Larry's head with the peculiar intimacy of a shared joke, a sweet weakness washed over her, like a soft, gentle wave washing over a waiting shore. Terrified, she dropped her eyes, attempting to dispel the reaction he drew from her without effort.

"Do you always frighten so easily?" Bret's voice was calm, with a hint of mockery, the tone causing her chin to lift in defiance. She glared, helplessly angry with his ability to read her thoughts as if they were written on her forehead. "That's better," he approved, fending off the fire with cool composure. "Anger suits you. It darkens your eyes and puts rose in your cheeks. Spirit is an essential trait for women and—" his mouth lifted at the corner as he paused "—for horses."

She choked and sputtered over the comparison, willing her temper into place with the knowledge that if she lost it she would be powerless against him in a verbal battle. "I suppose that's true," she answered carelessly after swallowing the words that had sprung into her head. "In my observation, men appear to fall short of the physical capacity of one and the mental capacity of the other."

"Well, that hairstyle certainly makes you look competent." Larry turned to study Hillary critically, oblivious to anything that had occurred since he had last spoken. With a sigh of defeat, Hillary gazed at the ceiling for assistance.

"Yes," Bret agreed, keeping his features serious. "The woman executive, very competent, very smart."

"Assertive, aggressive, and ruthless," Hillary interrupted, casting him a freezing look. "I shall emulate you, Mr. Bardoff."

His brows rose fractionally. "That should be fascinating. I'll leave you then to get on with your work, while I get on with mine."

The door closed behind him, and the room was suddenly larger and strangely empty. Hillary shook herself and got to work, attempting to block out all thoughts of Bret Bardoff from her mind.

For the next hour Larry moved around the room, clicking his camera, adjusting the lighting, and calling out directions as Hillary assumed the poses of a busy woman executive.

"That's a wrap in here." He signaled for her to relax, which she did by sinking into a soft leather chair in a casual, if undignified, pose.

"Fiend!" she cried as he snapped the camera once more, capturing her as she sprawled, slouched in the chair, legs stretched out in front of her.

"It'll be a good shot," he claimed with an absent smile. "Weary woman wiped out by woesome work."

"You have a strange sense of humor, Larry," Hillary retorted, not bothering to alter her position. "It comes from having a camera stuck to your face all the time."

"Now, now, Hil, let's not get personal. Heave yourself out of that chair. We're going into the boardroom, and you, my love, can be chairman of the board."

"Chairperson," she corrected, but his mind was already involved with his equipment. Groaning, she stood and left him to his devices.

The remainder of the day's shooting was long and tedious. Dissatisfied with the lighting, Larry spent more than half an hour rearranging and resetting until it met with his approval. After a further hour under hot lights, Hillary felt as fresh as week-old lettuce and was more than ready when Larry called an end to the day's work.

She found herself searching for Bret's lean form as she made her way from the building, undeniably disappointed when there was no sign of him and angry with her own reaction. Walking for several blocks, she breathed in the brisk autumn air, determined to forget the emotions stirred by the tall man with sharp gray eyes. Just a physical attraction, she reasoned, tucking her hands in her pockets and allowing her feet to take her farther down the busy sidewalk. Physical attraction happens all the time; it would pass like a twenty-four-hour virus.

A diversion was what she required, she decided—something to chase him from her mind and set her thoughts back on the track she had laid out for herself. Success in the field she had chosen, independence, security—these were her priorities. There was no room for romantic entanglements. When the time came for settling down, it certainly would not be with a man like Bret Bardoff, but with someone safe, someone who did not set her nerves on end and confuse her at every encounter. Besides, she reminded herself, ignoring the sudden gloom, he wasn't interested in her romantically in any case. He seemed to prefer well-proportioned redheads.

Shooting resumed the next morning, once again in *Mode*'s offices. Today, dressed in a dark blue shirt and boot-length skirt of a lighter shade, Hillary was to take on the role of working girl. The session was to take place in Bret's secretary's office, much to that woman's delight.

"I can't tell you how excited I am, Miss Baxter. I feel like a kid going to her first circus."

Hillary smiled at the young woman whose eyes were alight with anticipation. "I'll admit to feeling like a trained elephant from time to time—and make it Hillary."

"I'm June. This is all routine to you, I suppose." Her head shook, causing chestnut curls to bounce and sway. "But it seems very glamorous and exciting to me." Her eyes drifted to where Larry was setting up for the shooting with customary absorption. "Mr. Newman's a real expert, isn't he? He's been fiddling with all those dials and lenses and lights. He's very attractive. Is he married?"

Hillary laughed, glancing carelessly at Larry. "Only to his Nikon."

"Oh." June smiled, then frowned. "Are you two, ah, I mean, are you involved?"

"Just master and slave," Hillary answered, seeing Larry as an attractive, eligible man for the first time. Looking back at June's appealing face, she smiled in consideration. "You know the old adage, 'The way to a man's heart is through his stomach.' Take my advice. The way to that man's heart is through his lenses. Ask him about f-stops."

Bret emerged from his office. He broke into a slow, lazy smile when he saw Hillary. "Ah, man's best friend, the efficient secretary."

Ignoring the pounding of her heart, Hillary forced her voice into a light tone. "No corporate decisions today. I've been demoted."

"That's the way of the business world." He nodded understandingly. "Executive dining room one day, typing pool the next. It's a jungle out there."

"All set," Larry announced from across the room. "Where's Hillary?" He turned to see the trio watching him and grinned. "Hello, Bret, hi, Hil. All set?"

"Your wish is my command, O master of the thirty-five millimeter," Hillary said, moving to join him.

"Can you type, Hillary?" Bret inquired cheerily. "I'll

give you some letters, and we can kill two birds with one stone."

"Sorry, Mr. Bardoff," she replied, allowing herself to enjoy his smile. "Typewriters and I have a longstanding agreement. I don't pound on them, and they don't pound on me."

"Is it all right if I watch for a while, Mr. Newman?" June requested. "I won't get in the way. Photography just fascinates me."

Larry gave an absent assent, and, after casting his secretary a puzzled look, Bret turned to reenter his office. "I'll need you in a half hour, June—the Brookline contract."

The session went quickly with Larry and Hillary progressing with professional ease. The model followed the photographer's instructions, often anticipating a mood before he spoke. After a time, June disappeared unobtrusively through the heavy doors leading to Bret's office. Neither Hillary nor Larry noticed her silent departure.

Sometime later, Larry lowered his camera and stared fixedly into space. Hillary maintained her silence, knowing from experience this did not signal the end, but a pause while a fresh idea formed in his mind.

"I want to finish up with something here," he muttered, staring through Hillary as if she were intangible. His face cleared with inspiration. He focused his eyes. "I know. Change the ribbon in the typewriter."

"Surely you jest." She began an intense study of her nails.

"No, it'll be good. Go ahead."

"Larry," she protested in patient tones. "I haven't the foggiest notion how to change a ribbon."

"Fake it," Larry suggested.

With a sigh, Hillary seated herself behind the desk and stared at the typewriter.

"Ever harvested wheat, Larry?" she hazarded, attempting to postpone his order. "It's a fascinating process."

"Hillary," he interrupted, drawing his brows together.

With another sigh, she surrendered to artistic temperament. "I don't know how to open it," she muttered, pushing buttons at random. "It has to open, doesn't it?"

"There should be a button or lever under it," Larry returned patiently. "Don't they have typewriters in Kansas?"

"I suppose they do. My sister... Oh!" she cried, and grinned, delighted out of all proportion, like a small child completing a puzzle, when the release was located. Lifting the lid, she frowned intently at the inner workings. "Scalpel," she requested, running a finger over naked keys.

"Keep going, Hil," Larry commanded. "Just pretend you know what you're doing."

She found herself falling into the spirit of things and attacked the thin black ribbon threaded through various guides with enthusiasm. Her smooth brow was puckered in concentration as she forgot the man and his camera and gave herself over to the job of dislodging ribbon from machine. The more she unraveled, the longer the ribbon became, growing with a life of its own. Absently, she brushed a hand across her cheek, smearing it with black ink.

An enormous, ever-growing heap tangled around her fingers. Realization dawned that she was fighting a losing battle. With a grin for Larry, she flourished the mess of ribbon as he clicked a final picture.

"Terrific," he answered her grin as he lowered his camera. "A classic study in ineptitude."

"Thanks, friend, and if you use any of those shots, I'll sue." Dumping the mass of loose ribbon on the open typewriter, she expelled a long breath. "I'll leave it to you to explain to June how this catastrophe came about. I'm finished."

"Absolutely." Bret's voice came from behind, and Hillary whirled in the chair to see both him and June staring at the chaos on the desk. "If you ever give up modeling, steer clear of office work. You're a disaster."

Hillary attempted to resent his attitude, but one glance at the havoc she had wrought brought on helpless giggles. "Well, Larry, get us out of this one. We've been caught red-handed at the scene of the crime."

Bret closed the distance between them with lithe grace and gingerly lifted one of Hillary's hands. "Black-handed, I'd say." Putting his other hand under her chin, he smiled in the lazy way that caused Hillary's reluctant heart to perform a series of somersaults. "There's quite a bit of evidence on that remarkable face as well."

She shook off the sweet weakness invading her and peered down at her hands. "Good Lord, how did I manage that? Will it come off?" She addressed her question to June, who assured her soap and water would do the trick. "Well, I'm going to wash away the evidence, and I'm leaving you—" she nodded to Larry "—to make amends for the damage." She encompassed June's desk with a sweeping gesture. "Better do some fast talking, old man," she added in a stage whisper, and gave June the present of her famous smile.

Reaching the door before her, Bret opened it and took a few steps down the long hall beside her. "Setting up a romance for my secretary, Hillary?"

"Could be," she returned enigmatically. "Larry could do with more than cameras and darkrooms in his life."

"And what could you use in yours, Hillary?" His question was soft, putting a hand on her arm and turning her to face him.

"I've…I've got everything I need," she stammered, feeling like a pinned butterfly under his direct gaze.

"Everything?" he repeated, keeping her eyes locked on his. "Pity I've an appointment, or we could go into this in more detail." Pulling her close, his lips brushed hers, then formed a crooked smile that was devastatingly appealing. "Go wash your face—you're a fine mess." Turning, he strode down the hall, leaving Hillary to deal with a mixture of frustration and unaccustomed longing.

She spent her free afternoon shopping, a diversionary tactic for soothing jangled nerves, but her mind constantly floated back to a brief touch of lips, a smile lighting gray eyes. The warmth seemed to linger on her mouth, stirring her emotions, arousing her senses. A cold blast of wind swirling in her face brought her back to reality. Cursing her treacherous imagination, she hailed a cab. She would have to hurry in order to make her dinner date with Lisa.

It was after five when Hillary entered her apartment and dumped her purchases on a chair in the bedroom. She released the latch on the front door for Lisa's benefit and made her way to the bath, filling the tub with hot, fragrant water. She intended to soak for a full twenty minutes. Just as she stepped from the tub and grabbed a towel, the bell sounded at the front door.

"Come on in, Lisa. Either you're early, or I'm late." Draping the towel saronglike around her slim body, she walked from the room, the scent of strawberries clinging to her shining skin. "I'll be ready in a minute. I got carried away in the tub. My feet were…" She stopped dead in her tracks, because instead of the small, blond Lisa, she was confronted by the tall, lean figure of Bret Bardoff.

"Where did you come from?" Hillary demanded when she located her voice.

"Originally or just now?" he countered, smiling at her confusion.

"I thought you were Lisa."

"I got that impression."

"What are you doing here?"

"Returning this." He held up a slim gold pen. "I assumed it was yours. The initials H.B. are engraved on it."

"Yes, it's mine," she concurred, frowning at it. "I must have dropped it from my bag. You needn't have bothered. I could have gotten it tomorrow."

"I thought you might have been looking for it." His eyes roamed over the figure scantily clad in the bath towel and lingered on her smooth legs, then rested a moment on the swell of her breast. "Besides, it was well worth the trip."

Hillary's eyes dropped down to regard her state of disarray and widened in shock. Color stained her cheeks as his eyes laughed at her, and she turned and ran from the room. "I'll be back in a minute."

Hastily, she pulled on chocolate brown cords and a beige mohair sweater, tugged a quick brush through her hair, and applied a touch of makeup with a deft hand. Taking a deep breath, she returned to the living room, attempting to assume a calm front that she was far from feeling. Bret was seated comfortably on the sofa, smoking a cigarette with the air of someone completely at home.

"Sorry to keep you waiting," she said politely, fighting back the embarrassment that engulfed her. "It was kind of you to take the trouble to return the pen to me." He handed it to her and she placed it on the low mahogany table. "May I...would you..." She bit her lip in frustration, finding her poise had vanished. "Can I get you a drink? Or maybe you're in a hurry—"

"I'm in no hurry," he answered, ignoring her frown. "Scotch, neat, if you have it."

Her frown deepened. "I may have. I'll have to check." She retreated to the kitchen, searching through cupboards for her supply of rarely used liquor. He had followed her, and she turned, noting with a quickening of pulse how his presence seemed to dwarf the small room. She felt an intimacy that was both exciting and disturbing. She resumed her search, all too conscious of his casual stance as he leaned against the refrigerator, hands in pockets.

"Here." Triumphantly, she brandished the bottle. "Scotch."

"So it is."

"I'll get you a glass. Neat, you said?" She pushed at her hair. "That's with no ice, right?"

"You'd make a marvelous bartender," he returned, taking both bottle and glass and pouring the liquid himself.

"I'm not much of a drinker," she muttered.

"Yes, I remember—a two-drink limit. Shall we go sit down?" He took her hand with the usual familiarity, and her words of protest died. "A very nice place, Hillary," he commented as they seated themselves on the sofa. "Open, friendly, colorful. Do the living quarters reflect the tenant?"

"So they say."

"Friendliness is an admirable trait, but you should know better than to leave your door unlatched. This is New York, not a farm in Kansas."

"I was expecting someone."

"But you got someone unexpected." He looked into her eyes, then casually swept the length of her. "What do you think would have happened if someone else had come across that beautiful body of yours draped in a very insufficient towel?" The blush was immediate and impossible to control, and she dropped her eyes. "You should keep your door locked, Hillary. Not every man would let you escape as I did."

"Yes, O mighty emperor," Hillary retorted before she could bite her tongue, and his eyes narrowed dangerously. He captured her with a swift movement, but whatever punishment he had in mind was postponed by the ringing of the phone. Jumping up in relief, Hillary hurried to answer.

"Lisa, hi. Where are you?"

"Sorry, Hillary." The answering voice was breathless. "The most wonderful thing happened. I hope you don't mind, but I have to beg off tonight."

"Of course not—what happened?"

"Mark asked me to have dinner with him."

"So you took my advice and tripped him, right?"

"More or less."

"Oh, Lisa," Hillary cried in amused disbelief, "you didn't really!"

"Well, no," she admitted. "We were both carrying all these law books and ran smack into each other. What a beautiful mess."

"I get the picture." Her laughter floated through the room. "It really has more class than a mugging."

"You don't mind about tonight?"

"Do you think I'd let a pizza stand in the way of true love?" Hillary answered. "Float along and have fun. I'll see you later."

She replaced the receiver and turned to find Bret regarding her with open curiosity. "I must admit that was the most fascinating one-ended conversation I've ever heard." She flashed him a smile with full candlepower and told him briefly of her friend's long unrequited love affair.

"So your solution was to land the poor guy on his face at her feet," he concluded.

"It got his attention."

"Now you're stood up. A pizza, was it?"

"My secret's out," she said, carefully seating herself in a chair across from him. "I hope I can trust you never to breathe a word of this, but I am a pizza junkie. If I don't have one at well-ordered intervals, I go into a frenzy. It's not a pretty sight."

"Well, we can't have you foaming at the mouth, can we?" He set down his empty glass and stood with a fluid motion. "Fetch a coat, I'll indulge you."

"Oh, really, there's no need," she began with quick panic.

"For heaven's sake, let's not go through this again. Get a coat and come on," he commanded, pulling her from her chair. "I could do with some food myself."

She found herself doing his bidding, slipping on a short suede jacket as he picked up his own brown leather. "Got your keys?" he questioned, reengaging the latch and propelling her through the door.

Soon they were seated in the small Italian restaurant that Hillary had indicated. The small table was covered with the inevitable red and white checkered cloth, a candle flickering in its wine bottle holder.

"Well, Hillary, what will you have?"

"Pizza."

"Yes, I know that," he countered with a smile. "Anything on it?"

"Extra cholesterol."

White teeth flashed as he grinned at her. "Is that all?"

"I don't want to overdo—these things can get out of hand."

"Some wine?"

"I don't know if my system can handle it." She considered, then shrugged. "Well, why not, you only live once."

"Too true." He signaled the waiter and gave their order. "You, however," he continued when they were once more alone, "look as though you had lived before. You are a reincarnation of an Indian princess. I bet they called you Pocahontas when you were a kid."

"Not if they were smart," Hillary returned. "I scalped a boy once for just that."

"Do tell?" Bret's attention was caught, and he leaned forward, his head on his hands as his elbows rested on the table. "Please elaborate."

"All right, if you can handle such a bloodthirsty subject over dinner." Pushing back her hair with both hands, she mirrored his casual position. "There was this boy, Martin Collins. I was madly in love with him, but he preferred Jessie Winfield, a cute little blond number with soulful brown eyes. I was mad with jealousy. I was also too tall, skinny, all eyes and elbows, and eleven years old. I passed them one day, devastated because he was carrying her books, and he called out 'Head for the hills, it's Pocahontas.' That did it, I was a woman scorned. I planned my revenge. I went home and got the small scissors my mother used for mending, painted my face with her best lipstick, and returned to stalk my prey.

"I crept up behind him stealthily, patiently waiting for the right moment. Springing like a panther, I knocked my quarry to the ground, holding him down with my body and cutting off as much hair as I could grab. He screamed, but I showed no mercy. Then my brothers came and dragged me off and he escaped, running like the coward he was, home to his mother."

Bret's laughter rang out as he threw back his head. "What a monster you must have been!"

"I paid for it." She lifted the glass of wine that Bret had poured during her story. "I got the tanning of my life, but it was worth it. Martin wore a hat for weeks."

Their pizza arrived, and through the meal their conversation was more companionable and relaxed than Hillary would have believed possible. When the last piece was consumed, Bret leaned back and regarded her seriously.

"I'd never have believed you could eat like that."

She grinned, relaxed by the combination of wine, good food, and easy company. "I don't often, but when I do, I'm exceptional."

"You're a constant amazement. I never know what to expect. A study of contradictions."

"Isn't that why you hired me, Bret?" She used his name for the first time voluntarily without conscious thought. "For my versatility?"

He smiled, lifted his glass to his lips, and left her question unanswered.

Hillary felt her earlier nervousness return as they walked down the carpeted hall toward her apartment. Determined to remain calm, she bent her head to fish out her keys, using the time to assume a calm veneer.

"Would you like to come in for coffee?"

He took the keys from her hand, unlocked the door, and gave her a slow smile. "I thought you didn't drink coffee."

"I don't, but everyone else in the world does, so I keep some instant."

"With the Scotch, no doubt," he said leading her into the apartment.

Removing her jacket, Hillary assumed the role of hostess. "Sit down. I'll have coffee out in a minute."

He had shed his own coat, carelessly dropping it down over the arm of a chair. Once more she was aware of the strong build beneath the dark blue rib-knit sweater and close-fitting slacks. She turned and made for the kitchen.

Her movements were deft and automatic as she set the kettle on the burner and removed cups and saucers from cupboards. She set a small sugar bowl and creamer on the glass and wicker tray, and prepared tea for herself and coffee for the man in her living room. She moved with natural grace to the low table, to set the ladened tray down. She smiled with professional ease at the tall man who stood across the room leafing casually through her collection of record albums.

"Quite an assortment." He addressed her from where he stood, looking so at ease and blatantly masculine that Hillary felt her veneer cracking rapidly and fought back a flutter of panic. "Typical of you though," he went on, sparing her from the necessity of immediate comment. "Chopin when you're romantic, Denver when you're homesick, B. B. King when you're down, McCartney when you're up."

"You sound like you know me very well." She felt a strange mixture of amusement and resentment that he had pinpointed her mood music with such uncanny accuracy.

"Not yet," he corrected, putting down an album and coming over to join her. "But I'm working on it."

Suddenly, he was very close, and there was an urgent need in Hillary to be on a more casual footing. "Your coffee's getting cold." She spoke quickly and bent to remove the clutter from the tray, dropping a spoon in her agitation. They bent to retrieve it simultaneously, his strong, lean fingers closing over her fine-boned hand. At the contact a current of electricity shot down her arm and spread through her body, and her eyes darkened to midnight. She raised her face to his.

There were no words as their eyes met, and she realized the inevitability of the movement. She knew they had been drifting steadily toward this since the first day in Larry's studio. There was a basic attraction between them, an undefinable need she did not pause to question as he lifted her to her feet, and she stepped into his arms.

His lips were warm and gentle on hers as he kissed her slowly, then with increasing pressure, his tongue parted her lips, and his arms tightened around her, crushing her breasts against the hardness of his chest. Her arms twined around his neck. She responded as she had never responded to any man before. The thought ran through her clouded brain that no one had ever kissed her like this, no one had ever held her like this. Then all thought was drowned in a tidal wave of passion.

She made no resistance as she felt herself lowered onto the cushions of the couch, her mouth still the captive of his. The weight of his body pushed hers deep into the sofa as his legs slid between hers, making no secret of his desire. His mouth began to roam, exploring the smooth skin of her neck. The fire of a new and ageless need raged through her veins. She felt the thudding of a heart—hers or his, she could not tell—as his lips caressed her throat and face before meeting hers with possessing hunger. His hand moved under her sweater to cup the breast that swelled under his touch. She sighed and moved under him.

She was lost in a blaze of longing such as she had never known, responding with a passion she had kept buried until that moment, as his lips and hands moved with expertise over her warm and willing body.

His hands moved to the flatness of her stomach, and when she felt his fingers on the snap of her pants, she began to struggle against him. Her protests were ignored, his mouth devouring hers, then laying a trail of heat along her throat.

"Bret, please don't. You have to stop."

He lifted his head from the curve of her neck to look into the deep pools of her eyes, huge now with fear and desire. His own breathing was ragged. She knew a sharp fear that the decision to stop or go on would be taken out of her hands.

"Hillary," he murmured, and bent to claim her lips again, but she turned her head and pushed against him.

"No, Bret, no more."

A long breath escaped from his lips as he removed his body from hers, standing before removing a cigarette from the gold case he had left on the table. Hillary sat up, clutching her hands together in her lap, keeping her head lowered to avoid his eyes.

"I knew you were many things, Hillary," he said after

expelling a swift and violent stream of smoke. "I never thought you were a tease."

"I'm not!" she protested, her head snapping up at the harshness of his tone. "That's unfair. Just because I stopped, just because I didn't let you…" Her voice broke. She was filled with confusion and embarrassment, and a perverse longing to be held again in his arms.

"You are not a child," he began with an anger that caused her lips to tremble. "What is the usual outcome when two people kiss like that, when a woman allows a man to touch her like that?" His eyes were dark with barely suppressed fury, and she sat mutely, having been unprepared for the degree his temper could reach. "You wanted me as much as I wanted you. Stop playing games. We've both been well aware that this would happen eventually. You're a grown woman. Stop behaving like an innocent young girl."

The remark scored, and the telltale flush crept to her cheeks before she could lower her lashes to conceal painful discomfort. Bret gaped at her, anger struggling with stunned disbelief. "Good heavens, you've never been with a man before, have you?"

Hillary shut her eyes in humiliation, and she remained stubbornly silent.

"How is that possible?" he asked in a voice tinged with reluctant amusement. "How does a woman reach the ripe old age of twenty-four with looks like yours and remain as pure as the driven snow?"

"It hasn't been all that difficult," she muttered, and looked anywhere in the room but at him. "I don't normally let things get so out of hand." She made a small, helpless shrug.

"You might let a man know of your innocence before things get out of hand," he advised caustically, crushing out his cigarette with undue force.

"Maybe I should paint a red V for virgin on my fore-head—then there'd be no confusion." Hillary flared, lifting her chin in bold defiance.

"You know, you're gorgeous when you're angry." He spoke coolly, but the steel vibrated in his tone, casual elegance wrapped around a volatile force. "Watch your-self, or I'll have another go at changing your status."

"I don't think you would ever stoop to forcing a woman," she retorted as he moved to pick up his jacket.

Pausing, he turned back to her, gray eyes narrow-ing into slits as he hauled her to her feet, possessing her again until her struggles had transformed into limp clinging.

"Don't count on it." His voice was deadly soft as he gave her a firm nudge back onto the couch. "I make a point of getting what I want." His eyes moved lazily over her slim body, pausing on the lips still soft from his. "Make no mistake," he went on as she began to tremble under his prolonged gaze. "I could have you here and now without forcing, but—" he moved to the door "—I can afford to wait."

Chapter 4

For the next few weeks shooting moved along with few complications. Larry was enthusiastic about the progress that was being made and brought Hillary a file of work prints so that she could view the fruits of their labor.

Studying the pictures with a professional objectivity, she admitted they were excellent, perhaps the best work Larry and she had done together or separately. There was a touch of genius in his choice of angles and lighting, using shadows and filters with a master hand. Added to this was Hillary's ability to assume varied roles. The pictures were already beginning to form a growing study of womanhood. They were nearly halfway through the planned shooting. If everything continued to go as well, they would be finished ahead of schedule. Bret was now planning a crash publication, which would put the issue on the stands in early spring.

Sessions would resume following the Thanksgiving weekend, while the art director and staff, with Bret's approval, began the selection of what would be printed in the final copy. Hillary was grateful for the time off, not only for the rest, but for the separation from the man who filled her thoughts and invaded her dreams.

She had expected some constraint between them when she returned to work after their evening together, but Bret had greeted her in his usual way, so casually, in fact, that she thought for a moment that she had imagined the feel of his lips on hers. There was no mention of their meal together or the scene that followed, while he slipped with apparent ease into the partly professional, partly mocking attitude he invariably directed toward her.

It was not as simple a task for Hillary to mirror his nonchalance after the emotions he had awakened in her—emotions that had lain sleeping within her until his touch had brought them to life—but outwardly she displayed a casualness at odds with her inner turmoil.

All in all, the remainder of the shooting time passed easily, and if Larry was forced to admonish her from time to time to relax and not to scowl, he was characteristically preoccupied and saw nothing amiss.

Hillary stood staring from the window of her apartment, her state of mind as bleak as the scene that greeted her. The late November sky was like lead, casting a depressing spell over the city, the buildings and skyscrapers taking on a dismal hue. Leaves had long since deserted the trees, leaving them naked and cheerless, and the grass, where sidewalks made room for it, had lost its healthy green tone, looking instead a sad, dreary yellow. The somberness of the day suited her mood precisely.

A sudden wave of homesickness washed over her, a strong desire for golden wheat fields. Moving to the stereo, she placed a Denver album on the turntable, halting in her movements when the image of Bret standing in the very spot she now occupied swept through her mind. The memory of the hardness of his body against hers and the intimacy briefly shared filled her with a painful longing, replacing homesickness. With a flash of insight, she realized that her attraction for him was more than physical. She switched on the player, filling the room with soft music.

Falling in love had not been in her plans, she reminded herself, and falling for Bret was out of the question, now or ever. That road would lead nowhere but to disaster and humiliation. But she could not quiet the voice that hammered in her brain telling her it was already too late. She sank down in a chair, confusion and depression settling over her like a fog.

It had grown late when Hillary let herself into her apartment after having joined Lisa and Mark for Thanksgiving dinner. The meal had been superb, but she had hidden her lack of appetite under the guise of keeping a careful watch on her figure. She had hidden her depression and concentrated on appearing normal and content. As she closed the door behind her, she breathed a sigh of relief, at last removing the frozen smile and relaxing. Before she could move to the closet to hang up her coat, the phone rang.

"Hello." Her voice reflected her weariness and annoyance.

"Hello, Hillary. Been out on the town?"

There was no need for the caller to identify himself. Hillary recognized Bret immediately, glad that the thumping of her heart was not audible over the wire.

"Hello, Mr. Bardoff." She schooled her voice to coolness. "Do you always call your employees so late?"

"Grouchy, aren't we?" He seemed unperturbed. The thrill of hearing his voice warred with irritation at his composure. "Did you have a nice day?"

"Lovely," she lied. "I'm just home from having dinner with a friend. And you?"

"Spectacular. I'm very fond of turkey."

"Did you call to compare menus or was there something on your mind?" Her voice grew sharp at the picture of Bret and Charlene enjoying a beautifully catered dinner in elegant surroundings.

"Oh, yes, I've something on my mind. To begin with, I had thought to share a holiday drink with you, if you still have that bottle of Scotch."

"Oh." Her voice cracked, panic-filled. Clearing her throat, she stumbled on. "No, I mean, yes, I have the Scotch, but it's late and..."

"Afraid?" he interrupted quietly.

"Certainly not," she snapped. "I'm just tired. I'm on my way to bed."

"Oh, really?" She could hear the amusement in his voice.

"Honestly." To her disgust, she felt herself blushing. "Must you continually make fun of me?"

"Sorry." His apology lacked conviction. "But you will insist on taking yourself seriously. Very well, I won't dip into your liquor supply." Pausing, he added, "Tonight. I'll see you Monday, Hillary, sleep well."

"Good night," she murmured, filled with regret as she replaced the receiver. Glancing around the room, she felt a swift desire to have him there, filling the emptiness with the excitement of his presence. She sighed and pushed at her hair, realizing she could hardly call him back and issue the invitation had she known where to reach him.

It's better this way, she rationalized, better to avoid him whenever possible. If I'm going to get over this infatuation, distance is my best medicine. He'll tire soon enough without encouragement. I'm sure he gets an ample supply of it from other quarters. Charlene is more his style, she went on, digging at the wound. I could never compete with her sophistication, I haven't the knack. She probably speaks French and knows about wines and can drink more than one glass of champagne before she starts to babble.

On Saturday Hillary met Lisa for lunch, hoping the short outing would boost her flagging spirits. The elegant restaurant was crowded. Spotting Lisa at a small table, Hillary waved and made her way through the room.

"Sorry, I know I'm late," Hillary apologized, picking up the menu set before her. "Traffic was dreadful, and I had a terrible time getting a cab. Winter's definitely on its way. It's freezing out there."

"Is it?" Lisa grinned. "It feels like spring to me."

"Love has apparently thrown you off balance. But," she added, "even if it's affected your brain, it's done wonders for the rest of you. I believe you could glow in the dark."

The blissful smile that lighted Lisa's face was a heart-catching sight, and Hillary's depression evaporated.

"I know my feet haven't touched the ground in weeks. I guess you're sick of watching me float around."

"Don't be silly. It's given me a tremendous lift watching you light up like a neon sign."

The two women ordered their meal, slipping into the easy camaraderie they enjoyed.

"I really should find a friend with warts and a hooked nose," Lisa commented.

Hillary's fork paused on its journey to her mouth. "Come again?"

"The most fascinating man just came in. I might as well be invisible for all the attention he paid me. He was too busy staring at you."

"He's probably just looking for someone he knows."

"He's got someone he knows hanging on to his arm like an appendage," Lisa declared, staring boldly at the couple across the room. "His attention, however, is riveted on you. No, don't turn around," she hissed as Hillary started to turn her head. "Oh, good grief, he's coming over. Quick," she whispered desperately, "look natural."

"You're the one standing on her head, Lisa," Hillary returned calmly, amused by her friend's rapid capitulation.

"Well, Hillary, we just can't keep away from each other, can we?"

Hillary heard the deep voice and her wide eyes met Lisa's startled ones before she looked up to meet Bret's crooked smile. "Hello." Her voice was oddly breathless. Her glance took in the shapely redhead on his arm. "Hello, Miss Mason, nice to see you again," she said quietly.

Charlene merely nodded. From the expression in her frosty green eyes, it was apparent she couldn't have disagreed more. There was a short pause. Bret raised his brow in inquiry.

"Lisa MacDonald, Charlene Mason and Bret Bardoff," Hillary introduced quickly.

"Oh, you're *Mode* magazine," Lisa blurted out, her eyes shining with excitement. Hillary looked in vain for a hole to open up and swallow her.

"More or less."

Hillary watched, helpless, as Bret turned his most charming smile on Lisa.

"I'm a great fan of your magazine, Mr. Bardoff," Lisa bubbled. She appeared to be unaware of the darts shooting at her from Charlene's narrowed eyes. "I can barely wait for this big layout of Hillary's. It must be very exciting."

"It's been quite an experience so far." He turned to Hillary with an annoying grin. "Don't you agree, Hillary?"

"Quite an experience," she agreed carelessly, forcing her eyes to remain level.

"Bret," Charlene interrupted. "We really must get to our table and let these girls get on with their lunch." Her eyes swept both Hillary and Lisa, dismissing them as beneath notice.

"Nice to have met you, Lisa. See you later, Hillary." His lazy smile had Hillary's heart pounding in its now familiar way. But she managed to murmur goodbye. Nervously, she reached for her tea, hoping Lisa would not discuss the encounter.

Lisa stared at Bret's retreating back for several seconds. "Wow," she breathed, turning huge brown eyes on Hillary. "You didn't tell me he was so terrific! I was literally liquified when he smiled at me."

Dear heaven, Hillary thought wearily, does he affect all women that way? Aloud, she spoke with mock censure. "Shame on you—your heart's supposed to be taken."

"It is," Lisa affirmed. "But I'm still a woman." Looking at Hillary, she went on shrewdly, "Don't tell me he leaves you unmoved. We know each other too well."

A deep sigh escaped. "I'm not immune to Mr. Bardoff's devastating charm, but I'll have to develop some kind of antidote during the next couple of months."

"Don't you think the interest might be mutual? You're not without substantial charm yourself."

"You did notice the redhead clinging to him like ivy on a brick wall?"

"Couldn't miss her." Lisa grimaced. "I had the feeling she expected me to rise and curtsy. Who is she, anyway? The Queen of Hearts?"

"Perfect match for the emperor," Hillary murmured.

"What?"

"Nothing. Are you done? Let's get out of here." Rising without waiting for an answer, Hillary gathered her purse and the two women left the restaurant.

The following Monday Hillary walked to work. She lifted her face to the first snow of the season. Cold flakes drifted to kiss her upturned face, and she felt a thrill of anticipation watching soft white swirl from the lead-colored sky. Snow brought memories of home, sleigh rides, and snow battles. Sluggish traffic was powerless against her mood of excitement, and Hillary arrived at Larry's studio as bright and exuberant as a child.

"Hi, old man. How was your holiday?" Wrapped in a calf-length coat, a matching fur hat pulled low over her head, and cheeks and eyes glowing with the combination of cold and excitement, she was outrageously beautiful.

Larry paused in his lighting adjustment to greet her with a smile. "Look what the first snow blew in. You're an ad for winter vacations."

"You're incorrigible." She slipped out of her outdoor clothing and wrinkled her nose. "You see everything cropped and printed."

"Occupational hazard. June says my eye for a picture is fascinating," he added smugly.

"*June* says?" Delicate brows rose inquiringly.

"Well, yeah, I've, uh, been teaching her a little about photography."

"I see." The tone was ironic.

"She's, well, she's interested in cameras."

"Ah, her interest is limited to shutter speeds and wide-angle lenses," Hillary agreed with a wise nod.

"Come on, Hil," Larry muttered, and began to fiddle with dials.

Gliding over, she hugged him soundly. "Kiss me, you fox. I knew you had it in you somewhere."

"Come on, Hil," he repeated, disentangling himself. "What are you doing here so early? You've got half an hour."

"Amazing, you noticed the time." She batted her eyes, received a scowl, and subsided. "I thought I might look over the work prints."

"Over there." He indicated his overloaded desk in the back corner of the room. "Go on now and let me finish."

"Yes, master." She retreated to search out the file filled with the prints of the layout. After a few moment's study, she drew out one of herself on the tennis court. "I want a copy of this," she called to him. "I look fiercely competitive." Receiving no response, she glanced over, seeing him once more totally involved and oblivious to her presence. "Certainly, Hillary, my dear," she answered for him. "Anything you want. Look at that stance," she continued with deep enthusiasm, glancing back at the picture in her hands. "The perfect form and intense concentration of a champion. Look out, Wimbledon, here I come. You'll tear them apart, Hil." She again assumed Larry's role. "Thanks, Larry. All that talent and beauty too. Please, Larry, you're embarrassing me."

"They lock people up for talking to themselves," a deep voice whispered in her ear. Hillary jumped. The picture dropped from her hands to the pile on the desk. "Nervous, too—that's a bad sign."

She whirled and found herself face to face with Bret—

so close, in fact, she took an instinctive step in retreat. The action did not go unnoticed, and the corner of his mouth twitched into a disarmingly crooked smile.

"Don't creep up on me like that."

"Sorry, but you were so engrossed in your dialogue." His shoulders moved eloquently, and he allowed his voice to trail away.

A reluctant smile hovered on Hillary's lips. "Sometimes Larry lets the conversation drag a mite, and I'm obliged to carry him." She gestured with a slender hand. "Just look at that. He doesn't even know you're here."

"Mmm, perhaps I should take advantage of his preoccupation." He tucked a silky strand of hair behind her ear. The warmth of his fingers shot through her as he made the disturbingly gentle gesture, and her pulse began to jump at an alarming rate.

"Oh, hi, Bret. When did you get in?"

At Larry's words, Hillary let out a sigh, unsure whether it was born of relief or frustration.

December was slipping slowly by. Progress on the layout was more advanced than expected, and it appeared that actual shooting would be completed before Christmas. Hillary's contract with Bret ran through March, and she speculated on what she would do when the shooting stage was over and she was no longer needed. It was possible that Bret would release her, though she admitted this was highly unlikely. He would hardly wish her to work for a competitor before his pet project was on the stands.

Maybe he'll find some other work for me through

the next couple of months, she theorized during a short break in a session. Or maybe she could be idle for a time. Oddly, the latter prospect appealed to her, and this surprised her. She enjoyed her work, didn't she? Hard work, yes, but rarely boring. Of course she enjoyed her work. It was enough for her, and she intended to keep it first in her life for the next few years. After that, she could retire if she liked or take a long vacation, travel— whatever. Then, when everything was in order, there would be time for a serious romance. She'd find some- one nice, someone safe, someone she could marry and settle down with. That was her plan, and it made per- fect sense. Only now, when thought through, it sounded horribly cold and dull.

Larry's studio was more crowded than usual during the second week of December. This particular morn- ing, voices and bodies mingled in the room in delightful chaos. In this shooting, Hillary was sharing the spot- light with an eight-month-old boy as she portrayed the young mother.

A small section of the room was set to resemble part of a living area. When Hillary emerged from the hair- dresser's hands, Larry was busy double-checking his equipment. Bret worked with him, discussing ideas for the session, and she chided herself for staring at his strong, lean back.

Leaving the men to their duties, she went over to meet the young mother and the child who would be hers for a few minutes in front of the camera. She was both sur- prised and amused by the baby's resemblance to her.

Andy, as his mother introduced him, had a tuft of hair as dark and shining as Hillary's, and his eyes, though not as deep as hers, were startlingly blue. She would be taken without question for his mother by any stranger.

"Do you know how hard it was to find a child with your looks?" Bret asked, approaching from across the room to where Hillary sat with Andy on her lap. Bret stopped in front of her as she laughed and bounced the baby on her knee, and both woman and child raised deep blue eyes. "A person could be struck blind by all that brilliance. Perhaps you two should turn down the wattage."

"Isn't he beautiful?" Her voice was warm as she rubbed her cheeks against the soft down of his hair.

"Spectacular," he agreed. "He could be yours."

A shadow clouded over dark blue, and Hillary lowered her lashes on the sudden longing his words aroused. "Yes, the resemblance is amazing. Are we ready?"

"Yes."

"Well, partner." She stood and rested Andy on her hip. "Let's get to work."

"Just play with him," Larry instructed. "Do what comes naturally. What we're looking for is spontaneity." He looked down at the round face, and Andy's eyes met his levelly. "I think he understands me."

"Of course," Hillary agreed with a toss of her head. "He's a very bright child."

"We'll keep the shots candid and hope he responds to you. We can only work with children a few minutes at a time."

And so they began, with the two dark heads bent near

each other as they sat on the carpeted area with Hillary building alphabet blocks and Andy gleefully destroying her efforts. Soon both were absorbed in the game and each other, paying scant attention to Larry's movements or the soft click of the camera. Hillary lay on her stomach, feet in the air, constructing yet another tower for ultimate demolition. The child reached out, diverted by a strand of silky hair. His stubby fingers curled around the softness, tugging on it and bringing it to his mouth wrapped in a small fist.

Rolling on her back, she lifted the child over her head, and he gurgled in delight at the new game. Setting him on her stomach, he soon became enchanted by the pearl buttons on her pale green blouse. She watched his concentration, tracing his features with her fingertip. Again, she felt the pull of sudden longing. She lifted the baby over her body, making the sounds of a plane as she swayed him over her. Andy squealed in delight and she stood him on her stomach, letting him bounce to his own music.

She stood with him, swinging him in a circle before hugging him against her. This is what I want, she realized suddenly, holding the child closer. A child of my own, tiny arms around my neck, a child with the man I love. She closed her eyes as she rubbed her cheek against Andy's round one. When she opened them again, she found herself staring up into Bret's intense gaze.

She held her eyes level a moment as it drifted over her quietly that this was the man she loved, the man whose child she wanted to feel in her arms. She had known the truth for some time, but had refused to acknowledge it. Now, there was no denying it.

Andy's none-too-gentle tug on her hair broke the spell, and Hillary turned away, shaken by what she had just been forced to admit to herself. This was not what she had planned. How could this happen? She needed time to think, time to sort things out. Right now she felt too confused.

She was profoundly relieved when Larry signaled the finish. With a supreme effort, Hillary kept her professional smile in place while inside she trembled at her new awareness.

"Outstanding," Larry declared. "You two work together like old friends."

Not work, Hillary corrected silently, a fantasy. She had been acting out a fantasy. Perhaps her entire career was a fantasy, perhaps her entire life. A hysterical giggle bubbled inside her, and she choked it back. She could not afford to make a fool of herself now. She could not allow herself to think about the feelings running through her or the questions buzzing inside her brain.

"It's going to take some time to break down and set up for the next segment, Hil." Larry consulted his watch. "Go grab a bite before you change. Give it an hour."

Hillary assented with a wave of relief at the prospect of some time alone.

"I'll go with you."

"Oh, no," she protested, picking up her coat and hurrying out. His brow lifted at her frantic tone. "I mean, don't bother. You must have work to do. You must have to get back to your office or something."

"Yes, my work never ceases," he acknowledged with a heavy dose of mockery. "But once in a while I have to eat."

He took her coat to help her with it. His hands rested on her shoulders, their warmth seeping through the material and burning her skin, causing her to stiffen defensively. His fingers tightened and he turned her to face him.

"It was not my intention to have *you* for lunch, Hillary." The words were soft, at odds with the temper darkening his eyes. "Will you never cease to be suspicious of me?"

The streets were clear, but there was a light covering of white along the sidewalks and on the cars parked along the curb. Hillary felt trapped in the closed car sitting so close to the man who drove, long fingers closed over the steering wheel of the Mercedes. He skirted Central Park, and she endeavored to ease her tension and slow the incessant drumming of her heart.

"Look, it's beautiful, isn't it?" She indicated the trees, their bare branches now robed in white, glittering as if studded with diamonds. "I love the snow," she chattered on, unable to bear the silence. "Everything seems clean and fresh and friendly. It makes it seem more like..."

"Home?" he supplied.

"Yes," she said weakly, retreating from his penetrating gaze.

Home, she thought. Home could be anywhere with this man. But she must not reveal her weakness. He must never know the love that rushed through her, tossing her heart like the winds of a tornado that swept through Kansas in late spring.

Sitting in a small booth, Hillary babbled about whatever innocuous subject came to mind. Chattering to avoid a lull where he might glimpse the secret she held within her, securely locked like a treasure in a fortress.

"Are you okay, Hillary?" Bret asked suddenly when she paused to take a breath. "You've been very jumpy lately." His eyes were sharp and probing, and for a terrifying moment Hillary feared they would penetrate her mind and read the secret written there.

"Sure, I am." Her voice was admirably calm. "I'm just excited about the layout." She grasped at the straw of an excuse. "We'll be finished soon, and the issue will be on the stands. I'm anxious about the reception."

"If it's only business that bothers you," he said abruptly, "I believe I'm qualified to predict the reaction will be tremendous." His eyes reached out and held hers. "You'll be a sensation, Hillary. Offers will come pouring in—magazines, television, products for your endorsement. You'll be in a position to pick and choose."

"Oh" was all that she could manage.

His brows knitted dangerously. "Doesn't it excite you? Isn't that what you've always wanted?" he asked brusquely.

"Of course it is," she stated with a great deal more enthusiasm than she was feeling. "I'd have to be demented not to be thrilled, and I'm grateful for the opportunity you gave me."

"Save your gratitude." He cut her off curtly. "This project has been a result of teamwork. Whatever you gain from it, you've earned." He drew out his wallet. "If you're finished, I'll drop you back before I return to the office."

She nodded mutely, unable to comprehend what she had said to arouse his anger.

The final phase of shooting was underway. Hillary changed in the small room off Larry's main studio. Catching sight of her reflection in the full-length mirror, she held her breath. She had thought the negligee lovely but uninspired when she had lifted it from its box, but now, as it swirled around her, she was awed by its beauty. White and filmy, it floated around her slim curves, falling in gentle folds to her ankles. It was low cut, but not extreme, the soft swell of her breasts merely hinted at above the neckline. Yes, Hillary decided as she moved, the drifting material following in a lovingly lazy manner, it's stunning.

Earlier that day, she had modeled an exquisite sable coat. She remembered the feel of the fur against her chin and sighed. Larry had captured the first expression of delight and desire as she had buried her face against the collar. But Hillary knew now that she would rather have this negligee than ten sables. There was something special about it, as though it had been created with her in mind.

She walked from the dressing room and stood watching as Larry completed his setup. He has outdone himself this time, she mused with admiration. The lighting was soft and gentle, like a room lit with candles, and he had set up backlighting, giving the illusion of moonlight streaming. The effect was both romantic and subtle.

"Ah, good, you're ready." Larry turned from his task, then, focusing on her directly, let out a low whistle. "You're gorgeous. Every man who sees your picture will be dying for love of you, and every woman will be putting herself in your place. Sometimes you still amaze me."

She laughed and moved to join him as the studio door opened. Turning, the gown drifting about her, she saw Bret enter the room with Charlene on his arm. Blue eyes locked with gray before his traveled slowly over her with the intensity of a physical caress.

He took his time in bringing his eyes back to her face. "You look extraordinary, Hillary."

"Thanks." She swallowed the huskiness of her voice and her gaze moved from his to encounter Charlene's icy stare. The shock was like a cold shower and Hillary wished with all her heart that Bret had not chosen to bring his shapely companion with him.

"We're just getting started." Larry's matter-of-fact tone shattered the spell, and three heads turned to him.

"Don't let us hold things up," Bret said easily. "Charlene wanted to see the project that's been keeping me so busy."

His implication that Charlene had a stake in his life caused Hillary's spirits to plummet. Shaking off encroaching depression, she reminded herself that what she felt for Bret was strictly one-sided.

"Stand here, Hil," Larry directed, and she drifted to the indicated spot.

Muted lighting lent a glow to her skin, as soft on her cheek as a lover's caress. Soft backlighting shone through the filmy material, enticingly silhouetting her curves.

"Good," Larry stated, and, switching on the wind machine, he added, "perfect."

The easy breeze from the machine lifted her hair and rippled her gown. Picking up his camera, Larry began to shoot. "That's good, now lift your hair. Good, good, you'll drive them crazy." His instructions came swiftly, and her expressions and stances changed in rapid succession. "Now, look right into the camera—it's the man you love. He's coming to take you into his arms." Her eyes flew to the back of the studio where Bret stood linked with Charlene. Her eyes met his and a tremor shook her body. "Come on, Hillary, I want passion, not panic. Come on now, baby, look at the camera."

She swallowed and obeyed. Slowly, she allowed her dreams to take command, allowed the camera to become Bret. A Bret looking at her not only with desire, but with love. He came to her with love and need. He was holding her close as she remembered him holding her. His hands moved gently over her as his lips claimed hers after he whispered the words she longed to hear.

"That does it, Hillary."

Lost in her own world, she blinked and stared at Larry without comprehension.

"That was great. I fell in love with you myself."

Letting out a deep breath, she shut her eyes a moment and sighed at her own imagination. "I suppose we could get married and breed little lenses," she murmured as she headed for the dressing room.

"Bret, that negligee is simply marvelous." Charlene's words halted Hillary's progress. "I really must have it, darling. You can get it for me, can't you?" Charlene's voice was low and seductive as she ran a well-manicured hand along Bret's arm.

"Hmm? Sure," he assented, his eyes on Hillary. "If you want it, Charlene."

Hillary's mouth fell open with astonishment. His casual gift to the woman at his side wounded her beyond belief. She stared at him for a few moments before fleeing to her dressing room.

In the privacy of the dressing room, she leaned against the wall battling the pain. How could he? she cried inwardly. The gown was special, it was hers, she belonged in it. She closed her eyes and stifled a sob. She had even imagined him holding her in it, loving her, and now... it would be Charlene's. He would look at Charlene, his eyes dark with desire. His hands would caress Charlene's body through the misty softness. Now a fierce anger began to replace the pain. If that was what he wanted, well, they were welcome to it—both of them. She stripped herself from frothy white folds and dressed.

When she left the dressing room, Bret was alone in the studio, sitting negligently behind Larry's desk. Summoning all her pride, Hillary marched to him and dropped the large box on its cluttered surface.

"For your friend. You'll want to have it laundered first."

She turned to make her exit with as much dignity

as possible, but was outmaneuvered as his hand closed over her wrist.

"What's eating you, Hillary?" He stood, keeping his grip firm and towering over her.

"Eating me?" she repeated, glaring up at him. "Whatever do you mean?"

"Drop it, Hillary," he ordered, the familiar steel entering both voice and eyes. "You're upset, and I mean to know why."

"Upset?" She tugged fiercely at her arm. As her efforts for liberation proved fruitless, her anger increased. "If I'm upset, it's my own affair. It's not in my contract that I'm obliged to explain my emotions to you." Her free hand went to his in an attempt to pry herself free, but he merely transferred his hold to her shoulders and shook her briskly.

"Stop it! What's gotten into you?"

"I'll tell you what's gotten into me," she snapped as her hair tumbled around her face. "You walk in here with your redheaded girlfriend and just hand over that gown. She just bats her eyes and says the word, and you hand it over."

"Is that what all this is about?" he demanded, exasperated. "Good heavens, woman, if you want the damn thing, I'll get you one."

"Don't you patronize me," she raged at him. "You can't buy my good humor with your trinkets. Keep your generosity for someone who appreciates it and let me go."

"You're not going anywhere until you calm down and we get to the root of the problem."

Her eyes were suddenly filled with uncontrollable tears. "You don't understand." She sniffed as tears coursed down her cheeks. "You just don't understand anything."

"Stop it!" He began to brush her tears away with his hand. "Tears are my downfall. I can't handle them. Stop it, Hillary, don't cry like that."

"It's the only way I know how to cry," she said, weeping miserably.

He swore under his breath. "I don't know what this is all about. A nightgown can't be worth all this! Here, take it—it's obviously important to you." He picked up the box, holding it out to her. "Charlene has plenty." The last words, uttered in an attempt to lighten her mood, had precisely the reverse effect.

"I don't want it. I don't ever want to see it again," she shouted, her voice made harsh by tears. "I hope you and your lover thoroughly enjoy it." With this, she whirled, grabbed her coat, and ran from the studio with surprising speed.

Outside, she stood on the sidewalk, stomping her feet against the cold. Stupid! she accused herself. Stupid to get so attached to a piece of cloth. But no more stupid than getting attached to an arrogant, unfeeling man whose interests lay elsewhere. Spotting a cab, she stepped forward to flag it down when she was spun around to face the buttons on Bret's leather coat.

"I've had enough of your tantrums, Hillary, and I don't tolerate being walked out on." His voice was low and dangerous, but Hillary tilted back her head to meet his gaze boldly.

"We have nothing more to say."

"We have plenty more to say."

"I don't expect you to understand." She spoke with the exaggerated patience an adult uses when addressing a slow-witted child. "You're just a man."

She heard the sharp intake of his breath as he moved toward her.

"You're right about one thing, I am a man," she heard him whisper before he pulled her close, crushing her mouth in an angry kiss, forcing her lips to open to his demands. The world emptied but for his touch, and the two stood locked together, oblivious to the people who walked the sidewalk behind them.

When at last he freed her, she drew back from him, her breath coming quickly. "Now that you've proven your masculinity, I really must go."

"Come back upstairs. We'll finish our discussion."

"Our discussion is finished."

"Not quite." He began to drag her back toward the studio.

I can't be alone with him now, she thought wildly. Not now, when I'm already so vulnerable. He could see too much too easily.

"Really, Bret." She was proud of the calmness of her voice. "I do hate to create a scene, but if you continue to play the caveman I shall be forced to scream. And I can scream very loud."

"No, you wouldn't."

"Yes," Hillary corrected, digging in her heels. "I would."

"Hillary." He turned, maintaining possession of her arm. "We have things to clear up."

"Bret, it's gotten blown out of proportion." She spoke sweetly, ignoring the weakness in her legs. "We've both had our outburst of temper—let's just leave it at that. The entire thing was silly anyway."

"It didn't seem silly to you upstairs."

The slender hold on her control was slipping rapidly, and she looked up at him in a last ditch attempt. "Please, Bret, drop it. We're all temperamental sometimes."

"Very well," he agreed after a pause. "We'll drop it for the time being."

Hillary sighed tremulously. She felt that if she stayed any longer she ran the risk of agreeing to whatever he asked. Out of the corner of her eye she glimpsed a passing cab, and she put her fingers to her mouth to whistle it down.

Bret's mouth lifted in irrepressible amusement. "You never cease to surprise me."

Her answer was lost as she slammed the cab door behind her.

Chapter 5

Christmas was approaching, and the city was decorated in its best holiday garb. Hillary watched from her window as cars and people bustled through the brightly lit streets. The snow fell upon city sidewalks, the drifting white adding to her holiday mood. She watched the huge flakes float to earth like down from a giant pillow.

Shooting of the layout was complete, and she had seen little of Bret in the past few days. She would be seeing less of him, she realized, a shaft of gloom darkening her cheerful mood. Now that her part in the project was over, there would be no day-to-day contact, no chance meetings. She sighed and shook her head. I'm going home tomorrow, she reminded herself, home for Christmas.

That was what she needed, she told herself, closing her eyes on the image of Bret's handsome features. A complete change of scene. Ten days to help heal her heart, time to reevaluate all the plans she had laid out, which now seemed hopelessly dull and unsatisfying.

The knock on the door caused her to remove her face, which had been pressed against the glass. "Who is it?" she called as she placed her hand on the knob.

"Santa Claus."

"B-Bret?" she stammered, thrown off balance. "Is that you?"

"Just can't fool you, can I?" After a slight pause, he asked, "Are you going to let me in, or do we have to talk through the door?"

"Oh, sorry." She fumbled with the latch and opened the door, staring at his lean form, which leaned negligently against the frame.

"You're locking up these days." His eyes swept her pearl-colored velour housecoat before he brought them back to hers. "Are you going to let me in?"

"Oh, sure." Hillary stood back to let him enter, desperately searching for lost composure. "I, ah, I thought Santa came down the chimney."

"Not this one," he returned dryly, and removed his coat. "I could use some of your famous Scotch. It's freezing out there."

"Now I'm totally disillusioned. I thought Santa thrived on cookies and milk."

"If he's half the man I think he is, he's got a flask in that red suit."

"Cynic," she accused, and retreated to the kitchen. Finding the Scotch easily this time, she poured a measure into a glass.

"Very professional." Bret observed from the doorway. "Aren't you going to join me in some holiday cheer?"

"Oh, no." Hillary wrinkled her nose in disgust. "This stuff tastes like the soap I had my mouth washed out with once."

"You've got class, Hillary," he stated wryly, and took the glass from her hand. "I won't ask you what your mouth was washed out for."

"I wouldn't tell you anyway." She smiled, feeling at ease with the casual banter.

"Well, have something, I hate to drink alone."

She reached into the refrigerator and removed a pitcher of orange juice.

"You do live dangerously, don't you?" he commented as she poured. She raised the glass in toast and they returned to the living room.

"I heard you're off to Kansas in the morning," he said as he seated himself on the sofa. Hillary strategically made use of the chair facing him.

"That's right, I'll be home until the day after New Year's."

"Then I'll wish you both a Merry Christmas and a Happy New Year early." He lifted his glass to her. "I'll think of you when the clock strikes twelve."

"I'm sure you'll be too busy to think of me at the stroke of midnight," she retorted, and cursed herself for losing the calm, easy tone.

He smiled and sipped his Scotch. "I'm sure I'll find a minute to spare." Hillary frowned into her glass and refrained from a comment. "I've something for you, Hillary." He rose and, picking up his jacket, removed a small package from its pocket. Hillary stared at it dumbly, then raised her expressive eyes to his.

"Oh, but…I didn't think…that is…I don't have anything for you."

"Don't you?" he asked lazily, and color rushed to her cheeks.

"Really, Bret, I can't take it. I wouldn't feel right."

"Think of it as a gift from the emperor to one of his subjects." He took the glass from her hand and placed the package in its stead.

"You have a long memory." She smiled in spite of herself.

"Like an elephant," he said, then, with a touch of impatience: "Open it. You know you're dying to."

She stared at the package, conceding with a sigh. "I never could resist anything wrapped in Christmas paper." She tore the elegant foil away, then caught her breath as she opened the box and revealed its contents. Earrings of deep sapphire stones blinked up from their backing of velvet.

"They reminded me of your eyes, brilliantly blue and exquisite. It seemed a crime for them to belong to anyone else."

"They're beautiful, really very beautiful," she murmured when she found her voice. Turning her sapphire eyes to his, she added, "You really shouldn't have bought them for me, I—"

"I shouldn't have," he interrupted, "but you're glad I did."

She had to smile. "Yes, I am. It was a lovely thing to do. I don't know how to thank you."

"I do." He drew her from the chair, his arms slipping around her. "This will do nicely." His lips met hers and, after a moment's hesitation, she responded, telling herself she was only showing her gratitude for his thoughtfulness. As the kiss lingered, her gratitude was forgotten. He lifted his mouth, and dazedly she made to move from the warm circle of his arms. "There are two earrings, love." His mouth claimed possession again, now more demanding, and her lips parted beneath his insistence. Her body seemed to melt against his, her arms twining around his neck, fingers tangling in his hair. She was lost in the feel of him, all thought ceasing, her only reality his mouth on hers, and his hard body blending with her yielding softness.

When at last their lips separated, he looked down at her, his eyes darkened with emotion. "It's a pity you've only got two ears." His voice was husky, and his head lowered toward hers.

She dropped her forehead to his chest and attempted to catch her breath. "Please, Bret," she whispered, her hands slipping from his neck to his shoulders. "I can't think when you kiss me."

"Can't you now?" His mouth tarried a moment in her hair. "That's very interesting." He brought his hand under her chin and lifted her face, his eyes moving over her features slowly. "You know, Hillary, that's a very dangerous admission. I'm tempted to press my advantage." He paused, continuing to study the fragile, vulnerable face. "Not this time." He released her, and she checked the impulse to sway toward him. Walking to the table, he downed the remainder of his Scotch and lifted his coat. At the door, he turned, giving her his charming smile. "Merry Christmas, Hillary."

"Merry Christmas, Bret," she whispered at the door he closed behind him.

The air was brisk and cold, carrying the clean, pure scent that meant home, the sky brilliantly blue and naked of clouds. Hillary let herself into the rambling farmhouse and for a moment gave in to memories.

"Tom, what are you doing coming in all the way around the front?" Sarah Baxter bustled from the kitchen, wiping her hands on a full white apron. "Hillary." She stopped as she caught sight of the slim, dark woman in the center of the room. "Well, time's just gotten away from me."

Hillary ran and enveloped her mother in a fierce hug. "Oh, Mom, it's good to be home."

If her mother noticed the desperate tone of Hillary's words, she made no comment, but returned the embrace with equal affection. Standing back, she examined Hillary with a mother's practiced eye. "You could use a few pounds."

"Well, look what the wind blew in all the way from New York City." Tom Baxter entered through the swinging kitchen door and caught Hillary in a close embrace. She breathed deeply, reveling in the smell of fresh hay and horses that clung to him. "Let me look at you." He drew her away and repeated his wife's survey. "What a beautiful sight." He glanced over Hillary's head and smiled at his wife. "We grew a real prize here, didn't we, Sarah?"

Later, Hillary joined her mother in the large kitchen that served the farm. Pots were simmering on a well-used range, filling the air with an irresistible aroma. Hillary allowed her mother to ramble about her brothers and their families, fighting back the deep longing that welled inside her.

Her hand went unconsciously to the blue stones at her ears, and Bret's image flooded her mind, bringing him almost close enough to touch. She averted her face, hoping that the bright tears that sprung to her eyes would not be observed by her mother's sharp glance.

On Christmas morning, Hillary woke with the sun and snuggled lazily in her childhood bed. She had fallen into the bed late the night before, but, having slipped between the covers, had been unable to sleep. Tossing and turning, she had stared at a dark ceiling until the early hours. Bret had remained in her mind no matter how strenuously she had tried to block him out. His image broke through her defenses like a rock through plate glass. To her despair, she found herself aching to be close to him, the need an ache deep inside her.

In the morning, in the clear light of day, she once more stared at the ceiling. There's nothing I can do, she realized hopelessly. I love him. I love him and I hate him for not loving me back. Oh, he wants me all right—he's made no secret of that—but wanting's not loving. How did it happen? Where did all my defenses go? He's arrogant, she began, mentally ticking off faults in an effort to find an escape hatch in her solitary prison. He's short-tempered, demanding, and entirely too self-assured. Why doesn't any of that matter? What's happened to my brain? Why can't I stop thinking about him for more than five minutes at a time?

It's Christmas, she reminded herself, shutting her eyes against his intrusion. I am not going to let Bret Bardoff spoil my day!

Rising, she threw back the quilt, slipped on a fleece robe, and hurried from the room.

The house was already stirring, the quiet morning hush vanishing into activity. For the next hour, the scene around the Christmas tree was filled with gaiety, exclamations for the gifts that were revealed, and the exchange of hugs and kisses.

Later Hillary slipped outside, the thin blanket of frost crunching under her boots as she pulled her father's worn work jacket tighter around her slimness. The air tasted of winter, and the quiet seemed to hang like a soft curtain. Joining her father in the barn, she automatically began to measure out grain, her movements natural, the routine coming back as if she had performed the tasks the day before.

"Just an old farm hand after all, aren't you?" Though the words had been spoken in jest, Hillary halted and looked at her father seriously.

"Yes, I think I am."

"Hillary." His tone softened as he noticed the clouding of her eyes. "What's wrong?"

"I don't know." She let out a deep sigh. "Sometimes New York seems so crowded. I feel closed in."

"We thought you were happy there."

"I was...I am," she amended, and smiled. "It's a very

exciting place, busy and filled with so many different kinds of people." She forced back the image of clear gray eyes and strong features. "Sometimes I just miss the quiet, the openness, the peace. I'm being silly." She shook her head and scooped out more grain. "I've been a bit homesick lately, that's all. This layout I just finished was fascinating, but it took a lot out of me." Not the layout, she corrected silently, but the man.

"Hillary, if you're unhappy, if there's anything on your mind, I want to help you."

For a moment, she longed to lean on her father's shoulder and pour out her doubts and frustrations. But what good would it do to burden him? What could he do about the fact that she loved a man who saw her only as a temporary diversion, a marketable commodity for selling magazines? How could she explain that she was unhappy because she had met a man who had broken and captured her heart unknowingly and effortlessly? All these thoughts ran through her brain before she shook her head, giving her father another smile.

"It's nothing. I expect it's just a letdown from finishing the layout. Postphotography depression. I'll go feed the chickens."

The house was soon overflowing with people, echoing with mixed voices, laughter, and the sound of children. Familiar tasks and honest affection helped to erase the ache of emptiness that still haunted her....

When only the echoes of the holiday lingered, Hillary remained downstairs alone, unwilling to seek the comfort of her bed.

Curled in a chair, she stared at the festive lights of

the tree, unable to prevent herself from speculating on how Bret had celebrated his holiday. A quiet day with Charlene, perhaps, or a party at the country club? Right now they were probably sitting in front of a roaring fire, and Charlene was snuggled in his arms draped in that beautiful negligee.

A pain shot through her, sharp as the point of an arrow, and she was enveloped by a torturous combination of raging jealousy and hopeless despair. But the image would not fade.

The days at home went quickly. They were good days, following a soothing routine that Hillary dropped into gratefully. Kansas wind blew away a portion of her depression. She took long, quiet walks, gazing out at the rolling hills and acres of winter wheat.

People from the city would never understand, she mused. How could they comprehend this? Her arms were lifted wide as she spun in a circle. In their elegant apartments looking out at steel and concrete they could never feel the exuberation of being a part of the land. The land; she surveyed its infinity with wondering eyes. The land is indomitable; the land is forever. There had been Indians here, and plainsmen and pioneers and farmers. They came and went, lived and died, but the land lived on. And when she was gone, and another generation born, wheat would still wave in the bright summer sun. The land gave them what they needed, rich and fertile, generously giving birth to acres of wheat year after year, asking only for honest labor in return.

And I love it, she reflected, hugging herself tightly. I

love the feel of it in my hands and under my bare feet in the summer. I love the rich, clean smell of it. I suppose, for all my acquired sophistication, I'm still just a farm girl. She retraced her steps toward the house. What am I going to do about it? I have a career; I have a place in New York as well. I'm twenty-four. I can't just throw in the towel and come back to live on the farm. No. She shook her head vigorously, sending her hair swirling in a black mist. I've got to go back and do what I'm qualified to do. Firmly, she ignored the small voice that asserted her decision was influenced by another resident of New York.

The phone jangled on the wall as she entered the house, and, slipping off her jacket, she lifted it.

"Hello."

"Hello, Hillary."

"Bret?" She had not known pain could come so swiftly at the sound of a voice.

"Very good." She heard the familiar mockery and pressed her forehead to the wall. "How are you?"

"Fine, I'm just fine." She groped for some small island of composure. "I...I didn't expect to hear from you. Is there a problem?"

"Problem?" he returned in a voice that mirrored his smile. "No permanent one in any case. I thought you might be needing a reminder of New York about now. We wouldn't want you to forget to come back."

"No, I haven't forgotten." Taking a deep breath, she made her voice lightly professional. "Have you something in mind for me?"

"In mind? You might say I had one or two things in

mind." There was a slight pause before he continued. "Anxious to get back to work?"

"Uh, yes, yes, I am. I wouldn't want to get stale."

"I see."

You couldn't see through a chain-link fence, she thought with growing frustration.

"We'll see what we can do when you get back. It would be foolish not to put your talents to use." He spoke absently, as though his mind was already formulating a suitable project.

"I'm sure you'll think of something advantageous for both of us," she stated, trying to emulate his business-like tone.

"Mmm, you'll be back at the end of the week?"

"Yes, on the second."

"I'll be in touch. Keep your calendar clear." The order was casual, confident, and brisk. "We'll get you in front of the camera again, if that's what you want."

"All right. I…well…thanks for calling."

"My pleasure. I'll see you when you get back."

"Yes. Bret…" She searched for something to say, wanting to cling to the small contact, perhaps just to hear him say her name one more time.

"Yes?"

"Nothing, nothing." Shutting her eyes, she cursed her lack of imagination. "I'll wait to hear from you."

"Fine." He paused a moment, and his voice softened. "Have a good time at home, Hillary."

Chapter 6

The first thing Hillary did upon returning to her New York apartment was to put a call through to Larry. When greeted by a feminine voice, she hesitated, then apologized.

"Sorry, I must have the wrong number..."

"Hillary?" the voice interrupted. "It's June."

"June?" she repeated, confused, then added quickly, "How are you? How were your holidays?"

"Terrific to both questions. Larry told me you went home. Did you have a good time?"

"Yes, I did. It's always good to get home again."

"Hang on a minute. I'll get Larry."

"Oh, well, no, I'll..."

Larry's voice broke into her protestations. She immediately launched into an apology, telling him she would call back.

"Don't be dumb, Hil, June's just helping me sort out my old photography magazines."

It occurred to Hillary that their relationship must be moving along at light speed for Larry to allow June to get her hands on his precious magazines. "I just wanted you to know I was back," she said aloud. "Just in case anything comes up."

"Mmm, well, I guess you really should get in touch with Bret." Larry considered. "You're still under contract. Why don't you give him a call?"

"I won't worry about it," she returned, striving to keep her tone casual. "I told him I'd be back after the first." Her voice dropped. "He knows where to find me."

Several days passed before Bret contacted Hillary. Much of the interim she spent at home because of the snow, which seemed to fall unceasingly over the city, alternating with a penetrating, bitter sleet. The confinement, coming on the heels of the open freedom she had experienced in Kansas, played havoc with her nerves, and she found herself staring down from her window at ice-covered sidewalks with increasing despair.

One evening, as the sky dropped the unwelcome gift of freezing rain, Lisa arranged to have dinner and spend a few hours in Hillary's company. Standing in the kitchen, Hillary was separating a small head of lettuce when the phone rang. Looking down at her wet, leaf-filled hands, she rubbed her nose on her shoulder and asked Lisa to answer the ring.

Lifting the receiver, Lisa spoke into it in her most formal voice. "Miss Hillary Baxter's residence, Lisa Mac-

Donald speaking. Miss Baxter will be with you as soon as she gets her hands out of the lettuce."

"Lisa." Hillary laughed as she hurried into the room. "I just can't trust you to do anything."

"It's all right," she announced loudly, holding out the receiver. "It's only an incredibly sexy male voice."

"Thanks," Hillary returned with deep sincerity, and rescued the phone. "Go, you're banished back into the kitchen." Pulling a face, Lisa retreated, and Hillary gave her attention to her caller. "Hello, don't mind my friend, she's just crazy."

"On the contrary, that's the most interesting conversation I've had all day."

"Bret?" Until that moment, Hillary had not realized how much she needed to hear his voice.

"Right the first time." She could almost see the slow smile spread across his features. "Welcome back to the concrete jungle, Hillary. How was Kansas?"

"Fine," she stammered. "It was just fine."

"Mmm, how illuminating. Did you enjoy your Christmas?"

"Yes, very much." Struggling to regain the composure that had fled at the sound of his voice, she spoke quickly. "And you? Did you have a nice holiday?"

"Delightful, though I'm sure it was a great deal quieter than yours."

"Different anyway," Hillary rejoined, annoyed.

"Ah, well, that's behind us now. Actually, I'm calling about this weekend."

"Weekend?" Hillary repeated dumbly.

"Yes, a trip to the mountains."

"Mountains?"

"You sound like a parrot," he said shortly. "Do you have anything important scheduled from Friday through Sunday?"

"Well, I...ah..."

"Lord, what an astute conversationalist you are." His voice reflected growing annoyance.

Swallowing, she attempted to be more precise. "No. That is, nothing essential. I—"

"Good," he interrupted. "Ever been skiing?"

"In Kansas?" she retorted, regaining her balance. "I believe mountains are rather essential for skiing."

"So they are," he agreed absently. "Well, no matter. I had an idea for some pictures of a lovely lady frolicking in the snow. I've a lodge in the Adirondacks near Lake George. It'll make a nice setting. We can combine business with pleasure."

"We?" Hillary murmured weakly.

"No need for panic," he assured her, his words heavy with mockery. "I'm not abducting you to the wilderness to ravish you, although the idea does have some interesting angles." He paused, then laughed outright. "I can feel you blushing right through the phone."

"Very funny," she retorted, infuriated that he could read her so easily. "I'm beginning to recall an urgent engagement for the weekend, so—"

"Hold on, Hillary," he interrupted again, his words suddenly brooking no argument. "You're under contract. My rights hold for a couple more months. You wanted to get back to work; I'm putting you back to work."

"Yes, but—"

"Read the fine print if you like, but keep this weekend clear. And relax," he continued as she remained silent. "You'll be well protected from my dishonorable advances. Larry and June will be coming with us. Bud Lewis, my assistant art director, will be joining us later."

"Oh," she replied inadequately, unsure whether she was relieved or disappointed.

"I—the magazine, that is—will provide you with suitable snow gear. I'll pick you up at seven-thirty Friday morning. Be packed and ready."

"Yes, but—" Hillary stared at the dead receiver with a mixture of annoyance and trepidation. He had not given her the opportunity to ask questions or formulate a reasonable excuse to decline. Hanging up, she turned around, her face a study in bewilderment.

"What was all that? You look positively stunned." Lisa regarded her friend from the kitchen doorway.

"I'm going to the mountains for the weekend," she answered slowly, as if to herself.

"The mountains?" Lisa repeated. "With the owner of that fascinating voice?"

Hillary snapped back and attempted to sound casual. "It's just an assignment. That was Bret Bardoff. There'll be plenty of others along," she added.

Friday morning dawned clear and cloudless and cold. Hillary was packed and ready as instructed, sipping a second cup of tea, when the doorbell sounded.

"Good morning, Hillary," Bret said as she opened the door. "Ready to brave the uncharted wilderness?"

He looked quite capable of doing just that in a hiplength sheepskin jacket, heavy corded jeans, and sturdy boots. Now he appeared rugged, not the cool, calculating businessman to whom she had grown accustomed. Gripping the doorknob tightly, she maintained a cool exterior and invited him in.

Assuring him she was quite ready, she walked away to place the empty cup in the sink and fetch her coat. Slipping her coat over her sweater and jeans, she pulled a dark brown ski hat over her hair. Bret looked on silently.

"I'm ready." Suddenly aware of his intense regard, she moistened her lips nervously with her tongue. "Shall we go?"

Inclining his head, he bent to pick up the case she had waiting beside the sofa, his movements coinciding with hers. Straightening with a jerk, she flushed awkwardly. His brow lifted with his smile as he captured her hand and led her to the door.

They soon left the city as Bret directed the Mercedes north. He drove quickly and skillfully along the Hudson, keeping up a light conversation. Hillary found herself relaxing in the warm interior, forgetting her usual inhibition at being in close contact with the man who stirred her senses. As they began to pass through small towns and villages, she could hardly believe they were still in New York, her experience with the state having been limited exclusively to Manhattan and the surrounding area. Ingenuously, she voiced her thoughts, pulling off her hat and shaking out her rich fall of hair.

"There's more in New York than skyscrapers," he informed her with a crooked smile. "Mountains, valleys, forests—it has a bit of everything. I suppose it's time we changed your impression."

"I've never thought of it except as a place to work," she admitted, shifting in her seat to face him more directly. "Noisy, busy, and undeniably exciting, but draining at times because it's always moving and never seems to sleep. It always makes the sound of the silence at home that much more precious."

"And Kansas is still home, isn't it?" He seemed to be thinking of something else as he asked, his expression brooding on the road ahead. Hillary frowned at his change of mood, then gave her attention to the scenery without answering.

They continued northward, and she lost track of time, intoxicated by the newness and beauty of her surroundings. At her first glimpse of the Catskills, she let out a small cry of pleasure, spontaneously tugging on Bret's arm and pointing. "Oh, look—mountains!"

Turning her eyes from the view, she gave him her special smile. He returned the smile, and her heart did a series of acrobatics. She turned back to the scene out the window. "I suppose I must seem terribly foolish, but when you've only known acres of wheat and rolling hills, this is quite a revelation."

"Not foolish, Hillary." His voice was gentle, and she turned to face him, surprised at the unfamiliar tone. "I find you utterly charming."

Picking up her hand, he turned it upward and kissed her palm, sending shooting arrows of flame up her arm and down to her stomach. Dealing with his mockery and amusement was one thing, she pondered dizzily, she was quite used to that by now. But these occasional gentle moods turned her inside out, making her spark like a lighted match. This man was dangerous, she concluded, very dangerous. Somehow she must build up an impregnable defense against him. But how? How could she fight both him and the part of herself that wanted only to surrender?

"I could do with some coffee," Bret said suddenly, bringing Hillary back from her self-interrogation. "How about you?" He turned to her and smiled. "Want some tea?"

"Sure," she answered casually.

The Mercedes rolled into the small village of Catskill and Bret parked in front of a cafe. He opened his door and stepped from the car, and she quickly followed suit before he circled the front and joined her on the curb. Her eyes were fixed on the overpowering encircling mountains.

"They look higher than they are," Bret commented. "Their bases are only a few hundred feet above sea level. I'd love to see the expression on that beautiful face of yours when you encounter the Rockies or the Alps."

Interlocking his hand with hers, he led her out of the cold and into the warmth of the cafe. When the small table was between them, Hillary shrugged out of the confines of her coat, concentrating on the view, attempting to erect a wall of defense between herself and Bret.

"Coffee for me and tea for the lady. Are you hungry, Hillary?"

"What? Oh no,…well, yes, actually a little." She grinned, remembering the lack of breakfast that morning.

"They serve an outstanding coffee cake here." He ordered two slices before Hillary could protest.

"I don't usually eat that kind of thing." She frowned, thinking of the half grapefruit she had had in mind.

"Hillary, darling," Bret broke in with exaggerated patience. "One slice of cake is hardly likely to affect your figure. In any case," he added with irritating bluntness, "a few pounds wouldn't hurt you."

"Really," she retorted, chin rising with indignation. "I haven't had any complaints so far."

"I'm sure you haven't, and you'll get none from me. I've become quite enchanted with tall, willowy women. Though," he continued, reaching over to brush a loose strand of hair from her face, "the air of frailty is sometimes disconcerting."

Hillary decided to ignore both gesture and remark. "I don't know when I've enjoyed a drive more," she said, determined to remain casual. "How much farther do we have to go?"

"We're at the halfway point." Bret added cream to his coffee. "We should arrive around noon."

"How is everyone else coming? I mean, are they driving together?"

"Larry and June are coming up together." He smiled and ate a forkful of cake. "I should say Larry and June are accompanying Larry's equipment. I'm amazed he allowed her to travel in the same car with his precious cameras and lenses."

"Are you?" Hillary questioned, grinning into her tea.

"I suppose I shouldn't be," he admitted wryly. "I have noticed our favorite photographer's increasing preoccupation with my secretary. He seemed inordinately pleased to have her company on the drive."

"When I phoned him the other day, he was actually allowing her to sort out his photography magazines." Hillary's voice was tinged with disbelief. "That's tantamount to a bethrothal." She gestured with her fork. "It might even be binding. I'm not sure of the law. I still can't believe it." She swallowed a piece of cake and looked at Bret in amazement. "Larry's actually serious about a flesh-and-blood woman."

"It happens to the best of us, love," Bret agreed gently.

But would it ever to Bret? She could not meet his eyes.

On the road once more, Hillary contented herself with the scenery as Bret kept up a general conversation. The warmth of the Mercedes' interior and its smooth, steady ride had lulled her into a state of deep relaxation, and leaning back, she closed her suddenly heavy lids as they crossed the Mohawk River. Bret's deep voice increased her peaceful mood, and she murmured absently in response until she heard no more.

Hillary stirred restlessly as the change in road surface disturbed her slumber. Her eyes blinked open, and after a moment's blankness, reality returned. Her head was nestled against his shoulder, and, sitting up quickly, she turned her sleep-flushed face and heavy dark eyes to him.

"Oh, I'm sorry. Did I fall asleep?"

"You might say that," he said, glancing over as she pushed at tumbled hair. "You've been unconscious for an hour."

"Hour?" she repeated, attempting to clear the cobwebs. "Where are we?" she mumbled, gazing around her. "What did I miss?"

"Everything from Schenectady on, and we're on the road that leads to my lodge."

"Oh, it's beautiful." She came quickly awake as she focused on her surroundings.

The narrow road they traveled was flanked with snow-covered trees and rugged outcroppings of rock. Snow draped the green needles of pine, and what would have been dark, empty branches glistened with icicles and pure, sparkling white. Dense and thick, they seemed to be everywhere, rising majestically from a brilliant virgin blanket.

"There're so many." She scooted in her seat to experiment with the view from Bret's window, her knees brushing his thigh.

"The forest is full of them."

"Don't make fun." She punched his shoulder and continued to stare. "This is all new to me."

"I'm not making fun," he said, rubbing his shoulder with exaggerated care. "I'm delighted with your enthusiasm."

The car halted, and Hillary turned from Bret to look out the front window of the car. With a cry of pleasure, she spotted the large A-frame dwelling nestled in a small clearing so much a part of the surroundings it might have grown there. Picture windows gleamed and glistened in the filtered sunlight.

"Come get a closer look," Bret invited, stepping from the car. He held his hand out to her, and she slipped hers into his grasp as they began to crunch through the untouched snow. An ice-crusted stream tumbled swiftly on the far side of the house and, like a child wishing to share a new toy, Hillary pulled Bret toward it.

"How marvelous, how absolutely marvelous," she proclaimed, watching water force its way over rocks, its harsh whisper the only disturbance of peace. "What a fabulous place." She made a slow circle. "It's so wild and powerful, so wonderfully untouched and primitive."

Bret's eyes followed her survey before staring off through a dense outcropping of trees. "Sometimes I escape here, when my office begins to close in on me. There's such blessed peace—no urgent meetings, no deadlines, no responsibilities."

Hillary regarded him in open amazement. She had never imagined his needing to escape from anything or seeking deliberate solitude in a place so far from the city and its comforts and pleasures. To her, Bret Bardoff had represented the epitome of the efficient businessman, with employees rushing to do his bidding at the snap of his imperious finger. Now, she began to see another aspect of his nature, and she found the knowledge brought her a swift rush of pleasure.

He turned and encountered her stare, locking her eyes to his with a force that captured her breath. "It's also quite isolated," he added, in such a swift change of mood it took her a moment to react.

Blue eyes deepened and widened and she looked away, staring at the trees and rocks. She was here in the middle of nowhere, she realized, unconsciously chewing on her lip. He had told her the others were coming, but there was only his word. She had not thought to check with Larry. What if he had made the whole thing up? She would be trapped with him, completely alone. What would she do if...

"Keep calm, Hillary." Bret laughed wryly. "I haven't kidnapped you, the others will be along to protect you." He had deliberately provoked her reaction, and Hillary whirled to tell him what she thought of him, but he went on before she could speak. "That is, if they can find the place," he muttered, his brow creasing before his features settled in a wide smile. "It would be a shame if my directions were inadequate, wouldn't it?" Taking her hand once more, he led a confused and uneasy Hillary toward the lodge.

The interior was spacious, with wide, full windows bringing the mountains inside. The high ceiling with exposed beams added to the openness. Rough wooden stairs led to a balcony that ran the length of the living room. A stone fireplace commanded an entire wall, with furniture arranged strategically around it. Oval braid rugs graced the dark pine floor, their bright colors the perfect accent for the rustic, wood-dominated room.

"It's charming," Hillary said with delight as she gazed about her. She walked over to the huge expanse of glass. "You can stand here and be inside and out at the same time."

"I've often felt that way myself," Bret agreed, moving to join her and slipping her coat from her shoulders. "What is that scent you wear?" he murmured, his fingers massaging the back of her neck, their strength throbbing through her. "It's always the same, very delicate and appealing."

"It's, ah, it's apple blossom." She swallowed and kept her eyes glued to the window.

"Mmm, you mustn't change it, it suits you.... I'm starving," he announced suddenly, turning her to face him. "How about opening a can or something, and I'll start the fire? The kitchen's well stocked. You should be able to find something to ward off starvation."

"All right," she agreed, smiling. "We wouldn't want you to fade away. Where's the kitchen?" He pointed, and leaving him still standing by the window, she set off in the direction he indicated.

The kitchen was full of old-fashioned charm, with a small brick fireplace of its own and copper-bottomed pots hanging along the wall. The stove itself Hillary regarded doubtfully, thinking it resembled something her grandmother might have slaved over, until she observed that it had been adapted for modern use. The large pantry was well stocked, and she located enough cans for an adequate midday meal. Not precisely a gourmet feast, she reflected as she opened a can of soup, but it will have to do. She was spooning soup into a pan when she heard Bret's footsteps behind her.

"That was quick!" she exclaimed. "You must have been a terrific Boy Scout."

"It's a habit of mine to set the fire before I leave," he explained, standing behind her as she worked. "That way all I have to do is open the flue and light a match."

"How disgustingly organized," Hillary observed with a sniff, and switched the flame under the soup.

"Ah, ambrosia," he proclaimed, slipping his arms around her waist. "Are you a good cook, Hillary?"

The hard body pressed into her back was very distracting. She struggled to remain cool. "Anyone can open a can of soup." The last word caught in her throat as his hand reached up to part the dark curtain of her hair, his lips warm as they brushed the back of her neck. "I'd better make some coffee." She attempted to slip away, but his arms maintained possession, his mouth roaming over her vulnerable skin. "I thought you were hungry." The words came out in a babbling rush as her knees melted, and she leaned back against him helplessly for support.

"Oh, I am," he whispered, his teeth nibbling at her ear. "Ravenous."

He buried his face in the curve of her neck, and the room swayed as his hands slid upward under her sweater.

"Bret, don't," she moaned as a rush of desire swept over her, and she struggled to escape before she was lost.

He muttered savagely and spun her around, roughly crushing her lips under his.

Though he had kissed her before, demanding, arousing kisses, there had always been a measure of control in his lovemaking. Now it was as if the wildness of their surroundings had entered him. Like a man whose control has been too tightly bound, he assaulted her mouth, parting hers and taking possession. His hands pressed her hips against him, molding them together into one form. She was drowning in his explosion of passion, clinging to him as his hands roamed over her, seeking, demanding, receiving. The fire of his need ignited hers, and she gave herself without reservation, straining against him, wanting only to plunge deeper into the heat.

The sound of a car pulling up outside brought a muffled curse from Bret. Lifting his mouth from hers, he rested his chin on top of her head and sighed.

"They found us, Hillary. Better open another can."

Chapter 7

Voices drifted through the building, June's laughter and Larry's raised tones in some shared joke. Bret moved off to greet them, leaving Hillary battling to regain some small thread of composure. The urgent demand of Bret's lovemaking had awakened a wild, primitive response in her. She was acutely aware that, had they been left undisturbed, he would not have held back, and she would not have protested. The need had been too vital, too consuming. The swift beginning and sudden end of the contact left her trembling and unsteady. Pressing hands to burning cheeks, she went back to the stove, to attend to soup and coffee, hoping the simple mechanical tasks would restore her equilibrium.

"So, he's got you slaving away already." June entered the kitchen, arms ladened with a large paper bag. "Isn't that just like a man?"

"Hi." Hillary turned around, showing a fairly normal countenance. "It appears we've both been put in our places. What's in the bag?"

"Supplies for the long, snowbound weekend." Unpacking the bag, June revealed milk, cheese, and other fresh goods.

"Always efficient," Hillary stated, and, feeling the tension melt away, flashed her smile.

"It is difficult being perfect," June agreed with a sigh. "But some of us are simply born that way."

Meal preparations complete, they carried bowls and plates into the adjoining room to a large, rectangular wooden table with long benches running along each side. The group devoured the simple meal as though months had passed since they had seen a crust of bread. Mirroring Bret's now casual manner was at first difficult, but, summoning all her pride, Hillary joined in the table talk, meeting his occasional comments with an easy smile.

She retreated with June upstairs as the men launched into a technical discussion on the type of pictures required, and found the room they would share as charmingly rustic as the remainder of the house. The light, airy room with a breathtaking view of forest and mountains held two twin beds covered in patchwork quilts. Again wood predominated, the high sloping ceiling adding to the space. Brass lamps ensured soft lighting once the sun had descended behind the peaks outside.

Hillary busied herself with the case containing her wardrobe for the photo session as June threw herself heavily on a bed.

"Isn't this place fantastic?" Stretching her arms to the

ceiling, June heaved a deep sigh of contentment. "Far from the maddening crowd and typewriters and telephones. Maybe it'll snow like crazy, and we'll be here until spring."

"We'd only be able to stick it out if Larry brought enough film for a couple of months. Otherwise, he'd go into withdrawal," Hillary commented. Removing a red parka and bibbed ski pants from the case, she studied them with a professional eye. "Well, this should stand out in the snow."

"If we painted your nose yellow, you'd look like a very large cardinal," June commented, clasping her hands behind her head. "That color will look marvelous on you. With your hair and complexion, and the snow as a backdrop, you'll be smashing. The boss never makes a mistake."

The sound of a car caught their attention, and they moved to the window looking down as Bud Lewis assisted Charlene from the vehicle. "Well—" June sighed and grimaced at Hillary "—maybe one."

Stunned, Hillary stared at the top of Charlene's glossy red head. "I didn't...Bret didn't tell me Charlene was coming." Infuriated by the intrusion on her weekend, Hillary turned from the window and busied her hands with unpacking.

"Unless I'm very much mistaken, he didn't know." Scowling, June turned and leaned against the windowsill. "Maybe he'll toss her out in the snow."

"Maybe," Hillary countered, relieving some of her frustration by slamming the top of her suitcase, "he'll be glad to see her."

"Well, we won't find out anything standing around up here." June started toward the door, grabbing Hillary's arm along the way. "Come on, let's go see."

Charlene's voice drifted to Hillary as she descended the stairs. "You really don't mind that I came to keep you company, do you, Bret? I thought it would be such a lovely surprise."

Hillary entered the room in time to see Bret's shrug. He was seated on a love seat in front of the blazing fire, Charlene's arm tucked possessively through his. "I didn't think the mountains were your style, Charlene." He gave her a mild smile. "If you'd wanted to come, you should have asked instead of spinning a tale to Bud about my wanting him to drive you up."

"Oh, but, darling, it was just a little fib." Tilting her head, she fluttered darkened lashes. "A little intrigue is so amusing."

"Let's hope your 'little intrigue' doesn't lead you to 'a lot of boredom.' We're a long way from Manhattan."

"I'm never bored with you."

Soft and coaxing, the voice grated on Hillary's nerves. Perhaps she made some small sound of annoyance for Bret's eyes shifted to where she stood with June in the doorway. Charlene followed his gaze, her lips tightening for a moment before settling into a vague smile.

There followed an unenthusiastic exchange of greetings. Opting for distance, Hillary seated herself across the room with Bud as Charlene again gave Bret her full attention.

"I thought we'd never get here," Charlene complained with a petulant pout. "Why you would own a place in this godforsaken wilderness is beyond me, darling." She glanced up at Bret with cool green eyes. "All this snow, and nothing but trees and rocks, and so cold." With a delicate shiver, she huddled against him. "Whatever do you find to do up here all alone?"

"I manage to find diversions," Bret drawled, and lit a cigarette. "And I'm never alone—the mountains are teeming with life." He gestured toward the window. "There are squirrels, chipmunks, rabbits, foxes—all manner of small animal life."

"That's not precisely what I meant by company," Charlene murmured, using her most seductive voice. Bret granted her a faint smile.

"Perhaps not, but I find them entertaining and undemanding. I've often seen deer pass by as I stood by that window, and bear."

"Bears?" Charlene exclaimed, and tightened her hold on his arm. "How dreadful."

"Real bears?" Hillary demanded, eyes bright with adventure. "Oh, what kind? Those huge grizzlies?"

"Black bear, Hillary," he corrected, smiling at her reaction. "But big enough just the same. And safely in hibernation at the moment," he added with a glance at Charlene.

"Thank heaven," she breathed with genuine feeling.

"Hillary's quite taken to the mountains, haven't you?"

"They're fabulous," she agreed with enthusiasm. "So wild and untamed. All this must look nearly the same as it did a century ago, unspoiled by buildings and housing developments. Nothing but undisturbed nature for miles and miles."

"My, my, you are enthusiastic," Charlene observed.

Hillary shot her a deadly glance.

"Hillary grew up on a farm in Kansas," Bret explained, observing danger signals in dark blue eyes. "She'd never seen mountains before."

"How quaint," Charlene murmured, lips curving in a smile. "They grow wheat or something there, don't they? I would imagine you're quite accustomed to primitive conditions coming from a little farm."

The superior tone had Hillary bristling with anger, her rising temper reflected in her voice. "The farm is hardly little or primitive, Miss Mason. Impossible, I suppose, for one of your background to visualize the eternity of wheat, the miles of gently rolling hills. Not as sophisticated as New York, perhaps, but hardly prehistoric. We even manage to have hot and cold running water right inside the house most of the time. There are those who appreciate the land and respect it in all forms."

"You must be quite the outdoor girl," Charlene said in a bored voice. "I happen to prefer the comforts and culture of the city."

"I think I'll take a walk before it gets dark." Hillary rose quickly, needing to put some distance between herself and the other woman before her temper was irrevocably lost.

"I'll go with you." Bud stood, moving to join her as she slipped on her outdoor clothing. "I've been cooped up with that woman all day," he whispered with a conspirator's smile. "I think the fresh air will do me a world of good."

Hillary's laughter floated through the room as she

strolled through the door, arm in arm with Bud. She was oblivious of the frown that darkened the gray eyes that followed her.

Once outside, the two breathed deeply, then giggled like children at their private joke. By mutual consent, they headed for the stream, following its tumbling progress downstream as they ambled deeper into the forest. Sunlight winked sporadically through the trees, glistening on the velvet snow. Bud's easy conversation soothed Hillary's ruffled spirits.

They stopped and rested on a mound of rock for a moment of companionable silence.

"This is nice," Bud said simply, and Hillary made a small sound signifying both pleasure and agreement. "I begin to feel human again," he added with a wink. "That woman is hard to take. I can't imagine what the boss sees in her."

Hillary grinned. "Isn't it strange that I agree with you?"

They walked home in the subtle change of light that signified encroaching dusk. Again, they followed the stream, easily retracing the footsteps they had left in the pure, white snow. They were laughing companionably as they entered the A-frame.

"Don't either of you have more sense than to wander about the mountains after dark?" Bret asked them, scowling.

"Dark? Don't be silly." Hillary hopped on one foot as she pried off a boot. "We only followed the stream a little way, and it's barely dusk." Losing her balance, she collided with Bud, who slipped an arm around her waist to right her, keeping it there while she struggled with her other boot.

"We left a trail in the snow," Bud stated with a grin. "Better than bread crumbs."

"Dusk turns to dark quickly, and there's no moon tonight," Bret said. "It's a simple matter to get lost."

"Well, we're back, and we didn't," Hillary told him. "No need for a search party or a flask of brandy. Where's June?"

"In the kitchen, starting dinner."

"I better go help then, hadn't I?" She gave him a radiant smile and brushed past them, leaving Bud to deal with his boss's temper.

"A woman's work is never done," Hillary observed with a sigh as she entered the kitchen.

"Tell that to Miss Nose-in-the-Air." June wrinkled her own as she unwrapped the steaks. "She was so fatigued from the arduous drive—" June placed a dramatic hand to her forehead "—she simply had to lie down before dinner."

"That's a blessing. Anyway," Hillary went on as she joined in the meal preparation, "who voted us in charge of kitchen duty? I'm quite sure it's not in my contract."

"I did."

"Voluntarily?"

"It's like this," June explained, searching through cupboards. "I've had a small example of Larry's talents, culinary talents, and I don't want another bout of ptomaine. The boss even makes lousy coffee. And as for Bud—

well, he might be Chef Boy-Ar-Dee as far as I know, but I was unwilling to take the chance."

"I see what you mean."

In easy companionship they prepared the meal. The kitchen came to life with the clatter of dishes and sizzling of meat. Larry materialized in the doorway, breathing deeply.

"Ah, exquisite torture. I'm starving," he announced. "How much longer?"

"Here." June thrust a stack of dishes in his hands. "Go set the table—it'll keep your mind off your stomach."

"I knew I should have stayed out of here." Grumbling, he vanished into the adjoining room.

"I guess it's the mountain air," Hillary commented between bites as the group sat around the long table. "I'm absolutely ravenous."

The slow smile that drifted across Bret's face brought back the memory of the earlier scene in the kitchen, and warm color seeped into her cheeks. Picking up her glass containing a red wine Bret had produced from some mysterious place, she took a deep, impulsive swallow and firmly gave her attention to the meal.

The clearing up was confused and disorganized as the men, through design or innocence, served only to get in the way, causing June to throw up her hands and order them away.

"I'm the boss," Bret reminded her. "I'm supposed to give the orders."

"Not until Monday," June returned, giving him a firm shove. She watched with a raised brow as Charlene floated with him.

"Just as well," she observed, turning back to Hillary. "I probably couldn't have prevented myself from drowning her in the sink."

The party later spread out with lazy contentment in the living room. Refusing Bret's offer of brandy, Hillary settled herself on a low stool near the fire. She watched the dancing flames, caught up in their images, unaware of the picture she created, cheeks and hair glowing with flickering light, eyes soft and dreamy. Her mind floated, only a small portion of it registering the quiet hum of conversation, the occasional clink of glass. Elbows on knees, head on palms, she drifted with the fire's magic away from conscious thought.

"Are you hypnotized by the flames, Hillary?" Bret's lean form eased down beside her as he stretched out on the hearth rug. Tossed suddenly into reality, she started at his voice, then smiled as she brushed at her hair.

"Yes, I am. There're pictures there if you look for them," she answered, inclining her head toward the blaze. "There's a castle there with turrets all around, and there's a horse with his mane lifted in the wind."

"There's an old man sitting in a rocker," Bret said softly, and she turned to stare at him, surprised that he had seen the image too. He returned her look, with the intensity of an embrace, and she rose, flustered by the weakness his gaze could evoke.

"It's been a long day," she announced, avoiding his eyes. "I think I'll go up to bed. I don't want Larry to complain that I look washed out in the morning."

Calling her good nights, she went swiftly from the room without giving Bret the opportunity to comment.

* * *

The room was dim in early morning light when she awoke. She stretched her arms to the ceiling and sat up, knowing sleep was finished. When she had slipped under the blankets the night before, her emotions had been in turmoil, and she had been convinced the hours would be spent tossing and turning. She was amazed that she had slept not only immediately but deeply, and the mood with which she greeted the new day was cheerful.

June was still huddled under her quilt, the steady rhythm of her breathing the only sound in the absolute silence. Easing from the bed, Hillary began to dress quietly. She tugged a heavy sweater in muted greens over her head, mating it with forest green cords that fit with slim assurance. Forgoing makeup, she donned the snowsuit Bret had provided, pulling the matching ski cap over her hair.

Creeping down the stairs, she listened for the sounds of morning stirring, but the house remained heavy in slumber. Pulling on boots and gloves, Hillary stepped outside into the cold, clear sunlight.

The woods were silent, and she looked about her at the solitude. It was as if time had stopped—the mountains were a magic fairyland without human habitation. Her companions were the majestic pines, robed in glistening ermine, their tangy scent permeating the air.

"I'm alone," she said aloud, flinging out her arms. "There's not another soul in the entire world." She raced through the snow, drunk with power and liberation. "I'm free!" She tossed snow high above her head, whirling in dizzying circles before flinging herself into the cold snow.

Once more, she contemplated the white-topped mountains and dense trees, realizing her heart had expanded and made room for a new love. She was in love with the mountains as she was with the free-flowing wheat fields. The new and old love filled her with jubilation. Scrambling up, she sped once more through the snow, kicking up mists of white before she stopped and fell on her back, the soft surface yielding beneath her. She lay, spread-eagle, staring up at the sky until a face moved into her view, gray eyes laughing down at her.

"What are you doing, Hillary?"

"Making an angel," she informed him, returning his smile. "You see, you fall down, and then you move your arms and legs like this." She demonstrated, and her smile faded. "The trick is to get up without making a mess of it. It requires tremendous ability and perfect balance." Sitting up carefully, she put her weight on her feet and started to stand, teetering on her heels. "Give me a hand," she demanded. "I'm out of practice." Grabbing his arm, she jumped clear, then turned back to regard her handiwork. "You see," she stated with arrogant pride, "an angel."

"Beautiful," he agreed. "You're very talented."

"Yes, I know. I didn't think anyone else was up," she added, brushing snow from her bottom.

"I saw you dancing in the snow from my window. What game were you playing?"

"That I was alone in all this." She whirled in circles, arms extended.

"You're never alone up here. Look." He pointed into the woods, and her eyes widened at the large buck that stared back at her, his rack adorning his head like a crown.

"He's magnificent." As if conscious of her admiration, the stag lifted his head before he melted into the cover of the woods. "Oh, I'm in love!" she exclaimed, racing across the snow. "I'm absolutely madly in love with this place. Who needs a man when you've got all this?"

"Oh, really?" A snowball thudded against the back of her head, and she turned to stare at him narrowly.

"You know, of course, this means war."

She scooped up a handful of snow, balling it swiftly and hurling it back at him. They exchanged fire, snow landing on target as often as it missed, until he closed the gap between them, and she engaged in a strategic retreat. Her flight was interrupted as he caught her, tossing her down and rolling on top of her. Her cheeks glowed with the cold, her eyes sparkled with laughter, as she tried to catch her breath.

"All right, you win, you win."

"Yes, I did," he agreed. "And to the victor go the spoils." He touched her mouth with his, his lips moving with light sensuality, stilling her laughter. "I always win sooner or later," he murmured, kissing her eyes closed. "We don't do this nearly often enough," he muttered against her mouth, deepening the kiss until her senses whirled. "You've snow all over your face." His mouth roamed to her cheek, his tongue gently removing flakes, instilling her with exquisite terror. "Oh, Hillary, what a delectable creature you are." Lifting his face, he stared into her wide, anxious eyes. He let out a deep breath and brushed the remaining snow from her cheeks with his hand. "The others should be stirring about now. Let's go have some breakfast."

"Stand over there, Hil." Hillary was once more out in the snow, but this time it was Larry and his camera joining her.

He had been taking pictures for what seemed to Hillary hours. Fervently, she wished the session would end, her mind lingering on the thought of steaming chocolate in front of the fire.

"All right, Hillary, come back to earth. You're supposed to be having fun, not floating in a daze."

"I hope your lenses freeze." She sent him a brilliant smile.

"Aw, cut it out, Hil," he mumbled, continuing to crouch around her.

"That'll do," he announced at last, and she fell over backwards in a mock faint. Larry leaned over her, taking still another picture. Shutting her eyes in amusement, she laughed up at him.

"Are the sessions getting longer, Larry, or is it just me?"

"It's you," he answered, shaking his head, allowing the camera to dangle by its strap. "You're over the hill, past your prime. It's all downhill from here."

"I'll show you who's over the hill." Hillary scrambled up, grabbing a handful of snow.

"No, Hil." Placing a protective hand over his camera, Larry backed away. "Remember my camera, don't lose control." Turning, he ran through the snow toward the lodge.

"Past my prime, am I?" The snowball hit him full on the back as Hillary gave chase. Catching him, she leaped on his back, beating him playfully on the top of the head.

"Go ahead," he told her, carrying her without effort. "Strangle me, give me a concussion—just don't touch my camera."

"Hello, Larry." Bret strolled over as they approached the house. "All finished?"

Hillary noted with some satisfaction that, with the advantage of being perched on Larry's back, she could meet Bret's eyes on level.

"I shall have to speak to you, Mr. Bardoff, about a new photographer. This one has just inferred that I am over the hill."

"I can't help it if your career's shot," Larry protested. "I've been carrying you figuratively for months, and now that I've carried you literally, I think you're putting on weight."

"That does it," Hillary decided. "Now I have no choice—I have to kill him."

"Put it off for a while, would you?" June requested, joining them by the door. "He doesn't know it yet, but I'm dragging him off for a walk in the woods."

"Very well," Hillary agreed. "That should give me time to consider. Put me down, Larry—you've been reprieved."

"Cold?" Bret asked as Hillary began to strip off her outdoor clothing.

"Frozen. There are those among us who have developing fluid rather than blood in their veins."

"Modeling is not all glamour and smiles, is it?" he commented as she shook snow from her hair. "Are you content with it?" he asked suddenly, capturing her chin with his hand, his eyes narrowed and serious. "Is there nothing else you want?"

"It's what I do," she countered. "It's what I'm able to do."

"Is it what you *want* to do?" he persisted. "Is it *all* you want to do?"

"All?" she repeated, and, battling the urgent longing, she shrugged. "It's enough, isn't it?"

He continued to stare down at her before he mirrored her shrug and walked away. He moved, even in jeans, with a rather detached elegance. Puzzled, Hillary watched him disappear down the hall.

The afternoon passed in vague complacency. Hillary sipped the hot chocolate of her dreams and dozed in a chair by the fire. She watched Bret and Bud play a long game of chess, the three of them unconcerned by Larry's occasional, irrepressible intrusions with his camera.

Charlene remained stubbornly by Bret's side, following the contest with ill-concealed boredom. When the match was over, she insisted that he show her through the forest. It was apparent to Hillary that her mind was not on trees and squirrels.

The day drifted away into darkness. Charlene, looking disgruntled after her walk, complained about the cold, then stated regally that she would soak in a hot tub for the next hour.

Dinner consisted of beef stew, which left the redhead aghast. She compensated by consuming an overabundance of wine. Her complaints were genially ignored, and the meal passed with the casual intimacy characteristic of people who have grown used to each other's company.

Again accepting kitchen detail, Hillary and June worked in the small room, the latter stating she felt she was due for a raise. The job was near completion when Charlene strolled in, yet another glass of wine in her hand.

"Almost done with your womanly duties?" she demanded with heavy sarcasm.

"Yes. Your assistance was greatly appreciated," June answered, stacking plates in a cupboard.

"I should like to have a word with Hillary, if you don't mind."

"No, I don't mind," June returned, and continued to clatter dishes.

Charlene turned to where Hillary was now wiping the surface of the stove. "I will not tolerate your behavior any longer."

"Well, all right—if you'd rather do it yourself." Hillary offered the dishcloth with a smile.

"I saw you this morning," Charlene flung out viciously, "throwing yourself at Bret."

"Did you?" Hillary shrugged, turning back to give the stove her attention. "Actually, I was throwing snowballs. I thought you were asleep."

"Bret woke me when he got out of bed." The voice was soft, the implication all too clear.

Pain throbbed through Hillary. How could he have left one woman's arms and come so easily into hers? How could he degrade and humiliate her that way? She shut her eyes, feeling the color drain from her face. The simple fun and precious intimacy they had shared that morning now seemed cheap. Holding on to her pride desperately, she turned to face Charlene, meeting triumphant green eyes with blue ice. "Everyone's entitled to his own taste." She shrugged indifferently, tossing the cloth on the stove.

Charlene's color rose dramatically. With a furious oath, she threw the contents of her glass, splattering the red liquid over Hillary's sweater.

"That's going too far!" June exploded, full of righteous anger on Hillary's behalf. "You're not going to get away with this one."

"I'll have your job for speaking to me that way."

"Just try it, when the boss sees what you—"

"No more," Hillary broke in, halting her avenger. "I don't want any more scenes, June."

"But, Hillary."

"No, please, just forget it." She was torn between the need to crawl away and lick her wounds and the urge to pull out handfuls of red hair. "I mean it. There's no need to bring Bret into this. I've had it."

"All right, Hillary," June agreed, casting Charlene a disgusted look. "For your sake."

Hillary moved quickly from the room, wanting only to

reach the sanctuary of her bedroom. Before she reached the stairs, however, she met Bret.

"Been to war, Hillary?" he asked, glancing at the red splatters on her sweater. "Looks like you lost."

"I never had anything to lose," she mumbled, and started to walk by him.

"Hey." He halted her, taking her arms and holding her in front of him. "What's wrong?"

"Nothing," she retorted, feeling her precious control slipping with each passing moment.

"Don't hand me that—look at you." His hand reached out to tilt her chin, but she jerked back. "Don't do that," he commanded. His fingers gripped her face and held her still. "What's wrong with you anyway?"

"Nothing is the matter with me," she returned, retreating behind a sheet of ice. "I'm simply a bit weary of being pawed."

She watched, his eyes darkening to a thunderous gray. His fingers tightened painfully on her flesh. "You're darned lucky there're other people in the house, or I'd give you a fine example of what it's really like to be pawed. It's a pity I had a respect for fragile innocence. I shall certainly keep my hands off you in the future."

He relaxed his grip, and with chin and arm aching from the pressure, she pushed by him and calmly mounted the stairs.

Chapter 8

February had drifted into March. The weather had been as cold and dreary as Hillary's spirits. Since the fateful weekend in the Adirondacks, she had received no word from Bret, nor did she expect to.

The issue of *Mode* with Hillary's layout was released, but she could build up no enthusiasm as she studied the tall, slim woman covering the pages. The smiling face on the glossy cover seemed to belong to someone else, a stranger Hillary could neither recognize nor relate to. The layout was, nevertheless, a huge success, with the magazines selling as quickly as they were placed on the stands. She was besieged by offers as the weeks went by, but none of them excited her. She found the pursuit of her career of supreme indifference.

A call from June brought an end to her listlessness. The call brought a summons from the emperor. She debated refusing the order, then, deciding she would rather face Bret in his office than to have him seek her out at home, she obeyed.

She dressed carefully for the meeting, choosing a discreetly elegant pale yellow suit. She piled her hair up from her neck, covering it with a wide-brimmed hat. After a thorough study, she was well pleased with the calm, sophisticated woman reflected in her mirror.

During the elevator ride to Bret's office, Hillary schooled herself to remain aloof and detached, setting her expression into coolly polite lines. He would not see the pain, she determined. Her vulnerability would be well concealed. Her ability to portray what the camera demanded would be her defense. Her years of experience would not betray her.

June greeted her with a cheery smile. "Go right on in." She pushed the button on her phone. "He's expecting you."

Swallowing fear, Hillary fixed a relaxed smile on her face and entered the lion's den.

"Good afternoon, Hillary," Bret greeted her, leaning back in his chair but not rising. "Come sit down."

"Hello, Bret." Her voice matched the polite tone of his. Her smile remained in place though her stomach had begun to constrict at the first contact with his eyes.

"You're looking well," he commented.

"Thank you, so are you." She thought giddily, What absurd nonsense!

"I've just been looking over the layout again. It's certainly been every bit as successful as we had hoped."

"Yes, I'm glad it worked out so well for everyone."

"Which of these is you, Hillary?" he muttered absently, frowning over the pictures. "Free-spirited tomboy, elegant socialite, dedicated career woman, loving wife, adoring mother, exotic temptress?" He raised his eyes suddenly, boring into hers, the power almost shattering her frail barrier.

She shrugged carelessly. "I'm just a face and body doing what I'm told, projecting the image that's required. That's why you hired me in the first place, isn't it?"

"So, like a chameleon, you change from one color to the next on command."

"That's what I'm paid to do," she answered, feeling slightly ill.

"I've heard you've received quite a number of offers." Once more leaning back in his chair, Bret laced his fingers and studied her through half-closed eyes. "You must be very busy."

"Yes," she began, feigning enthusiasm. "It's been very exciting. I haven't decided which ones to accept. I've been told I should hire a manager to sort things out. There's an offer from a perfume manufacturer—" she named a well-known company "—that involves a long-term contract—three years endorsing on TV and, of course, magazines. It's by far the most interesting, I think." It was at the moment the only one she could clearly remember.

"I see. I'd heard you'd been approached by one of the networks."

"Oh, yes." She made a dismissive gesture, racking her brains for the details. "But that involves acting. I have to give that a great deal of thought." I'd win an Oscar for this performance, she added silently. "I doubt if it would be wise to jump into something like that."

He stood and turned his back, staring out at the steel and glass. She studied him without speaking, wondering what was going on in his mind, noting irrelevantly how the sunlight combed his thick blond hair.

"Your contract with me is finished, Hillary, and though I'm quite prepared to make you an offer, it would hardly be as lucrative as a television contract."

An offer, Hillary thought, her mind whirling, and she was grateful his back was to her so that he could not observe her expression. At least she knew why he had wanted to see her—to offer her another contract, another piece of paper. She would have to refuse, even though she had no intention of accepting any of the other contracts. She could never endure continuous contact with this man. Even after this brief meeting, her emotions were torn.

She rose before answering, and her voice was calm, even professional. "I appreciate your offer, Bret, but I must consider my career. I'm more than grateful to you for the opportunity you gave me, but—"

"I told you before, I don't want your gratitude!" He spun to face her, the all-too-familiar temper darkening his eyes. "I'm not interested in perfunctory expressions of gratitude and appreciation. Whatever you receive as a result of this—" he picked up the magazine with Hillary's face on the cover "—you earned yourself. Take that hat off so I can look at you." He whipped the hat from her head and thrust it into her hands.

Hillary resisted the need to swallow. She met his angry, searching gaze without flinching.

"Your success, Hillary, is of your own making. I'm not responsible for it, nor do I want to be." He seemed to struggle for a measure of control and went on in calm, precise tones. "I don't expect you to accept an offer from me. However, if you change your mind, I'd be willing to negotiate. Whatever you decide, I wish you luck—I should like to think you're happy."

"Thank you." With a light smile, she turned and headed for the door.

"Hillary."

Hand on knob, she shut her eyes a moment and willed herself the strength to face him again. "Yes?"

He stared at her, giving her the sensation that he was filing each of her features separately in his brain. "Goodbye."

"Goodbye," she returned, and turning the knob, she escaped.

Shaken, she leaned her back against the smooth other side of the door. June glanced up from her work.

"Are you all right, Hillary? What's the matter?"

Hillary stared without comprehension, then shook her head. "Nothing," she whispered. "Oh, everything." With a muffled sob, she streaked from the room.

Hillary hailed a cab a few nights later with little enthusiasm. She had allowed herself to be persuaded by Larry and June to attend a party across town in Bud Lewis's penthouse apartment. She must not wallow in self-pity, cut off from friends and social activities, she had decided. It was time, she told herself, pulling her shawl closer against the early April breeze, to give some thought to the future. Sitting alone and brooding would not do the job.

As a result of her self-lecturing, she arrived at the already well-moving party determined to enjoy herself. Bud swung a friendly arm over her shoulders and, leading her to the well-stocked bar, inquired what was her pleasure. She started to request her usual well-diluted drink when a punch bowl filled with a sparkling rose pink liquid caught her eye.

"Oh, that looks nice—what is it?"

"Planter's punch," he informed her, already filling a glass.

Sounds safe enough, she decided as Bud was diverted by another of his guests. With a tentative sip, Hillary thought it remarkably good. She began to mingle with the crowd.

She greeted old and new faces, pausing occasionally to talk or laugh. She glided from group to group, faintly amazed at how light and content was her mood. Depression and unhappiness dissolved like a summer's mist. This is what she needed all along, she concluded—some people, some music, a new attitude.

She was well into her third glass, having a marvelous time, flirting with a tall, dark man who introduced himself as Paul, when a familiar voice spoke from behind her.

"Hello, Hillary, fancy running into you here."

Turning, Hillary was only somewhat surprised to see Bret. She had only agreed to attend the party when June had assured her Bret had other plans. She smiled at him vaguely, wondering momentarily why he was slightly out of focus.

"Hello, Bret, joining the peasants tonight?"

His eyes roamed over her flushed cheeks and absent smile before traveling down the length of her slim form. He lifted his gaze back to her face, one brow lifting slightly as he answered. "I slum it now and then—it's good for the image."

"Mmm." She nodded, draining the remainder of her glass and tossing back an errant lock of hair. "We're both good with images, aren't we?" She turned to the other man at her side with a brilliant smile that left him slightly dazed. "Paul, be a darling and fetch me another of these. It's the punch over there—" she gestured largely "—in that bowl."

"How many have you had, Hillary?" Bret inquired, tilting her chin with his finger as Paul melted into the crowd. "I thought two was your limit."

"No limit tonight." She tossed her head, sending raven locks trembling about her neck and shoulders. "I am celebrating a rebirth. Besides, it's just fruit punch."

"Remarkably strong fruit I'd say from the looks of you," he returned, unable to prevent a grin. "Perhaps you should consider the benefits of coffee after all."

"Don't be stuffy," she ordered, running a finger down the buttons of his shirt. "Silk," she proclaimed and flashed another smile up at him. "I've always had a weakness for silk. Larry's here, you know, and," she added with dramatic emphasis, "he doesn't have his camera. I almost didn't recognize him."

"It won't be long before you have difficulty recognizing your own mother," he commented.

"No, my mother only takes Polaroid shots on odd occasions," she informed him as Paul returned with her drink. Taking a long sip, she captured Paul's arm. "Dance with me. I really love to dance. Here—" she handed her glass to Bret "—hang on to this for me."

She felt light and free as she moved to the music and marveled how she had ever let Bret Bardoff disturb her. The room spun in time to the music, drifting with her in a newfound sense of euphoria. Paul murmured something in her ear she could not quite understand, and she gave an indefinite sigh in response.

When the music halted briefly, a hand touched her arm, and she turned to find Bret standing beside her.

"Cutting in?" she asked, pushing back tumbled hair.

"Cutting out is more what I had in mind," he corrected, pulling her along with him. "And so are you."

"But I'm not ready to leave." She tugged at his arm. "It's early, and I'm having fun."

"I can see that." He continued to drag her after him, not bothering to turn around. "But we're going anyway."

"You don't have to take me home. I can call a cab, or maybe Paul will take me."

"Like hell he will," Bret muttered, pulling her purposefully through the crowd.

"I want to dance some more." She did a quick spin and collided full in his chest. "You want to dance with me?"

"Not tonight, Hillary." Sighing, he looked down at her. "I guess we do this the hard way."

In one swift movement, he had her slung over his

shoulder and began weaving his way through the amused crowd. Instead of suffering from indignation, Hillary began to giggle.

"Oh, what fun, my father used to carry me like this."

"Terrific."

"Here, boss." June stood by the door holding Hillary's bag and wrap. "Got everything under control?"

"I will have." He shifted his burden and strode down the hall.

Hillary was carried from the building and dumped without ceremony into Bret's waiting car. "Here." He thrust her shawl into her hands. "Put this on."

"I'm not cold." She tossed it carelessly into the back seat. "I feel marvelous."

"I'm sure you do." Sliding in beside her, he gave her one despairing glance before the engine sprang to life. "You've enough alcohol in your system to heat a two-story building."

"Fruit punch," Hillary corrected, and snuggled back against the cushion. "Oh, look at the moon." She sprang up to lean on the dash, staring at the ghostly white circle. "I love a full moon. Let's go for a walk."

He pulled up at a stoplight, turned to her, and spoke distinctly. "No."

Tilting her head, she narrowed her eyes as if to gain a new perspective. "I had no idea you were such a wet tire."

"Blanket," he corrected, merging with the traffic.

"I told you, I'm not cold." Sinking back into the seat, she began to sing.

Bret parked the car in the garage that serviced Hillary's building, turning to her with reluctant amusement. "All right, Hillary, can you walk or do I carry you?"

"Of course I can walk. I've been walking for years and years." Fumbling with the door handle, she got out to prove her ability. Funny, she thought, I don't remember this floor being tilted. "See?" she said aloud, weaving dangerously. "Perfect balance."

"Sure, Hillary, you're a regular tightrope walker." Gripping her arm to prevent a spill, he swept her up, cradled against his chest. She lay back contented as he carried her to the elevator, twining her arms around his neck.

"I like this much better," she announced as the elevator began its slow climb. "Do you know what I've always wanted to do?"

"What?" His answer was absent, not bothering to turn his head. She nuzzled his ear with her lips. "Hillary," he began, but she cut him off.

"You have the most fascinating mouth." The tip of her finger traced it with careful concentration.

"Hillary, stop it."

She continued as if he had not spoken. "A nicely shaped face too." Her finger began a slow trip around it. "And I've positively been swallowed up by those eyes." Her mouth began to roam his neck, and he let out a long breath as the elevator doors opened. "Mmm, you smell good."

He struggled to locate her keys, hampered with the bundle in his arms and the soft mouth on his earlobe.

"Hillary, stop it," he ordered. "You're going to make me forget the game has rules."

At last completing the complicated process of opening the door, he leaned against it a moment, drawing in a deep breath.

"I thought men liked to be seduced," she murmured, brushing her cheek against his.

"Listen, Hillary." Turning his face, he found his mouth captured.

"I just love kissing you." She yawned and cradled her head against his neck.

"Hillary...for heaven's sake!"

He staggered for the bedroom while Hillary continued to murmur soft, incoherent words in his ear.

He tried to drop her down on the spread, but her arms remained around his neck, pulling him off balance and down on top of her. Tightening her hold, she once more pressed her lips to his.

He swore breathlessly as he struggled to untangle himself. "You don't know what you're doing." With a drowsy moan, she shut her eyes. "Have you got anything on under that dress?" he demanded as he removed her shoes.

"Mmm, a shimmy."

"What's that?"

She gave him a misty smile and murmured. Taking a deep breath, he shifted her over, released the zipper at the back of her dress, pulled the material over smooth shoulders, and continued down the length of the slimly curved body.

"You're going to pay for this," he warned. His cursing became more eloquent as he forced himself to ignore the honey skin against the brief piece of silk. He drew the spread over the inert form on the bed. Hillary sighed and snuggled into the pillow.

Moving to the door, he leaned wearily on the frame, allowing his eyes to roam over Hillary as she lay in blissful slumber. "I don't believe this. I must be out of my mind." His eyes narrowed as he listened to her deep breathing. "I'm going to hate myself in the morning." Taking a long, deep breath, he went to search out Hillary's hoard of Scotch.

Chapter 9

Hillary awoke to bright invading sunlight. She blinked in bewilderment attempting to focus on familiar objects. She sat up and groaned. Her head ached and her mouth felt full of grit. Placing her feet on the floor, she attempted to stand, only to sink back moaning, as the room revolved around her like a carousel. She gripped her head with her hands to keep it stationary.

What did I drink last night? she wondered, squeezing her eyes tight to jar her memory. What kind of punch was that? She staggered unsteadily to her closet to secure a robe.

Her dress was tossed on the foot of the bed, and she stared at it in confusion. I don't remember undressing, she thought. Shaking her head in bemusement, she pressed a hand against her pounding temple. Aspirin, juice, and a cold shower, she decided. With slow, careful steps, she walked toward the kitchen. She stopped abruptly and leaned against the wall for support as a pair of men's shoes and a jacket stared at her in accusation from her living room sofa.

"Good heavens," she whispered as a partial memory floated back. Bret had brought her home, and she had… She shuddered as she remembered her conduct on the elevator. But what happened? She could only recall bits and pieces, like a jigsaw puzzle dumped on the floor— and the thought of putting them together was thoroughly upsetting.

"Morning, darling."

She turned slowly, her already pale face losing all color as Bret smiled at her, clad only in slacks, a shirt carelessly draped over his shoulder. The dampness of his hair attested to the fact that he had just stepped from the shower. *My shower.* Hillary's brain pounded out as she stared at him.

"I could use some coffee, darling." He kissed her lightly on the cheek in a casual intimate manner that tightened her stomach. He strode past her into the kitchen, and she followed, terrified. After placing the kettle to boil, he turned and wrapped his arms around her waist. "You were terrific." His lips brushed her brow, and she knew a moment's terror that she would faint dead away. "Did you enjoy yourself as much as I did?"

"Well, I—I guess, I don't…I don't remember…exactly."

"Don't remember?" He stared in disbelief. "How could you forget? You were amazing."

"I was... Oh." She covered her face with her hands. "My head."

"Hungover?" he asked, full of solicitude. "I'll fix you up." Moving away, he rummaged in the refrigerator.

"Hungover?" she repeated, supporting herself in the doorway. "I only had some punch."

"And three kinds of rum."

"Rum?" she echoed, screwing up her eyes and trying to think. "I didn't have anything but—"

"Planter's punch." He was busily involved in his remedy, keeping his back toward her. "Which consists, for the most part, of rum—amber, white, and dark."

"I didn't know what it was." She leaned more heavily on the doorway. "I had too much to drink. I'm not used to it. You—you took advantage of me."

"I took advantage?" Glass in hand, he regarded her in astonishment. "Darling, I couldn't hold you off." He lifted his brow and grinned. "You're a real tiger when you get going."

"What a dreadful thing to say," she exploded, then moaned as her head hammered ruthlessly.

"Here, drink." He offered the concoction, and she regarded it with doubtful eyes.

"What's in it?"

"Don't ask," he advised. "Just drink."

Hillary swallowed in one gulp, then shivered as the liquid poured down her throat. "Ugh."

"Price you pay, love," he said piously, "for getting drunk."

"I wasn't drunk exactly," she protested. "I was just a

little…a little muddled. And you—" she glared at him "—you took advantage of me."

"I would swear it was the other way around."

"I didn't know what I was doing."

"You certainly seemed to know what you were doing—and very well too." His smile prompted a groan from Hillary.

"I can't remember. I just can't remember."

"Relax, Hillary," he said as she began to sniffle. "There's nothing to remember."

"What do you mean?" She sniffed again and wiped her eyes with the back of her hand.

"I mean, I didn't touch you. I left you pure and unsullied in your virginal bed and slept on that remarkably uncomfortable couch."

"You didn't…we didn't…"

"No to both." He turned in response to the shrilling kettle and poured boiling water into a mug.

The first flood of relief changed into irritation. "Why not? What's wrong with me?"

He turned back to stare at her in amazement, then roared with laughter. "Oh, Hillary, what a contradiction you are! One minute you're desperate because you think I've stolen your honor and the next you're insulted because I didn't."

"I don't find it very funny," she retorted. "You deliberately led me to believe that I, that we—"

"Slept together," Bret offered, casually sipping his coffee. "You deserved it. You drove me crazy all the way from the elevator to the bedroom." His smile widened at her rapid change of color. "You remember that well enough. Now remember this. Most men wouldn't have left a tempting morsel like you and slept on that miserable couch, so take care with your fruit punch from now on."

"I'm never going to take another drink as long as I live," Hillary vowed, rubbing her hands over her eyes. "I'm never going to look at a piece of fruit again. I need some tea or some of that horrible coffee, *something.*" The sound of the doorbell shrilled through her head, and she swore with unaccustomed relish.

"I'll fix you some tea," Bret offered, grinning at her fumbling search for obscenities. "Go answer the door."

She answered the summons wearily, opening the door to find Charlene standing at the threshold, taking in her disheveled appearance with glacial eyes.

"Do come right in," Hillary said, shutting the door behind Charlene with a force that only added to her throbbing discomfort.

"I heard you made quite a spectacle of yourself last night."

"Good news travels fast, Charlene—I'm flattered you were so concerned."

"You don't concern me in the least." She brushed invisible lint from her vivid green jacket. "Bret does, however. You seem to make a habit of throwing yourself at him, and I have no intention of allowing it to continue."

This is too much for anyone to take in my condition, Hillary decided, feeling anger rising. Feigning a yawn, she assumed a bored expression. "Is that all?"

"If you think I'm going to have a little nobody like you

marring the reputation of the man I'm going to marry, you're very much mistaken."

For an instant, anger's heat was frozen in agony. The struggle to keep her face passive caused her head to pound with new intensity. "My congratulations to you, my condolences to Bret."

"I'll ruin you," Charlene began. "I'll see to it that your face is never photographed again."

"Hello, Charlene," Bret said casually as he entered the room, his shirt now more conventionally in place.

The redhead whirled, staring first at him, then at his jacket thrown carelessly over the back of the sofa. "What…what…are you doing here?"

"I should think that's fairly obvious," he answered, dropping to the sofa and slipping on his shoes. "If you didn't want to know, you shouldn't have taken it upon yourself to check up on me."

He's using me again, Hillary thought, banking down on shivering hurt and anger. Just using me to make her jealous.

Charlene turned on her, her bosom heaving with emotion. "You won't hold him! You're only a cheap one-night stand! He'll be bored with you within the week! He'll soon come back to me," she raved.

"Terrific," Hillary retorted, feeling her grip on her temper slipping. "You're welcome to him, I'm sure. I've had enough of both of you. Why don't you both leave? Now, at once!" She made a wild gesture at the door. "Out, out, out!"

"Just a minute," Bret broke in, buttoning up the last button of his shirt.

"You keep out of this," Hillary snapped, glaring at him. She turned back to Charlene. "I've had it up to the ears with you, but I'm in no mood for fighting at the moment. If you want to come back later, we'll see about it."

"I see no reason to speak to you again," Charlene announced with a toss of her head. "You're no problem to me. After all, what could Bret possibly see in a cheap little tramp like you?"

"Tramp," Hillary repeated in an ominously low voice. "Tramp?" she repeated, advancing.

"Hold on, Hillary." Bret jumped up, grabbing her around the waist. "Calm down."

"You really are a little savage, aren't you?" shot Charlene.

"Savage? I'll show you savage." Hillary struggled furiously against Bret.

"Be quiet, Charlene," he warned softly, "or I'll turn her loose on you."

He held the struggling Hillary until her struggles lost their force.

"Let me go. I won't touch her," she finally agreed. "Just get her out of here." She whirled on Bret. "And you get out too! I've had it with the pair of you. I won't be used this way. If you want to make her jealous, find someone else to dangle in front of her! I want you out— out of my life, out of my mind." She lifted her chin, heedless of the dampness that covered her cheeks. "I never want to see either of you again."

"Now you listen to me." Bret gripped her shoulders more firmly and gave her a brief but vigorous shake.

"No." She wrenched herself out of his grip. "I'm through listening to you. Through, finished—do you understand? Just get out of here, take your friend with you, and both of you leave me alone."

Picking up his jacket, Bret stared for a moment at flushed cheeks and swimming eyes. "All right, Hillary, I'll take her away. I'll give you a chance to pull yourself together, then I'll be back. We haven't nearly finished yet."

She stared at the door he closed behind him through a mist of angry tears. He could come back all right, she decided, brushing away drops of weakness. But she wouldn't be here.

Rushing into the bedroom, she pulled out her cases, throwing clothes into them in heaps. I've had enough! she thought wildly, enough of New York, enough of Charlene Mason, and especially enough of Bret Bardoff. I'm going home.

In short order, she rapped on Lisa's door. Her friend's smile of greeting faded at the sight of Hillary's obvious distress.

"What in the world—" she began, but Hillary cut her off.

"I don't have time to explain, but I'm leaving. Here's my key." She thrust it into Lisa's hand. "There's food in the fridge and cupboards. You take it, and anything else you like. I won't be coming back."

"But, Hillary—"

"I'll make whatever arrangements have to be made about the furniture and the lease later. I'll write and explain as soon as I can."

"But, Hillary," Lisa called after her, "where are you going?"

"Home," she answered without turning back. "Home where I belong."

If Hillary's unexpected arrival surprised her parents, they asked no questions and made no demands. Soon she fell into the old, familiar pattern of days on the farm. A week drifted by, quiet and undemanding.

During this time it became Hillary's habit to spend quiet times on the open porch of the farmhouse. The interlude between dusk and sleep was the gentlest. It was the time that separated the busy hours of the day from the reflective hours of the night.

The porch swing creaked gently, disturbing the pure stillness of the evening, and she watched the easy movement of the moon, enjoying the scent of her father's pipe as he sat beside her.

"It's time we talked, Hillary," he said, draping his arm around her. "Why did you come back so suddenly?"

With a deep sigh, she rested her head against him. "A lot of reasons. Mostly because I was tired."

"Tired?"

"Yes, tired of being framed and glossed. Tired of seeing my own face. Tired of having to pull emotions and expressions out of my hat like a second-rate magician, tired of the noise, tired of the crowds." She made a helpless movement with her shoulders. "Just plain tired."

"We always thought you had what you wanted."

"I was wrong. It wasn't what I wanted. It wasn't all I wanted." She stood and leaned over the porch rail, staring into the curtain of night. "Now I don't know if I've accomplished anything."

"You accomplished a great deal. You worked hard and made a successful career on your own, and one that you can be proud of. We're all proud of you."

"I know I worked for what I got. I know I was good at my job." She moved away and perched on the porch rail. "When I left home, I wanted to see what I could do for myself by myself. I knew exactly what I wanted, where I was going. Everything was cataloged in neat little piles. First A, then B, and down the line. Now I've got something most women in my position would jump at, and I don't want it. I thought I did, but now, when all I have to do is reach out and take it, I don't want it. I'm tired of putting on the faces."

"All right, then it's time to stop. But I think there's more to your decision to come home than you're saying. Is there a man mixed up in all this?"

"That's all finished," Hillary said with a shrug. "I got in over my head, out of my class."

"Hillary Baxter, I'm ashamed to hear you talk that way."

"It's true." She managed a smile. "I never really fit into his world. He's rich and sophisticated, and I keep forgetting to be glamorous and do the most ridiculous things. Do you know, I still whistle for cabs? You just can't change what you are. No matter how many images you can slip on and off, you're still the same underneath." Shrugging again, she stared into space. "There was never really anything between us—at least not on his side."

"Then he must not have too many brains," her father commented, scowling at his pipe.

"Some might claim you're just a little prejudiced." Hillary gave him a quick hug. "I just needed to come home. I'm going up now. With the rest of the family coming over tomorrow, we'll have a lot to do."

The air was pure and sweet when Hillary mounted her buckskin gelding and set off on an early morning ride. She felt light and free, the wind blowing wildly through her hair, streaming it away from her face in a thick black carpet. In the joy of wind and speed, she forgot time and pain, and the clinging feeling of failure was lost. Reining in the horse, she contemplated the huge expanse of growing wheat.

It was endless, stretching into eternity—a golden ocean rippling under an impossibly blue sky. Somewhere a meadowlark heralded life. Hillary sighed with contentment. Lifting her face, she enjoyed the caressing fingers of sun on her skin, the surging scent of land bursting into life after its winter sleep.

Kansas in the spring, she mused. All the colors so real and vivid, the air so fresh and full of peace. Why did I ever leave? What was I looking for? She closed her eyes and let out a long breath. I was looking for Hillary Baxter, she thought, and now that I've found her, I don't know what to do with her.

"Time's what I need now, Cochise," she told her four-legged companion, and leaned forward to stroke his strong neck. "Just a little time to find all the scattered pieces and put them back together."

Turning the horse toward home, she set off in an easy, gentle lope, content with the soothing rhythm and the spring-softened landscape. As the farm and outbuildings came into view, however, Cochise pawed the ground, straining at the bit.

"All right, you devil." She tossed back her head and laughed, and with a touch of her heels sent the eager horse racing. The air vibrated with the sound of hooves on hard dirt. Hillary let her spirits fly as she gave the gelding his head. They cleared an old wooden jump in a fluid leap, touched earth, and streaked on, sending a flock of contented birds into a flurry of protesting activity.

As they drew nearer the house, her eyes narrowed as she spotted a man leaning on the paddock fence. She pulled back sharply on the reins, causing Cochise to rear in insult.

"Easy," she soothed, stroking his neck and murmuring soft words as he snorted in indignation. Her eyes were focused on the man. It appeared half a continent had not been big enough for a clean escape.

Chapter 10

"Quite a performance." Bret straightened his lean form and strode toward them. "I couldn't tell where the horse left off and the woman began."

"What are you doing here?" she demanded.

"Just passing by—thought I'd drop in." He stroked the horse's muzzle.

Gritting her teeth, Hillary slipped to the ground.

"How did you know where to find me?" She stared up at him, wishing she had kept her advantage astride the horse.

"Lisa heard me pounding on your door. She told me you'd gone home." He spoke absently, appearing more interested in making the gelding's acquaintance than enlightening her. "This is a fine horse, Hillary." He turned his attention from horse to woman, gray eyes sweeping over windblown hair and flushed cheeks. "You certainly know how to ride him."

"He needs to be cooled off and rubbed down." She felt unreasonably annoyed that her horse seemed so taken with the long fingers caressing his neck. She turned to lead him away.

"Does your friend have a name?" He fell into step beside her.

"Cochise." Her answer was short. She barely suppressed the urge to slam the barn door in his face as Bret entered beside her.

"I wonder if you're aware how perfectly his coloring suits you." He made himself comfortable against the stall opening. Hillary began to groom the gelding with fierce dedication.

"I'd hardly choose a horse for such an impractical reason." She kept her attention centered on the buckskin's coat, her back firmly toward the man.

"How long have you had him?"

This is ridiculous, she fumed, wanting desperately to throw the curry comb at him. "I raised him from a foal."

"I suppose that explains why the two of you suit so well."

He began to poke idly about the barn while she completed her grooming. While her hands were busy, her mind whirled with dozens of questions she could not find the courage to form into words. The silence grew deep until she felt buried in it. Finally she was unable to prolong the gelding's brushing. She turned to abandon the barn.

"Why did you run away?" he asked as they were struck with the white flash of sunlight outside.

Her mind jumped like a startled rabbit. "I didn't run

away." She improvised rapidly. "I wanted time to think over the offers I've had—it wouldn't do to make the wrong decision at this point in my career."

"I see."

Unsure whether the mockery in his voice was real or a figment of her imagination, she spoke dismissively. "I've got work to do. My mother needs me in the kitchen."

The fates, however, seemed to be against her as her mother opened the back door and stepped out to meet them.

"Why don't you show Bret around, Hillary? Everything's under control here."

"The pies." Hillary sent out rapid distress signals.

Ignoring the silent plea, Sarah merely patted her head. "There's plenty of time yet. I'm sure Bret would like a look around before supper."

"Your mother was kind enough to ask me to stay, Hillary." He smiled at her open astonishment before turning to her mother. "I'm looking forward to it, Sarah."

Fuming at the pleasant first-name exchange, Hillary spun around and muttered without enthusiasm, "Well, come on then." Halting a short distance away, she looked up at him with a honey-drenched smile. "Well, what would you care to see first? The chicken coop or the pig sty?"

"I'll leave that to you," he answered genially, her sarcasm floating over him.

Frowning, Hillary began their tour.

Instead of appearing bored as she had expected, Bret appeared uncommonly interested in the workings of the farm, from her mother's vegetable garden to her father's gigantic machinery.

He stopped her suddenly with a hand on her shoulder and gazed out at the fields of wheat. "I see what you meant, Hillary," he murmured at length. "They're magnificent. A golden ocean."

She made no response.

Turning to head back, his hand captured hers before she could protest.

"Ever seen a tornado?"

"You don't live in Kansas for twenty years and not see one," Hillary said briefly.

"Must be quite an experience."

"It is," she agreed. "I remember when I was about seven, we knew one was coming. Everyone was rushing around, securing animals and getting ready. I was standing right about here." She stopped, gazing into the distance at the memory. "I watched it coming, this enormous black funnel, blowing closer and closer. Everything was so incredibly still, you could feel the air weighing down on you. I was fascinated. My father picked me up, tossed me over his shoulder, and hauled me to the storm cellar. It was so quiet, almost like the world had died, then it was like a hundred planes thundering right over our heads."

He smiled down at her, and she felt the familiar tug at her heart. "Hillary." He lifted her hand to his lips briefly. "How incredibly sweet you are."

She began walking again, stuffing her hands strategically in her pockets. In silence, they rounded the side of the farmhouse, while she searched for the courage to ask him why he had come.

"You, ah, you have business in Kansas?"

"Business is one way to put it." His answer was hardly illuminating, and she attempted to match his easy manner.

"Why didn't you send one of your minions to do whatever you had in mind?"

"There are certain areas that I find more rewarding to deal with personally." His grin was mocking and obviously intended to annoy. Hillary shrugged as if she were indifferent to the entire conversation.

Hillary's parents seemed to take a liking to Bret, and Hillary found herself irritated that Bret fit into the scene so effortlessly. Seated next to her father, on a firm first-name basis, he chatted away like a long-lost friend. The numerous members of her family might have intimidated anyone else. However, Bret seemed undaunted. Within thirty minutes, he had charmed her two sisters-in-law, gained the respect of her two brothers, and the adoration of her younger sister. Muttering about pies, Hillary retreated to the kitchen.

A few minutes later, she heard: "Such domesticity."

Whirling around, she observed Bret's entrance into the room.

"You've flour on your nose." He wiped it away with his finger. Jerking away, she resumed her action with the rolling pin. "Pies, huh? What kind?" He leaned against the counter as though settling for a comfortable visit.

"Lemon meringue," she said shortly, giving him no encouragement.

"Ah, I'm rather partial to lemon meringue—tart and sweet at the same time." He paused and grinned at her averted face. "Reminds me of you." She cast him a withering glance that left him undaunted. "You do that very well," he observed as she began rolling out a second crust.

"I work better alone."

"Where's that famous country hospitality I've heard so much about?"

"You got yourself invited to dinner, didn't you?" She rolled the wooden pin over the dough as if it were the enemy. "Why did you come?" she demanded. "Did you want to get a look at my little farm? Make fun of my family and give Charlene a good laugh when you got back?"

"Stop it." He straightened from the counter and took her by the shoulders. "Do you think so little of those people out there that you can say that?" Her expression altered from anger to astonishment, and his fingers relaxed on her arms. "This farm is very impressive, and your family is full of warm, real people. I'm half in love with your mother already."

"I'm sorry," she murmured, turning back to her work. "That was a stupid thing to say."

He thrust his hands in the pockets of slim-fitting jeans and strolled to the screen door. "It appears baseball's in season."

The door slammed behind him, and Hillary walked over and looked out, watching as Bret was tossed a glove and greeted with open enthusiasm by various members of her family. The sound of shouting and laughter carried by the breeze floated to her. Hillary turned from the door and went back to work.

Her mother came into the kitchen and Hillary responded to her chattering with occasional murmurs. She felt annoyingly distracted by the activity outside.

"Better call them in to wash up." Sarah interrupted her thoughts, and Hillary moved automatically to the door, opening it and whistling shrilly. Her fingers retreated from her mouth in shock, and she cursed herself for again playing the fool in front of Bret. Stomping back into the kitchen, she slammed the screen behind her.

Hillary found herself seated beside Bret at dinner, and ignoring the bats waging war in her stomach, she gave herself over to the table chaos, unwilling for him or her family to see she was disturbed in any way.

As the family gravitated to the living room, Hillary saw Bret once more in discussion with her father, and pointedly gave her attention to her nephew, involving herself with his game of trucks on the floor. His small brother wandered over and climbed into Bret's lap, and she watched under the cover of her lashes as he bounced the boy idly on his knee.

"Do you live with Aunt Hillary in New York?" the child asked suddenly, and a small truck dropped from Hillary's hand with a clatter.

"Not exactly." He smiled slowly at Hillary's rising color. "But I do live in New York."

"Aunt Hillary's going to take me to the top of the Empire State Building," he announced with great pride. "I'm going to spit from a million feet in the air. You can come with us," he invited with childlike magnanimity.

"I can't think of anything I'd rather do." Lean fingers ruffled dark hair. "You'll have to let me know when you're going."

"We can't go on a windy day," the boy explained, meeting gray eyes with six-year-old wisdom. "Aunt Hillary says if you spit into the wind you get your face wet."

Laughter echoed through the room, and Hillary rose and picked up the boy bodily, marching toward the kitchen. "I think there's a piece of pie left. Let's go fill your mouth."

The light was muted and soft with dusk when Hillary's brothers and their families made their departure. A few traces of pink bleeding from the sinking sun traced the horizon. She remained alone on the porch for a time, watching twilight drifting toward darkness, the first stars blinking into life, the first crickets disturbing the silence.

Returning inside, the house seemed strangely quiet. Only the steady ticking of the old grandfather clock disturbed the hush. Curling into a chair, Hillary watched the progress of a chess game between Bret and her father. In spite of herself, she found herself enchanted by the movements of his long fingers over the carved pieces.

"Checkmate." She started at Bret's words, so complete had been her absorption.

Tom frowned at the board a moment, then stroked his chin. "I'll be darned, so it is." He grinned over at Bret and lit his pipe. "You play a fine game of chess, son. I enjoyed that."

"So did I." Bret leaned back in his chair, flicking his lighter at the end of a cigarette. "I hope we'll be able to play often. We should find the opportunity, since I intend to marry your daughter."

The statement was matter-of-factly given. As the words passed from Hillary's ear to brain, her mouth opened, but no sound emerged.

"As head of the family," Bret went on, not even glancing in her direction, "I should assure you that financially Hillary will be well cared for. The pursuit of her career is, of course, her choice, but she need only work for her own satisfaction."

Tom puffed on his pipe and nodded.

"I've thought this through very carefully," Bret continued, blowing out a lazy stream of smoke. "A man reaches a time when he requires a wife and wants children." His voice was low and serious, and Tom met laughing gray eyes equally. "Hillary suits my purposes quite nicely. She is undoubtedly stunning, and what man doesn't enjoy beauty? She's fairly intelligent, adequately strong, and is apparently not averse to children. She is a bit on the skinny side," he added with some regret, and Tom, who had been nodding in agreement to Hillary's virtues, looked apologetic.

"We've never been able to fatten her up any."

"There is also the matter of her temper," Bret deliberated, weighing pros and cons. "But," he concluded with a casual gesture of his hand, "I like a bit of spirit in a woman."

Hillary sprang to her feet, unable for several attempts to form a coherent sentence. "How dare you?" she managed at length. "How dare you sit there and discuss me as if I were a—a brood mare! And you," she chastised her father, "you just go along like you were pawning off the runt of the litter. My own father."

"I did mention her temper, didn't I?" Bret asked Tom, and he nodded sagely.

"You arrogant, conceited, son of a—"

"Careful, Hillary," Bret cautioned, stubbing out his cigarette and raising his brows. "You'll get your mouth washed out with soap again."

"If you think for one minute that I'm going to marry you, you're crazy! I wouldn't have you on a platter! So go back to New York, and...and print your magazines," she finished in a rush, and stormed from the house.

After her departure, Bret turned to Sarah. "I'm sure Hillary would want to have the wedding here. Any close friends can fly in easily enough, but since Hillary's family is here, perhaps I should leave the arrangements to you."

"All right, Bret. Did you have a date in mind?"

"Next weekend."

Sarah's eyes opened wide for a moment as she imagined the furor of arrangements, then tranquilly returned to her knitting. "Leave it to me."

He rose and grinned down at Tom. "She should have cooled off a bit now. I'll go look for her."

"In the barn," Tom informed him, tapping his pipe. "She always goes there when she's in a temper." Bret nodded and strode from the house. "Well, Sarah." With a light chuckle, Tom resumed puffing on his pipe. "Looks like Hillary has met her match."

The barn was dimly lit, and Hillary stomped around the shadows, enraged at both Bret and her father. The two of them! she fumed. I'm surprised he didn't ask to examine my teeth.

With a groan, the barn door swung open, and she spun around as Bret sauntered into the building.

"Hello, Hillary, ready to discuss wedding plans?"

"I'll never be ready to discuss anything with you!" Her angry voice vibrated in the large building.

Bret smiled into her mutinous face unconcernedly. The lack of reaction incensed her further and she began to shout, storming around the floor. "I'll never marry you—never, never, never. I'd rather marry a three-headed midget with warts."

"But you will marry me, Hillary," he returned with easy confidence. "If I have to drag you kicking and screaming all the way to the altar, you'll marry me."

"I said I won't." She halted her confused pacing in front of him. "You can't make me."

He grabbed her arms and surveyed her with laconic arrogance. "Oh, can't I?"

Pulling her close, he captured her mouth.

"You let go of me," she hissed, pulling away. "You let go of my arms."

"Sure." Obligingly, he relinquished his hold, sending her sprawling on her back in a pile of hay.

"You—bully!" she flung at him, and attempted to scramble to her feet, but his body neatly pinned her back into the sweet-smelling hay.

"I only did what I was told. Besides," he added with a crooked smile, "I always did prefer you horizontal." She pushed against him, averting her face as his mouth descended. He contented himself with the soft skin of her neck.

"You can't do this." Her struggles began to lose their force as his lips found new areas of exploration.

"Yes, I can," he murmured, finding her mouth at last. Slow and deep, the kiss battered at her senses until her lips softened and parted beneath his, her arms circled his neck. He drew back, rubbing her nose with his.

"Wretch!" she whispered, pulling him close until their lips merged again.

"Now are you going to marry me?" He smiled down at her, brushing hair from her cheek.

"I can't think," she murmured and shut her eyes. "I can't ever think when you kiss me."

"I don't want you to think." He busied his fingers loosening her buttons. "I just want you to say it." His hand took possession of her breast and gently caressed it. "Just say it, Hillary," he ordered, his mouth moving down from her throat, seeking her vulnerability. "Say it, and I'll give you time to think."

"All right," she moaned. "You win, I'll marry you."

"Good," he said simply, bringing his lips back to hers for a brief kiss.

She fought the fog of longing clouding her senses and attempted to escape. "You used unfair tactics."

He shrugged, holding her beneath him easily. "All's fair in love and war, my love." His eyes lost their laughter as he stared down at her. "I love you, Hillary. You're in every part of my mind. I can't get you out. I love every crazy, beautiful inch of you." His mouth crushed hers, and she felt the world slip from her grasp.

"Oh, Bret." She began kissing his face with wild abandon. "I love you so much. I love you so much I can't bear it. All this time I thought… When Charlene told me you'd been with her that night in the mountains, I—"

"Wait a minute." He halted her rapid kisses, cupping her face with his hands. "I want you to listen to me. First of all, what was between Charlene and me was over before I met you. She just wouldn't let go." He smiled and brushed her mouth with his. "I haven't been able to think of another woman since the first day I met you, and I was half in love with you even before that."

"How?"

"Your picture—your face haunted me."

"I never thought you were serious about me." Her fingers began to tangle in his hair.

"I thought at first it was just physical. I knew I wanted you as I'd never wanted another woman. That night in your apartment, when I found out you were innocent, that threw me a bit." He shook his head in wonder and buried his face in the lushness of her hair. "It didn't take long for me to realize what I felt for you was much more than a physical need."

"But you never indicated anything else."

"You seemed to shy away from relationships—you panicked every time I got too close—and I didn't want to scare you away. You needed time. I tried to give it to you. Hanging on in New York was difficult enough." He traced the hollow of her cheek with a finger. "But that day in my lodge, my control slipped. If Larry and June hadn't come when they did, things would have progressed differently. When you turned on me, telling me you were sick of being pawed, I nearly strangled you."

"Bret, I'm sorry, I didn't mean it. I thought—"

"I know what you thought," he interrupted. "I'm only sorry I didn't know then. I didn't know what Charlene had said to you. Then I began to think you wanted only your career, that you didn't want to make room in your life for anything or anyone else. In my office that day, you were so cool and detached, ticking off your choices, I wanted to toss you out the window."

"They were all lies," she whispered, rubbing her cheek against his. "I never wanted any of it, only you."

"When June finally told me about the scene with Charlene at the lodge, and I remembered your reaction, I began to put things together. I came looking for you at Bud's party." He pulled up his head and grinned. "I intended to talk things out, but you were hardly in any condition for declarations of love by the time I got there. I don't know how I stayed out of your bed that night, you were so soft and beautiful...and so smashed! You nearly drove me over the edge."

He lowered his head and kissed her, his control ebbing as his mouth conquered her. His hands began to mold her curves with an urgent hunger, and she clutched him closer, drowning in the pool of his desire.

"Good God, Hillary, we can't wait much longer." He removed his weight from her, rolling over on his back, but she went with him, closing her mouth over his. Drawing her firmly away, he let out a deep breath. "I don't think your father would think kindly of me taking his daughter in a pile of hay in his own barn."

He pushed her on her back, slipping his arm around her, cradling her head against his shoulder. "I can't give you Kansas, Hillary," he said quietly. She turned her head to look at him. "We can't live here—at least not now. I've obligations in New York that I simply can't deal with from here."

"Oh, Bret," she began, but he pulled her closer and continued.

"There's upper New York or Connecticut. There are plenty of places where commuting would be no problem. You can have a house in the country if that's what you want. A garden, horses, chickens, half a dozen kids. We'll come back here as often as we can, and go up to the lodge for long weekends, just the two of us." He looked down, alarmed at the tears spilling from wide eyes and over smooth cheeks. "Hillary, don't do that. I don't want you to be unhappy. I know this is home to you." He began to brush the drops from her face.

"Oh, Bret, I love you." She pulled his cheek against hers. "I'm not unhappy. I'm wonderfully, crazily happy that you care so much. Don't you know it doesn't matter where we are? Anyplace I can be with you is home."

He drew her away and regarded her with a frown. "Are you sure, love?"

She smiled and lifted her mouth, letting her kiss give him the answer.

* * * * *

**Fall under the spell of *New York Times*
bestselling author**

Nora Roberts

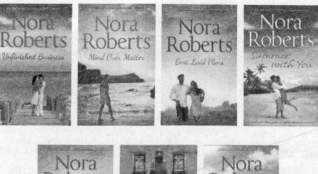

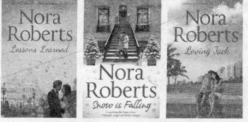

**450 million of her books in
print worldwide**

www.millsandboon.co.uk

Introducing
Cordina's Royal Family...

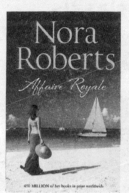

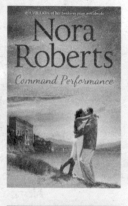

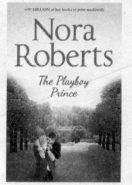

450 million of her books in
print worldwide

www.millsandboon.co.uk

Introducing
the Stanislaskis...

**Fall under the spell of *New York Times*
bestselling author**

Nora Roberts

Get ready to meet the MacKade family...

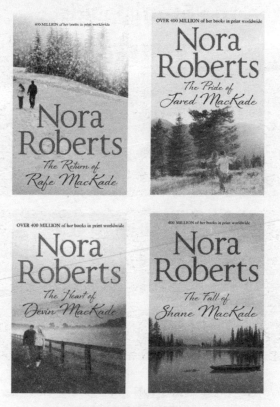